Remeg drove her mount toward Rai as another blazing arrow split the sky.

The barn roof went up with a hungry *WHOOSH!* The doors sprang open and a torrent of panicked horses boiled out, splitting like a river to either side of the fray and disappearing across the grassland.

A vision appeared in the gaping doorway.

The grey horse, made hazy with drifting smoke, stood firm and resolute in the face of combat. The thick neck bunched as the animal tucked its chin close to its chest and danced its feet in the battle dressage of the Carraid. The rider, cloaked and cowled, swung the bright nimbus of a blade into the air as a voice rang out, not in the thin, high tones of an adolescent boy, but in the clear tenor of a man.

"WEATHERCOCK!"

Other Books by Melissa Crandall

Darling Wendy and Other Stories – Seventh Circle Press, 2008
Earth 2 – Ace Books, 1994
Quantum Leap – Search and Rescue – Ace Books, 1994
Star Trek #63 – Shell Game – Pocket Books, 1993
Star Trek #60 – Ice Trap (written in collaboration as L.A. Graf) – Pocket Books, 1992

As Contributor

Amoskeag: The Journal of Southern New Hampshire University, Spring 2009
5.5 BW – Poems and Stories – Seventh Circle Press, 2006
The Geranium Farm Cookbook – Church Publishing, 2006
STRIDES, The Official Publication for the North American Riding for the Handicapped Association – Summer 2003
ASPCA Animal Watch – Winter 2002
STRIDES, The Official Publication for the North American Riding for the Handicapped Association – Fall 2002
New England Writers Network – Summer 2002
STRIDES, The Official Publication for the North American Riding for the Handicapped Association – Fall 2001
The Resident – December 2000
Main Street News – December 2000
McKrells.com – Bio of Kevin McKrell – June 2000
Steed Read – December 1998
Pictorial Gazette, September 8, 1998
High Hopes Happenings – various articles
Serve It Forth – Cooking with Anne McCaffrey – Warner Books, 1996

WEATHERCOCK

A NOVELBY

MELISSA CRANDALL

WEATHERCOCK

PRINTING HISTORY
Tortuga Loca, first edition 2011

ISBN: 978-1-9364760-1-5

Library of Congress Control Number: 2010917663

PRINTED IN THE UNITED STATES OF AMERICA

This book is dedicated to

IAN ANDERSON

The author wishes to gratefully acknowledge the following people:

My husband Ed – Where would I be without you? You mean the world to me and I love you with all my heart.

Risë Shamansky – Who has been with me through it all.

Pam Hohmann – My twin, awesome friend, and brutal copy editor. One of these days we'll build that dimensional doorway.

MJ Allaire and Ryan Twomey – You guys rock on so many levels it's not even funny.

Wendy Carofano – Over 40 years of friendship connects us (yow!). Thanks for putting life into perspective.

Daniel Forward – Writer, poet, actor, artist and fledgling lawyer, whose unexpected kindness and generosity of heart to a stranger on a really bad day made a profound difference in my life.

Liz Cole, Stacey Coleman, John Hodges, Brittany Lester, Adina Pelle, Roberta Pyzel, Elizabeth Roth, and Joanne Sanford – for the gift of their time and insight.

"The Fates guide those who will; those who won't they drag."

-- Joseph Campbell
The Hero with a Thousand Faces

ONE

Ren's eyes flashed open underground. She lay still, feigning sleep, her breath slow and regular, and wondered what it was that had woken her.

The fire in her small hearth, long since gone to embers, pulsed a faint ruddy glow against the shadows that filled the room. On the rug beside the bed, lean piebald shanks twitching as he chased phantom sheep, Jak lay undisturbed. That was evidence enough that there was no real danger, so what had roused her in the deep hours of the night?

She sat up to listen and heard only her heartbeat. Nothing ordinary or otherwise stirred in the great warren of caves and tunnels her people called home. All seemed well.

But she was awake.

She lay down again and knew at once that it was a lost cause. Sleep had fled, not to be recaptured that night. Sitting up, she ran a hand through her hair, scratched the back of her neck, and sighed. "Bugger all," she muttered, and threw the covers back.

Jak looked up the instant her feet hit the floor and blinked sleepy dog eyes at her, clearly wondering what the deuce had possessed her to rise at this hour. "Peace, Jak," she murmured, letting him know it was none of his concern. That might be, but canine loyalty demanded he follow her from the tiny sleeping alcove into the slightly larger main room where he curled up on the hearth rug and sighed deeply, much put-upon.

Stepping over him, Ren stirred the coals with a long iron poker and tossed a couple of logs onto the fire. She swirled the contents of the kettle, added water from a wooden ewer to the dregs of last night's tea, and placed it over the flames. Hooking a short-legged stool with one foot, she dragged it close to the hearth and sat down with her shirt-tail hanging between her knees.

Her spartan living quarters held little beyond the basic necessities of her shepherding life – a low square table, some cushions on which to sit, and several thick woven rugs. A goat-skin bag hung from a small promontory of rock that curled from the cave wall like a beckoning finger. Beneath it leaned her crook, the wood polished to a natural gloss by generations of hands. Tucked into a corner near the curtained doorway were a longbow and a quiver of arrows, a pair of snowshoes, and a set of narrow wooden skis with poles. Shelves hewn from the rock walls held clothing, tools, and an assortment of odds and ends. A slender ledge above the fire displayed a collection of stream-tumbled stones, hawk feathers, and other gifts given to her by her grandchildren.

As she waited for the kettle to boil, Ren picked at the knee of her breeches where the material was almost worn through and wondered what this day would bring. There was a list of chores longer than her arm, but most of them would have to wait or get passed on to someone else. Her first duty, as soon as it was light, was to hike down the mountain to the village of Cadasbyr and learn what news they had to share. Rumors of evil behavior on the part of Queen Kedar Trevelyan had seeped north from the royal city of Caerluel. Were the stories of her depredations true or was it all just talk created by idle gossips to stir the soup and pass the time? Ren had to know the truth beyond any doubt. The safety of her people – particularly the men – depended upon it.

Steam curled from the kettle's spout in a lazy ribbon, bringing the welcome scent of hot tea. In stocking feet, she left her seat and crossed the room to take a pottery mug from the shelf. As her fingers closed around her favorite (glazed in blue with a belly as fat as a friar's), the wood in the fireplace gave a sudden loud SNAP. She flinched at the noise *(a tad jumpy, aren't you Ren?)* and dropped the mug, which landed on the one bit of stone floor not covered by a rug, breaking the handle. "Damn it all t' –"

Behind her, Jak growled.

Ren turned around fast, the mug forgotten, but there was no one in the room except her and the dog. He crouched on the rug as if to spring and stared at the fire with the fixed 'eye' he used to control sheep. His top lip quivered.

"What d' ye ken, Jak?" she said softly. She knew better than to question his instincts.

The dog whined and the tip of his tail wavered. He crouched lower, haunches bunched, finding his balance, ready to spring. His intent gaze flicked her way for an instant and then riveted back on the fire, telling her in the only way he knew how that something was there.

Nothing was there.

Without looking away, Ren reached behind her and felt for the crook leaning against the wall. Taking it in both hands, balanced as a quarterstaff, she moved forward.

The hearthstone, raked coals, and burning logs all looked as they had a moment before. The tea kettle was blasting steam and she used the end of her crook to swing aside the iron arm from which it hung. That was when she saw it.

The log whose pitch-filled knot had snapped in the heat had shifted, knocking free a spray of grey ash across the hearthstone. Printed in the ash was the four-clawed track of a rooster. It was larger than that of a normal bird, but there was no mistaking it for anything else, no means by which Ren might explain away its appearance as she would the pictures in a cloud. The spoor lay as clear as if the beast had just strutted its way across the hearth, but there was no animal present save the dog.

Ren's heart gave a funny little hitch, a conflicted blend of fear and joy, and she sank to her knees. Snatches of old songs, portents, and prophecies cascaded through her mind so fast she could not catch hold of a single one. Reaching out, she held her open hand above the sharp definition of those claws …

… then slapped her palm down, scattering ash and obliterating the sign.

The jumble of logs in the grating erupted as if kicked from within and a curtain of sparks flew into her face. Ren cried out and fell back, one hand raised to shield her eyes, the other clenched deep in the fur of Jak's ruff to hold back the lunging, wildly barking dog. Cinders fell around them like falling stars, singeing holes in the rugs. Ren went after them on her hands and knees, patting furiously to extinguish them before they could blaze to life.

When all that remained were dots of ash and the smell of charred wool, she sat back on her heels and looked once more at the hearth. What she saw there sent a convulsive shudder down the length of her back and buried cold fingers at the base of her spine.

A scattering of embers had landed on the hearthstone where the swipe of Ren's hand through the ash was still apparent. They clustered in bright, pulsing glory along specific lines, giving her no option to deny their message. Here was the uplift of mighty wings, the curved stroke of an open beak, and a twinkling gallinaceous eye.

Ren's heart lurched in her chest with an enormous *thump!* She pulled Jak into her lap and held him close. "I dinna ken I'm ready for this," she whispered to the image as it slowly faded into grey, dead clinkers. "But I promise I'll gie it my best go." A smile whispered across her lips, turning her mouth up at the corners, and she buried her face in the dog's soft fur.

Two

Kinner was in the kitchen finishing up the day's chores, but his heart wasn't in it. He was too aware of other things going on in the Household, an undercurrent of tension that seemed to hover just above his skin like static electricity.

When the door to the common room opened and immediately slammed shut again, the noise came as something of a relief, although he couldn't imagine which of the Secondwives had possessed the temerity to do such a thing in front of his mother. He held very still, straining to hear, but there was no further uproar. The house settled back into its ominous silence like a toad into mud.

This was not a good sign.

"Aren't you done *yet,* Seedless?"

He flinched and ducked his head, eyes downcast. The words were ugly and the tone uglier still. He knew without having to look that it was Mairgy; the broad, flat tones of her northern dialect gave her away.

From the corner of his eye, he glimpsed the frothy swirl of a lacy nightdress hem as the barefoot girl brushed past. She had been fostered into the Household to provide new blood to the family line. At first, Kinner had found her shy ways appealing, but four years under this roof had transformed her from a doe-eyed, slightly chubby eleven-year-old into a robust, self-absorbed teenager. Since the onset of her menses, powerful with the sense of her growing sexuality, she had pursued him with ardent and single-minded zeal.

But not anymore.

"You shouldn't be downstairs without slippers," he said. He reached for the broom and began to sweep.

"Mind your own business," she replied and filled a ladle with cool water from the cistern.

"It *is* my business."

She smiled with malicious joy. "Not for long," she sang. She drank, arching her back to thrust her breasts against the nightgown's simple homespun in an altogether mendacious invitation.

Kinner briefly entertained the fantasy of swatting her ample backside with the broom, but that was, of course, impossible. It was not given to men to do such things. Instead, he scooped the debris he'd collected into the dustpan and emptied it into the bin.

Mairgy snorted derisive laughter through her nose. When she was finished drinking, she hung the ladle back on its nail and leaned against the sink, scrutinizing Kinner from head to heel like a buyer appraising stock at an auction. He fidgeted under that scornful gaze and gnawed self-consciously at his lower lip. Like every adolescent boy since the dawn of time, he was acutely aware of his vague resemblance to an unfinished pie – an unskilled fusion of malformed dough with knobby knees, enormous feet, and jug-handle ears.

The girl wound a strand of dark hair around her finger and brought it to her lips. "Auntie Dwinn says you're as good as gone. That's what the meeting is about."

Kinner remained silent. Did she think him too stupid to understand why the common room was barred this evening to all but the Wives? Crisis lay over the Household like a hand poised to swat. He felt the weight of it pressing down against his head.

She wrinkled her nose at his lack of response and chewed the side of a thumbnail. "The outside breeding schedule will be suspended until we review finances." She spoke with the authority of a Secondwife (which she was not, never having borne a child), as if she knew everything there was to know about the business of pedigree and breeding. "There won't be stud fees taken in to off-set those we pay out, and now we'll have to refund money to the families who received nothing for their investment because someone I won't mention by name couldn't perform."

Kinner felt an almost overwhelming desire to apologize. He bit the inside of his cheek to keep from doing so.

She prattled on, impressed with her grasp of the situation. "Even if we eventually get a male birth from one of the outside pairings, it'll be years before he's of any use." The word *'If'* hung in the air, unspoken but sharply felt. Better not to jinx the event before it happened.

Sighing with teenaged angst, Mairgy shoved away from the sink and breezed past Kinner close enough for him to smell the fresh scent of soap and her own particular musk. A flip of the hips and a flirty twirl of nightgown was the last he saw of her.

He listened as her footsteps crossed the foyer, pattered briskly up the stairs, and trotted down the hallway to the big room at the end which served as the girls' dormitory. Only after the door had opened and closed again, cutting off a peal of girlish laughter, did he set the broom aside. He swished the dish cloth in the pan of tepid wash water, wrung it out … and in a sudden and rare display of temper, flung it across the room. It landed skewed on the drying rack where it hung for a moment like a wayward thought before crumpling to the floor in a sad little heap.

"To the Hells with it." His voice cracked with bitterness and worry. "Let them clean up their own mess for a change." For the first time in his life, the seventeen-year-old left the kitchen without finishing his chores.

Slouching to the stairs, he paused with a foot on the first riser and glanced toward the common room. Behind the heavy door, voices rose and fell. Their words were indistinct, but the discordant tone was unmistakable. Kinner raised a hand to his chest and massaged the knot lodged tight beneath his heart.

Ragged coughing suddenly cut through the storm of argument. The tide of painful sound crested and gave way to thick, phlegmy rumbles that sounded like the muffled crumple of snow sliding off a roof. Holan's symptoms – the horrible cough, the mucus, the crippled breathing – always grew worse when she was upset.

The door to the common room jerked open and Auntie Milda hurried out. She was still in her work clothes and stank of horses and manure. Kinner imagined her chair riddled with hay chaff and hair. It would never have occurred to her to put down an old towel to protect the upholstery, or to change her clothing before going in to the meeting. Tomorrow he would be in there for hours, picking the chairs clean to make them suitable for company.

If he was still here, that is.

She took two quick strides toward the kitchen, caught sight of him standing in the shadows, and whirled about. "Kinner!" One hand fluttered in command. "Get your mother a –" She stopped and rethought what she was about to say. He could almost hear the gears shifting in her brain; the last thing they wanted right now was for *him* to walk into that room. "Never mind," she said with a brisk shake of the head. "I'll do it myself. You get to bed." She disappeared toward the kitchen.

Without leaving his place on the stairs, Kinner leaned to one side in an attempt to peek beyond the slightly open vee of the door. All he could see were the backs of a couple of chairs and the women seated there (Aunties Cully and Prueth). Their heads were turned toward the top of the table where his mother sat in pride of place as Firstwife, but that was behind the door and out of his line of sight. He listened to the rough draw of shallow breathing between each cough. Was this it? Was this the fit that would kill the blacksmith? If it did, his only champion would be gone.

Milda's rummaging made a racket as she searched the kitchen for what she wanted, something that Kinner could have laid his hands on in an instant had she cared to ask. What sort of chaos would she leave for him to set right? Should he offer to help, despite her order to go to bed? Would she see the mess he had left behind and call for him to clean it up?

Back she came at a careful trot with a cup of water in one hand. She stopped short, surprised to find him still there. "Go on, now!" she said sharply and shooed him like a chicken with her free hand. "Stop loitering around doorways and get upstairs. If there's anything that needs telling, you'll hear it; otherwise keep your nose out of other people's business. And for pity's sake, stand up straight!" She didn't wait to see if he would follow her directive (it was assumed that he would), but hurried back into the common room and closed the door. The coughing continued for a moment longer and then there was silence as Holan drank. Another cough or two cleared her throat, followed by more silence as she finished the water. When it was clear that the present difficulty had passed, the voices began their vigorous argument anew, each rising to speak above the last.

"Other people's business?" Kinner said. He swallowed hard, feeling sick to his stomach. "Whose business do you think it *is* but mine?"

He climbed the stairs toward the third floor and the small bedroom tucked under the eaves beside the attic. Last week, that room had belonged to a three-year-old cousin. Now it was his, as it had been in childhood; a demotion from the roomy expanse of the Husband's quarters.

On the second floor landing, a bundle of scrawny limbs clad in a flannel nightgown propelled itself backward on its rump to get out of his way. The five-year-old girl sat with her face hidden against her drawn up knees, arms curled protectively around her head.

"What are you doing out here, Ferlie?" Kinner said, surprised to see her. "You were supposed to be in bed hours ago."

She sniffled, a thoroughly soggy noise, and said nothing.

He sat down beside her, legs crossed like a tailor. "What's the matter? The big girls teasing you again?"

The child shook her head, but did not look up. An exhalation that was more sob than sigh trembled through her like the delicate riffle of wind across still water. When Kinner touched the tip of her elbow with one finger –"Come on, you can tell me" – she burst into tears.

He pulled her into his lap and held her close. "Hey, now, what is this?" he said, rocking gently from side to side. Shoulders heaving, she buried her face against his chest and wailed like her best friend had just died.

At the end of the hallway, the dormitory door opened. Steeling himself for more ridicule, Kinner looked up and met the gaze of his half-sister Pegeen.

She was eighteen, the offspring of Kessler and Auntie Dwinn. Like Kinner, she favored their father (which in her case was a blessing, considering Auntie Dwinn).

For a moment they just looked at each other. When Pegeen spoke, it was without scorn. "I wondered where she'd gotten to. It doesn't take this long to do a piddle. Do you want me to take her?"

Kinner shook his head.

Pegeen nodded. There was a moment of uncomfortable silence and then she spoke in a soft voice tense with anger. "It's not *fair.*" She gave him a sad little smile and closed the door.

Kinner stayed where he was, humming and rocking until Ferlie's tears ceased. When she settled more comfortably against him and crooked a thumb into her mouth, he wiped her face with the hem of her nightgown and waited to see if she would fall asleep. When she didn't, he said, "Do you want to talk about it now?"

In the way of small children, she responded to his question with one of her own. "Are you really going away?"

The simple query lanced his heart. Kinner took a slow, deep breath and nodded, his chin moving against her hair. "Very likely." The only question remained the *means* of his departure, but he wasn't about to discuss that with a five-year-old.

"Don't you like it here?"

"Of course I do." Well, that wasn't precisely true, but he might be excused a tiny white lie this one time. Ferlie was still too young to understand the particulars involved in running a Household. "Sometimes people go away, is all. That's just the way things are."

She sat up, jabbing him sharply in the groin with her knee, and threw her arms around his neck. "I don't want you to go!"

"Oh, sweetie." He pressed his face against her hair. "I don't want to leave. You know that, don't you?"

She nodded, then leaned back in his arms with her eyes streaming and looked him straight in the face. "Will you come say goodbye before you go?"

He could see his reflection in her eyes, a little Kinner momentarily trapped there. How long would she remember him once he was gone? A month? As long as a year? Would she forget him entirely? Would she retain little bits of their time together or would he end up as a shadowy figure from childhood, a vague memory? "Yes," he said. "If they'll let me, I'll come say goodbye."

She rubbed her sleeve across her runny nose and climbed out of his lap to stand barefoot in front of him. With a grave demeanor more in keeping with an adult than a little child, she placed her hands on his shoulders and leaned in to kiss him on both cheeks. "Someday I'll be a wife," she said, looking straight into his eyes. "Then I'll come find you and bring you home. I promise."

Kinner's throat closed. Before he could find the wit or ability to reply, Ferlie walked away and let herself into the girls' room, closing the door behind her without a backward glance. Kinner drew a shaky breath and wiped a sleeve across his eyes. Pushing to his feet, he took the last flight of stairs.

The room on the third floor was little more than a closet, with barely enough space for the narrow bed, a small table, and a chair with a rush seat. The walls were white-washed, but a rust-colored stain shaped like a seagull marred the ceiling above the bed. A small window, open a fraction to let air circulate, was curtained with a leftover scrap of cloth that stirred in the breeze. Tonight, the wind was from the south. He smelled the sea.

It took little effort to conjure a picture of his childhood self in this room: stick-thin, bucky front teeth, and brown hair airy as dandelion fuzz. Night after night he had lain in this bed and listened to stories of the Weathercock. Holan had sworn him to secrecy over those tales, explaining that the legendary hero was something special between mother and son and not to be shared with the others, not even his father. He could hear her still, as if an echo inhabited the room:

"When the Weathercock rides, the sight of him will pierce our enemies to the heart. Bright as the banner of morning he'll be and the world will never be the same for his coming." She spoke in a hush, her eyes fixed upon the opposite wall with such rapt attention that he half expected the hero to come bursting through the whitewash.

Held in the circle of her arms, Kinner tucked his ear against her chest and listened to her heartbeat. Her shirt smelled of smoke and sweat, metal and fire, the homey and pleasant odors of her forge and his life. "Will he really come some day, Mum?"

The fine strands of his hair caught and tugged against the rough skin of her palm as she stroked his head. "So says the legend."

He looked up at her. "When?" he demanded.

She chuckled and kissed the freckled tip of his nose. "Why, I don't know, child. When it suits him, I expect."

Kinner beat his stuffed rabbit against his leg. "I wish he'd come now!"

The blacksmith's arms tightened around him. "As do I, child," she murmured. There was longing in her voice and a sadness that Kinner did not understand. She kissed the top of his head. "As do I."

He closed the door and undressed in the dark. No more fine bed linens and expensive silks for him! That lovely apparel, soft as doeskin and cool as water, was folded away in the bottom drawer of the bureau in the Husband's room to await its next occupant. It was back to nubbly flannel and cheap cotton.

The latticed ropes supporting the bed's straw mattress creaked as they took his weight. Kinner clasped his knees to his chest in unconscious mimicry of Ferlie and sighed.

Sterile.

No one knew why so many pregnancies resulted in girl babies, or why the rarer male offspring were often sterile. It was just the way things were in Duine, the way things had always been. Such circumstances had given rise to Households composed of women, the most fortunate of which were organized around a Husband. Breeding arrangements were negotiated between Households, for which the servicing family received a hefty fee. Law required the strict maintenance of pedigree books as well as the regular introduction of new blood as insurance against inbreeding, and Husbands rarely left the security of their homes. Those men rendered sterile through infirmity, old age, or fate (*Like me*, Kinner thought with bitterness) were dispatched as quickly as possible. Retaining them was not an option.

"Keeping a man after he's gone blank is like feeding a dry cow just because you like its eyes," Auntie Cully had declared one night when the topic came up at dinner. "If a man can't breed, what good is he? Better to put him out of his misery as soon as possible."

The other wives (all but his mother, who had remained peculiarly silent) had wholeheartedly agreed.

The deep tolling of a bell came faint on the wind from the hillside church that served their village. The three-note chime – the last of the day in these remote parts, although city cathedrals were said to ring the Church Offices throughout the night – extolled the virtues of the Three-Headed Goddess, the Triune Lady, the Triple-She. Besides death, Her Church was the only option available to infertile men, provided their families were willing to take the trouble and expense of sending them to the monastery at Dara. As titular members of the religious community there, the sterile lived out their lives committed to the devotion of prayer. Once they took up residence, they were considered dead to their families and never seen in the outside world again.

But Holan hated the Church. No matter how much she loved him, Kinner thought it unlikely that she would send her only son to serve a deity she despised.

Knuckles rapped gently against the door; a soft sound meant to awaken rather than startle. The iron latch rattled as it lifted and the door creaked open to admit a skeletal hand bearing a cheap yellow candle in a wooden holder. Holan peered around the door jamb. She was old – fifty last spring – but illness had made her ancient. Her eyes, pouched with darkness, shone fever-bright, like two stars gleaming in the back of a cave. "Thought I'd find you up," she said with a wan smile. "May I come in?"

She was the only one who ever asked permission. "Of course," Kinner said. He shifted to make room, but she put the candle down on the table and crossed to the window instead, drawn there by the sound of voices and the tramp of feet in the street below. Standing to one side of the casement, where movement would not be seen should anyone chance to look up, she parted the curtain a fraction with one finger.

Six months ago, a rumor had come to town via a band of gypsy tinkers that Queen Kedar Trevelyan had ordered a squadron of soldiers to procure for her men of breedable age. Gossip ran rampant and sooner or later Kinner overheard every version there was to the tale – how the queen did not pay for the Husbands she took ("That's thievery, that is!" Auntie Dwinn had shouted and pounded her fist on the table until the crockery rattled and Holan was forced to call her to order); how she used more than one male as "Husband" (that proud title turning derogatory in the mouths of those who spoke of it); how the men discarded by the queen were offered to her court favorites as playthings and sluts. What happened to the men after that, no one knew. Certainly none of them had been returned to their families or found their way home on their own. The worst rumor of all was that Kedar Trevelyan had ordered the deaths of proven, viable studs – men with a long line of healthy descendents – when she failed to conceive.

It was the one tale at which Kinner's aunts had scoffed.

"That's nothin' but idle, slanderous tripe, that is," Auntie Bellini had said just a few weeks ago as the women gathered in the common room after dinner. She toed her mud-caked boots off onto the rug that Kinner had hung over the clothesline only that morning to whack free of dirt. "Say what you like about her, but you get right down to the old brass tacks, regality aside and all that, and the queen's a woman like us, ain't she? She understands about business. She wouldn't do nothin' stupid." The other women had nodded their agreement and murmured over their pipes and glasses of whisky. Holan, seated in the chair nearest the fire, had remained silent on the topic.

As the sound of footsteps faded, she twitched the curtain closed and looked at her son. "No worries. It's only a crowd of locals rowdying their way home from the pub. They'll get the rough side of someone's tongue for coming in so late."

Kinner nodded. Holan could be sharp-tongued herself on occasion. He took a deep breath, smelled the sea again, and tried to still the quaking of his heart. "Is it over, Mum? Downstairs, I mean."

The line of her mouth turned bitter. "Oh, yes. We're quite done, us." She sat beside him and took his hand. Once hers had been warm and strong. Now they were a gnarled bundle of sharp sticks, angular bird bones trapped beneath the thin, faintly blue translucence of her flesh.

Kinner's heart felt bruised. Here it came at last, the end of his life laid out for all to see. He could scarce believe this was happening. There was nothing he could do to change the outcome, nothing he could say that would make any difference to the women downstairs. "How will you –" *Do it*, he meant to say, wishing in some perverse way to know the manner of his death, but he could not make the words come. Would the Household abandon him in the hills to die or would it fall to one of the Secondwives to kill him? Surely they wouldn't make his mother do it?

Holan had been speaking. Caught up in his worry, Kinner had missed half of what she said and only now caught the last word. "Go?'" he repeated in confusion. "Go where?"

She looked annoyed. "Weren't you listening? I said you're going to Dara."

Confusion swept him even as a weight lifted from his chest. Suddenly, he could breathe again. "But you hate the Church!"

"I just saved your life and you're arguing?" She clutched his sleeve and gave it a shake. "Would you rather be dead? That's what the others want."

"Of course I wouldn't rather be …" Words failed him. He stared at her, working hard to get his head around the idea. "How does this work?" he said. "Do I take a wagon from here or do I go somewhere else to catch it?"

"Neither," she said, and smoothed out a crease in her trousers. "I'm going to take you."

Kinner blinked, brain spinning like a stick tossed into a rollicking stream. "Mum, Dara is half a world away."

"I'm not stupid, boy. I know where Dara is."

He felt a flush of annoyance. "Then you know that you're not fit to travel such a distance."

"*Pah!*" She pushed him away and folded her arms across her prominent breast bone. "Thank you so much for your concern, not to mention your vote of confidence, but *I'll* decide what I'm fit for, laddybuck." The wave of one claw-like hand took in the room, the house, the entire world for all he knew. "I'd rather die on the road than stay here with these carrion crows." She shook her head. "I should have made this trip a long time ago. I knew I'd have to sooner or later. I had plenty of warning. But I …" Her voice trembled and faltered. "… had to do … what needed … doing …" Her eyes grew dreamy and unfocused. "… to insure …" Her expression went lax and her words became unintelligible.

Kinner waited. It was the only thing he *could* do when she was in the grip of one of her spells. She hadn't always been this way, or so the aunties said. The fits (as they called them) had begun the year after his birth, as if the bearing of a son had changed the blacksmith in some fundamental way. The seizures left her vague and silent, prone to making curious calculations in the air. At night, when most tradeswomen closed up shop and went home or to the pub for a pint or two with the neighbors, Holan had shut herself alone in the smithy. The clangor that issued from behind those locked and iron-banded doors had made it impossible for anyone in the house to get a decent night's rest. In the morning, the shop would be swept clean with nothing to show for all the noise except a tired woman ravenous for breakfast and infuriatingly adept at turning aside every question.

The Secondwives whispered to anyone who would listen that Holan was insane. Such talk had frightened Kinner when he was small. He had quizzed his father about it, climbing into Kessler's lap where he sat mending clothes under the screening leaves of the grape arbor. Still young in years, but already exhausted by the demands of his responsibilities within the Household, Kinner's father had made some noises of reassurance and sent the boy off to complete the simple chores that were already expected of him. Although dissatisfied with the explanation, Kinner had read the worry in Kessler's eyes and never asked again.

Holan's voice abruptly cleared. "If they found it … found it … they'd sell it … or worse. Melt it … but that's not for awhile yet."

Kinner stroked her brittle fingers in an attempt to gently call her back to him. "Melt what, Mum?"

Her dark eyes were silver-limned in the candlelight. She twitched … blinked several times fast, her lashes fluttering like a hummingbird's wings … and in a heartbeat was herself once more. "Oh, damn!" Her mouth pursed in disgust. "I never told you that part, did I?" She rolled her eyes. "Never told you any of it really and now's a bit late to begin, but there you have it." She slapped her thighs. "Despite what I've led you to believe, my darling, your mother is not always the sharpest nail in the horse shoe." The bony point of her shoulder pressed against his. "You listen to what I'm about to say, son of mine, and remember every word."

She smelled of medicine and a papery, almost desiccated odor that made Kinner want to wrinkle his nose. He tried to draw away without being obvious. "Mum …"

Holan placed a finger against his lips. "Hush. And hearken. This is a story about the Weathercock." Her voice dropped into the tone and cadence he remembered from old. "The Weathercock," she repeated. "And what he has done with me."

THREE

You can't breathe through mud.

That fundamental truth came to Rai as she struggled face down in the glop of the stable yard with Banya's boot sole pressed firmly against the back of her head.

"Had enough?" the Carraid asked in a brightly conversational tone.

Unable to speak, Rai thrust the middle finger of each fist straight out.

Banya tutted. "Such language in a young girl." The boot lifted and a beefy hand descended to grab the back of Rai's sodden jacket and give it a yank. She came off the ground with the sucking kiss of mud, staggered, and nearly fell. Banya steadied her with a solicitous hand under one elbow until she found her balance, then stepped back and gave her a once-over. "Wow." She grinned with satisfaction. "You look like shit."

Rai glared and spat perilously close to the Carraid's boot. Digging a finger into her ear, she glanced at the women gathered in a loose circle around them and snarled. "What are you skanks looking at?"

The garrison soldiers laughed and replied with catcalls and a few illustrative gestures. If they'd found any entertainment value at all in watching Banya kick Rai's ass again, it only proved what Rai had been saying all along – that things in Caerau had gotten dull.

The group shifted and broke apart, reforming in huddles of two and three for the exchange of wagered coins. Overcast light caught the grimy brass of four-sided dins and holed sens as they passed from hand to hand. An unexpected flash of light caught the edge of a silver dobler thrown into the pot by some overconfident fool.

Banya swiped the palm of her hand at the rain dripping off her nose and lightly biffed Rai's shoulder with the tips of her massive knuckles. "Come on, little girl. Let's get cleaned up."

Rai tugged her wet pants out of her butt. "Don't call me little girl," she said and fell into step beside the big woman, boots splashing in the ankle-deep mud.

They were a lesson in contrasts. Banya was not quite thirty; tall, muscular, and built like the dray horse she somewhat resembled. Her blonde hair was braided into countless thin plaits that hung past her shoulders, and she favored traditional horseclan garb when off duty (although the bright colors were a muddy rainbow at present). Tiny bells, each smaller than the nail on Rai's pinky, were sewn to the tops of her boots. They rang a soft chime with every step as her bow-legged, equestrian stride took her across the compound.

Rai was shadow to the Carraid's sun. Small and finely made, her black hair was cropped short (she'd had head lice the summer before), and her eyes were a murky hazel. Her fair cheeks were pink with old sunburn, the slope of her nose patchy with peeling skin. Impoverished by even the standards of soldiery, the nineteen-year-old possessed only that which the garrison provided – two pairs of boots, a sword and dagger, and two black-and-beige uniforms. The upright half-collar of her jacket bore a copper pip to denote her rank as a lowly grunt. The brass star beside it identified her as a member of the Caerau garrison.

Months of crippling boredom coupled with bad weather had brought her to this day. Twitchy with malcontent, Rai had doled her unhappiness onto the rest of the garrison with the liberality of a half-wit disbursing an inheritance. When that didn't make her feel any better, she had imprudently cast derision on the rag-tag orphans that worked under Banya in her role as garrison horse mistress.

It was a stupid move on Rai's part, and she knew it. The Carraid was sentimental about the oddest of things, not least of which was the mongrel brood in her employ. Although by trade a canny and dangerous warrior, Banya largely viewed the world through calm and ironic eyes. It took real talent to antagonize her to the point of physical retaliation.

Rai was the most talented idiot Banya had ever known.

The barracks that housed the Caerau garrison was a long, narrow, white-washed stone building with a sagging roofline and wooden shutters. The main room, lit by cheap oil lamps and a few random windows, held grey-blanketed cots set into two rows. Each bed had a wooden trunk at its foot and a wall cubby at its head, all of them scarred by years of graffiti. A stone fireplace at either end of the structure roasted those who slept closest and froze the soldiers whose beds were furthest away. A curtained doorway in one long wall led to the bath house. The air, indeed the very stones and roof thatch, stank with the aggregate aromas of sweat, menstrual blood, pipe tobacco, and farts.

Banya dipped her head beneath the door lintel to avoid concussion and turned sideways to let pass a comrade heading off to duty. Fallon grunted (a universal sign of acknowledgement among soldiers) and went on her way. The room was almost empty, the rest of the garrison being occupied elsewhere. Von and Jobin were seated before the fire with their legs stretched toward the heat, enjoying a smoke and a quiet conversation. Duan and Tullia sat cross-legged on opposite ends of the same bunk, a deck of dog-eared playing cards between them on the thin mattress. Tynar stood watching the game with mild interest, her pants around her ankles. Her shanks had the color and consistency of poorly-kneaded dough.

Tullia drew a card from her hand and placed it face-up on the blanket. She folded the cards together, fanned them again, and paused to take in Rai's bemired appearance. "Soldier," she said seriously, her eyelids crinkling with humor. "You look like someone just yanked you head first out of a horse's ass."

Duan laughed, exposing several bad teeth rotted black to the gum-line.

Tynar kicked her pants aside and scratched her naked crotch with unenthusiastic vigor. "Should have left her up there, you ask me." She leveled a finger at Rai. "I lost money because of you, crowbait."

"Cry me a river," Rai said and followed Banya along the aisle toward their bunks.

The rat-faced northerner shook out a fresh pair of uniform pants, pulled them on, and tied the waist. "A *lot* of money," she said with inflated self-importance.

Rai toed off the muddy ruin of her boots, wondering if they were worth trying to salvage or should she just chuck them. Standing first on one foot, then the other, she peeled off her holey socks and dropped them onto the floor like dead snakes. She glanced at Tynar with a tired and jaundiced eye. "Spare me that line of crap. You don't have any money."

"Even if you did, you couldn't wager it," Banya said. "Everyone knows you owe half the corps for past debts."

"Right you are there, girlie-girl," Duan said. She drew a card from those she held and tapped it against her disastrous teeth as she considered her next move. She placed the card atop the one Tullia had discarded. "She owes me a three-sen."

"Din-six, here," Von offered from in front of the fire.

"Dobler-half," Jobin pitched in.

Tynar's face darkened. "Shut up, the lot of you."

Duan's gaze, flat as a snake's, lifted from her cards. "Watch your mouth, Northerner, unless you want a fat lip."

The women locked eyes, but the challenge lasted only a moment before Tynar dropped her gaze. She gave a little shrug, like a horse shuddering off a pesky fly, and turned away as if the argument was beneath her notice. Behind her back, Duan rolled her eyes and returned her attention to the game.

Banya, bent over her open footlocker, straightened with one hand on the upright lid. "Wait a second. You bet *against* me, Ty? In a fight with *Rai?*" She grimaced. "Ouch. That hurts."

Tynar squirmed, discomfited. "Well, I thought –"

"Aw, Ty," Von cooed. "That's *sweet*, stickin' up for the underdog like that." She wriggled her eyebrows. "Have you got a thing for our Miss Rai?"

Rai made a face. "Don't make me puke."

Tullia folded her cards, tapped them against her knee, and reordered the spread. "Anyone dumb enough to bet against Banya in a fight deserves to lose," she remarked to the air.

"You got that right," Jobin said.

Rai nodded. "I didn't think there was anyone alive *that* stupid."

Tynar came at her fast. Her fist clipped Rai's shoulder, spinning her halfway around. Rai ducked a second blow aimed at her head, hooked a foot behind Tynar's ankle, and jerked. As Tynar went over backward, a flailing hand caught the edge of a nearby thunder jug and sent the crapper flying.

In the Barracks Rules as set forth by Black Hirn – a.k.a. cook, doctor, battle surgeon, soldier, and general *major domo* of the garrison, second only to Captain Remeg – every chamber pot was to be emptied and scrubbed twice a day, at dawn and at dusk. Rai could not recall who had drawn the odious duty this week, but whoever it was had missed one. With balletic grace, a single turd spun through the air and landed squarely on Tynar's chest, pointed at her chin like an accusatory brown finger.

There was a moment of silence … and then the room erupted with bellows of laughter. Grimacing with disgust, Tynar twitched the shit onto the floor, scrambled to her feet, and stalked out of the building, slamming the door behind her. Fine dust shifted down from the rafters.

Banya brayed, bent double, hands on her knees. "Oh!" She gasped and clutched at her side. "Oh, help me, Mother, I'm *dyin'!*"

Tullia sprawled backward on the bunk, arms clasped across her stomach, bouncing with hilarity and gulping for air. She tried to speak, failed twice, and gave it up as a lost cause. Duan scooped up the deck of cards and flung them into the air in celebration.

Von cackled and wiped tears from her eyes. "Oh, that was *beautiful!* Rai, I love you. You could'na done that better if you'd tried."

"Thanks." Rai could not help but preen just a little. All at once, the day seemed vastly improved.

Banya wiped her eyes with the heel of her hand. "That was so sweet, buddy, I'm going to buy you a drink after dinner." She snagged a towel from her wall cubby and flipped it over her shoulder. "C'mon, hero," she said with bright cheer and passed through the curtained doorway into the bath house. Rai snatched up her own towel and followed, leaving the others to their mirth.

The bath house was a marvel of modern engineering that never failed to impress and fascinate Rai. Half the size of the barracks, its walls and floor were thick stone lined with cedar. A row of nine metal tubs were connected via a confusing welter of copper and brass piping to two enormous, wood-fired coppers. Since drawing fresh water for every bath was wasteful, the soldiers rotated through the tubs one after the other like a large family on Sunday morning, until the water grew too cold and scummy for use. A hearty competition existed among the women on how best to time their arrival at the baths, to be either the first into the water or to breeze in at the exact moment when it must be changed.

Banya strolled the line, inspecting the tubs with an experienced eye. Recognizance complete, she thumped the sides of two adjacent baths. They *bonged* a hollow note and the water rippled, releasing faint tendrils of steam. "We lucked out," she said and tossed her towel onto a wooden bench. "Someone must've drawn these and then got called away before they could use them." She skinned out of her muddy attire and climbed into a tub. As the water closed over her shoulders, she sighed with bliss and closed her eyes.

Rai followed, settling into the warm water with a grunt of pure pleasure. Fresh bruises the color of plum jam decorated her arms and legs like a jester's motley. An angry welt on the underside of one wrist showed the marks of Banya's teeth printed into her flesh like a craftsman's emblem pressed into the bottom of a tankard. A mottled lump the size of a cobblestone raised the skin beside her right knee and shifted with a fluid ease she found nauseating when she prodded it with a scarred and knuckly forefinger. "I need to get out here. This town is making me screwy."

"You were born screwy." Banya tipped her head back against the raised edge of the tub, her expression one of luxurious contentment. Her braids floated like water weeds and curtained the swell of her breasts.

Rai jabbed a middle finger at her, careful to keep her hand beneath the water and out of sight.

"Don't do that," the Carraid warned.

Rai's finger darted back inside the curl of her fist. "Do what?"

Banya opened one eye to look at her. "You know what."

"How do you know I did anything? Your eyes were closed."

Banya settled more comfortably against the back of the tub. "I know *everything* you do, little girl."

"Don't call me little girl." Rai picked up a worn chunk of thick black soap the size and heft of a brick and rolled it between her hands. "Fucking hot all summer," she groused. "No duty except townie stuff." She scrubbed her face and spoke through the suds, blowing bubbles. "Do you realize we never got out of the city once this summer? Not once!"

Banya sighed. "Yes, Rai," she murmured. "I was here, too, remember?"

"Yeah, but *nothing* bothers you."

"*Some* things bother me." She glanced at her friend to underscore the remark. "I just don't go on and on about it for months on end, making everyone else miserable right along with me."

Rai rinsed her face. "What's that supposed to mean?"

"Nothing."

"Right nothing." She kicked the water in frustration. "There wasn't even a single bandit uprising all summer. Can you believe that?"

"Well, it *was* hot," Banya opined in a laconic tone. "Maybe this year they opted to visit the seaside on holiday."

"Ooh, funny." Rai scrubbed her armpits. "What the hell's the point of having bandits if they don't uprise on a regular schedule?"

Banya snorted laughter. "You're the only person I know who would wish for a bandit attack as an antidote to boredom." Her fingers dabbled in the water. "It was a good summer, you know, despite the heat. Crops did well and the harvest should be good. With full bellies, the hill folk have no reason to steal."

Rai goggled at her. "*Reason?* It's their *job!*"

The Carraid smiled and sank deeper into the tub until the water reached her chin. "If the queen's tax collectors don't take it all, there may even be enough food to get everyone through the winter." Her tone hinted at a dubious faith in that belief. "Ah, well, the hill folk aren't stupid. They'll pay out their share and more in taxes, but they'll hide things away as well. They know how to glean the woods and meadows and strip the fields for what's left behind. They'll get by." Her voice took on a tone of admiration. "Somehow, they always do."

"I don't give a rat's ass," Rai said. "I'm talking about expectations. Bandits are supposed to rise in the summer because the roads are full of travelers. If they don't do their job, how are we supposed to do ours? Where does that leave us?" She plied the soap across her scalp and scrubbed with her fingers. Mud-colored suds trickled down her shoulders and turned the bathwater grey. "I'll tell you where it leaves us," she said. "Stuck with the same old shit. Guard the gates and walk the watch," she sing-songed through a dribble of soap.

"Practice arms we never use against enemies we never fight in case we have to protect a bunch of pox-ridden townies who couldn't pour piss out of a boot if you printed the directions on the heel."

Banya arched an eyebrow. "I suppose you'd prefer battle and its tantalizing allure of poor rations, lice, rats, and dysentery." She raised a finger to make a point. "Not to mention imminent death, of course."

"You know what I mean. You're just being difficult."

Banya smiled. "Ah, well, someone has to do it."

Rai kicked the water again and a wave sloshed over the side of the tub. As if in response to this petulant display, thunder growled overhead and a sudden barrage of rain hammered the roof like fists.

"Shit!" Rai exploded.

Banya raised both hands, palms upturned and dripping. "You see how you are? There's no pleasing you. You were bored, so I threw a nice fight, but did you like it? No. You were unhappy with the heat. Now it's cold and rainy and you're miserable." She shook her head in dismay. "It seems like the Goddess has gone out of her way to accommodate your every request, Rai. You ought to be more grateful." She smirked and blew bubbles in a watery raspberry.

"Asshole."

"Puke-face."

Rai rinsed and got out of the tub. She buffed herself pink on the emery-rough towel, then tossed it and her filthy clothing onto the pile of dirty laundry by the door and returned naked to the barracks. The room was deserted and the turd, retrieved from the floor by some hardy soul, lay in the middle of Tynar's pillow like a token of affection. Rai grinned in anticipation of the fireworks that would follow its discovery and began to get dressed. From the bath house came the splash of water and Banya's atonal whistling. The tune was one Rai didn't know, a haunting lament with a somewhat martial undertone.

She was on her hands and knees searching under the bunk for her spare pair of boots when she realized the whistling had stopped. Lifting her head, she peered over the edge of the cot and met Banya's steady gaze from the bath house doorway. "Something I can do for you, songbird?"

Naked with a towel clutched in one hand, the Carraid studied her. "You're not really serious about leaving town, are you? Not serious enough to actually do it, I mean."

"Said I was, didn't I?" Rai fished out her boots from beneath the bed and shifted around onto her rump to pull them on.

"Not in so many words." Banya dressed with the alacrity of an experienced soldier – black breeches with beige piping, plain muslin shirt, black vest and boots. Her braids, towel-dried, shed water in a dark patch over each breast like she was milk-heavy and leaking. “There’s a word for when someone leaves their post without orders, Rai. It’s desertion. They hang people for that around here, you know.”

Rai grinned. “Only if they catch you.” When Banya failed to respond with laughter, her smile faded. She draped her arms across her cocked up knees. “Relax, Mother. I’m not going to throw away a perfectly lousy job by getting myself strung up for desertion. Give me credit for more brains than that.”

Banya shrugged acquiescence. “Maybe a few more.”

“Thanks.” Rai stood and stomped her feet to settle the old boots. “Hey, what’s the name of that tune you were whistling?”

“This?” The big woman hummed a few bars. When Rai nodded, she shrugged. “It’s an old Carraid folk song.”

“It’s pretty.”

“You think?” She snagged their jackets from a long rack on the wall and tossed Rai’s to her. “Let’s get some supper.”

They paused on the stoop to draw up their hoods against the steady fall of rain. Rai chuffed breath and watched the white fog rise. “It’s turning colder. There’ll be frost before you know it.”

“Aye,” Banya said. A wistful longing crept into her voice. “Round-up will start in another week or two.” Her expression was difficult to read in the shadows.

Rai looked up at her. “You miss Carraidland, don’t you? Miss being home?”

Banya shrugged. She stuffed her hands into her pockets and led the way down the steps. Beneath their feet, the deserted yard was a morass of mud churned into a heavy stew by the passage of boots, hooves, and wheels.

The reasons behind Banya’s decision to leave her beloved homeland in exchange for a soldier’s life outside its borders were a mystery to Rai. The Carraid had never offered an explanation and Rai had never asked because you didn’t pry into a person’s life without invitation. She knew little about the Carraid and their way of life beyond their disproportionate love of horses and a fondness for garish clothing.

“I don’t know what it’s like to miss home,” she said, taking two strides for every one of Banya’s. “I got out of Cadasbyr as soon as I could and ended up making a living the same way as my mother.” Her bark of laughter was devoid of humor. “Life’s weird that way.”

“Life’s weirder than you know, little girl.”

For once, Rai didn’t parrot her usual response. She trotted along beside Banya, head bent against the cold rain, and was not altogether surprised when their path diverted toward the stable.

"I just want to check on things," the Carraid said. "It won't take but a minute." She hauled one of the big doors open just far enough for them to squeeze though the gap and slid it closed behind them. A lantern, its flame turned low, hung from an iron arm secured to an overhead beam. The ruddy throb of its light did little to lessen the gloom, turning black shadows to umber and charcoal. Hoods pushed back, jackets dripping onto the scarred wooden floor, the women paused to let their eyes adjust as they breathed in the warm smell of contented animals. Mice and rats rustled in the hay as narrow-flanked, amber-eyed cats ghost-footed along the rafters. High in the mow, safely out of reach from all but the most intrepid feline, pigeons shifted on coral-colored feet and cooed idiotic remarks.

Banya smiled when several of the horses nickered, turning their heads to look at them. "Bunch of greedy pigs. They're less interested in us than they are in the chance for an extra ration of grain." She uttered a low two-toned whistle.

A door at the far end of the aisle opened, spilling a wedge of light onto the floor. A shadowy form appeared, carrying an iron skillet that sizzled and sent up the heavenly aroma of slab bacon. "Yes, Chief?"

"No worries, Teegan," Banya said. "Just wanted to let you know it was us."

The girl lifted the skillet. "We're about to have supper. You're welcome to join us."

Banya shook her head. "Thanks all the same, but we're away in a moment. You go on and enjoy your meal."

"All right, Chief. Good night." She stepped back into the room and the door closed.

Banya moved down the long center aisle, checking each stall as she went, patting an offered nose here or an arched neck there. One animal, black as a murderer's heart, flicked his ears at her approach.

"Watch it," Rai cautioned. "That horse of Remeg's is an evil old bastard."

"Him? Ah, he's just misunderstood." Banya's forehead creased in a frown. "There's no such thing as a bad horse, Rai, anymore than there are bad children or bad dogs. It all comes down to handling, how they're treated by those with power over them." She scratched at the base of the horse's ears and crooned a sing-song tone that made no sense to Rai, but which the horse appeared to love. His grunt of pleasure made her smile.

"Poor treatment is what gave this guy his bad manners," Banya said. "That can be difficult to train out once it's been learned. With some animals, heck with some people, you never can get rid of it. Those are the ones who are best destroyed, if they're lucky."

"How is that lucky?"

Banya's eyes were sad. "The alternative is to be beaten and tortured for the rest of their lives." Her fingers moved along the underside of the horse's jaw and his eyelids went heavy with bliss. "My girls can handle every animal in this barn without fear, but they were scared of him. I couldn't have that, so I started working with him a couple of times each day, whenever I had a minute to spare. He tried to take a chunk out of me more than once and still does, sometimes, when he feels out of sorts, but we've come to trust each other. You'd be surprised at how smart he is."

"I'll take your word for it." Rai boosted up onto a barrel and sat with her legs dangling, heels thudding gently against the wooden staves. She had no intention of getting any closer to the beast. "If Captain Remeg catches you messing with him, she'll have your head on a plate."

Banya scowled. Her hands traveled along the animal's neck, across his back and down his flank, where she gently traced the raised contours of scars – some old, others half-healed – left by the raking of spurs. "I wouldn't have to mess with him, as you put it, if she treated him like a living creature instead of a thing put here for her use. It's a wonder I've been able to retrain him at all." Her quiet vehemence startled Rai, for Banya rarely voiced an opinion on their commanding officer. "That's what I meant about him being smart. He knows who his friends are." She bestowed a final pat and turned away. "Everything's snug here. Let's go eat. I'm starving." Halfway to the door, Banya paused and looked back. Rai had not moved off her perch. "You coming?"

Rai smiled. "I have an idea about how we can get out of the city for awhile."

The horsewoman's eyes narrowed and her head tilted a wary fraction. "Why do I think I hate it?"

"You haven't even heard it!"

"Let's keep it that way, shall we?"

"No, listen, it's great! I've got it all figured out. We'll go to Captain Remeg and tell her that your mother just died and you have to go to Carraidland for the funeral and to take her place in the round up or some bullshit like that, but anyway you're really upset and don't want to travel alone so it would be best if I went along to keep an eye on –"

"No." Banya voice was flat and very firm. Her fingers made a warding off gesture in the air between them.

Rai screwed up her face and mimicked the gesture, fluttering her fingers in an exaggerated motion. "What the hell's that supposed to be?"

"You know what it is." The Carraid glowered at her. "I love my mother. I won't tempt Fate by speaking of her death before it happens."

Rai rolled her eyes. "Oh, for love of the Three! I'd always heard the Carraid were a bunch of Goddessless barbarians, but I didn't think *you* believed in that sort of shit." She snorted. "*Fate.*"

"Hear and think what you like, but I'm having no part of your stupid plan." Banya crossed her arms. "Why include me in it, anyway? I'm perfectly happy here. You're the one with the problem."

"Yeah, a six-foot-four problem." Rai hopped off the barrel and dusted the seat of her pants. "Look, if it'll make you feel better, we'll tell Remeg that it's my mother who died. Fate is welcome to the old bitch, if it doesn't already have her."

"You really hate her, don't you?"

The question, delivered with a gentle note of surprise, cut close to the bone. Bully for Banya's rosy childhood, but Rai's had been different and she still had the scars to prove it. "Let's just say that I've no reason to love her and leave it at that, all right?"

"Fine by me, but don't be foolish. Your plan is crap."

"You're the one who's foolish. It's a perfect plan. It'll get us out of town for a few weeks, let us blow off the stink, and we'll be back before snow flies with no one the wiser." Rai grinned and punched Banya lightly on the arm. "Think of the possibilities! By this time tomorrow, we could be eating dinner *anywhere.*"

"Including the stockade." Banya heaved a sigh and shook her head. "Look, Rai, I'm sorry. I know you're excited about this. Maybe it is a good plan and I'm just being a nervous nelly, but I can't be party to this."

Rai's expression fell. "Fine," she said with scorn. "Your loss. You go to dinner like a good girl. I'm going to go see Remeg right now." She shoved past Banya, opened the barn door, and flipped up her hood before stepping out into the rain. She had gone no more than a dozen paces before she heard a muttered oath and the rumble of the barn door sliding closed. Ducking her head against the downpour, Rai hid a smile as a pair of mud-clotted boots fell into pace beside her.

An irritable growl and a spate of profanity greeted the pound of Rai's fist against the tower door. There was the sound of something being slapped down, chair legs scraping against the floor, and the plod of heavy feet. A tiny metal plate set high in the door slid back and a pair of eyes – one gimlet, the other nonexistent – looked out. There was a grunt of annoyance and the plate snapped closed. Two locks snicked back and the door creaked open part-way to reveal a sinewy, tattooed forearm knotted with muscle and crisscrossed with scars. A square-jawed face stared at them. It had once been handsome, that face, perhaps even beautiful in its way, but that was no longer the case. The wide, smooth seam of a scar ran from the left temple, through where that eye had once been, across the bridge of the shattered nose, and ended at the base of the right cheek.

"What do you two clowns want?"

"Only one clown," Banya averred, hands thrust into her pockets. She blinked past the rain dripping off her hood. "I just came along for the ride."

Rai resisted the urge to kick her. "Evening, Orne," she said with solemn politeness. "May I see Captain Remeg, please?" She laid a hand on the woman's thick wrist as if to swing her aside like a gate and felt the hard muscles flex in warning.

"I don't recall her sending for you, pipsqueak." A spark of light reflected in the grey depths of Orne's single, ruthless eye. "Captain gave orders not to be disturbed. Least wise, not by the likes of you."

Rai tried to look sincere. "You don't think I'd interrupt the captain unless it was an emergency, do you?"

Orne sighed. "Give the other leg a pull, why don't you? It's got bells on."

Rai's shoulders slumped, making her the picture of abject despair. She raised a hand to her eyes as if to hide tears. "I just received word that …" She paused for effect and let her voice break just a little. "My mother is *dead*."

"Uh-huh." Orne's rigid stance relaxed not one bit. She thrust a crooked finger so close under Rai's nose that she could smell the pork grease from the guard's dinner. "You lie to me, I'll knock you silly."

Rai looked shocked. "Why would I invent such a thing?" She drooped, a mournful supplicant. "Please, Orne. May I see Captain Remeg?"

The battle-scarred warrior studied her, then suddenly cast her eyes past Rai and pinned Banya where she stood. "This true?" she demanded.

Rai's heart leapt into her throat. Would the Carraid's innate sense of honesty allow her to play along?

Banya's expression gave no hint to her thoughts. Her shoulders lifted in a tiny shrug. "I'm a little worried about her sanity at present," she said, gliding past the guard's question with complete honesty. She gave Rai a pointed look.

Orne's lips pursed as she considered the options. "All right," she said. "I'll tell Remeg you're here, but the choice to see you is hers. If she says no, out you go."

Rai nodded. "That's more than fair. Thank you."

The guard held the door open. "Banya, you coming in, too?"

The Carraid shook her head. "Thanks, no. I've got things to do. I'll leave Rai in your tender care."

"Well, if you change your mind, I've a deck and dice inside." Orne said it not wholly with enthusiasm, for Banya had the reputation as a wickedly successful card player, no matter what the game.

"Maybe I'll take you up on it after my shift," Banya said. She leaned inside to grab Rai's arm as Orne turned away and mounted the first few steps of the long stairway that led to Remeg's office. "I'm begging you." Her voice was a harsh whisper for their ears alone. "Don't do this. It's not right. Getting caught on the wrong side of Remeg is not a good idea."

Rai patted her hand. "Relax, Mother. I'm not going to get caught. Besides, what's the worst than can happen?" She closed the door in her face.

FOUR

Kinner sat before the fire hunched in misery, exhausted; helpless. In the two weeks since leaving home, he had endured saddle sores, sleepless nights, rain, cold, fear, and abduction. Now he was in a stone tower in a city that had been only a name until today, waiting for … what?

She who held the answer to that question was there with him, but she wasn't talking.

Holan sat ramrod straight in a worn leather camp chair before a plain wooden desk, her eyes fixed on the windows behind the desk where rain pummeled the diamond-shaped panes. The firm set of her jaw broadcast her state of mind more clearly than words.

"Mum?"

No response; not even the flicker of an eye to indicate she had heard him.

The office had little to recommend it, with its dingy whitewash and scuffed floor. It was clearly a place of labor, not of enjoyment. A small unadorned religious icon hung on one wall and two squat candles in shiny brass holders sat on the mantelpiece. A small cabinet, its unfinished wood gone a soft grey with age and use, held a ruby-bellied decanter and four delicate horn cups chased with silver.

Kinner sighed and rubbed his forehead, careful to avoid the tender spot in the middle of his brow where a blue *triskele,* the mark of sterility, had been pricked into his skin with needle and ink. Much of the pain and swelling had subsided, but none of the shame.

There was no ritual inherent in the marking of steriles. As far as the affected family was concerned, the less notice taken of the new pariah the better. Holan had taken him to a little shop down by the docks for the procedure. Had the circumstances been different, Kinner would have been fascinated by the wharves and ships, the bustle and mysterious cargo, and the sea-faring women with their weathered skin, exotic clothing, and rolling swagger. Several of the sailors bore colorful tattoos to which his seemed a poor relation.

He had recoiled at the first touch of the needle. The woman wielding it

– the first black woman he had ever seen, monkey-faced and wizened as shoe-leather – had sworn at him. "I'll tie you down, boy, you don't hold still." He had closed his eyes then and Holan had held his hand as tears ran down his face.

They had left home the next morning, in foggy weather that uncannily mimicked his mood. No one came to see them off. The Aunts could not be bothered and the girls were not allowed. He thought of Ferlie and hoped she would understand.

As they rode east through town, shopkeepers opening their stores for the day had stared with unabashed curiosity, their expressions a mixture of pity for the blacksmith and outright contempt for the boy who had failed his family. One woman, a cobbler by the sign above her door, had spit on the ground as Kinner rode past. "Good riddance, you useless git."

"Where you off to, smith?" another merchant called. "Going to leave him in the hills or kill him outright?"

"No," cried another voice, treacley with feigned compassion. "Didn't you hear? She's taking him to *Dara.*"

Laughter and exclamation had followed, some of the remarks downright foul. Kinner, his face flushed hot with blood, had ducked his head and hunched his shoulders in small defense against the harassment.

Holan, riding beside him, had raised her chin and set her eyes straight ahead. "Pay them no mind, boyo," she said and nudged her horse into a trot. "Big mouthed bitches, the lot of them."

Did she mean these women in particular, he wondered, or those at home who had obviously discussed the issue outside the family? Knowing Holan, it was probably both.

From the beginning, it was obvious the trip would take an enormous toll on her. By the end of the first day, Holan's profile was gaunt, the flesh seeming to melt away with every mile, her eyes looming large and bright in the sunken caverns of her skull.

Kinner watched in silent anguish. If she died before they reached Dara, what would become of him?

One night, as they sheltered within a travelers bothy, she caught him watching her. "Stop your staring," she said. Pipe smoke curled from her lips. "I'm not some strange bug come crawling out of the wall."

Kinner yanked his blankets closer around his neck. "You shouldn't smoke in your condition," he said in a crabby, accusatory tone.

She snorted with contemptuous ill humor. Firelight painted her cheeks rosy with false health. "*My condition.*" She tapped her chest with the pipe stem. "I'll worry about my condition and you mind your own business." She took a deep draw just to annoy him and jetted smoke from the corner of her mouth like a dragon in some child's book of bedtime stories. "This blend eases the cough. At this late date I'll take what comforts I can find."

Kinner focused on the edge of his blanket, working it back and forth with his fingers, folding and unfolding in endless repetition.

Holan watched him for a time, then huffed in annoyance and propped a bony elbow on one knee. "What's eating you?"

He shrugged.

She grunted. "Fine. Don't talk. It won't be my fault if you shrivel up like a dead cat and end up looking like Auntie Dwinn."

A smile twitched the line of his mouth. He fought to keep it at bay, but it was useless to try. He chuckled. "That's an awful thing to say!"

"But true all the same." She tossed a stick onto the fire. "You *can* talk to me, you know," she said. "You can even yell at me if it'll make you feel better."

Kinner's cheer bled away. For a moment, the strained silence threatened to return, and then he sat up, hands clutched in the blanket. "This whole thing is bollixed!" he cried, eyes filling with tears. "It's not *fair*, Mum!"

Holan's expression softened, but she did not move to console him. "Fairness. Now that's an interesting topic." She sucked on the pipe. The smoke released with her next words briefly crowned her thinning hair with a garland of grey. "The world turns to the Weathercock's cry, lad, no matter what the Lady Church says. We may not understand His methods, but that doesn't make them wrong." She clicked the pipe stem against her teeth. "I'm not happy with the turn of things, but no one asked my opinion. Would you prefer a different outcome?"

"To sterility?" he said with sarcasm. "Gee, let me think."

She swatted his leg. "You have a choice, Kinner. You can let this defeat you or you can use it to your advantage."

He snorted. "Choice," he muttered. "As if that figures into anything."

She thrust the pipe stem at him like a weapon. "There are *always* choices!" she declared. "Nothing is inevitable unless you make it so."

He drew breath to argue, but she spoke over him before he could get out a single word. "The best path is not always the easiest one. If it's easy you want, you'd best turn around and go home and let *them* decide your future. It won't be easy, but it'll be short. I can promise you that." She sucked hard on the pipe, a deep and angry draw, and the bowl glowed with ruddy color. "As for the rest of it … how do I make you understand its importance?" Her gnarled fingers curled into a fist and knocked against her breastbone. "This is as much a part of me as the beating of my heart and I'll do whatever it takes to see it to the end even if it means crawling to Dara." Her gaze burned for a moment with the fervid enthusiasm of a zealot, then her expression changed, deepening into regret. "Is it too late to say sorry, love? I had no business filling your head with those damned stories. If I'd acted earlier, as I should have, there'd be no need to include you in this fool's venture."

Kinner moved closer and touched the thin strands of her vanishing hair, recalling its former rich darkness with a pang that squeezed his heart. "You were right to tell me about the Weathercock, Mum," he said in a soft voice. "I – I'm *glad* you told me. I'm not happy with how things turned out, but my ... problem ... isn't your fault."

Holan's hand, dry as old boot leather, caressed his cheek and he leaned his face into her palm. "Shows what I get for vanity, though, doesn't it, being certain I'd march into Dara proud as punch?" Her expression faltered, allowing a rare and fleeting glimpse of the frightened dying woman beneath the blacksmith's bluff exterior. "Except now my time is up." She put the pipe down, cupped her son's face in both hands, and brought their foreheads together. "We may not like what's been set before us," she whispered. "But we can face it together."

He hugged her, careful not to squeeze those fragile bones too tightly, and stared over her shoulder into the darkness. *There are always choices,* she had said. *Nothing is inevitable unless you make it so.* Maybe that was true for women, but how those words applied to him, Kinner could not see at all.

His memories fragmented into dancing flame and fallen ash as the office door opened. The lean woman standing on the threshold paused there for a heartbeat as if to gauge the tension in the room, then she stepped inside and closed the door. Her handsome, somewhat severe features were accentuated by extremely short dark hair and sharply peaked brows. Two thumb-sized golden orbs affixed to the black wool collar of her uniform caught the light and winked.

Her cool gaze slid across Kinner, lingered on his forehead in brief speculation, and moved on as she silently dismissed him as being of no importance. "I'm Captain Remeg, commander of the Caerau garrison." Her voice was cool. She neither smiled nor offered a hand in greeting.

Neither did Kinner's mother. "My name is Holan. I'm from Moselle." Without turning, she gestured toward the fire. "That is my son, Kinner."

He stood, eyes downcast as was proper, and bowed slightly before resuming his seat.

Having already put him out of her mind, Remeg did not acknowledge the deference. "You appear ill, madam. If you've come carrying plague, I have just cause to turn you –"

Holan held up a hand to still her words. "No plague, I assure you. It's a wasting disease for which there is no cure, but utterly incommunicable if the condition of my family may be taken as proof."

"As your family is in Moselle and not here, I must take you at your word." Remeg's boots made a sharp sound against the floor as she crossed the room and stepped behind the desk. She rested a hand on the back of the chair, but her posture did not relax, nor did she move to sit. "You requested to see me."

Holan nodded. "Yes, Captain. I wish to lodge a complaint against your troop."

One dark eyebrow twitched slightly upward. "The entire troop or someone in particular?"

"The squadron of soldiers who detained us on the road and took my son prisoner."

Wood scraped against the floor as Remeg pulled the chair away from the desk and sat. Placing her elbows precisely on the desk top, she laced her fingers together. Her hands were long-boned, lean and strong, covered with a white cross-hatching of old scars and the healing pink of recent wounds. "Please explain."

Kinner thought that she must already know the details from her own soldiers. How could she not? Holan had made no secret of her displeasure and upon arrival in Caerau had caused such a ruckus that the woman in command of the squadron, had escorted them to the tower in self-defense and left them for Remeg to deal with.

"I am taking my son to the monastery at Dara," Holan said. She withdrew a document from her pouch, unfolded it, and pushed it across the desk. "He has a sincere calling."

Remeg gave the paper a cursory glance, noted the physician's signature and wax seal affixed to the affidavit, and pushed it back toward Holan with one finger as if loathe to touch it. "My condolences," she said with bland indifference.

"Thank you," Holan said in the same dry tone. "My Household would just as soon see him dead, but …" She shrugged. "I'm a sentimental old fool, I suppose. He *is* my son, after all."

Remeg remained impassive, as unblinking as a reptile. The blacksmith braved the crest of that silence like a ship mounting the curl of a wave. "My condition forced us to travel more slowly than we might otherwise and bad weather delayed us further. Several days ago we were …" She paused to search for the right word. "Intercepted by your soldiers."

Kinner shivered with remembrance. The *clop-suck* of hooves in mud had heralded the troop's approach long before they came into view, materializing out of the mist and cold slanting rain like a ghostly army from a by-gone era.

There had been seven riders and a wagon driver. Tall boots and hooded cloaks of boiled wool shielded them from the worst of the storm. The leader – The leader, a lanky middle-aged woman – had halted her mount across the road, impeding their progress as the other riders made a loose circle around Holan and Kinner. The draywoman had eased her team to a stop with a long, drawn out *whooaa.* While the big horses blew smoky air and stamped their feathered feet, she produced a pipe from an inside pocket and puffed it to life. One knee crossed over the other, she sat back with the reins lax in her hands and watched the proceedings with vague interest while the rain beat a steady rhythm against the wagon's heavy canvass roof. From inside came the sound of weeping.

"This is dirty weather to be caught out in," The leader had observed in a bantering tone.

"Indeed it is." Holan's reply had not invited camaraderie or conversation. "All the more reason to reach our destination as soon as possible."

"And where might that be, madam?" The soldier's voice had remained friendly, but Kinner sensed a worrisome undercurrent.

His mother had sat up straight in the saddle. "With all due respect ..." Her eyes sought the insignia on the woman's collar. "*Sergeant,* this is a free road."

Unfazed, the woman had scratched her nose. "Aye, that's true enough, but it's also the queen's road. Since we ride at her behest, that makes your business our own." She smiled. "With all due respect." Her gaze shifted from Holan to Kinner, sitting hooded and silent atop his horse. Her eyes narrowed. "Who's this then?"

"My son." Holan reached into her pouch for the same document she would later present to Remeg, and held it out. The beribboned wax seals had dangled in an obvious manner, turning in the wind. "We travel to Dara."

"My condolences." She examined the certificate and returned it. Kneeing her horse forward, she reached out and pushed Kinner's hood back from his face. She studied him with detachment and jerked the hood back over his damp hair. "Into the wagon."

"No!" Holan had struggled to drive her horse forward as the others closed in on her son. "You have no right! He has been examined by a registered physician and deemed sterile –"

"Of what use, then, is he to you?" the sergeant had demanded, her dark gaze penetrating. "Sentimentality is all well and good, but you should be grateful to have us take him off your hands and save you a long and difficult trip." She had jerked her head to those under her command. "Put him in the wagon with the rest. And *you* …" She leaned forward and shoved a finger against Holan's chest. "Be on your way."

One of the soldiers had spoken up. "Beck, Cap'n Remeg said the queen only wants –"

"I know what the queen wants!" Beck had snapped. "Half the frelling continent knows what she wants and we're all leaping at shadows in case we get it wrong. I'm not taking any chances. Put him in the wagon."

Kinner had tried to escape, jerking the reins and pummeling the horse with his heels. Encircled as it was and firmly held by a cheek strap, there was nothing the poor beast could do but pin its ears and roll its eyes in confusion. One of the soldiers attempted to pry Kinner's fingers from the reins. When he refused to let go, she slapped him across the face. The shock of the blow made him drop the wet leather, and she had scooped him from the saddle as neatly as an egg from its cup and tossed him into the wagon, shrieking with terror. Hands had caught him, easing the fall, and he found himself staring up into the faces of a dozen frightened men.

"At which point, your soldiers warned me off with drawn weapons." Holan's voice was tense with constrained emotion. "I had little choice but to do as they ordered or risk being killed for my bother. They couldn't move fast in that sort of weather, not with a wagonload of men they couldn't, so it wasn't difficult to keep up."

That was a lie. It had taken every ounce of strength and determination Holan possessed to keep up. She had ghosted their heels, stopping to rest and eat only when they did, afraid to sleep for fear of being left behind. Brazen, she had come to sit by their fire each night to get warm. Annoyed at first, the soldiers had quickly grown amused by the old woman's boldness and tenacity. Some shared their food with her, while others gave her extra blankets and let her speak briefly with Kinner to put her mind at ease. Finally even Beck took pity and allowed the blacksmith to ride in the wagon with her horse tied to the rear. The men inside had huddled around her like chicks drawn to a protective hen.

"Yes, I heard about all that." Remeg's voice was soft. Her eyes, opaque, gave nothing away.

"When we arrived in Caerau, I came here straight away." Holan tapped a finger against the sterility decree. Remeg, having already glanced at it, was not about to look a second time. "I want permission to leave Caerau immediately with my son."

A small line appeared between the captain's brows as if a headache might have bloomed there. "Granted," she said simply and without preamble. "Be on your way."

Holan was clearly surprised by the easy capitulation. "And we'll travel unmolested?"

Remeg folded her hands together. "I can guarantee no further harassment by my soldiers while you remain here, but I won't vouch for the behavior of Caerau's citizens. What transpires between you and them is your own go-around, subject to the laws of this city and the judgment of its mayor. What befalls you outside Caerau's walls is none of my affair." Her body language made it clear the interview was at an end.

"May I then ask a favor, Captain?"

Annoyance tightened the skin around Remeg's eyes. "You already have."

"Yes," Holan said with deference. "I've no wish to flog a dead horse or to impose on your good nature, but my failing health suggests that it might be prudent to have a guide, someone to take us through the mountains by the safest route. Would you assign one of your soldiers for the duration of our journey? That way, if I die before we reach Dara, she can see that my son gets there safely. The boy could never find the way alone." She leaned forward and lowered her voice. "You know how men are with directions."

"Ah." Remeg's tone suggested that Kinner's disappearance would be no great loss. Pushing her chair back, she stood and looked down at Holan. "As I need hardly point out, madam, the autumn rains have arrived. The rivers are swollen and many of the trails will be treacherous with mud. How you choose to endanger yourselves is your business, but I find no justification in putting one of my soldiers at risk for a venture that I am incapable of viewing as anything other than foolhardy. Perhaps you'll have greater success asking in town for a guide."

For a moment Holan sat in silence, starring at Remeg, then she toed off one boot and reached deep inside. Her hand emerged with the fingers curled into a fist. "Your logic is irrefutable, Captain, but may I stress that it means a great deal to me that we reach Dara as soon as possible." She opened her palm and placed a single gold darma on the desk.

Kinner nearly choked. He had never suspected his mother to possessed such wealth. Where had it come from? Had she hoarded this secret cache in order to spend it exactly this way?

Remeg's hand moved to rest beside the golden disc, her loosely curled fingers poised like a spider. When they moved, it was to trace across the embossed visage of Queen Kedar Trevelyan. "You realize that this could be construed as bribery."

Holan's gaze never wavered. "I prefer to think of it as compensation for your trouble. The guide will be paid as well, of course."

Remeg's mouth twitched and her chin dipped in a barely perceptible nod. Once more her finger ran along the Queen's profile and then she very deliberately pushed the coin toward Holan. "I'm afraid I can't help you."

The blacksmith's mouth dropped open with astonishment. Before she could speak, before she could even begin to voice an argument, there was a knock on the door.

"Come," said Remeg.

The door swung open to reveal a pair of soldiers stood on the landing. One was the disfigured guard who had admitted Holan and Kinner to the tower. Behind her, all but lost in shadow, was a younger, darker woman.

The cropped fringe of the guard's hair did not move as she dipped her head. "Sorry to interrupt, Captain, but this soldier requested an audience. I think you might want to talk to her."

Remeg inclined her head briefly to Holan. "Duty calls," she said. "Madam, this concludes our discussion. Take your money and your son and be on your way wherever you choose to go. It's no concern of mine."

Holan drew breath to argue, but a glance toward Orne's looming presence made her reconsider. Lips pressed into a disapproving line, she vanished the darma back into her boot with the swift ease of a magician and shoved her foot down on top of it. She tried to rise with dignity, but anger, dismay, and exhaustion conspired against her. Her hand slipped off the arm of the chair as she pushed herself up and she would have fallen had Kinner not leaped from his seat to catch her.

He looked up at Remeg, who had not so much as twitched a muscle when Holan faltered. Their eyes met in a fleeting glance he hoped never to repeat. "Excuse us, Captain," he said and put his arm around Holan's waist. "Come on, Mum." He helped her up and together they moved out onto the tiny landing.

From behind, Remeg spoke. "Come in, Rai, and close the door. Orne, show them out."

The scarred woman grunted and pushed past Kinner and Holan with a brusque "This way." At the bottom of the stairs, she held the outer door open and delivered them without a word into the wet and windy night.

FIVE

The tower door shut, followed by the flat snap of both locks being engaged. Kinner cringed from the sound as if it were a blow and plucked nervously at his mother's sleeve. "What do we do now, Mum?" His voice was raw with anxiety.

Holan shook him off. "Hush your noise. I have to think." She began to pace – three steps in one direction, five in another – always returning to where he stood waiting, only to pass by him as if he were invisible. Rain flattened the dry fuzz of her hair against her skull and tracked runnels down her face, sluicing off the end of her nose like a freshet. Her gaze darted from one spot to the next without sense or reason. The churned earth and rain-dimpled puddles offered no answers and the black sky wept at her futility.

Nailed to the spot by indecision, Kinner watched her track back and forth. His heart clenched with despair at the overwhelming sense of his own uselessness. A hot cup of tea and foot rub could not make things better, but there was little else he knew how to do. "Mum?"

She brushed past like they were strangers, the sodden length of her cloak barely stirring around her ankles as she walked.

He tried again. "Mum, why don't we get inside somewhere, find someplace warm where we can change into dry clothes, maybe get something hot to drink and a bit of supper? There must be a tavern or inn where we can –"

Her up-flung hand silenced him like a knife across the throat. She stopped short, facing away from him, and now leaned forward to peer into the darkness. Kinner looked as well and saw nothing … until a slight motion in the gloom of an alley revealed a dark and solitary figure with hunched shoulders and a cowled head. A faint thread of tune, whistled low and atonal, carried to him on the breeze.

Kinner's gut tightened and his heart began to pound. Every blood-curdling story his aunts had ever told about strangers in big cities raced through his mind in the same instant his mother grabbed a handful of his cloak. "Come on!" To his horror, she began to drag him *toward* the ominous figure rather than away from it.

"Excuse me," the blacksmith called. The whistling ceased, but there was no other response to her hail. "You're Carraid, are you not?"

The figure shifted and stepped out of the alley into the marginally better light thrown by a guttering street lamp. Kinner took an involuntary step backward, pulling at his mother's arm as the big head lifted on that massive frame and a large hand pushed the hood back slightly to reveal a broad and pleasant face framed by countless thin blonde braids.

The tall woman touched two fingers to her brow in greeting. "Banya Kiordasdotter." She startled Kinner by dipping her head to him in an amiable salute. "You've good eyes on a dark night, Grandmother."

"It wasn't my eyes that marked you as Carraid-born, Kiordasdotter, but my ears." Holan stepped closer and lowered her voice. "One does not usually hear certain songs beyond the circle of certain friends."

An emotion Kinner could not read swept across Banya's face. It flattened her gaze and brought a sobering line to her generous mouth. Her eyes narrowed a fraction, gauging Holan and her words. One arm shifted beneath her cloak and Kinner imagined a large hand curling around the hilt of a knife, ready in an instant to draw his mother's blood.

Unfazed by any implied threat, Holan grasped the soldier's wrist with a skeletal hand. Banya resisted for an instant, then brought her ear down as the blacksmith went up on her toes to meet it. "I need your help," Holan whispered. She pulled back slightly to look straight into the horseclanner's eyes. "In the Weathercock's name."

"In here." The faint stir of Banya's voice was whisper thin and barely there, her words masked by a white puff of breath. She inched open the barn door just far enough for them slip through the narrow gap and slid it shut again. A restive stirring went through the herd like the rustle of leaves in an easy wind. One of the horses chuckled a low and throaty question. "Quiet, you," the Carraid said in a soft voice, then added, "Wait here," and moved away into the darkness.

"Where –" The tight squeeze of Holan's fingers around his wrist silenced Kinner. Eyes wide, he stared at nothing, breathing in the sweet odor of animals at rest. Something suddenly bumped his ankle and he jumped, sucking air to scream *Rats!*, but before he could cry out the thing on the floor uttered a throaty *purrowl* and butted his leg again. Shaken, torn between laughter and tears, Kinner stooped and reached out a blind hand. When his wary fingers encountered fur, the cat arched the smooth contours of its back into his open palm and ran its body through his hand from head to tail and back again, purring all the while.

A small glow like a fairy candle appeared at the far end of the barn. Banya emerged from a side room and walked toward them carrying a lantern with the wick turned low. Her smile caught the faint light. "At least now we won't go stubbing our toes in the dark, eh?" she whispered. She nudged the cat with her boot. "Scoot," she said and whistled a single note, the faint sound all but lost in the black vastness of the barn.

Furtive motion stirred the hay in the mow overhead and a moment later a figure dropped from above, startling both Kinner and Holan. The lanky teenager landed in the aisle with ease and straightened. She glanced at the strangers, her dark gaze sharp with interest, and ran a hand over her hair to brush away loose chaff. "Chief?"

"Keep your voice down, Teegan. I need your help." Banya laid a hand on the girl's shoulder. "This lady and her son need somewhere quiet and out of the way to spend the night, maybe as much as a couple of days, with no one the wiser. I'm putting them in the mow under your care, eh? Feed 'em, bed 'em down warm, and keep 'em out of sight."

Teegan nodded without need for explanation. "Understood."

"The rest of you understand as well?" the Carraid asked into the air.

A score of sleep-tousled heads rose into view and peered down at them over the lip of the mow, each expression grave and serious. All in a row, the girls ranged in age from a freckled, tow-headed tyke of five up to the gypsy-dark Teegan. "Yes, Chief," they responded in unison, heads bobbing, voices high and soft.

"See that you do," Banya said. "If I hear that so much as one of you has noised barn business about, you'll all be cut loose and back on the streets. That understood as well?"

"Yes, Chief," they chorused.

Banya nodded. "They'll take good care of you," she said to Holan with assurance. "I need to tie up some loose ends if we're going to do this right. May take a day or two –"

"Whatever you think is best," Holan said. She grasped Banya's enormous paw between her bony hands. "Thank you, Kiordasdotter."

The Carraid did not smile. "Thank me when we get to Dara in one piece, Grandmother, and not before." She turned to the slender girl. "They're all yours now, Teegan. Their horses and baggage are out back. Put the animals at the far end of the barn where they're less likely to draw attention. Groom them, bed them down, and give them hay and an extra ration of grain. Add some molasses and a pinch or two of salt and give it a warm before you feed them. Stow the gear in the tack room back behind the stuff that needs repair. No one will notice an extra saddle or two lying about. Put the luggage up top with our friends." She handed the lantern to Kinner, touched two fingers to her brow in farewell, and was gone.

As the door closed behind her, deft fingers plucked the lantern from Kinner's grasp. Startled, his eyes met Teegan's for an instant before she turned away and began to issue orders. "Rigg and Stuka, you bring the horses in quiet-like and put them to bed. You heard the Chief tell how." A set of identical twins of perhaps seven years old with matching dirt smudges across their noses, leapt from the mow and disappeared into the darkness. "Senya and Triss, you bring in their bags and get 'em stowed." These girls, a few years younger than Teegan, nodded and were gone. "The rest of you, make a sleeping place out of sight in a dry corner under the eaves." The last of the children scurried off.

Teegan jerked her head toward the mow ladder and put her free hand under Holan's elbow. "Can you climb, Grandmother, or should we rig a sling?"

The blacksmith brushed away the suggestion with a snort. "The day I need a sling to get up a ladder, you may as well put me in the ground. If someone comes along behind to keep me steady, I think I can make it on my own." Her voice turned derogatory. "And if I can't, you have my permission to toss me up there like a sack of grain."

The girl flashed a brief grin. "Fair enough." She looked at Kinner. "You first, that way you can help her from above. Up you get." When he reached the mow, she climbed up half-way to hang the lantern on a hook, then returned to the aisle. "After you, Grandmother," she said and stepped in close behind Holan as the blacksmith put her hands on the first rung. "I'm right here, so don't you worry about falling."

"Believe me, young woman, falling is the least of my concerns." Mouth set with resolution, Holan began to scale the ladder. Though her intentions were good, ill health and the turmoil of the past days claimed her halfway to her goal. She stopped climbing and clung to the wooden rung with her forehead against her hands. "Give me a moment," she murmured, breathing hard.

"I'm sorry, Grandmother, but I don't have one to give." Teegan's next words emerged as a bark. "Grab her arms!" Kinner leaned down without question and grasped his mother's wrists as the girl put her shoulder under the blacksmith's bony rump and delivered an unceremonious shove that goosed Holan into the hay. She landed half atop her son and lay there, gasping with laughter.

Teegan's head popped up over the edge of the mow. "I took you at your word, Grandmother," she said with a grin.

Holan tried to respond, but the dust kicked up by her precipitous arrival made her cough. Her frail body curled forward and shuddered against the support of Kinner's arms as she fought for breath. "This is no good," he said. "She can't stay up here. It's too dirty."

"There's nowhere else," the girl said, climbing the rest of the way to join them. "Besides, it's a hay mow," she stated with annoyance. "What did you expect?"

Kinner had been raised to never talk back to a woman no matter what her age, but anger and worry overrode all of his training. "We didn't expect *anything* in this stupid town! We weren't even supposed to –"

Holan swatted his arm. "Hush and ... be ... grateful." Her lungs labored like a bellows. "They're ... doing us ... a ... favor."

Kinner felt ashamed. Were it not for Banya's kindness, they would still be standing in the rain outside Remeg's tower, wondering what to do. He rubbed his forehead and sighed. "I'm sorry," he said to Teegan. "I'm just ..." He shook his head, unwilling to explain and tired of making excuses. "Please, a drink of water would help her."

"I can do that." The teenager let the tense moment slide away with the ease of someone used to playing referee. She vanished back down the ladder (without use of the rungs, Kinner noticed), and returned a moment later to offer Holan a battered cup filled with cool water.

Kinner held it while his mother drank, one hand over his to steady the cup against her mouth. "Thank you," she said when she had finished it all. She wiped her lips on her sleeve. "That's much better."

Teegan didn't look convinced, but instead of arguing she took the lantern from its hook. "This way, please."

They shuffled through loose fodder to the rear of the mow and an area beneath the eaves. From the outside it looked like nothing but a haphazard stack of sheaves, but within that sanctuary was an open area floored deep in hay. Senya and Triss were putting on the finishing touches as the travelers arrived, spreading bedrolls and adding extra blankets redolent of horse. Holan and Kinner's meager luggage lay stacked along the back wall of the barn.

Teegan nodded approval as she hung the lantern from a knob of wood. "Good job, you two."

"Yes, this is lovely." Holan turned in a circle to admire the shelter. "It's much better than a room at a stinky old inn. Thank you so much."

The girls' chests puffed with pride. "You're welcome, Grandmother," Senya said with pleasure and tugged a dark forelock as she and Triss exited.

Two girls of nine or ten pushed into the shelter now, trailed by the youngest.

One carried a wooden tray which held a knife and two cups, a rolled scrap of towel, a small loaf of bread, a fist-sized chunk of cheese, and two withered apples. She put this down between the bedrolls and stepped back. Beside it, the other girl placed two steaming billy cans. "Them's tea in one." She spoke more to Teegan than to their guests, too shy to look directly at them. "Sugar in't. No milk, sorry. The other's for washing up, if one was wanting to."

"That's good thinking, Even, Odd." Teegan's pleasure in their efforts faded as her brows drew down in sudden suspicion. "Where'd you get that food? It's not from our stores."

Their faces fell. They glanced at one another and looked at their feet. Their hands reached out to each other, left to right, and closed.

The older girl's expression grew stern. "Out with it."

"We kiped it from the kitchen," Odd, on the left, whispered.

Teegan was on them in an instant. She wrenched them apart, shook them hard, and boxed their ears. "You stole from Black Hirn?" She was outraged, appalled. "Where's your brains? She catches you, she'll have all our heads. The Chief's, too! How'll that make the Chief look, eh? They'll say she can't handle her own, maybe take her away from us! How'll that make *us* look? We're above thievery, unless you're wanting back on the streets where you was found!"

"No, Teeg!" Even pleaded. Wide, fearful eyes searched the older girl's face for benevolence and did not find it.

"It's not the good stuff!" Odd added in a hurry, eyes flooding with tears. "We took from the pile set aside for the pigs!" Belatedly, she realized how that must sound and clapped both hands over her mouth, cheeks scarlet.

"Black Hirn's pigs must eat very well," Holan said with gentleness. "That's a handsome bit of cheese."

"They cutted all the green bits off," a small, helpful voice said by her leg.

She looked down into the open, honest face of the little blonde and smiled. "Did they?"

The child nodded with serious demeanor. "It were all *hairy,*" she said, and wrinkled her nose.

Holan placed a gentle hand on the child's head. "That was very thoughtful," she said. Her words trembled with suppressed laughter.

"The bread's a bit tough," Even admitted, emboldened to speak. "But we thought you could dunk it in the tea to soften it up."

"That's not the point!" Hands fisted in the cloth of their shirts, Teegan shook them again. "Look, it's grand that you wanted to give them something to eat, but you shouldn't have lifted it like a couple of common lightfingers." She shoved them away, wiped her hands on her pants like they were soiled, and stuck out a warning finger. "I won't turn you over to Hirn this time because the Chief wants things quiet and it's the first you've been so stupid and show-offy. But you so much as look at those scraps again – or anything else belonging to Black Hirn – without permission and I'll dump you at her feet and let her do as she likes with you. Got that?" Their heads bobbled in terrified affirmation. "Extra chores all week for both of you *and* you'll turn the manure pile. Now get to bed."

"Yes, Teegan," they murmured and scuttled away into hiding without once looking back.

When they were gone, the girl drew a steadying breath. "I apologize for that."

"This Black Hirn must be a formidable presence," Holan observed.

The corner of Teegan's mouth lifted. "You could say that." She rubbed the back of her neck. "They're basically good girls, you know. Don't judge 'em by this. They know better than to take without asking."

"I doubt they'll do so again," said Holan. "Quite honestly, pig fare or not, those apples look delicious."

Teegan took the hint. "I'll leave you to your supper and your beds. If you need anything in the night, I'm not far away. Just give a soft call and I'll hear –" She looked down. "What are you still doing here, Bug?"

The littlest girl paid her no mind. She was staring up at Kinner with serious intent, her tiny brow creased in deep thought. One hand reached out and fisted in the loose cloth of his pants leg. "Are you my da'?" she said.

His eyes bugged. "Um … ah … no. No, I don't think so." He squatted down to her level and pushed the hair away from his forehead. "Do you see this mark?"

She nodded solemnly and touched it with a gentle finger.

"That means I can't be anyone's da'."

Bug's eyes grew round with amazement. "They puts paint on your face and now you can't be a da'?" She was horrified.

Kinner shifted, not certain how to explain sexuality to a five-year-old. "Well … something like that." He noticed a wad of cloth bunched under her arm. Hoping to change the subject, he said, "What's that?"

"Bogus." She handed it to him. The bundle of rags unfolded into the soiled remains of a half-stuffed, one-eyed, bent-eared toy bunny that reminded him vaguely of the one he had owned as a child. "Teegan founded him in a dust bin and gived him to me."

The older girl's eyelids crinkled with affection. "Enough talk now, Bug. These folks need their supper and their rest. Time for all little girls and their rabbits to be in bed."

“’kay,” the child agreed around an enormous yawn. She took her toy from Kinner and let Teegan usher her toward the makeshift entry. On the threshold, she stopped and turned back. The expression on her sweet face was one of such profound sadness that Kinner felt his heart go tight with compassion. “The queen took my da,” Bug whispered. “But I’m going to find him someday and bring him home.” A single big tear wobbled at the corner of her eye, broke free, and trickled down her face. Stifling a sob against the rabbit’s worn and much-loved head, she hugged it tight against her chest and left the shelter.

Teegan met their eyes with an expression too old for her years. “That child followed the wagon when they took her father.” Her voice was low, meant not to be heard beyond the three of them. “Last year, that was. She meant to catch up and make the soldiers let him go. Of course she fell behind and got lost. Only the Three knows how she made it to Caerau. Black Hirn found her half-dead, hiding in the wash house, and brought her to me for saving. Chief let me keep her.” She worried her bottom lip, looking for a moment hardly older than the girls in her care. Then she murmured, “Good night,” and was gone.

Six

Rai could sense Remeg's eyes on her as she closed the office door. The knowledge made the skin between her shoulder blades creep. She wondered about the strangers, but her curiosity was a fleeting thing. The door latch clicked under her hand, the sound cutting across her thoughts, and she came to attention with her gaze fixed not on Remeg's face (no one stared straight into those shrewd eyes, not by choice they didn't), but on the wall beyond the captain's left shoulder.

Remeg had resumed her seat behind the desk. Now she leaned on the arm of the chair and looked at Rai with an expression of vague bemusement. "At ease." She rubbed tiredly at one eye and stifled a yawn. "Well? What's so important it can't wait?"

Rai cleared her throat, pushing aside the insistent warning of Banya's voice in her mind. "I've received some bad news, Captain."

Remeg grunted and shoved back her chair. Walking to the hearth, she lit a taper in the fire and set flame to the candles on the mantelpiece. The wicks flared white and settled to a blue-hearted gold, burning true and strong with the purity of fine wax, not guttering like the cheap tallow used in the barracks. She cupped one of the burnished holders between both hands like a chalice and carried it to her desk. Her reflection in the window wavered, distorted by a ripple in the glass as Remeg placed the candle on the desk. Her shadow loomed on the wall behind her, hunch-backed and dreadful. Lit from below, her face was macabre, the sharp line of her cheekbones heightened by shadows, her bright gaze trapped in the dusky eye cups of her skull.

A sudden image of Blas, the Queen of War and Death, darkest of the Goddess's three aspects, darted through Rai's mind and left behind an unsettled aura like the hint of smoke on a horizon.

"Well, go on," Remeg said. "What's happened?"

Rai swallowed and for an instant was positive that she tasted soot on the back of her tongue. "I received word tonight from back home in Cadasbyr that my mother is –" Her voice broke and she looked away, a strong woman attempting to hide embarrassing emotion from another strong woman. "Dead."

A faint noise curled from the back of Remeg's throat like a spider stretching out a single thin leg to test the warp and weft of its latticed web. "The cause?"

Rai had worked out the details on the way to Remeg's office. Even so, she winged a silent prayer to whichever of the Goddess's three heads might be tilted in her direction at this moment. "I don't have many details, Captain. The message said there was some sort of quarrel that got out of hand." She released a sad little laugh. "When it comes to my mother, there's always some sort of quarrel. She isn't ... wasn't ... known for her easy-going personality." That much was true. Muire – sullen, solitary, black-hearted as a storm crow and given to rages of extraordinary proportion – got along with no one.

The unexpected weight of a hand on her shoulder snapped Rai's head around so fast it made her dizzy. Remeg's snake-cool eyes were mere inches from her own. Rai's bladder tightened. She fought the wave of panic that threatened to send her bolting toward the door and prayed she wouldn't wet herself.

Remeg's mouth curled in a faint smile. "I'm sorry if I startled you." She gestured with one hand. "Please sit." As Rai gingerly settled onto the stool recently vacated by the boy, Remeg crossed to the wooden cabinet. She filled one of the small horn cups with the deep red fluid from the decanter and held it out. "Here. This should help to steady your nerves."

Rai's guilty mind whirled with notions of poison. She reached for the offering, dismayed to see a slight tremor in her hand. Drawing a steadying breath, she raised the delicate cup to her mouth. The silvered edge was cool against her lips, a pronounced counterpoint to the liquid fire that warmed her stomach when she swallowed. She stifled a cough.

"There now," Remeg said. "I'm sure that helps." She resumed her place at the desk and stood with her fingertips barely grazing its scarred surface. "You know, Rai, part of my job as commander of this garrison is to be concerned with those under my command. I confess, however, to being somewhat at a loss in this circumstance. What can I do for you beyond offering my profound sympathy?"

Rai couldn't tell if that was sarcasm or not. *Stay frosty,* she thought. *Nothing's wrong. Remeg's just being Remeg.* "The Household will handle the funeral arrangements," she said. *They'll heave her body over a cliff and throw a week-long celebration.* "I'd like to request some leave to go home and pay my respects." *Pissing on her corpse would be a good start.* "I wouldn't ask except that we were so close." She drank again to hide the sneer that came with those words. She'd learned before she was out of nappies to stay out of Muire's reach.

Remeg steepled her fingers beneath her chin. "Given the circumstances, that's a reasonable request."

A rush of adrenaline popped along Rai's nerves. Fie on Mother Banya's worry and fuss! This was going to work and Rai would laugh all the way to whichever town she chose as her vacation spot while the Carraid stayed behind and worked. "Thank you, Captain," she said with every ounce of gratitude she could muster. "You're very understanding."

Something between a smile and a tic flirted with the corner of Remeg's mouth. "Understanding my soldiers is part and parcel of what I do. As I see it, there's only one minor impediment to my granting your request."

Rai's congratulatory relief slithered into her vitals and lay there like a mass of frozen worms. She dredged up what innocence remained and forced herself to look straight at Remeg. "What's that, Captain?"

Remeg perched a hip on the corner of the desk. Her eyes followed the waving toe of her boot as her leg swung idly back and forth. "I was just thinking about when you enlisted as a *tawse.*" A tawse was what they called a girl too young to be trained in soldiery, one who served the garrison as a dogsbody until she came of age. The name derived from the thonged leather strap that some soldiers used on the girls as discipline. "I was only a lieutenant at the time," Remeg conceded, as if that made a difference. "But I'm almost certain you told Captain Pel your mother was already dead."

Breath hissed from Rai's cold lips. How, in the name of the Three, had she forgotten? Afraid that Captain Pel would send her packing if she knew that Rai had family, she'd woven a story of half-truths. Once she was accepted for service, she had put it all from her mind. She had been so *young* …

She fought the urge to dash her brains out on the hearth stones. "Captain …"

"Silence." The steel of Remeg's voice quelled any weak explanation Rai might have offered. In that instant, Remeg could have ground glass into Rai's eyeballs without a single noise of protest. "And you will stand at attention when in my presence."

Rai shot to her feet. Her hands, compromised with the half-empty cup, wavered, uncertain what to do, afraid of dropping it and hearing the fragile horn break. She settled for placing it on the mantel beside the solitary candlestick and then came to attention, her back as rigid as if someone had shoved a broom handle up her ass.

"Being not without my eyes and ears in the garrison, I am well aware of your present dissatisfaction with military life, although I couldn't care less. What I *do* care about is being played for a fool." Remeg never raised her voice, but the whiplash tone struck Rai dumb. "Beginning tomorrow morning, you will spend your days under the tutelage of Black Hirn. Perhaps you'll find the kitchen more to your liking. Your evenings shall be spent in the barracks. This reassignment will be so noted in the duty roster and will not change without my express consent and signature. Dismissed."

Rai wanted desperately to say something, to make an apology, to torture herself on the rack of her own stupidity, but could find no words. In miserable silence, she saluted. Remeg turned away without acknowledging the gesture.

Rai let herself out of the office, shutting the door softly behind her, and trudged downstairs to the ground floor. She waited in silence for Orne to emerge from the warmth of her little room and unlock the outer door. "So you're off home, then, eh?" the grizzled warrior said. "Lucky you." She looked contrite. "Sorry, Rai. It's not lucky your mum died, I didn't mean that. I just meant it will be nice for you to get away … even for a … funeral …" Her voice dropped to an embarrassed mumble and her face clenched like a fist.

Rai shoved her hands into her pockets and hunched her shoulders to her ears. *Shut your pie-hole and hurry up with the damned lock!* Too stupid to live, she was desperate to find Banya and have the Carraid kill her. "I'm not going to Cadasbyr," she said.

Orne, misunderstanding, shot a dour look up the stairs toward the light that shone beneath Remeg's door. She lowered her voice so as not to be overheard. "That stinks like shit on the wind. Don't see why she can't let you go. It's not like your mother dies more than once."

Rai grimaced. The locks clicked open and Orne swung the door wide. Cold air blew in and stippled them with rain.

Eschewing her hood, Rai stepped from beneath the lintel and ducked her head against the weather. Across the street, a shadow detached from the gloom beneath the sparse shelter of a protruding eave and squelched toward her. When Banya got close enough to see Rai's face in the street lantern's wavering light, she stopped dead. "I don't fucking believe it." She sighed and closed her eyes in momentary pain. "You got caught."

Orne paused with the door half-shut. "Caught?" She frowned in confusion, then glanced up at the light burning in Remeg's window. Illumination dawned behind that ruined visage and she flung open the door in a livid rage. "You *lied* to me?" Her fist caught Rai just behind the angle of her jaw and sent her sprawling face-first at Banya's feet. "You're lucky I don't kill you!"

"I wish she would," Banya said to the air as the door slammed shut. "It would save me the bother." She nudged Rai with her boot. "You alive?" When a mud-bubbly groan was the only response, she grabbed Rai under the armpits and hauled her up.

Rai's knees wobbled. The side of her face was numb and her probing tongue found a tooth in the back that felt loose. Her ear rang like a carillon. "Banya –"

"Save it." She gripped Rai's bicep and forced her to keep pace with the long Carraid stride.

"Where are we going?" Rai said. Her tongue felt thick and she tasted blood.

"Somewhere private," Banya said. "We need to talk."

Beyond the makeshift walls of hay, the barn was quiet in the middle hours of the night. No horses shifted below, no pigeons stirred above. Even the cats had gone away on private business, all except the silky black who had butted Kinner's ankles earlier. She had followed him into the mow and now lay curled atop his blankets, a warm and comforting presence fitted into the angle behind his knees.

Unable to sleep, he listened to the familiar pattern of his mother's breathing – the wheezing inhales and moist, rattling exhales that told him she was still alive. The round-bellied lantern Teegan had left them cast a faint ruddy light, allowing Kinner to watch the faint rise and fall of Holan's chest as she slept.

Only when they were finally alone had she let the day's travails overcome her. With a whisper of sigh, she had dropped into the hay with the boneless grace of a rag doll castoff by a disinterested child.

Kinner was beside her in an instant, taking the wet cloak from her shoulders and casting it over a rafter to dry. He wrapped her in a warm, somewhat smelly blanket, pulled off her boots, and peeled the damp hose from her chilled and bluish feet. "You need dry clothing and a warm bed."

"Perhaps, but a cup of tea would serve me better at the moment."

He tucked the blanket around her cold toes. "All right." He swirled the contents of the billy can, poured the strong brew into the ill-made mugs, and handed one to her. "Mum?"

"Hm?" Eyes closed, Holan breathed deep of the fragrant steam, a look of bliss on her face.

He picked up his mug, took a slurpy sip, and made a face. There was enough sugar in the tea to make his teeth ache. "Where did you get the darma that you tried to give Captain Remeg?"

"That's none of your affair," she said without rancor. She sipped the drink and grimaced at its sweetness. "I never expected her to turn down such a prize, I'll confess that much. Mark my words, boy, Captain Remeg has friends in high places or she'd have snatched that money up good."

"How long have you had it, the darma?"

"Again with the darma?" Holan scrutinized him through the steam coming off her mug. "What's the problem? You complaining about how you were raised? Bothered that we didn't spend it on ourselves?" She snorted and drank. "You were well taken care of and we had enough."

He thought about the tiny house crammed with women. "We could have had more."

"And done what with it, may I ask? Bought things we didn't need to impress people we don't like?" She made a raw, wet noise of disgust. "You sound like your aunts. The worst sort of folks are those who have enough, but continue to take long beyond their ability to use."

"Like Queen Kedar, you mean."

She grabbed his wrist so fast and with such ferocity that Kinner dropped his mug. Hands that appeared weak and wasted found strength enough to grind the bones together. "Those who keep their thoughts to themselves also keep their heads," she hissed. "Are you so stupid as to say such things aloud and in her own town? People have been *killed* for less, Kinner! I taught you better than that."

"Sorry, Mum." When neither her eyes nor her hand released him, he nodded rapidly. "You *did* teach me better, Mum. It was stupid; I'm sorry. Please, you're hurting me."

"Be glad it's only me doing the hurting." She squeezed his wrist tighter, using the pain to reinforce her message like an exclamation point, then released him and sat back with the frigid grace of an empress. She sucked up a hearty mouthful of tea and downed it in one swallow even though it was hot enough to scald pigs.

In the silence that followed, Kinner refilled his mug, sliced bread and cheese, pared an apple, and set it all before her. His mother ate without speaking, buried in her thoughts. He sat across from her, hunched and miserable, and ate his food in small, sad bites. Just when he thought the silence would drive him crazy, she cleared her throat. "This is very good. Thank you."

"You're welcome, Mum. Yes, it is."

A tiny smile sketched a dimple in one of Holan's cheeks. "Despite its being pig food?"

Kinner smiled, grateful that things were better between them once more. "In spite of that." He chuckled. "'It were all *hairy,*'" he said, mimicking Bug, and they both laughed.

When they had consumed every bite and all but the pulpy dregs of the tea, Kinner tidied up while his mother had a quick wash-up and changed into a flannel nightgown and thick woolen hose. When she was finished, he eased her into bed and tucked the covers snug around her. "All set?"

"Yes." The strain of travel and worry marked her face, deepening the lines brought on by disease. "It's nice being out of the weather and really warm for a change, isn't it?"

"We're very lucky, you and me." He stroked her forehead, willing her to health once more. "Anything you need?"

"Just some sleep," she said around a yawn and closed her eyes. "You're a good son, Kinner."

He swallowed hard and bent to kiss her cheek, hating the leathery feel of her skin against his lips and the pervasive, low-lying odor of disease. "Good night, Mum." The lantern swung at his touch as he turned the wick low, waltzing shadows across the ceiling. Wriggling out of his damp clothes, he spread them on the hay to dry, pulled a nightshirt on over his head, and got into bed. The blankets were warm and the hay felt softer than goose-down after so many nights on the road. He sighed and closed his eyes.

Sleep refused to come.

Hours later, he was still awake, listening to the beat of rain against the barn roof close above his head and thinking about how quickly his world had changed. Everything that had once defined his life was gone. Soon Holan would be gone as well and he would be truly alone, abandoned at Dara to survive among strangers, forced to spend his life praying to a Goddess in which he did not believe. Under the circumstances, blasphemy seemed inherent in the taking of such vows. Kinner had asked about that once they were on the road and there was no risk of being overheard by any of the women at home.

"You can't blaspheme against that which you don't believe," had been Holan's response, but the answer hadn't eased his mind. What about all those people who *did* believe in the Goddess? Did not the strength of that belief add weight to the likelihood of Her existence? The adherents of the Triple She seemed so adamant, so free from any doubt. Although he would rather have died than admit it to his mother, Kinner was not at all certain about the Weathercock being real, despite Holan's conviction. That bit of heresy filled him with nervous guilt even now. What if the Weathercock *was* real? What if he suddenly burst open the barn roof just to prove Kinner wrong?

The Weathercock …

Kinner rose from his bed. The cat behind his knees *mrowled* in irritation at the loss of body heat, then settled back to sleep as the boy gingerly stepped around his mother's recumbent form. The sharp ends of hay prickled the bottoms of his feet and then his knees as he knelt by their luggage. By necessity, they were traveling light – a couple of rucksacks apiece, some spare blankets … and a long, narrow reliquary of polished wood inlaid with decorative metal and abalone shell. Holan meant to donate it to the monastery once Kinner took his vows, although no saint's bones would ever rest within. What lay inside the slender rectangle had dictated the blacksmith's entire life, leading her to the anvil and forge at an early age, and a dusty barn far from home now that she was dying.

Kinner's memory echoed with the old tales. Lost in the fog of storybook legend taken as truth, he released the feretory from its protective wrapping of oiled cloth, flipped back the shining clasps, and lifted the lid. Red silk greeted his fingers as he parted the shroud and ran his hands lightly over what it concealed.

He'd seen the sword only once prior, a fleeting glimpse before Holan shut the prize away, but he remembered the glory of its workmanship. Holan had garnered the reputation as an adequate blacksmith, perhaps even a fine one, but no one, not even her son with his extreme loyalty, had ever guessed her capable of such work as that which now lay beneath his hands. It surpassed everything that anyone, except Holan, had dreamed possible.

The slim and unadorned blade ended in a hilt capped by an ardent cock, its throat stretched in mid-cry, its wings arched back to form a cage for the hand meant to wield it. The metal caught the lantern's tenuous gleam and sang back a line of light as clear and pure as ice. That this amazing weapon had been made for the Weathercock could scarce be sanctioned. That they were taking it to Dara – that distant, isolated bastion of the Three-Headed Goddess – seemed the most ludicrous thing of all, but Holan was obdurate. Her visions had told her that the sword must be delivered to Dara, so there it would go.

Kinner stared at the sword, pondering the many questions his mother could not – *would not* – answer. Only when his hands grew stiff with cold did he hide the treasure away again and burrow back into bed to await the dawn's slow, wet arrival.

Alone in her quarters, Remeg drank cup after cup of searing liquor as the whirl of her thoughts kept the welcome relief of both sleep and inebriation at bay. Rain wept black tears against the window glass.

Damn the woman! Why had she arrived on Remeg's doorstep to unwittingly unlock a memory long thought buried and forgotten? How little it took to make old wounds seep fresh blood.

That stupid Beck! Instead of doing the smart thing, she had brought the diseased bitch and her scrawny get into Caerau and then left the mess for

Remeg to sort out. What in the Goddess's name had possessed her to take custody of a sterile in the first place?

Remeg knew the answer to that. Kedar Trevelyan's obsession had everyone dancing a spastic gavotte, terrified of offending her. Well, the Nine Hells could take them all, especially that old woman and her useless child, soon to be discarded and locked away forever behind Dara's formidable walls.

Remeg raised the cup so that candlelight glowed through the thin wall. "A toast," she said and fell silent, lost for words. She shot the drink back and swallowed, feeling the liquor burn a hot trail. Rain hammered the glass like angry fists, but the din fell on deaf ears consumed by the rising howl of memory.

SEVEN

Chill wind buffeted Rai and Banya where they stood at the crest of the bridge that joined Caerau's two halves. This was the best place in the world for a private conversation. No one could hear them over the tumble of water and anyone approaching would be seen or heard long before they arrived.

Rai's jaw ached where Orne had struck her. What she wanted most was a hot drink and a dry bed. What she had gotten instead was lunacy. "I don't believe what I'm hearing."

Banya leaned on the stonework and stared down at the river. They could not see the water in the dark, but they could hear it foaming against the pilings. "Believe what suits you."

Rai shivered. The rain had ceased for the moment, but not the infernal wind and it sliced through her clothing. "You're nuts to even consider this."

"That's the pot calling the kettle black considering what you just tried to do." Banya's braids danced in the wind. "I'm not asking for your approval. I just wanted you to know, is all."

"You're leaving Caerau."

"Yes."

"Just like that." Rai snapped her fingers.

"Yes."

Rai made a sound low in her throat. "That's bullshit."

The Carraid raised an eyebrow and said nothing.

Rai grabbed her sleeve. "You said my plan was crap and you were right." A strong gust of wind plastered her wet clothing against her and set her teeth on edge. "Now you're going to do the same thing?"

"It's not the same thing at all. I'm not tricking my way out of town, I'm just going."

"Without a word to Remeg."

Banya sighed and shifted her weight.

Rai studied her profile. A sudden knot of fear tightened around her heart. "You'll come back." Her soft voice begged for reassurance.

The Carraid released a slow breath. "It's not likely."

Rai struggled for words, unable to fit her mind around what was happening. Finally, she settled on her old mantra. "That's bullshit."

"Rai –"

"No! You listen to *me* for a change! You're the most –" She cast about for the right word. "*Steadfast* person I know! You're duty-bound. You've never deserted anything in your life."

The horsewoman shrugged, her expression guarded. "There's a first time for everything."

"Maybe." Rai braced her bare and calloused hands on the bridge and leaned out over the water, lifting her face into the wind. Frigid air blew her hair in a wild tumble. "The way I figure it, though, for you to want to desert, –"

"I don't *want* to …"

Rai kept talking as if Banya had not interrupted. She spoke slowly, piecing her thoughts together bit by bit. "For you to want to desert," she repeated, "There must be a good reason. For you, of all people, to put aside a sworn duty, there must be another duty, one that you think is more important." She looked at her friend. "So what is it?"

Banya refused to meet her eyes. "It doesn't concern you."

Rai stepped back, stung. "Doesn't *concern* me? If it doesn't concern me, then why did you even bother to tell me you're going? Why didn't you just disappear and let me wake up to find you gone if that's all our friendship means to you?" She moved closer and lowered her voice. "Has something bad happened in Carraidland?"

Banya shook her head. "It's not Carraidland," she said and then added truthfully, "At least not directly."

"Well, then what *is* it?" Rai demanded again.

The Carraid drew a deep breath. "Look, Rai, I appreciate your interest, but –"

"*Interest?*" She swatted the big woman's arm. "This isn't about interest, you moron! It's about my best friend doing something stupid and not wanting me involved." Her fingers tightened on Banya's sleeve. "You know I'll go with you, don't you? Just say the word."

The offer brought a fleeting smile to Banya's generous mouth. Then it vanished and the line of her lips hardened again. "If I don't want you involved, it's not likely I'd ask you go with me."

Her vehemence made Rai's stomach hurt. "You don't want me to come?"

Banya's agony showed on her face. "It's not that I don't want you …"

Disregarding a fall that would surely have killed her, Rai scrambled onto the stonework, grabbed Banya by the front of her jacket, and shook her as hard as she could. Under different circumstances, Banya would have been reduced to helpless laughter by such an action. Now she just stood there and took it.

Nose to nose, Rai glared into those blue Carraid eyes. "*What ... is ... it?*" she demanded, punctuating each word with a shake.

Banya drew a deep breath … and told her. For hours afterward, Rai tried to talk her out of it. The scheme was the most numb-ass thing she had ever heard. Imagine risking your life (and it would be Banya's life if Remeg caught her) to help someone deliver her sterile brat to Dara. It was *nuts!*

They argued on the bridge until Banya left for duty. Rai stormed off to bed and spent the night twisting and turning, unable to sleep until Banya came in at shift's end and settled onto her bunk with a weary sigh. In the morning, as Rai was getting dressed, Banya rolled over in bed and without looking at her said yes, she could come along.

Rai had experienced some pretty ugly things, but few compared with the garbage heap that lay hidden at the back of the long yard behind the garrison kitchen. The change in weather helped to keep the stench down, but did little to alleviate the up-close-and-personal approach insisted upon by Black Hirn who, it must be said, did garbage the way she did everything … to perfection.

Digging the tines of her pitchfork deep, Rai lifted and turned the rotting mass, recoiling with sharp disgust as a heap of squirming maggots boiled to the surface. "That's it!" she said to no ears but her own. "I'm done."

Bending to pick up the bucket at her feet, she dumped the last of the wood ash onto the worms. "Come and get it," she said to the birds watching her from a nearby tree. "Grub's on." She laughed. "No pun intended." Bucket in hand, the pitchfork balanced on her shoulder, she slogged out of the mound, goo sucking at her boots with every step.

As she walked, the first snow flurries of the season eddied in the breeze and settled on her hair like a mantilla of lace. Somewhere overhead, hidden by clouds, the afternoon sun heeled westward.

The derision began before she was half-way across the yard, caught in the open between the compost bins and the sere and frost-burned remains of the vegetable gardens.

"Where'd you buy that *wonderful* perfume, Rai? I want to get some for my horse's arse!"

"Are you kidding? That *is* a horse's arse!"

Eyes locked on the ground in front of her, she kept walking and, more importantly, kept her mouth shut. To react would only incite further abuse from her amused comrades. Rai had often wished that she possessed Banya's fluid ability to embrace insult, transform it, and laugh loudest at herself. Were Banya in Rai's shoes right now, she would say something witty to deflect the humor and turn it back on her tormentors. Then again, Banya would never have gotten herself into this mess.

Bitch.

Near the kitchen door, Rai drove the fork tines into the hard soil beside the horse trough and bent to splash a double handful of cold water into her face.

"How's the incredible resurrecting mother this morning?" a jolly voice inquired.

Rai blew mucus out one nostril, snagged it with a pointedly raised middle finger, and wiped it on her pants.

Banya settled her rump onto the edge of the trough and flipped a little splash of water at her friend. "Did someone wake up on the wrong side of the rack this morning?"

Rai pressed her hands into the small of her back and stretched. "I am *such* an asshole," she moaned.

Banya retrieved a piece of straw from the ground, wiped it between two fingers, and stuck it into the corner of her mouth. "That's true."

"You don't have to be so damned ready to agree."

The Carraid splayed a hand across her chest. "Hey, I'm here for you, buddy! If you think you're an asshole, I'm ready to be nothing short of supportive."

"Thanks ever so." She went to sit, but a sharp cry –"*Rai!*" – brought her to her feet again. "Now what?" she muttered and turned to face the woman who stood on the kitchen's back stoop. "Yes, ma'am?"

Black Hirn's pants were dusted with flour, her dark arms white to the elbow. A momentary break in the clouds sparkled a watery rill of sunlight off the numerous small gold rings that adorned both ears. The smooth ebony dome of her skull was beaded with sweat and shone with a tint that was almost red. Her shirt stuck to her, plastered flat over the right side of her chest where she was missing a breast. There was much speculation among the garrison soldiers as to the fate of that breast, but no one had ever worked up the nerve to ask. Hirn was a stern task-master and the undisputed queen of kitchen, scullery and hospital. Her regime was hard but fair; she demanded obedience in all things and rewarded accordingly. It was rumored that not even Remeg would dare cross her.

"You done wid dat heap?" Hirn's voice was earth-deep and loam-rich, honey-toned in the parlance of her island home.

"Just finished it," Rai said.

“You done it like I tol’ you?”

Rai held out both hands. “Would I dare do it any other way?”

The saucy response made the cook’s eyelids droop a fraction in either humor or annoyance. “Better to have,” she said. She tossed a small bundle. Banya, quicker than her tired friend, snagged it out of the air before it landed in the dirt. “Dat’s for you,” Hirn said. “When you done, clean dat fork good, dry it and put it away in da shed. Take a bat’ and be here in time for supper crew.”

“Yes, ma’am,” Rai called with mock cheeriness.

Hirn’s earrings chimed as she tossed her head. “Ah, you go fuck yoursel’,” she said and returned inside.

Rai looked at the rag-wrapped bundle in Banya’s hand. “What is it? A horse-shit sandwich?”

“If I say yes, can I have it?” Banya opened the napkin. Nestled in the drape of fabric lay an enormous scone, hot from the oven, sliced down the middle and packed with butter, jelly, and thin strips of ham.

Rai snatched up the delicacy and took a huge bite, eyes rolling in gustatory ecstasy. “You’re my best friend in the whole world,” she said, flaky pastry crumbling from her lips as she spoke. “And I’d give you the shirt off my back if I thought it would fit, but please don’t ask me to share this because I’d have to kill you.”

“You’d try.” Banya patted Rai’s knee. “Enjoy yourself. You’ve earned it.”

“Too right.” Rai chewed, lost in the irresistible blend of flavors, the salty pungency of smoked meat against the taste of sweet berry jelly and creamy fresh-churned butter. For a moment, she was filled with utter peace. Then she caught the pensive expression on Banya’s face and her chewing slowed. She knew what had her friend so preoccupied. She had thought of little else since the Carraid first laid the issue before her two nights ago.

Swallowing the last of her treat, she licked the crumbs from her fingers. “Tonight, then, is it?” she said in a soft voice.

“Aye.” Banya’s head canted slightly in the direction of the stable yard, a corner of which could just be seen from where they sat. “After the midnight bell. If you’re late …”

“You’ll leave without me. I know.” Rai lifted a hand and flapped fingers against thumb, making a mouth. “Blah-de-blah-de-blah. You’ve told me a dozen times. I’ll be there.”

The clop of hooves heralded the appearance of Teegan, laden with a bucket of horse brushes and an armload of tack. In her wake trailed Bug, leading Remeg’s black by a thin strand of twine caught around the cheek piece of his halter. Had the horse wished, he could have pulled away without difficulty and trampled the child. Instead, he followed her like a big dog, lips moving in a gentle exploration of her scalp. She laughed and patted his neck.

Rai picked a stray wad of food out of her back teeth with a finger. "Where's Remeg off to?"

Banya smiled at the tiny girl and the big horse, eyes misty with a memory she chose not to share. "Captain doesn't discuss her personal affairs with me, Rai."

"She doesn't discuss anything with anyone. I've never seen a person play her cards so close to the vest. You ever known her to be friendly with anyone in the garrison?"

"It's hard to be friends when you're the boss." Banya's big hands slapped her knees. "You'd best get moving before Hirn decides to come out here again and poke you with a sharp stick. Besides, I've got things to do." Their eyes met in a brief but weighted communication and then the Carraid strolled away. The same whistled tune as before drifted back on the breeze.

Rai cleaned and stored her tools as directed, then hurried toward the barracks. She ran the gauntlet of abuse over the way she smelled ("Who brought in the dead dog?" "Is it low tide?"), grabbed a towel, and hustled into the bath house. When she stepped back into the barracks (shivering and blue; there'd been no hot water), she found the room empty. The off-duty women had gone to queue for supper, which meant she was running late. Hirn would have her head.

Having trashed all the clothes she owned, Rai now had nothing clean to wear. She stood beside her cot, jiggling with indecision, and her restless eyes settled on the wooden trunk at the foot of Tynar's bed.

She dressed fast so as not to get caught. Tynar's spare boots were well made and must have cost her a fair chunk of change (a good trick, considering her wailing state of constant poverty). They were snug across Rai's instep, but would stretch with wearing. She gave them a quick rub with fireplace ash to age them and grinned at her handiwork. Unless someone was particularly nosy, there was no reason to think the boots weren't hers to begin with.

She ran all the way to the kitchen and ducked through the doorway as the final bell rang. Pretending she didn't see Hirn's sour expression, Rai pulled an apron on over her head, tied the long strings twice around her waist, and joined the procession of kitchen workers as they hustled fish stew and hot bread into the mess hall.

When dinner was over and clean up and morning prep were complete, the work crew was free to go. With drum-tight bellies (one of the perks of working for Hirn), they hurried into the night, laughing and joking, slipping in the half-frozen mud. A thin, gamin-faced girl nudged Rai's elbow. "Drink, Rai?" Her eyes held a vague hopefulness, an invitation which Rai would have accepted on a different night.

"Sorry, Baz, I can't. Remeg's orders."

The girl's expression drooped. "I heard about that." She kicked the ground with her toe. "Another time, maybe? After Remeg cools off?"

Rai nodded, feeling bad about the lie. Bazile was a nice kid, not what one usually found in a garrison soldier, and she wondered what her story was. "For certain."

Bazile's face brightened with an enormous smile. "Great! That's great. That'll be ... um ... great." She lowered her gaze shyly. "Can I walk you back?"

Shit. Why tonight of all nights? "Better not." Rai rolled her eyes and clocked her forehead with the heel of her hand. "I've got a lot to think about, you know?"

The girl nodded. "Oh, right. Sure. See you tomorrow, then?"

"Bright and early," Rai said with false jollity. She waited for Bazile to move away first. When she didn't, Rai set off toward the barracks with no intention of returning there. It would be too difficult to sneak out again. Someone was sure to tell on her. Her few belongings were packed in a rucksack stowed in the barn's hay mow, and rendezvous with Banya was three hours away. If she waited in the barn, she'd go half-crazy with nothing to do and too much to think about. Where, then, to bide her time?

Her answer came in the form of a tolling bell, a single sonorous call to evening worship. Irreligious in the extreme, yet moved by something she could not name, Rai turned toward the sound, cutting through back streets and tiny gardens at a brisk walk until she emerged from a side street and faced the cathedral's imposing edifice.

Hundreds of years before, sharp-edged blocks of granite had been transported from the Corydon Mountains at great expense to the local population. What was money, the clergy argued, when compared with redemption? Rai had never understood how a bigger and more expensive church brought one closer to the Goddess. That sort of question had gotten her into trouble as a child. Consequently, she had learned to keep her mouth shut and play-act her faith.

She entered the Cathedral on the heels of a stooped crone in dark rags clutching the arm of a tiny child barely out of babyhood. The hag (who could have been the child's pimp as easily at its mother and might be both), hastened into one of the chapels and fell prostrate before an edifice of St. Siofra the Archer. Forced to its bare and chilblained knees, the filthy waif mined her runny nose with an industrious forefinger and wiped the results along the prayer rail.

Rai grinned and crossed the center aisle, boots echoing in the stillness. She slid into a vacant pew, paused to genuflect (surprised that she remembered how), and knelt. Wintry chill crept from the stones and gnawed at her knees as she clasped her hands on the back of the pew in front of her and raised her eyes.

The cathedral's gloom was broken by flame. Each chapel had its rack of lit votives left by supplicants. Thick waxy pillars, cousins to those in Remeg's office, flickered at intervals in iron wall sconces. A chandelier bearing at least three dozen tapers hung suspended on a thick chain in the middle of the vaulted ceiling. Three red candles (and what had *those* cost? she wondered) burned on the altar to signify the Presence of the Goddess. Light and shadow quivered across an enormous icon, making the three carved horns appear to writhe like serpents. The air was dense with the mixed odors of wax and incense.

A hooded priestess stepped into view. This was neither the High Lady in blue nor the Archbishop in claret, who sometimes attended evening services here rather than with the queen in her private chapel. This woman was a nameless priestess whose duty it was to provide religious guidance through the night offices. Dressed in a loose grey robe she circled the altar thrice, pausing to genuflect each time she passed in front of it, and then lowered her hood. Her head was shaved, the dome as smooth as a baby's ass. She bowed her head as if to accept the guillotine and faced the congregation as the other religious personnel filed in to take their place in the choir.

The priestess raised her arms and her voice rang out as clear as the tolling of the cathedral bell. Her call to worship was answered by those assembled, their voices lifting in harmonious cry to blend in a round like braided ropes of hair:

"I bind unto myself today
The strong name of the Horned Goddess,
She of the Three Ways.
By invocation of the same,I bind myself now and always
To the One in Three,
The Three in One.
I bind this day to me forever."

The litany fell from Rai's tongue with old familiarity as the voices circled and soared until, at some unseen cue, they filtered out one by one until only the voice of the priestess remained. The last line was hers alone and then the cathedral fell silent but for the faint whisper of prayer that came from those assembled. Penitents were now free to approach the altar to receive communion or petition the Goddess for a boon.

Rai sat back into the pew and bowed her head against her folded hands. It wasn't her memory for which she prayed, nor did she beg exculpation for having lied to Remeg. She prayed for Banya and for whatever it was that drove her to act as she had. She prayed that everything would work out for them once this stupid trip was over.

Just before midnight, Rai stepped into the barn and slid the door closed. Shadows moved, black on black, as the horses shifted, lifting curious noses to draw in her scent and wicker questions. "Banya?" she whispered, and almost shrieked when a tiny, mittened hand insinuated itself into hers.

"Don't you go bein' ascairt, Miss Rai." Bug's soft voice issued from the level of Rai's hip. "Teegan says there's nothin' to be afeared of in the dark. The Chief, she told me to wait and fetch you when you come."

Rai pressed a hand across her pounding heart and let herself be blindly led, wondering how the child could navigate between stalls and around the various bins and barrels without running into anything. Then again, this barn was Bug's world; she probably knew it better than anyone except Banya.

A hairline crack of light outlined a door at the far end of the aisle. Bug released Rai's hand to use both of hers on the metal latch, pressing down with one thumb atop the other until it clicked open, loud in the quiet. "Inside, Miss Rai," Bug ordered with all the authority of her mentor and stood aside to let her ease through the narrow opening. "I has to go be guard," she added with serious pride and closed the door.

A shuttered lantern hanging from an overhead beam cast a nebulous glow across those assembled. Poker-faced Teegan lounged against a saddle rack with two of the barn brats squatting at her feet, though Rai could not have named them on a bet. Banya lifted one shaggy eyebrow in question. *Are you coming?* When Rai nodded, the Carraid sighed and looked away. Rai couldn't tell if it was in relief or dismay.

Although her glimpse of the boy in Remeg's office had been brief, she recognized him at once, the tattletale sterility mark like a dark smutch of soot between his eyebrows. His mother sat to his left and now that Rai saw her up close, she instantly regretted the wayward generosity that had compelled her to join this ridiculous venture. Banya had told her the woman was sick, but it was more than that and Rai didn't need to be a physician to see it.

She looked at Banya. "Can I talk to you for a minute?"

The horsewoman's resigned expression said that she'd been expecting this. She gave the others a tight smile and moved to stand close beside her partner, their backs turned to give the illusion of privacy.

Rai's fingers dug into Banya's wrist. "You said she was sick!" she hissed in a whisper. "You never said anything about dying!"

The Carraid shrugged. "Semantics," she murmured.

"Sem –? I ought to clobber you! What if she dies on the trail?"

Banya looked at her. "It's not a question of 'if,' Rai. She knows that even if the boy doesn't. That's why she asked for help."

Rai controlled the urge to tear Banya's head from her shoulders and shit down her neck. "You should have told me! You should have said."

The Carraid's braids shifted against her coat with a sigh as she nodded. "You're right. I should have. I'm sorry."

Rai refused to be mollified. "I should stay here, let you make a damn fool of yourself on your lonesome, get yourself killed."

Banya's eyelids crinkled with her smile. "But you won't."

Rai shot her a look. "Don't bet on it. I can dump your sorry ass any time I choose." She heaved a sigh. "Let's just get this idiots' brigade on the road before I change my mind." She felt the grateful press of fingers on her arm as Banya turned to face the others.

"All right, everyone. Still as mice now."

The boy scrambled to his feet and offered Rai a tentative smile as he helped his mother to rise. "Hello. My name is Kinner. This is my mother Holan. Thank –"

She turned away with a grunt.

With Banya leading and Teegan bringing up the rear, they filed through the barn and exited at the back of the building. Four horses waited, each with a girl holding its head against her chest to keep it quiet.

Banya took her reins from Senya and jostled the pack and bedroll tied behind the saddle. It held steady and she nodded with satisfaction. Gathering the reins into one fist, she prepared to mount. "I'm sorry to leave everything in your lap, Teeg."

The teenager ran her fingers through the mare's mane and shrugged. "If there's one thing I've learned working for you, Chief, it's to be adaptable. We'll be fine, the lot of us. And if we're not …" She drew a deep breath, released it slowly, and blinked hard. For a second, the image of a self-assured young woman wavered and Rai glimpsed the frightened girl beneath. "There're other places we can go."

Banya pulled the girl close in a strong hug. "If it comes to that, if you fear for yourself or the others at any time, you get yourselves into Carraid any way you can. Give my name to the first person you meet and tell them I sent you to Balfor Oldinsdotter. She's Carraidleader. She'll make a place for you until I get there."

Teegan nodded, unable to speak, and dashed a quick hand across her eyes. As she stepped out of Banya's embrace, her crew drew close around her in a tight knot of support. Even Bug appeared, drawn by some unheard summons. Bundled to the eyebrows in cast-off clothing, she pressed close against Teegan's leg. A thumb stole into her mouth.

Banya looked away, her face tense with sadness, and mounted. She patted the mare's dappled neck and turned in the saddle. "Let's do this."

The plan was to approach the west gate via back alleys, at which point Holan and Kinner would go first. If the guard stopped them, which was unlikely, it would only be for a moment. There was nothing about them to draw attention and Holan had their papers all in order. Shortly after their departure, Banya and Rai would follow. Being guards, they would draw slightly more curiosity, but Banya was prepared for that. In her belt pouch she carried documents bearing Captain Remeg's forged signature attesting to their reassignment to the small garrison outpost in Gwernach on the western shore. Those on duty tonight would commiserate on Rai and Banya's rotten luck (Gwernach was a dinky pest-hole of a town), complain over the lack of a going-away party, and bid them farewell without question.

The whole thing gave Rai a stomach ache.

After a few minutes of riding, Banya drew rein. "This is where we split up," she whispered. "Grandmother, you'll see the gate to your right as soon as you enter the street. Just keep riding as you are and you'll be fine." She gave Holan a confident nod, then looked at Kinner and smiled. "You'd better pull up that hood and keep your face lowered, boy. You've got guilt written all over you and you haven't done anything wrong." She raised her head at the sudden sound of rapid hoof beats drawing near. "That's from the castle. Something must be up."

"Should we wait?" Holan said, worried.

The Carraid shook her head. "No. This may work to our advantage. If the guards are busy with a messenger from the castle, they won't pay so much as a fart's worth of attention to you. Get along."

They started forward. The clatter of hooves grew louder, but did not slow. Whoever was approaching the gate had no intention of stopping.

And that was when all hell broke loose.

Eight

"You're late, Remeg." The queen's voice held a note of imperial disdain.

Paused in the doorway awaiting permission to enter these private quarters, the garrison captain pushed her hood back and bowed low over a bent knee. "Apologies, Your Majesty. Garrison business delayed my immediate departure."

Kedar Trevelyan, Queen of Duine, turned toward the fire, snubbing Remeg but also displaying her profile to its best advantage. Court attire had been set aside in favor of a luxurious crimson robe stitched at every hem with intricate knotwork. The neckline, decorated with the additional sparkle of tiny jewels set amid the masterful embroidery, was cut to expose the queen's pale, perfect shoulders and the upper swelling of her breasts. Deep sleeves hid her hands and anything those clever hands chose to conceal. The gold circlet worn for everyday affairs was gone as well, tossed aside amid a scattering of frippery on a low table. Her hair, black as a brigand's heart, had been released from its coif and now hung over one naked shoulder in a loose braid, the end curled in her lap like a quiescent snake amid the folds of sanguine cloth.

The snake comparison was more than apt, as Remeg knew only too well. Please the queen and she would remain warm and placid, a jeweled reptile curled in contentment upon a warm rock. Oppose her and you'd soon feel the prick of fangs in your neck. She never forgot – and rarely forgave – a transgression.

Remeg did not acknowledge the well-dressed woman who stood behind the queen. Chella Quarm was a minor daughter of nobility and twice the monarch's age, a fawning court dog with the randy indiscretions of a bitch in heat. Remeg noted with quiet malice that Quarm's red hair (swept to one side in this season's most popular – and, in the captain's opinion, least attractive – style) had faded and gone grey at the roots. Her shipment of henna must be late. Her eyelids were painted with gold and green glitter, an effect that was almost certainly intended to impress, but which Remeg thought made Quarm look like a seaport doxy.

Not to insult the doxies, of course.

"Business that was more important than our summons, apparently," said Kedar in a chill voice.

Quarm smirked at the rebuke and rested a proprietary hand on the back of the monarch's chair, very near the white skin of the royal shoulder.

Remeg suppressed a desire to shove the woman's teeth down her throat. "On the contrary, Majesty. There is nothing of more importance to me than the fulfillment of your desires. However, since my role as garrison commander demands loyalty and accountability to you, I must perforce make difficult choices. In this circumstance, the responsibilities of my garrison – *your* garrison, Majesty – took precedence lest your royal person be exposed to danger or difficulty."

"Hm." The queen's eyes flicked in her direction and Remeg fancied she caught a hint of smile in their depths. "You may enter, Captain."

Remeg stepped across the threshold. Undoing the simple clasp at her throat, she let her wet cloak slide into the waiting arms of a servant who hung it on a hook behind the door.

"Saphira," said the queen. "You may retire for the night."

"Yes, Majesty." The girl bobbed a curtsy and withdrew, closing the door behind her.

An impeccably manicured hand ringed with rubies, emeralds, and diamonds, emerged empty from the depths of Kedar's sleeve and waved perfunctorily. "Chella, we wish to confer with Captain Remeg in private."

Quarm bowed low from the waist. "As Your Majesty desires." Full, red-lacquered lips curled in an unctuous smile. "Shall I remain in the ante chamber?"

"Blessed Goddess, am I not to be allowed a few hours free of your dogging steps?" Kedar snapped. "Go home, Quarm, or whatever hole it is you crawl into when you're not here. If I require your presence, you'll be summoned."

Remeg's features remained bland even as she savored Quarm's humiliation. The voluptuous mouth sucked into a thin line and the skin around her eyes tightened with embarrassment and anger. "Yes, Majesty," she said in a carefully neutral tone. She bowed again and took her leave, brushing past Remeg near enough to make most people step backward. Remeg held her ground, staring straight ahead as if the chamber wall was the most fascinating thing she had seen in days.

The door closed behind Quarm. When the sound of her footsteps had vanished down the corridor, Kedar chuckled and held her delicate hands out in front of her, turning them back and forth so that the jeweled rings caught the firelight and threw pale sparkles across the tapestried walls. After a moment, she shifted her gaze to contemplate the silent woman who remained. "That was quite the pretty little speech, Captain."

"Was it, Majesty?"

Kedar snorted. "You know it was. The question remains, was it for my benefit … or Quarm's?" When Remeg did not reply, the queen rose and came toward her. They were something of a size, with the soldier perhaps an inch or so taller. Where Remeg was all clefts and angles and narrow, slanting planes, Kedar was warm and softly rounded.

The queen touched one of the gold insignia on Remeg's collar with the tip of her finger. "So … there is nothing of more importance to you than the fulfillment of my desires, eh?" Her chin tilted up in a small challenge as her finger lingered along the edge of Remeg's jaw. "Well then, my pretty captain, I command you to fulfill them all."

Remeg took a single step forward, spanning the narrow distance between them, and fitted her hand along the outer curve of Kedar's breast. The ball of her thumb brushed across the nipple and the queen's head lolled back, eyes half closed as Remeg bent to kiss her throat. Kedar plucked at Remeg's shirt front, fouling the ties and cursing in whispered frustration. Remeg laughed softly and lost herself to lovemaking as the queen's robe parted and her questing hands caressed warm and willing flesh.

Afterward, they lay on the rug nested together like spoons in a drawer, covered by a blanket Remeg had pulled from the divan. Kedar faced the fire, eyes heavy with satiation, her hair a tangled sprawl across her lover's arm.

Remeg's gaze moved about the room, resting briefly on each familiar object – the favorite paintings, woven tapestries, and rosewood furniture carved with twining ivy. Firelight reflected off the surface of a pedestal mirror, illuminating the tooled leather surface of a lap desk on which lay an abandoned spread of well-thumbed tarot cards.

For two dins, she'd have thrown them into the street. Kedar's sudden and intense preoccupation with fortune-telling was preposterous and Remeg had said as much in private, but logic was overruled by a court that indulged every royal whim.

She sighed and shifted into a more comfortable position, careful to not disturb the royal head. Her eyes followed the curve of light along Kedar's cheek. How was it that she could lose so much time – and so much of herself – in the company of this extraordinary creature?

Remeg's past was littered with very few lovers. Those she had taken had been regarded as short-term and expendable, not utterly out of callousness, but because she was a warrior, a foot soldier before becoming a commander. A soldier's life wasn't the sort in which long-term attachments were made unless one wished to make a habit of a broken heart. The future was unstable; anything might come along. Life was much too short to commit to a single individual. Or so she had believed with unshakeable confidence until that day, ten years past, when she first saw the new queen. In that instant, Remeg's philosophy had undergone a profound and irreversible metamorphosis.

Kedar had been resplendent on the day of her coronation, a new sun outshining the old (she who had died and been buried the week before). Clad in gold and crimson, she sat upon the throne of her ancestors and smiled a beguiling welcome as each noble bent knee before her to declare homage. Well-versed in protocol, she had listened to their stories, laughed at their jokes, and dimpled prettily at each compliment.

Remeg knew a kindred spirit when she saw one. This young woman was no bit of pandering fluff. She would not rule as a figurehead easily led by counselors, nor would she flirt with gentry, ignorant of the consequences. In the depths of those angelic eyes lurked the heart of a predator. Despite herself, Remeg was impressed … and intrigued.

It was well into the evening's celebration before she made her move. Although Captain Pel had been presented to the new monarch and politely acknowledged, a lieutenant's rank did not guarantee Remeg an introduction. She had waited until she was certain that every noble in the room had been introduced before she contrived to place herself in the queen's path as she made her way around the great hall. Handsome in her black uniform, rank insignia gleaming silver at either side of her neck, Remeg had bowed low as Kedar strolled past and raised her head slightly to catch the new queen's eye. All these years later, she still marveled at her temerity.

Agostina Quarm, the queen's minister (mother of the deplorable Chella and as wily as her daughter was ox-stupid), had given the officer a narrow-eyed look of annoyance and paused to introduce her. "Lieutenant Remeg of the Caerau garrison, Your Majesty," she said in a flat tone that conveyed her displeasure.

Kedar had lowered those incredible eyes to Remeg's upturned face and offered the back of her hand. Remeg took it with gentle fingertips, kissed the soft skin, and flicked the tip of her tongue into the cleft between two fingers. She felt the shock travel up the queen's arm. The royal hand was withdrawn with no outward sign that anything untoward had occurred. Words were exchanged – a polite frippery, nothing of consequence – and Kedar moved on.

Several weeks passed – long enough for Remeg to believe that her attempt at seduction had failed – and then the order came for her to present herself at the castle. The private and unnecessarily prolonged meeting had left them both restless with desire. The long line of petitioners outside the door had not afforded the luxury of sexual fulfillment at that time, but they were quick to arrange a tryst soon afterward and had remained lovers ever since.

There were no secrets in a royal household; they both knew that. Remeg supposed that knowledge disguised as rumor had found its way into the town and the garrison, but insofar as she and Kedar were concerned their public behavior remained uncompromised. What took place in the privacy of the queen's apartments was their business alone, although Remeg liked to think that the details would uncurl the hair of the most creative courtier.

"You're not listening to me."

"Of course I am." Remeg hoped that she hadn't missed anything vital. Kedar could be the Goddess's own fury if she thought she was being ignored.

"Liar." The queen snuggled her round little backside against her lover's stomach. "Anyway, *as I was saying* ..." She glanced over her shoulder to make certain she now had Remeg's full attention. "I sent that cloth merchant packing. Imagine trying to foist cheap goods off onto me of all people. Does she think I'm an idiot not to know good material from bad?" Her eyes narrowed. "What was that look for?" She had caught Remeg rolling her eyes.

"It's not directed at you, love. I had a run-in with a cloth merchant myself earlier this week."

Kedar rolled onto her back and laced her fingers together across her flat stomach. "Tell me about it. I want to hear something besides the usual boring court babble."

"It's far from interesting, believe me. And it might be wise to have a care when describing your court as boring. Walls have ears, you know."

"Let them listen," Kedar said with a snort. "Half of them wouldn't recognize an intelligent conversation if it bit them on the ass. The other half ..." She paused in consideration and chewed the corner of her mouth. "Well, they do bear watching, you're correct. They know how to sift through the chaff of words for the succulent kernel of truth." She smiled with obvious pleasure at the simile. "Never mind them. Tell me the story."

Remeg pulled the blanket up over her angular hip. "There's nothing to tell, really. She got drunk in town and wandered onto garrison property where she caused a bit of an uproar. She was arrested, presented to the town magistrate, and fined the contents of her warehouse."

Kedar frowned. "That seems excessive punishment for a bit of drunken tomfoolery."

"So it would be, but for her history of such behavior. Judge Alaria may prefer to not squeeze the local merchants too tightly, but neither does she want relations between the town and the garrison to be anything but cordial. She's good at her job. I like her." She lifted her arm from beneath the queen's head and massaged it to restore blood flow. "What was Quarm's business here earlier?" she said, mindful to keep her voice neutral.

Kedar's impish grin bore more than a touch of malice. "She's a member of my court," she said lightly. "One of the *favored.*" She skated her eyes toward Remeg to see what reaction that remark might bring. "Her presence was requested as was yours."

"For the same purpose?"

"That's hardly your business." An edge crept into Kedar's voice. "When I summon her, she comes."

Despite Remeg's determination to not let such a remark bother her, the double entendre dug under her skin. She sat up with nonchalant grace and reached for her shirt. "As you say, it is entirely Your Majesty's business whom you entertain in private. If you prefer to sport with riff-raff –"

Kedar's laughter was sharp as scissors. "Chella Quarm is hardly riff-raff. She is descended from one of the finest bloodlines in the kingdom." Her smile grew mean. "Unlike someone I could mention."

Her expression stony, Remeg pulled the shirt on over her head and slid her arms into the sleeves. "Apologies, Majesty. Apparently, this particular riff-raff has spoken out of turn. May I recommend that you study your peerage, however? You'll find that the Quarm family tree does not branch." She made as if to rise. "With your permission, I'll return to the garrison."

Kedar pulled Remeg down beside her. "My, but aren't we prickly this evening." She kissed her soundly. "You do not have permission to leave. We're supposed to be making love, not having a fight."

"You started it."

"That's what you deserve for going all jealous on me."

A sudden swell of emotion tightened Remeg's chest. "But I *am* jealous of you," she whispered. She ran a gentle hand along the contours of her lover's face, down the side of her neck, and over her torso to cup a naked breast. Kedar sighed a kittenish purr and rolled toward her.

The rise of passion was abruptly quenched by a strident cry from the street. "He comes!" It was an old woman's voice, trembling with the weight of years. "He comes in fire! In storm! He comes for all!"

Kedar spat an oath and sprang to her feet. Snatching up the discarded robe, she thrust her arms into the sleeves and rushed to fling open the shutters over one window. Cold air spilled into the room as she leaned over the sill.

"SILENCE!"

Moonlight was made fickle by the scud of clouds. Standing in the shadows behind the queen, Remeg could see the street below and the pale oval of an upturned face. The crone raised a finger toward the window. "He comes for you, Kedar Trevelyan," the scratchy voice continued. "Teach you to take Husbands without asking or payment! Teach you what happens when –"

Kedar screamed – an inarticulate shriek of rage – and slammed the shutters closed. She raced for the door and wrenched it open hard enough to bounce it off the inner wall. "Wellyn!"

Her secretary – clothing awry, frizz-haired and bleary-eyed from sleep – appeared in the doorway of a room three doors down and hurried toward her mistress. "Yes, Majesty?"

"That old woman is back! I told you to get rid of her!"

"I did, Majesty, only –"

"You didn't, more's to the point!" The queen grabbed Wellyn by the front of her shirt and shook her hard. "I want that old bitch *silenced,* do you understand?" The intent of her words hung blatant between them. "If that street isn't quiet in five minutes, you'll take her place in the dungeon."

Wellyn stuttered. "I – I understand, Majesty! I'll take care of it at once! I –"

Kedar slammed the door closed in her face and leaned against it, panting with fury. Remeg came to her and rested her hands on the queen's trembling shoulders. "What's the matter, love? What's some mindless old crone to you?"

"She's been out there night after night crying about that blasted Weathercock!"

Remeg blinked in astonishment and then laughed, her voice a soft chuckle against Kedar's hair as she drew her into an embrace.

The queen stiff-armed away, her hands cold on Remeg's chest. "Don't you dare laugh at me!"

"I'm not laughing at you, Kedar, but really. The Weathercock's a myth, an ignorant hill folk legend from a past so remote that even the peasants who believe in it don't remember how it began. It's got nothing at all to do with you."

"It's easy to assume a cavalier attitude when it's not you they say will be brought down! They don't talk about *your* rule being shattered, but *mine!*" Kedar's eyes brimmed with tears.

Remeg drew her close and this time the queen let her, twining her arms around the captain's narrow waist as Remeg stroked the long length of her back. "They're just stories, pet."

"Stories have power when people believe them." Kedar's voice, muffled against Remeg's chest, was firm with conviction. "Thinner tales than those have brought walls crashing down."

"Maybe so," Remeg said with sternness. "But there have been tales of the Weathercock for more years than I can number and no one has ever tried to make them come true."

"What about the Carraid?" The queen's bark of laughter was joyless. "Their entire territory practically oozes Weathercock."

Remeg held her at arm's length so she could look into Kedar's eyes. "Their territory is part of *your* entire country, my queen. It's you who rules this land, not the Carraid."

"Tell that to that damned barbarian leader of theirs, that Balfor Oldinsdotter! She behaves as if Carraidland were a separate country. And what can I do about it? Nothing! Their cavalry ..." Kedar gestured, momentarily at a loss for words to describe the strength of Carraidland on horseback. "You have a couple of riders in the garrison, don't you?" She pushed on without waiting for Remeg's confirming nod. "Would you willingly go against a thousand of *them?* Not bloody likely! The best I can hope for where Carraidland is concerned is to maintain a respectful truce. They'll let me play at being their queen so long as I leave them alone to run things as they like." Her slender frame shook with frustration. "Thank the Goddess the other nobles find them as outlandish as I do or they'd be running the world!"

The first part of that observation was not precisely accurate, but Remeg didn't feel like arguing the point right now. This was the sort of foolishness that came from steeping oneself in idle chatter and fortune telling. When you whiled away your hours in such a manner and those about you did nothing except confirm your own strongly-held beliefs, then cool reasoning fled and dark things came to feed at your table.

They stood in silent tableau with their arms about each other, the queen's rant having finally run its course. "Come," Remeg said. She led Kedar back to the fire and coaxed her down onto the rug. She wrapped a blanket around her and tucked the loose ends around her cold feet. "Now listen to me." She pulled Kedar close and gently rocked. "Neither that old woman nor her stupid prophesizing can hurt you. I promise." She glanced down at the queen's pensive face, its beauty marred by worry. "Would you like to hear a story?"

Kedar sniffed delicately. "What sort of story?" she said, her voice pitched like a child's.

It took effort, but Remeg kept the annoyance from her face. She despised this little-girl aspect of Kedar's, the part of her that was prone to tantrums, whining, and petulant spitefulness. This was the side of her lover that was catered to by the sycophants who clustered around her like flies to rotten meat.

Remeg abhored the pandering liars. She abhored Kedar as well (a little) for buying into the shit they spewed, but she would not allow that prejudice to draw her into another argument with the queen. Not tonight. There had been enough histrionics for one evening.

Remeg had no real stories to tell (save one that had never been told, not even to Kedar), but there were other things she could talk about, snippets of gossip she might share to distract the queen and ease her heart. "I had a visit from a stranger the other day who wanted an escort to Dara."

Kedar's kissable nose wrinkled in distaste. "What did she want with that old place?"

"Have you ever been there?"

Dark hair shifted around the queen's shoulders with the sound of silk as she shook her head. "It's too remote to include on any tour through the kingdom. If I went there, I'd have to visit Delma and Per and every other little mud-clump town. Why should I trek through the mountains just to look at dead seals and unwashed babies? That's what tax collectors are for."

Remeg could hardly fault Kedar for not wanting to make such a journey, but she wondered if the people living in those remote areas – those who sacrificed to pay the heavy, self-serving hands of the tax collectors – even realized they had a queen, let alone knew her name.

"The High Priestess came from Dara to pay homage at my coronation," Kedar added. She pursed her lips, musing, and shrugged away the memory because it didn't matter. "Why did they build a monastery in such a forsaken place?"

"I suspect the original chapel was erected over a pagan site to more easily convert the locals to Goddess worship. The remoteness serves as a good place to put away unacceptable sons."

The queen shifted. "I don't understand why the families don't just kill them outright."

Remeg stared past her. In the shifting fire she saw dark eyes and an angular chin like hers. "Because some mothers are soft-hearted."

"Hmph! Soft-headed is more like it. Those boys are useless."

Abruptly, Remeg felt old. She desperately wanted a drink – not the smooth wine of the queen's ample cellars, but the sharp burn of the liquor in her office. "Not so useless if you look at it from the point of view of the Church. Being free of family duty allows those men to devote their lives to worship of the Goddess which, in turn, frees able-bodied women for work which the men would find either physically taxing or too complicated to understand."

Kedar thumped the rug with one small fist. "I'm not a dunce, Remeg. I know all that. What does it have to do with the woman who came to see you?"

"She had her son with her." Kinner's face flashed across Remeg's mind – pale skin and haystack hair, blue tattoo between wide brown eyes. "She wanted him delivered to the monastery."

"How touching." Kedar's voice was thick with acrimony. She abruptly rose and stood before the mirror. Picking up a brush, she began to work the bristles through the dark length of her unbraided hair. Her eyebrows pinched together. She looked as if she might cry.

Remeg felt her heart clench. What Kedar wanted more than anything was a child, a daughter to be queen once she was gone. Birthing a son – a *fertile* son, not one of those useless steriles – would be a feather in her cap, but Kedar was pragmatic enough to know the odds against that were extremely high. Because the Household from which she sprang was without Husband at present, she had begun her quest for motherhood by approaching those nobles most devoted to her. They were flattered and gladly offered use of their studs for free, imagining the grateful bounty that would ensue once the queen conceived.

Except she hadn't.

Male after male was tried with no success. Once, in the privacy of her chambers with only Remeg as witness, Kedar had flown into a screaming rage. The thought that it might be *she* who was sterile was not to be borne (although Remeg secretly thought it likely). In a growing tide of desperation, the queen searched farther afield, no longer considerate of blood-lines and nobility. She stopped asking for the use of Husbands and began taking them (although not from landed families or the locals, whose displeasure she could not risk). But the hill folk and gypsies – those who lived and worked the far flung fields and forests, who plied their trades along the coast and in the mountain vastness, who lived too far away for her to visit – those families might be *bargained* with.

If not bargained with, then coerced.

If not coerced, then threatened.

And if threats did not work, then her soldiers would prey like wolves upon a herd of deer.

Remeg had lost count of how many males had been brought into Caerluel Castle to service the queen. Kedar used every one. She even shared them with a few court favorites, but Goddess protect the woman who conceived before her. Remeg knew for a fact that it had happened a few times, but those women had prudently excused themselves due to 'pressing business back home' and were not seen at court until months after the suspected birth. If another child played among the dogs and rushes in their family hall, what of it?

Kedar's despair had birthed in Remeg a small knot of pain. She hated to see her darling heartbroken, but this was one difficulty from which she could not rescue the queen, no matter how willing she would have done so.

"What did you tell her?"

Caught out once more as the queen's words broke into her thoughts, Remeg blinked. Whence had come this preoccupation? She was usually more alert. "What?"

"The woman," Kedar said with pointed asperity. "I assume you told her the garrison is not an escort service."

Remeg did not appreciate being told how to run her business, not even by this woman. "As a matter of fact, I did. Then she tried to bribe me."

"What with?"

Remeg snorted. "A darma, if you can believe it. I showed her the door."

The hairbrush halted in mid-stroke, a smudge of pale wood against the mahogany darkness of Kedar's hair. "What about her son?"

The question was posed in such a neutral manner that Remeg was instantly on the alert. She reached for her pants. "What about him?" she said, stepping into them.

"Are you certain he's infertile?"

Remeg did up the front of her trousers. "Don't be ridiculous."

"Don't be impertinent." Kedar's robe swirled about her in a storm of claret as she turned. "Are you *certain?*"

Remeg made her wait while she finished tucking in her shirt. "I saw the mark on his forehead and the paperwork was in order, if that's what you mean." She pulled on her boots. "Why are we even discussing this?" She wished to her bones that she had never brought up Holan of Moselle and had, instead, bedded the queen a second time.

"Don't be naïve. Paperwork can be forged."

"To what purpose?" Remeg sighed. "No one is going to take a fertile son to Dara just to protect him from you."

Kedar drew herself up with self-righteous indignation. "The Households don't like that I take their men."

"Can you blame them? I hardly think that you, of all people, need a lesson in the ways of the world." Remeg hunted around for her uniform jacket, saw it laying across the arm of a chair, and picked it up. "Sometimes all the wealth a family has is tied up in their Husband. You are monarch. The people owe you their fealty. If you want their men, then so be it. I'm the last one to argue that point. But perhaps they would be more accommodating if you were willing to pay a reasonable stud fee instead of just appropriating their men outright because you're desperate."

Kedar's face was bloodless with wrath. "Don't you dare call me that! And don't tell me how to run my affairs! We shall do as we like. Bring them here."

"What?"

"That woman and her son. Bring them to us. We will discover whether or not he is sterile."

Remeg shoved her arms into her jacket and shrugged it onto her shoulders. All of the goodness had gone out of the evening and she desperately craved the silence of her quarters. "I don't know where they are and I don't care. I presume she found a guide and left town as soon as possible."

"Go after them and bring them back. Tonight! I want to see this boy for myself."

"As if 'seeing' has anything to do with it," Remeg said sourly.

The blow rocked her head sideways and her cheek blossomed like a fiery rose, scarlet and hot. She stood rooted, stunned, and stared at the queen in disbelief. The silence between them screamed.

When Kedar spoke, it was as Remeg's ruler, not her lover. "Do as you are ordered, Captain Remeg, and do not show your face to us with some puling excuse as to why you have failed."

Or else hung unspoken in the air. *Or else* promised an end to that which had gladdened and sustained Remeg for ten years. With something like horror, she realized that she could not bear the threat of that *or else.*

Only once in her life had Remeg let something be held over her. She had sworn then that it would never happen again and it hadn't … until now, when she realized that what she had believed to be personal fortitude and strength was actually nothing more than the absence of the correct *or else.*

She bowed, the picture of military correctness. "By your leave, Majesty." She waited until the queen nodded – a tense motion, her breath coming tight and fast through her nose – then she took her cloak from behind the door and departed. Her boot heels struck sharp echoes from the stone flags as she marched along the silent corridor. A sleepy servant let her out into the chill night. When her horse was brought from the stable, Remeg calmly pulled herself into the saddle and trotted away from the castle with utter decorum. Only when she was certain that she was out of sight of Kedar's windows did she rake the beast's sides with her heels and send him thundering toward the garrison.

Nine

Kinner's horse, plodding along behind Holan's, stopped dead in the middle of the street and pricked its ears toward the clatter of approaching hooves. He jiggled the reins and bounced a little in the saddle. The horse ignored him, taking advantage of his inexperience to do as it chose, and lifted its muzzle to scent the wind. "She won't move," he said, turning to look back at Rai and Banya.

"Whack her hard between the –" The word 'ears' died on Rai's lips as the oncoming horse burst into view. It took the street corner so tightly that it almost raked its rider off on a lamp post, and in the horrible instant before the two horses collided time seemed to slow and stretch. The clatter of galloping broke into a lagging cadence – *pok-e-ta, pok-e-ta* – the strike of each hoof an individual shock of sound – and then the animals slammed together with a grunting concussion that Rai felt deep in her chest.

Kinner screamed and grabbed the saddle as the mare slid sideways, fighting for balance on the wet cobblestones. The other horse spun in a full circle and bucked hard, tossing its rider against the nearest building.

Rai drove her heels against her horse's ribs. The animal squealed in surprise and shot from the alley. As it bore down on Kinner's mare, Rai leaned out of the saddle and grabbed the back of the boy's cloak. "LET GO!" she bellowed and dragged him out of the saddle to lie face-down across her thighs as the mare lost its footing and went down with a solid, teeth-jarring thump. The horse's leg shattered with a horrible *crack!* and splintered bone jutted through the skin, shinng bright and wet against the torn flesh as she shrieked and thrashed, spraying blood in a fine vermillion rain. Her gyrations tore loose the baggage behind the saddle. A narrow case bound with shiny clasps bounced across the cobbles and sprang open. Red silk spilled forth and metal pealed against the paving stones as a magnificent blade slipped free of its shroud.

Rai stared, dumbstruck, her brain stuttering. Before she could speak, motion at the edge of her vision tore her gaze away from the weapon and she found herself looking straight at Captain Remeg.

The tableau held long enough for astonishment to dawn on Remeg's face; long enough for her to identify the boy slung across Rai's lap; to notice Banya framed in the dark alley like a religious icon and Holan poised between flight and her child; long enough for her to get a good look at the fabulous sword laying naked in the street.

The moment shattered with a crack like breaking ice as Remeg snatched Rai's bridle. With one hand on the reins and the other fisted in the wool of the boy's cloak, Rai had no way to repel her save one. Kicking a foot free of the stirrup, she lashed out and caught Remeg in the sternum, sending her reeling backward, whooping for breath.

The Carraid mare sprang past them, sideswiping Remeg and driving her to her knees. Guiding the animal with legs and voice, Banya leaned down out of the saddle and, one-handed, swept up the blade. As she straightened, she let fly a piercing whistle. The sound, meant to carry above the din of battle, drew an instantaneous response from the horses.

Rai's shot into a full gallop, so close behind the Carraid mare that his muzzle almost touched her flank as they sped along the empty street toward freedom beyond the city walls. Holan's mount followed out of instinct, taking the blacksmith with it, while the wounded mare was left behind, trapped on her back like a turtle, flailing her shattered leg and crying out at the desertion.

Remeg snatched at her horse's trailing reins and fought to get a foot in the stirrup. "*Stop them!*" she bellowed to the gate guards.

To their credit, the two soldiers who were minding the gate that night made a game attempt to follow Remeg's orders, but the sight of a wild-eyed Carraid careening toward them with a naked blade in her hand – especially *this* Carraid, with whom they had so much experience – was enough to make even the threat of Remeg pale by comparison. They scattered like mice and the charging horses gained the open road.

Banya rode as all Carraid did – by instinct – as the miles slipped away beneath them. When she judged that the distance from immediate pursuit was great enough to allow them a breather, she led them away from the road, across the verge, and in among the trees. Rampant growth as yet untouched by autumn's colors closed behind them like a screen and hid them from view, but she pressed on, head tucked to avoid low-hanging branches as the horses, breathing heavily, picked their careful way in the dark. The woods were creepy-silent, hushed in the wake of this intrusion, with nary a cricket or frog to break the stillness. The air beneath the leaf canopy was cold and dank.

Banya strained to catch any sound of pursuit, but all behind them was quiet.

Finally, she called a halt. Leaning forward to run a tender hand along the mare's sweaty neck, she murmured, "Best horse in the world, that's what you are."

"You mind telling me why we can't even get out of town before everything goes to shit?" Rai said.

Banya ignored her and swung out of the saddle. "Let's give these animals a rest. That is unless the boy wants to ride to Dara slung over your lap."

"No, thank you." Kinner's froggy voice spoke from the vicinity of Rai's left knee. His arms and legs moved feebly. "Um … I don't think I can … would you mind …?"

"Sure." Rai fisted both hands into the back of his cloak and shoved him off her lap like a carcass. He landed hard, almost on his head, and curled immediately onto his side, moaning in misery.

"That could have been a little gentler," Banya said with reproach. "He *is* a man, after all."

"Not according to that tattoo," Rai said. She started to add something, but right then Kinner gave a strangled gurgle, lurched onto his hands and knees, and puked up the remains of his supper. "Gross," she said, and dismounted on the offside to avoid stepping in it.

Kinner sat back on his heels and used his sleeve to wipe the strings of mucus from around his mouth. Banya squatted beside him. "You okay?" When he nodded, she held out an open canteen. "Rinse your mouth, then take a tiny swallow. Just a sip, mind, or you'll be sick again." She took back the canteen when he was through, wiped the mouth with her gloved hand, took a long swallow, and palm-tapped the bung into place. "You still with us, Grandmother?"

"Barely, Kiordasdotter." Banya couldn't see well in the gloom, but she didn't need to. Holan sounded awful – haggard, spent, wrung dry – and one step closer to death if the Carraid was any judge.

The quaver in his mother's voice brought Kinner staggering to his feet. He shoved past Rai and reached for Holan, touching first her knee and then her hands as he peered up at her. "Mum, are you all right? Do you need anything?"

"A bit of that water and a little less fuss," Holan said in a cranky tone. She coughed. The sound came from her toes, deep and ragged, rich with moisture and thick as mud. It put a run of gooseflesh up Banya's arms that made her shiver. She glanced at Rai as the canteen passed to Kinner, but she only shrugged and shook her head.

Holan drank like a bird, lifting her chin after each sip to help her swallow. She poured a small amount of water into her hand and wiped it over her face and neck. Kinner lifted the edge of his cloak for her to dry her face and she pushed him away with a gentle hand. "Stop nattering. I'm fine." A self-deprecating note came into her voice. "As fine as I have hope to be, at any rate." She looked at Banya. "Is the sword all right?"

"That's not for me to say, Grandmother." The big woman held the weapon point up and turned it back and forth. Nebulous moonlight lacquered the metal and made the eyes of the rampant cock appear to wink. "There might be a few scratches."

"Give it to me!" The blacksmith's hands shook as the blade was passed to her. She held it in her arms with a tenderness usually reserved for newborns and ran her knotted fingers across every contour. "It seems well," she said after a moment and sighed heavily. "And the box?"

"That's a bit worse for wear, I'm afraid," Banya said. She handed it to Kinner, who held it up for his mother's inspection. One latch hung askew, the wood around it splintered. Bits of shell had broken off, leaving gaps in the inlay like missing teeth in a smile.

"Well, it's not pretty," said Holan. "But it's far from ruined. It can be repaired when there's time." She stroked a finger along the head of the fighting cockerel. "This could have been so much worse."

"You mind telling me how?" Rai said.

Banya made a move as if to slap her on the side of the head. "Leave it, will you?" She turned back to Holan. "Take some rest, Grandmother, but stay in the saddle. If we have to move fast, I'd rather not have to sling you up there like a haunch of meat."

Holan chuckled. "Oddly enough, that's my preference as well."

Banya grinned, amused by the old woman's verve. She glanced at her partner, said, "Rai," in a flat tone, and walked off a discrete distance.

As Rai moved to join her, there came the sound of something large forcing its way through the undergrowth behind them. "Oh, Holy Three," Rai whispered. "She's found us." The soldiers drew their weapons and moved to stand in front of Holan and Kinner, dropping into combat stance. Kinner moaned with fear and pressed against his mother's leg. The sound of crackling brush grew louder. The undergrowth before them rustled, parted, and a dark horse stepped into the clearing. With a cry, Rai brought her sword around and steel rang against steel as Banya turned the blow aside with the flat of her blade.

Rai rounded on her in fury. "What the fuck –?"

"Relax, little girl," the Carraid said. "He's unmounted."

Rai's breath escaped in a rush. She drove the point of her sword into the ground and leaned on the hilt. "Shit." She ran a shaky hand across her face and watched as Banya approached the black animal and scratched between its ears. Breathing hard, the horse dropped his forehead against her chest.

"It's a wonder he didn't step on his reins and break his fool neck," Banya mused as she stroked his shoulder. "If Remeg was half the rider she thinks she is, she'd have gotten on him before he could respond to the whistle."

"Well, I don't know about you, but I'm grateful she sucks," Rai said. She yanked her weapon from the ground and sheathed it. Fitting her hand around as much of Banya's wrist as she could manage, she drew her away from the others. "This is an utter clusterfuck," she said, keeping her voice low.

"Thanks," Banya said. "I wasn't aware."

"You ready to tell me what's really going on?"

"I don't know what you're talking about."

"Oh?" Rai said with sarcasm. "Well, how about that sword for starters? What's the story on that? You never mentioned that pretty little piece of goods when you told me about this trip. What is it, the boy's dowry or something? I thought steriles got into Dara for free."

Banya thumbed grime out of the corner of one eye and sighed, knowing she had no one but herself to blame. "Look, we don't have time to get into it right now. There *is* more to tell and I will, just not right this minute, okay?"

"Do I have a choice?"

Banya smiled. "There are always choices."

Rai snorted. "Didn't think so." She kicked the ground. "Will she come after us?"

"Remeg?" Banya pondered, shuffling the loose sheaf of dead leaves beneath her feet. "I doubt it. We're only a couple of worthless grunts, after all."

Rai touched her sleeve. "But I lied to her."

"You did"

"And now I've left town against orders."

"*We've* left town, little girl. You're hardly alone in this venture."

"That's desertion."

"The idea didn't seem to bother you before."

"That's when it was temporary!" Rai snapped. She looked around the clearing as if she expected a bogey to leap from the shadows. "We knocked her off her horse."

Banya held up a finger. "That was an accident."

"And we stole him!"

"We didn't steal him! He came along of his own accord. It's not our fault that he's trained to obey signals."

Rai's lip curled. "I'm sure Remeg will be very understanding when we explain it like that."

Silence grew between them. Frost-curled leaves crunched beneath Rai's boots as she shifted her weight. "She'll come after us," she said with certainty.

"You don't know that," Banya said.

They looked at each other and something passed between them, an unspoken accord. As one, they moved across the clearing to join the others.

"Time to go," Banya said. "Rai, you take the black and let the boy have your horse."

"Forget it," she said. "That animal's crazy."

"We can't put an inexperienced rider on him."

"Then you ride him and I'll take your mare."

"Fat fucking chance I'd put *you* on Carraid horseflesh." Banya leaned into her face. "Look, we're losing time, so just do it, will you? There are four horses; let's use them."

Rai glared at her. "You're pretty keyed up for someone who thinks she's not being pursued," she said in a snotty tone. She motioned to Kinner. "Go on, kid. Up you get." He didn't move. She glanced at Banya.

"Come on, boy," the Carraid said none-too-gently.

"Everything's gone." Kinner's voice was small and filled with sorrow. "It all spilled into the street. My clothes. My books. The bracelet Mum made me when I was …" His words wobbled with unshed tears.

"That's just stuff," Holan said in a withering tone. "We have what's most important." She coiled the muddied silk around the sword and returned it to its box.

Kinner's hurt was obvious to everyone except his mother. Busy securing the box to her saddle, she either didn't see his pain or chose to disregard it. When he realized this, his lips thinned into a bitter line and he looked at the ground.

"Go on, kid," Rai said again, more gently this time. She laced her fingers together to make a step and waited. He came to her without a word, placed his boot in the cradle of her hands, and let her boost him into the saddle. When he was settled, she reached for the black's reins. The stallion's ears flattened against his head and he whickered low with displeasure. Rai snatched her hand away and did a quick back-step.

"You knock off that shit!" Banya snapped. The horse's ears sprang forward and his malevolent eyes went doe-soft as if to ask, "Me? Did I do something wrong?"

Cursing under her breath, Rai took up the reins and mounted. The animal jittered sideways, but did not buck. Drawing the reins tight, she nodded her readiness.

Banya swung into the saddle and turned to regard her little troupe. She knew that Rai would stick by her no matter what. Kinner was clearly frightened, but there was a hint of determination in the set of his jaw that had not been there before. Holan …

The Carriad nearly laughed aloud. Holan, with her bony shoulders thrown back, looked like she ate adventure every morning and crapped out danger at night.

The glint in the old woman's eyes became a sparkle. "Some day I want to hear the full story behind this night, Kiordasdotter."

Banya's smile was cheerless. "If we live to tell it, Grandmother. If we live to tell it."

TEN

A sliver of sun broached the eastern horizon and bloodied the line between earth and heaven, bruising the clouds in colors to match Remeg's mood. She studied the sky beyond the bubbled window glass, watching the hue change from scarlet and rose to saffron and pearl as the sun slipped free of the land and vanished again behind the low welter of clouds. The rain resumed, pattering spectral fingers against the glass.

Time was marked by the slow blink of her eyes and the measured rise and fall of her breathing. The print of Rai's boot sole on her chest burned through her shirt like a brand. A mug of strong tea laced with whiskey sat untouched in the middle of the desk, gone tepid in the hours since Black Hirn had left it there.

Somewhere beyond Caerau, life was normal. Morning arrived as always, burnishing lovers and killers alike, and the day's smoky hand passed unseen, ushering babes into the world and old women out of it.

Old women.

Out.

Of.

It.

With the meticulous care of a spider, Remeg walked the web of her thoughts. With deft and delicate touch, she felt where each bit of knowledge joined the next. Where the thread broke, its end raveled like the rotted weave of an old tapestry, she back-tracked to find the next join and moved on.

She was not altogether surprised by Rai's desertion, but Banya was another matter. Part of Remeg's job was to monitor the shifting alliances that existed in the garrison. A handful of trusted lieutenants kept her well informed in that regard. She knew Rai and Banya were long-time friends, but friendship was not enough in Remeg's view to make an exemplary soldier like Banya behave in such a manner. And yet, in fact, she had appeared to be leading the merry little band that had quit Caerau so precipitously.

And what of that woman, Holan of Moselle, and the seedless brat whose name Remeg could not recall? She had assumed – treacherous word! – that they had left town days ago, with or without a guide. Yet there they were, still in Caerau despite everything she had told Kedar. What twist of fate had tied their star to that of two sly and deceitful soldiers?

Her soldiers.

A discreet knock interrupted her thoughts. Remeg held her breath for five heartbeats and then slowly released it as she turned. "Come."

Asabi, lean and dark as a river eel and muddy from hard riding, stood like a length of dour shadow against the lighter grain of the door. She saluted and rubbed the side of her nose with a gnarled stub, all that remained of a forefinger. "We tracked 'em as far as the forest, Captain, then lost the trail." She shook her head in grudging admiration. "That Banya, she could cross snow and not leave a track."

"Any sign of that woman or the boy?"

"No. We found a place where someone upchucked, but that's it. Rain's washed away most everything else. What there is to see …" Asabi shrugged. "We may as well be hunting willy-wisps."

Behind her back, Remeg's short fingernails bit red crescents into her palms. "Are they still together?"

Asabi swiped her nose with a gauntleted wrist and sniffed. "They were before we lost the trail. What they've done since, I can't say."

Remeg nodded and turned away, deep in thought. In and of themselves, Rai and Banya meant little to her. They were a pair of expendable grunts, two in the long line she had seen come through the garrison. Rai's deception rankled, that was true, and the question behind Banya's desertion was certainly of interest, but what, really, could Remeg do about it? Neither was worth the expense and effort it would take to hunt them down. Banya would undoubtedly vanish behind the borders of Carraidland and Rai, being the good little duckling she was, would follow her. But Holan and her brat were another matter. Kedar had demanded their presence and that was a duty which Remeg must fulfill or risk losing the queen forever.

She pushed that black fear away with force of will and brought to bear her pragmatism. The difficulties as presented were not insurmountable. She knew her quarry's destination. Once the fugitives were located, the offer of a hefty financial inducement and a pardon for past offences would almost certainly guarantee Rai and Banya's cooperation. If not, then there were penalties for desertion, none of them pleasant.

With her way now clear, Remeg faced Asabi. "Have Black Hirn outfit a long-term patrol to leave in three hours."

Asabi's expression remained carefully enigmatic. "That's not much time,

Captain."

"That's not my problem, Lieutenant. Handpick a dozen soldiers, those who don't mind hunting their own without question and killing them if need be."

If Asabi was surprised by the order, it didn't show. "Anything else?"

"Yes. Send Gair to me. She'll handle things in my absence, but right now I want her to question those foundlings of Banya's, see if they know anything. I'll lead the patrol and you'll be second. And get yourself something to eat."

"Aye, Captain." The slender, jet-skinned woman touched her fingers lightly to her brow and departed.

Remeg closed the door and leaned against it, feeling the rough texture of unplaned wood against her shoulder blades. Unbidden, the image of a silver blade rose in her mind. Stepping away from the door, she rubbed a hand across her tired eyes as if to wipe away the sight of the shining weapon and rooster hilt. In the Goddess's name, what was she to make of that? Worse still, what would Kedar, with all her superstitious dabbling, make of it were she to learn of that sword's existence? Holy hell would boil over.

Holy *war.*

On a whim, Remeg grabbed her cloak and slung it around her shoulders. Leaving the office, she hurried downstairs, where she stuck her head briefly into the tower guard's small anteroom. Hebbady, who had duty from midnight to noon, looked up. "Yes, Captain?"

"I'm going out on an errand, Heb. Gair's due in. Have her wait in my office."

"Aye, Captain."

Remeg pulled up her hood as she stepped outside. A fine, soaking mist beaded the expensive wool like watery pearls. Turning, she bent her head against the rain and strode toward the center of town. There was someone she had to see.

"Captain Remeg! A delight, as always!"

"The pleasure is mine, Archbishop." Remeg waited until the servant who had led her to this room had departed before she approached the woman sitting behind a table laid with a plain damask cloth. A rack of candles danced golden light across a simple clay cup and a wooden trencher on which an apple core and a few crumbs were all that remained of breakfast. Bowing her head, Remeg dropped to one knee and kissed the offered amethyst ring. "Thank you for seeing me on such short notice."

Archbishop Clary was a lean, athletic woman in her sixties who rode daily and practiced both archery and religious needlepoint. She waved away the apology. "No need." She indicated that Remeg should take a seat. "I've just finished breakfast, but can I offer you something?" There was a basket of fresh rolls on the table, plus a bowl of fruit and a brown, round-bellied teapot.

"Thank you, no," Remeg said as she pulled out a chair. "I've eaten."

"At daybreak, no doubt," Clary said with startling accuracy.

Not for the first time, Remeg pondered just how much the Archbishop knew – not only about last night's goings-on, but about everything that happened in Caerau. Like Remeg, Clary had her spies. It would be foolishness on Remeg's part not to accept that one of them must reside in the garrison, although who it was remained a mystery. "Yes, Your Grace."

"Up and out early, that's what I like to hear. None of this lolling in bed at all hours." Clary's grey curls made her look like everyone's favorite granny, a deception that Remeg admired. The Archbishop was a kind and benevolent soul when the situation warranted, but beneath that friendly exterior was a spine of solid steel and a superlative intelligence.

Clary picked up a pipe from beside her plate and went about the routine of filling it with fragrant tobacco from a lidded silver pot. "So, tell me, Captain. How can I be of service this fine morning?" Her eyes twinkled as she glanced up from her work. "No deep dark confessions, I warrant?"

Remeg smiled with practiced ease. "None today, I'm afraid, Your Grace. I'm here with a question."

The Archbishop lit a taper from a candle and applied it to the pipe bowl. She sucked twice, blew smoke, and waved the taper to put it out. Laying it across her plate, she settled back in her chair. "Go on."

Remeg folded her hands together on the table and leaned forward. "What can you tell me about the Weathercock?"

Clary's shrewd gaze did not waver. "That's an unusual line of inquiry. You're not thinking of changing alliances, are you?"

Remeg laughed politely because it was expected. "No, Your Grace. I belong to the Goddess, first and last."

"That's good to hear. I wish half my parishioners were so dedicated." The archbishop blew smoke from the corner of her mouth. "The Weathercock's a myth, as you must know. An everlasting hero sort of thing." She removed the pipe from her mouth and held the stem against her cheek. "What is it precisely that you wish to know?"

Remeg evaded the question by ignoring it. "The tales speak of a boy who will end the rule of queens and bring about equality between the sexes."

Clary nodded. "There isn't much more to the story than that, I'm afraid.

Ridiculous, of course. Imagine a man running a business or doing manual labor." She snorted at the notion. Resting an elbow on the table, she leaned toward Remeg. "Imagine the disaster with one of them as ruler!" She sat back and shivered in mock horror. "If that isn't enough to put your off your food and give you nightmares for a week, I don't know what is!"

"Very true, Your Grace." Remeg sat back in her chair, wondering how to proceed. She pieced her words together with care. "Are portents mentioned in the stories, a birthmark or celestial event by which the child will be known? Are there clues to his identity or images connected with the tales? Banners, perhaps, or sigils?"

Clary's gaze sharpened. "Have you seen or heard something suspicious, Captain?"

Remeg shook her head. "No, Your Grace." Devout in her own way, she hoped the Goddess would forgive one that little white lie. "Nothing concrete. Nothing on which to place a hand or base a hypothesis. But I do hear things from time to time, as you must know. Stories filter down from the mountains and villages and end up here. Is it wise to ignore them entirely, given Her Majesty's interest in –"

Clary cut her off, mouth pursed with disapproval. "I presume you're referring to her current infatuation with the occult."

"I would not be so bold as to describe it thus, Your Grace, but –"

"Put aside the pretence, Captain," Clary said sharply. "You and I and this teapot …" she tapped the mouthpiece of the pipe against the brown crockery to underscore her words. "… all know it's a load of codswallop. I've wasted hours talking to Kedar about this very thing, but she won't listen. She would rather put her immortal soul at risk than to stand on the side of reason." She sighed heavily. "It's like talking to a wall."

Remeg knew that better than anyone. Her next words came slowly and with care. "In the bit of study I've done, Your Grace, it seems that there's never been an uprising in the Weathercock's name, yet the legend and its rumors persist. If I – if *we* – were to prove them to be entirely without foundation, perhaps the queen would see reason at last."

Clary smiled a bit condescendingly. "That's a grand notion, Captain, but I question our ability to banish every glimmer of the Weathercock from this land. The peasantry *will* have their little legends." She puffed on the pipe. "And maybe they should," she mused, blowing smoke and watching it rise.

"We needn't silence every whisper, Your Grace," Remeg said. "Merely gain enough proof to put Her Majesty's mind at ease. At that point, her attention could be redirected to other matters." Remeg kept her features bland under Clary's scrutiny. Let her look all day, if she liked; she would find nothing to read on Remeg's face.

"You've wisdom of your own, Captain, something I've known for quite some time." The archbishop placed the pipe beside the wooden plate and steepled her fingers beneath her chin. When she next spoke, her voice had the cadence of a chant. "From the ashes of our fathers shall he rise. Red and silver his colors shall be and his sign a rampant cock, blah-de-blah-de-blah." She chuckled.

Remeg smiled politely, but in her mind rose the events of the night before – the spilled richness of red silk and silver blade; the heart-stopping beauty of the fighting cock captured at the moment of battle. Her vitals felt cold.

Clary pushed back her chair and rose, making it clear that the audience was over. "Well, I support your endeavor, Captain, and wish you luck in it. If there's a more explicit way I can aid you, please let me know."

Remeg took her cue and stood. "Thank you, Archbishop. I shall." She bowed low, kissed Clary's ring once more, and showed herself out.

There was one more stop to make before she returned to her tower and made ready for departure.

Remeg nodded to the barkeep as she stepped through the doorway of The Bishop's Cat, a favorite watering-hole of the garrison. The woman's eyebrows lifted in inquiry, but Remeg shook her head and instead of buying a drink, wended her way among the scatter of mostly empty tables and chairs toward the back of the room where sat a solitary figure.

She noisily pulled out a chair, turned it back to front and straddled the seat. "Hello, Gorach."

The bleary, red-rimmed eyes of a career alcoholic lifted from their study of the table's scarred surface and blinked at her. Remeg could not recall the last time she had seen the disgraced Carraid sober. Certainly not since her discharge.

"Cap'n." The woman's breath was foul, her gums mottled with black and her teeth rotted to stumps. Only the Goddess knew when she had last bathed – months ago? Years? Her skin was pale with addiction and her hair hung in feculent ropes around her swollen face.

"I need some information," Remeg said. When the woman did not reply, she dug a ten-sen piece out of her pocket and tapped it sharply against the table. Gorach flinched at the sound and her eyes tracked slowly to focus on the coin. Remeg held it up between two fingers. "I need some information," she repeated. "When I have it, I'll buy you a drink and give you this coin so you can buy more. All right? Do you understand?"

The big woman's head moved with the ponderous slowness of a drugged bear. "Yous alls good to me, Cap'n." She reached for the coin with thick, uncoordinated fingers.

Remeg held it out of reach. "Information first, Gorach, then the money. What I want to know is, do the Carraid really believe in the Weathercock or is that all merely part of the legend?"

A light kindled deep in the drunkard's faded eyes. With effort, she pushed herself to sit up straight. "Weathercock's no story," she said with contempt. Her voice had taken on a surprisingly firm and clear timbre. "Weathercock's *real.*"

"To you or to all of Carraidland?"

"T' ev'ryone."

"Is the Weathercock here?" Remeg said. "Has he been born?"

Gorach shook her head. "Not yet, but soon, they say."

"*Who* says?" When she made no reply, Remeg tried another tack. "What would the Carraid do to see the Weathercock succeed?"

"Anything," Gorach replied at once. "Ever'thing."

"Even commit treason against the queen?"

The big woman shook. It took Remeg a moment to realize it was laughter and not palsy. Gorach looked at her out of eyes as rheumy and poached as a couple of eggs, but the expression in them sat Remeg back in her chair with surprise. "Carraidland's got no queen," the former soldier said clearly. "Carraidland has Carraidland."

Remeg nodded and slipped the coin into the woman's big paw. She patted her arm as she rose. "Thank you, Gorach. I'll have them send over a pint of lager."

"Thank'ee, Cap'n," the woman slurred. Her head sank deeper between her shoulders. Her next words were muffled.

Halfway to the bar, Remeg turned. "What was that?"

"The sword," Gorach repeated. "Th' Weathercock's sword. S'posed to be made special, for his hand alone."

Blood hammered suddenly in Remeg's temples. "What does it look like?"

"Dunno." Gorach's head tipped forward and she snored.

Remeg debated shaking her awake, then decided against it. She ordered the promised drink and left the tavern. Her brief glimpse of the sword shone bright in her mind as she walked toward her tower. The mere fact of the blade's existence implicated the boy and his mother, although precisely how Remeg was not yet sure. Add in Banya of Carraidland and her puppet-partner Rai, and the situation almost screamed with treachery. If, by some chance, that proved to not be the case, what of it? It would take little effort to make it seem so. Remeg could paint whatever picture she chose, so long as betrayal of the queen lay at its center.

When she quenched this uprising, when she put to the sword all those who threatened her queen, then she would have Kedar right where she wanted her – loving, compliant and, most important of all, *grateful.*

Eleven

Concealed amid a tall jumble of rock in a lee warmed by the sun, Rai undid the front of her coat and fanned it open. The heavy garment was a cast-off from a soldier who had died a few years back. An impromptu raffle had dispersed the dead woman's personal effects and Rai had won the coat. It had never fitted her properly, being a bit long in both body and sleeve, but it was warm and that was all she cared about.

Overnight the weather had transformed from a seasonal chill to a rare treat, an autumn gift known as Peasants' Summer, so-called because the poor put the cheater days to use foraging for nuts, late berries, wild onions, and honey. The remainder of the field crops – every last seed and stalk, anything that was not rotted or pest-chewed – went into their larders to see them through the hell of deep winter. The occasional deer might also be taken, but that was a risky venture that would lose someone a hand if she were caught. Sheep and cattle were herded from their pastures to pass the cold months secure in pens and barns close to the house or (in the case of some families) indoors with people. As a little child, having the animals inside had seemed like great fun to Rai … until the mixed stench of smoke, manure, and unwashed bodies made you want to gag. It was all a game until a goat shit where you slept or some stupid cow, frightened by the howling of wolves outside the door, trod on you in the night and broke your hand.

The sere grass of the meadow over which she looked was bent low, driven flat by a strong wind from the southwest. Rai glanced at the sky. The peasants had better work fast. Suspiciously fat clouds were massing in the north and east, and the wind kept threatening to shift.

The scrape of pebbles beneath a boot sole announced Banya's arrival. Rai shifted aside to give her room and the Carraid settled down beside her. "See anything?"

Rai shook her head. "Nah. Some birds is all and a badger and a pokey-spine pig." She tilted her face to the sky and briefly closed her eyes, relishing the gypsy warmth. "I think Remeg's let us go. I told you we weren't that important."

"As I recall, you were the one convinced that she would hunt us down."

"Didn't argue the point, did you?" Rai folded her arms and settled against the stone. "Are you ready to tell me what the deal is with that sword?"

Banya turned her attention to the countryside. "It's a long story."

"Meaning we don't have time for it right now?"

The Carraid shrugged. "More or less."

Rai grunted and glanced toward the makeshift campsite far below. The horses were picketed loosely together, rumps turned to the wind. They cropped the dry grass with a lethargy entirely at odds with their usual ardor over food. Salt stiffened the hair on their chests and necks, latticing their hides in irregular lines like a child's chalk drawing.

The boy sat cross-legged on the ground beside his mother, who lay wrapped in blankets with her head pillowed on a saddlebag. The rigors of last night's hard road had been familiar to the two soldiers, but pure torture on their companions. Holan had clung to her saddle with whey-faced tenacity, her head rocking on its spindle of neck like a heavy melon on a too-thin vine. Kinner, pale and frightened, had remained as silent and solemn as a priestess. As the hours shifted toward daylight, however, a subtle change had occurred in the boy. The color in his face had heightened and his eyes had grown bright with excitement. Rai had found the transformation altogether unbecoming in a man.

"How's she doing?" she said.

Banya flicked a wind-blown braid out of her eyes. "It won't be –" A sudden shout from below cut her off. They sprang to their feet, swords drawn, and careered down the escarpment like a couple of mountain goats.

Holan's face was bloodless; not the white of milk, but vaguely blue, waxy and luminous, as if a ghostly light shone beneath her skin. Shadows – grey, plum, smudgy brown and indigo – nestled at the base of her throat, in the hollows beneath the prominent ridge of each cheek, and crowded along the rims of her eyes. Her breathing was labored, as wet and bubbly as thin gruel.

Kinner tenderly stroked her left hand. The flesh was cold, as if kissed by frost, and the tips of her fingers were blue. The outline of each tendon and bone pressed into his palm. "Can I get you anything, Mum?" he said, and swallowed around the painful lump in his throat.

Her head made a faint, negative motion against the saddlebag. "No, my dear. I'm fine."

Fine, he thought. How could she say so? Then again, maybe she was fine. Maybe there really was nothing left to be done, nothing she either needed or wanted beyond a wish to have this ordeal at an end.

Holan slowly turned her face toward the nearby woods and stared at the trees. A tiny frown plucked a faint track between her eyebrows, but Kinner had witnessed enough of her trances to know that this was not one of them. This was a moving away, his mother's first steps on an inevitable journey. Her lips moved without sound.

He leaned closer. "What was that, Mum? I didn't catch it."

She blinked as if it hurt to do so. "It's a damn shame."

"What is?"

Her free hand twitched in a vague gesture. "All of this." Her mouth curled in a little moue. "I've based my entire life on something I couldn't even touch."

Kinner bit his lip. Now was not the time for recrimination or regret, not on his part at least. "You did what you thought right, Mum. You told me more than once that you didn't have any choice."

Holan's brow puckered in consternation. "I don't believe I ever used those words." She looked at him. "I told you before, boy. There are always choices. You don't have to do what someone tells you to do, not even if that someone holds your life in their hands. The path you take is your business alone and no one else's. If the choice you make doesn't work out as you planned, you change it and try again. Nothing is fixed while you still draw breath. You can always walk away."

"So why didn't you?" There was no meanness in his question, only curiosity. "If that's how you feel, why didn't you walk away from the Weathercock?"

"Because I didn't want to." Her eyes burned with a familiar fever that all but broke Kinner's heart. "Instead, I chose to live a selfish life."

He stroked her fingers. "You did fine, Mum."

She shook her head. "That's kind of you to say but no, I didn't. I should have paid more attention to you and to Kessler."

"What are you talking about?" Kinner said with gentle admonishment. "You tucked me into bed every night and you almost never missed a bath time or a story. There are few mothers who can say the same. As for Father … well, you know he loved you best."

A puckish smile dimpled one wasted cheek. "He did, didn't he?" Holan's voice was wistful.

For a moment, Kinner caught a glimpse of the young girl she had been, the woman-child un-Housed by circumstance and not yet twenty, who had bartered everything she owned in a game of chance against a fat, drunken sow of a merchant who had placed her Family's Husband into the pot in a blind panicked attempt to get out of debt.

Kessler had told him the story many times, relating those hours of worry in a dockside tavern as he wondered which of the players would own him in the end. His eyes always shone when he spoke of the resolute and wily young woman who, with a final roll of the dice, had won the means to begin her own Household without having to pay for the services of someone else's Husband.

In thinking of his father's life, Kinner felt suddenly overwhelmed by the memory of his death. Gone were the soft voice and kindly manners, the ready chuckle and patient corrections, the equal delight in his son's fascination with sunsets and spider webs. Lost without the gentle guidance of that loving man to teach him the ways of the world and his role in it, the boy had grown silent and withdrawn.

The over-played grief of the Secondwives had been an embarrassment and would have humiliated Kessler had he been alive to witness the display. Holan was disgusted by their histrionics. If the blacksmith shed a single tear over the loss of her beloved, no one saw it. Dry-eyed and stoic, she had arranged for the funeral service and burial and left it to the Secondwives to handle the details of the reception. They managed to lay out the meal with an odd combination of austerity and pomp, as if unable to decide how best to honor Kessler's memory or which demonstration of grief would make the better impression on the neighbors.

In what was considered a horrific breach of etiquette, Holan had refused to attend the reception, leaving Kinner alone at the head of the table, uncomfortable in that place of honor as the new Husband. He had tried not to listen while his aunts argued with his mother through the closed door of the forge, but their voices were shamefully audible to those who gathered in the parlor to pay their respects to the Family.

Holan had ignored their entreaties and refused to open the door. In a few minutes, the muffled *woof!* of the forge bellows was heard through the wall, followed by the *clang!* of a hammer against the anvil. The aunts had returned to the house, their faces pruned with anger and embarrassment, and spent the remainder of the evening making shrewish remarks to the assembled guests. As the neighbors came and went, Kinner noticed that some cast a thoughtful glance toward the smithy. Maybe they understood and sympathized with the blacksmith more than they let on. Then again, maybe the one they felt sorry for was *him.*

"Kinner?"

He leaned closer. "Yes, Mum?"

Something of the old Holan surfaced in her eyes and sudden strength entered her voice. "You know I love you, don't you?"

"Yes, Mum," he whispered. "I love you, too."

She nodded as if that were a given. "You do understand that I'm going to die soon and won't be able to take you to Dara?"

"Yes." His voice broke on the word. How would he get there, but for her?

"Good. There's no sense in pretending otherwise." She folded both hands around his. "Now listen carefully. It's important that you pay close attention to what I'm about to tell you. Will you do that?"

"Of course, Mum, but don't you think –"

"Good boy." Her eyes held his. "You're not sterile."

The words struck him like a blow and reverberated with an odd echo. "What?"

"You heard me. You're not sterile."

Brutal sadness stabbed his heart. This was it; her mind had gone at last. He remembered what it was like when Auntie Prueth went "round the bend" (as the neighbors put it) and ran off down the middle of the street stark naked claiming she was made of flowers.

He squeezed his mother's fingers. "It's all right, Mum. I'm here."

Holan swatted his hand with unexpected strength. "I *know* you're here! Don't be patronizing. I may be dying, but I'm not senile!" She grabbed his wrist and gave it a shake. "Listen to me! You're ... not ... sterile."

Next she would be calling him Kessler or believing that they were home in Moselle. "Of course I am, Mum," Kinner said, thinking as he did so that it was probably pointless to disagree. When had he ever won an argument with Holan? "Doctor Swainy filled out the paperwork. You showed it to Captain Remeg. Don't you remember?"

She waved a hand, dismissing his question as if it held no more merit than a bad smell on the breeze. "I remember taking you to get that infernal tattoo as well, but things aren't always as they appear. Believe me, boy, you're as fertile as a spring field."

Kinner felt a flicker of annoyance and pushed it away. "Then why did I never get any of the girls pregnant?"

Holan smiled. "That's because I fixed it so you couldn't."

Silence pressed against his ears for a heartbeat, two ... and then he exploded. "*What?*" From somewhere up among the rocks came a cry and a skitter of loose gravel; Rai and Banya on the move. "You ... you *fixed* it? How in the world do you fix something like that?"

Holan shrugged with false modesty. "It's simple enough if you stay observant. Each time you had sex, I slipped an abortifacient into the girl's tea. If she *had* quickened, that took care of it with little muss, no fuss, and no one much the wiser." She grinned, clearly pleased with herself. "By my own reckoning, you planted healthy seeds better than a dozen times." She patted his hand. "Well done, boy!"

"*Well done?*" Kinner's voice was strident. That she had willingly, purposely, done such a horrendous thing to him was impossible. How could she, of all people, have tampered with his life that way? *Why* would she, when the begetting of children was his chief purpose?

He pulled away and scrambled to his feet. "I trusted you, Mum!" He stood with his hands apart in supplication, aware of Rai and Banya behind him and mortally embarrassed that this scene should take place in front of strangers. "Why did you do such an awful thing?"

Holan's face was without expression. "Because it made a good cover."

Kinner reeled as if physically struck. His legs folded and he hit the ground hard.

"I knew I was sick long before the doctor confirmed it," Holan continued. "I knew my time was up, that it was now or never to get the sword to Dara. Since I could no longer go there on my own, I needed your help and you couldn't help me if you were busy making babies and raising a family."

Revulsion and incredulity pooled through Kinner's soul like black ink. "You ruined my life because of the *Weathercock?*"

Holan rolled her eyes. "Don't be so melodramatic. Your life is hardly ruined. I've given you a second chance, is all. You've got years ahead of you."

"To spend in a monastery where I don't belong!" The stench of her betrayal made the air fetid and difficult to breathe. "What am I supposed to do now that you've *fixed* everything?"

Her eyes glimmered. "That's the big question, isn't it? Will you hear me out?"

Kinner drew his knees to his chest and shivered, feeling cold despite the weather. "I'm listening."

"You're not, but I hope you will be by the time I'm through." Holan turned her wasted cheek against the saddlebag. "For a long time, the only visions I had were of making the sword. I had no idea what I was supposed to do with it. That information came barely a year ago."

Kinner hugged himself tighter. Banya dropped into a squat beside him, sword propped tip-down between her knees as she listened. Rai stood behind her, watching the trees.

"The vision showed me taking the sword to Dara. Imagine my confusion over that! Take the Weathercock's blade to a stronghold of the Goddess and deliver it into the hands of those sworn to Her service? It made no sense, but the message was quite clear. Well, I couldn't just up and leave, could I? Responsibilities aside, my illness made travel difficult and the journey would have aroused suspicion. I couldn't risk drawing too much attention because the sword had to remain a secret. And then Kessler died."

Pain moved across her face like an unseen hand working the clay of her flesh. "I stayed out late in the forge that night, making a lot of racket so everyone would leave me alone to think. I realized that if you failed to sire children, the Household would turn you out. As Firstwife, I could insist on taking you to Dara rather than having you killed and the sword could go with us. You'd end up with a different sort of life, of course, but is that really such a bad thing? Besides, the price was worth it."

Anger laid a heavy hand upon Kinner's chest. For the first time ever, he felt a worm of hatred coil around his heart. "Easy words when you're not the one paying that price," he said with acrimony. "Did it never occur to you to ask me for help? When have I ever refused you? Haven't I kept the Weathercock a secret all these years because you asked me to? Did you never consider what I might want?"

"What you wanted didn't matter." Her words were like a slap in the face. "What I wanted didn't matter. Do you think I enjoyed deceiving you and cheating you of your birthright?"

"There are always choices," he said with bitter irony.

"Yes," she agreed, adamant. "And I chose to sacrifice both of us to the Weathercock's cause."

"*Both* of us?" Kinner all but spat the words. "What have you lost? You've had your life! You've done as you bloody damn well please! You haven't thought about anyone but yourself!"

"Is that Household all you ever wanted out of life?" she countered. "To spend your years cleaning up after more and more unappreciative women and then to be discarded in the end anyway?" She shifted position, clearly in pain.

Kinner clenched his hands against the instinct to offer comfort. "They called me 'Seedless.'" His voice was filled with pain. He drove the heels of his hands against his eyes to keep the tears at bay. "How could you let them hurt me like that? How could *you* hurt me like that?"

Holan's fingers toyed with the frayed hem of one sleeve. "I never wanted to hurt you, love." Her eyes were shadowed with regret. "But there were forces at work in our lives larger than I ever realized, forces that I didn't have the strength or desire to refuse." Her cough was tiny, held back by force of will, and packed solid with moisture. "I believe in the Weathercock and what he stands for," she said. "Do you?"

Kinner stopped the first hateful words that leaped into his mouth. As a child, he had believed fervently in the Weathercock for no other reason than because his mother, whom he adored, wished him to. How did he feel now, with her duplicity revealed? Could he still believe in a child's fable? Could he separate her actions from the dream of a warrior for the land and its people?

He thought about the tangible and weighty presence of the Goddess – Her churches, cathedrals, and shrines; Her archbishop, priestesses, and monks; Her candles, incense, and prayers. He thought of the Weathercock – intangible as a wish, weighty as a summer's breeze – and was assailed by memory. Once again he heard his mother's voice and saw, through a child's eyes, the gaudy blood of a rising sun reflected in a upheld blade. Emotion swelled his heart. Holan was still his mother and he loved her despite her machinations. There were enough lies between them that one more would not hurt. "Yes, Mum," he said. "I still believe."

She sighed. "Well, that's something, at least." She held out a skeletal hand toward Banya and Rai. "Thank you for your help and for getting us this far."

Banya enclosed the offered hand in a gentle grip, as if she held a hatching egg. "You're welcome, Grandmother. We'll take credit where it's due, but our meeting in Caerau was coincidence."

Holan patted the Carraid's big knuckles. "You know better than that, Kiordasdotter." A line of drool tainted with blood formed at the corner of her mouth and broke free across the hollow line of her cheek. "May I ask a favor of you?"

"Shit," Rai muttered.

Banya reached back and swatted her leg. "Anything, Grandmother."

"Will you finish what I've begun? Will you see the sword into safekeeping at Dara?"

The Carraid nodded. "I'd have done that without your asking."

"And will you not abandon my son? Will you take him wherever he chooses to go?"

"Of course, Grandmother."

Holan sighed, her work done. "Thank you." She released Banya and reached for her son. Blinded by tears, Kinner knelt and clutched her icy fingers. She looked at him as if she meant to memorize him for all eternity. "There are always choices," she reminded him in a whisper. Her eyes grew soft and unfocused. For a moment she looked lost. Then suddenly, delight lit her face. "Oh, my *darling!*" she cried with joy. Her breath faded on a faint sigh and she died.

Grief strangled Kinner like an incoming tide, unstoppable, deep and green and immeasurably vast, filling his lungs with the salty weight of tears. He curled forward over their joined hands, laid his head against his mother's chest, and sobbed.

"Can we go now?" Rai said.

Banya rounded on her. "You've got all the compassion of a kick in the teeth!"

"What do you want me to do? She's dead. Let's bury her and get moving."

Kinner raised his swollen and splotchy face at her words. "The Weathercock's people don't go into the ground."

"She's dead," Rai needlessly pointed out again. "What difference does it make where she goes? It's not like she's going to complain or anything."

"For the love of…" Banya turned to Kinner. "Please excuse my friend. She fell down a flight of stairs when she was a baby and landed on her manners."

"I was *pushed* down that flight of stairs," Rai amended. She kicked a stone across the clearing and glanced at the sorrowful boy. "I suppose we could make a cairn. That's not in the ground, it's under a pile of rocks."

"Shut *up*, Rai," Banya growled. She ran a hand over her face. "I know that purge by fire is the way to go, but the fact is we'd be days finding enough wood. What if we put her up a tree and let the elements have her? Will that do, boy?"

Kinner wiped his face with a sleeve. "Thank you. That would be fine." He folded Holan's hands across her chest, kissed her, and pulled the wide hood of her cape across her face. Then he stood and turned to face the women into whose charge he had been placed. "And my name is Kinner, not boy."

Humor lit Banya's eyes with new respect. "Fair enough."

They chose an ancient maple for Holan's resting place, a tree whose strong and sprawling branches blazed with fiery splendor. Where three limbs came together to form a secure perch, Banya laid the blacksmith's body to rest.

While the soldiers made ready to move out, Kinner stayed at the foot of the tree, one hand against the trunk, staring up at the wind-tossed mass of red and orange foliage that hid his mother's bier. "Goodbye, Mum," he whispered. He listened for an answer on the wind, but Holan was gone as if she had never been. All that remained was the echo of her voice and the sound of Banya calling him to mount up.

Then again, maybe that *was* an answer, at least for now.

TWELVE

Rai woke to a pre-dawn sky speckled with stars and blissfully free of rain. The moon's waning disc hung over the horizon, encircled by a faint white ring. The sight of it brought to mind a childhood rhyme: *When there's a ring around the moon, rain or snow is coming soon.*

Her father had taught her that, the two of them standing in the farmstead's darkened yard wrapped in the wool of his shawl, armor against the penetrating cold of a highland winter morning. Rai had crooked a skinny arm around his neck and leaned her dark head against his. *Ith that true, Da?* At four years old, she had a lisp … and a bruised lip courtesy of her mother, who insisted that Rai did it for attention.

Brendie had smiled and kissed her temple. *We'll have to wait and see, Rai-bird.* Their idyll was interrupted by a bellow from indoors – Muire, awake and hungry and on the rampage, wanting to know *what the fuck* Brendie was doing out in the freezing dark with the child, staring at the sky like a couple of moonstruck idiots. Rai's father had kissed her again, a moth-light touch of whiskery lips against her temple, and taken her inside. He managed to get her safely tucked into a corner by the fireplace with a bowl of porridge and a slice of buttered bread before Muire stamped into the room and slapped him hard for his foolishness.

Rai pushed the memory aside and sat up. Banya was awake and feeding bits of fresh wood to the fire, nurturing it like a chick. Rai stretched, grunting with pleasure when the length of her spine popped. "How long have you been awake?" she whispered, mindful of the sleeping boy.

The Carraid placed a kettle of water on to boil. "Couple of hours," she said around a yawn. Her breath steamed.

Rai chafed her hands together and peered around. There was precious little to see beyond the circle of trees and the vague outline of the horses. "Dark as a whoremaster's heart," she said. "Where are we?"

"Northwest of Caerau." Banya dug into a rucksack and removed a lidded canister. "The Leith's off that way," she said and jerked her head to the east where a faint pearly-pink lightened the sky.

If she listened hard, Rai could catch the faint murmur of that slow and mighty river speaking its secretive tongue. The Leith began life as the Lon, a fierce and mean-spirited stretch of water birthed high among the Corydon peaks. The river quieted as it descended into the lowlands and plains, slowing and broadening and becoming an altogether different sort of creature with a different name to prove it.

"I gotta go see a woman about a dog," Rai said. She tossed her blankets aside and went into the bushes to do as Nature intended. When she returned, Kinner was awake and sitting up, scootched closer to the fire with his blankets around his shoulders.

Steam curled from the spout of the kettle, filling the campsite with the life-affirming scent of hot tea, and Banya was doing something creative that looked suspiciously like batter for griddle scones. Rai settled cross-legged on her blankets and reached for the kettle.

"That's hardly steeped," Banya warned.

"I don't care," she said and poured a cup. "By the time I get to seconds, it'll be strong enough to walk spiders on." She hefted the kettle in Kinner's direction and raised her eyebrows in question. When he nodded, she filled a second mug and handed it across to him.

"Thank you," he murmured. The rims of his eyes were swollen and red.

Rai knew the look. She's seen it on the faces of soldiers whose lovers had perished in battle. Now, as then, she had no idea what to say in the face of such grief. "You're welcome." She smiled. "I'm not used to good manners. In the garrison, it's always fuck-this and shit-that." She winced and bit her lip. That probably hadn't been the right thing to say, not to a man at any rate. "Is there any sugar?" she asked the Carraid, desperate to change the subject.

Without looking up from her work, Banya tossed a small sack in her direction. Rai caught it one-handed, loosened the drawstrings, and dumped enough into her tea to turn it into syrup.

"Have a care with that," Banya said. "It has to last until Dara."

"Yes, Mother." Rai swirled the liquid, took a loud slurp, and smacked her lips with pleasure. "So what's the plan, then?"

Banya laid a small iron griddle atop the coals and ran a piece of salt pork across it. "You know the plan. We do as we promised. We deliver the sword to Dara and take Kinner wherever he wants to go."

Rai held up a finger. "May I point out that it was *you* who did all the promising? I never agreed to anything."

"Guilt by association."

"I don't think so." Rai blew across her mug. "And what do you mean wherever he wants to go? He's a man."

"Stop talking like he's not here." The Carraid poured a row of creamy batter circles onto the hot griddle. As they bubbled and turned crisp around the edges, a heavenly smell filled the campsite. The scent arrowed straight up Rai's nose and impaled her brain so completely that she almost lost her train of thought.

"You know what I mean. He can't think for himself."

"Oh, ta. Thanks very much," Kinner said. "Why is it that just because I'm male, you assume I'm stupid as well? I'm not, you know."

Banya tossed him a wink as she flipped the scones over to cook the other side. "Well said, lad."

"Oh, horse pucky." Rai drank more of the overly-sweet tea and hefted the mug at Kinner in salute. "Okay. You're so smart, prove it."

"He doesn't have to prove anything to you," Banya said.

"Shut up and cook." Rai looked at Kinner through the ribbon of steam coming off her drink. "You're free to go anywhere in the world. What's it to be?"

Kinner's mouth gaped opened … and then slowly closed. He sat in thought for a minute or two and finally shrugged. "I don't know."

Rai smiled with satisfaction. "My point exactly. Men can't make decisions."

Banya whacked her on the knee with the spatula. "Your point, my fanny. A question like that can't be answered on the fly."

"You're just sticking up for him because you want to get into his pants!"

Banya's expression tightened and Rai felt the sudden weight of an impending beating. "I'm warning you, little girl. Do *not* go there."

"She's right, though," Kinner said. Both women blinked at him, surprised to silence. "Not about you wanting to …" He blushed. "But I *do* have to make a decision." A faint expression of pain tightened the skin around his eyes. "Until yesterday, I didn't even know I had a choice," he said softly.

Banya slid two scones onto a wooden trencher and handed it to him, pointedly ignoring Rai's outstretched hand. "You could return home."

"No," he said, his voice adamant. The answer had come fast; there was no need to think it over. "After Mum's little … arrangements … I doubt they'd believe I'm fertile." Kinner shook his head in bewilderment. "I'm not sure I believe it myself."

Banya put a couple of scones onto a plate for herself and then handed Rai the remainder. Stirring the batter, she poured more circles and sat back to eat while they cooked. "It only takes one pregnancy to change their minds," she said.

Kinner bit into a scone and chewed, deep in thought. "I'm not sure they'd give me a chance to prove myself. Even if they did, then what?" His expression turned sullen. "Bed woman after woman like a bull until I'm too old and worn out to be of any use?" His voice rose. "Spend my life doing laundry and sweeping floors, scared to death that one day I'll sire a son to –" He broke off and looked away.

"You don't have that many options, kid," Rai said, trying to be kind. "Far as I know, men are husbands, whores, monks, or dead."

Banya lifted the edge of a scone to check the underside. "Could you be a little more blunt?"

"What?" Rai said in confusion. The observation had been made in good faith, not as a sarcastic dig. "Am I the only one here who understands the facts of life?"

"I understand them better than anyone." The bitter quality of Kinner's voice surprised her. He sighed. "I'm going with you to Dara." He met their eyes. "It's not that I don't trust you, but I owe it to Mum to see the sword placed where it's meant to be. When that's done, I'll figure out what comes next." He peered into his mug, perhaps looking for his future in the tea leaves. All at once he seemed small and lost again, his bravado all but extinguished. "Who knows?" he said with a shrug. "Maybe I'll like the monastery and decide to stay." He didn't sound like he believed it.

Rai reached over and pinched a scone off the griddle with two fingers, tossing it from hand to hand to cool it. Banya raised the spatula like a bludgeon. "You pull a stunt like that again you'll lose a hand, little girl."

"Don't call me little girl." Rai bit into the scone and puffed air to keep from burning her tongue. "So, Kinner," she said in a supremely cheery voice. "Since my good buddy here doesn't seem to want to tell me about the sword, why don't you? What was all that twaddle your mother was spewing right before she died?"

Kinner bristled. "It's not twaddle. She made the sword for the Weathercock."

"I see. And the Weathercock is coming … *when?*"

"No one knows for sure."

"Uh-huh." She rooted dough out of her teeth with her tongue and washed it down with tea. "You do know the Weathercock is just a story, right?"

Kinner's next words were stout with belief. "One day he'll come in flame and glory to free this land."

Rai's snort echoed in the depths of her mug. "That's a load of crap."

"Actually," Banya said. "It isn't."

Rai's mouth hung open. "Oh, my sainted aunties! Don't tell me you believe in this shit, too? It doesn't even make sense!"

Banya flipped the second batch of scones off the griddle and onto a plate.

"It makes perfect sense if you set aside all the palaver spoon-fed to you by the Church." Banya stirred what remained of the batter and pointed the dripping spoon at Rai. "Imagine how much stronger our world would be if the skills of both sexes were encouraged."

"What are you talking about? They already are. Men make babies and take care of the Households, and women run businesses and –"

"And the government and the Church and every other institution of power." Banya swiped the griddle again with the salt pork and poured the last of the batter. "Does that sound equal to you?"

"*Equal?*" Rai yipped. She put down her mug with a thump and spread her hands. "Men are fragile. They're emotional. Breeding babies and taking care of the home is what they're made to do."

"They might do more, given half a chance."

"Like what?"

"Gee, I don't know." Banya made a sarcastic show of laying a forefinger against her cheek as if in deep thought. "Become doctors? Merchants? Travel the world?" She leered wickedly. "Take up arms?"

"Take up – ! Oh, now you're just talking tripe!" Rai took a savage bite from a scone, angrier than she could credence. "Answer me this, smart-ass. If men did all those things, when would they find time to make babies?"

"Oh, I think they'd manage." The Carraid winked broadly at Kinner, who blushed and ducked his head.

"What about the Households?" Rai persisted. "Who would cook and clean if the men were out doing …" She waved her hands randomly. "… all that other stuff?"

"The same people who already do it in every Household that doesn't have a Husband. Or didn't you think about that?"

Rai had not, but the idea sent a discordant echo down the years of her life. If her father had been given a choice, if Brendie had been able to escape Muire's tyranny, might he be alive today? Might they be living together somewhere, just the two of them, a father and daughter team?

She tried to imagine that; to imagine *him,* gathered together from wisps of memory. How old would he be? Somewhere in his forties, certainly. Strands of fine grey would have invaded his rich black hair and beard. What occupation would he have chosen? Sailor? Teacher? He had loved books and enjoyed reading to the Household's children, filling their heads with tales of far-off lands and talking animals …

Rai stood up fast and strode away from the fire. Behind her, Kinner said, "I'm sorry. Did I do that?" and Banya replied, "Don't worry about it."

She walked a short distance to where the tack was piled and knelt to pick up a set of beautifully tooled saddlebags. If Remeg's horse was now hers, it stood to reason that these were hers, too. She set about undoing a buckle.

The swish of dead grass against boots interrupted her curiosity. Banya squatted beside her, hands clasped loosely between her knees, a position she could assume for hours at a time. "Okay then?"

"Fine."

"You sure?"

"Yes."

The Carraid nodded. "Sounds like it. Find anything interesting?"

"Not yet." Rai picked at the buckle.

Banya sighed. "Look, I'm sorry, but you were coming down pretty hard on the boy."

"His name is *Kinner,*" Rai said with heavy sarcasm. She sat back on her heels. "Hang the kid. Why didn't you tell me any of this?"

"Any of what? About the sword and the Carraid and the Weathercock?"

"Yes!"

Banya snorted a tiny bemused laugh and rubbed her face. "Why do you think, Rai? You don't banter about the downfall of the queen in her own city. You want me executed?"

"Only if I'm the one to do it." She searched the first saddlebag, found nothing of interest, and flipped it over to open the other side. "It doesn't make sense, no matter what you two zealots believe. Why would the Weathercock want his sword sent to Dara of all places?"

Banya looked troubled. "I haven't been able to figure out that part."

"So why, in the name of all that's Three-Headed and holy, are we going through with this?"

Banya looked at her. There was no duplicity in her gaze, no ulterior motive, just plain, unadulterated Banya. "Because I said I would."

Rai felt a wash of hopelessness. There was nothing in the world more solid than a Carraid's word of honor, particularly the word of *this* Carraid.

Banya's mouth lifted in a hint of smile. "I'm acting on faith, Rai," she said. It was almost an apology. "You always said I was too soft-hearted for my own good."

"The word I used was soft-*headed.*" Rai glanced over her shoulder at the solitary figure near the fire, the boy who was conscientiously removing the last of the scones from the griddle before they burned. "He's scared, isn't he?"

"Wouldn't you be, if your only hope of aid lay in the two of us?"

"I'd be shitting my pants." She opened the saddlebag and reached inside. Out came a cloth drawstring sack the size of her fist, its bottom bulging with weight. Rai shook it and grinned at the jingle of money. "This looks promising."

Banya's agile fingers plucked the purse from her hand and vanished it into a jacket pocket.

"Hey, that's mine!"

"This is a joint venture, pal. What's yours is mine and what's mine is mine. We need supplies."

"My ass." Rai reached toward the pocket to take back the money and got her hand slapped hard. "We have plenty of supplies!"

"Food stuffs, yeah, but Kinner lost everything. He needs a change of clothes, at least." She peered at Rai. "You did bring other clothes, right?"

"I only have the two uniforms and both were dirty, thanks to you."

The Carraid tweaked the front of Rai's shirt. "You didn't think to steal a second uniform along with the boots you took?" She grinned at Rai's astonishment. "You didn't think I'd notice, did you? Honestly, I despair of you sometimes, I really do."

Rai folded her arms, grumpy. "We should have just taken Holan's clothes. She won't need them."

Banya's jollity vanished. "Don't you dare say that in front of Kinner," she said in a soft, dangerous voice. "I know that's what we should have done, but I couldn't ask him to leave his mother naked and neither could you, for all your rough talk." She checked the sky and rose. "Dawn's nearly here. Let's break camp and get moving. I want to reach Cadasbyr by dark."

Rai froze, as still as a hare who senses danger in the circling shadow of a hawk. "What?"

Banya looked down at her. "Cadasbyr. Look," she added quickly. "I know you don't like it there, but –"

"I hate it! Go somewhere else!"

"We're in the middle of numb-fuck nowhere. What do you suggest? The way you carry on, anyone would think you're still a little kid. It's just a town."

"Yeah, the town from hell." Rai upended the saddlebag and gave it a shake. A white silk scarf drifted out and landed at her feet. As she bent to pick it up, a heady whisper of scent lifted from the cloth. Rai sniffed and made a face. "Perfumed. Looks like Remeg has a rich squeeze."

"You know the rumors."

"The queen?" Rai waved a dismissive hand. "What would a woman like Kedar Trevelyan see in a simple grunt when the richest women in the world want to lick her toes?"

"Even you should have figured out by now that Remeg's not a simple grunt. Besides, we all have our tastes."

"I'll believe that when I see it." Rai shoved the scarf into a jacket pocket and tossed the empty saddlebags onto the pile as she turned to followed Banya back to the fire. The rising wind, dotted with the first airy snowflakes of the day, caught the trailing end of silk and tugged. The scarf slid free of Rai's pocket without her noticing and skirled away into the darkness.

An early snowfall dusted the countryside as Remeg led her troop at a hard gallop along the north road out of Caerau. She raked the sides of the buckskin beneath her with scouring heels. The animal tried to give her what she wanted, but all its swiftness could not help her out-run her demons, the worst of which had risen from its grave to stare at her with the dark eyes of a child.

She had penned a hasty note to Kedar while waiting for the patrol to assemble. The message conveyed only that information which Remeg deemed unlikely to drive the queen into a rant. She had dispatched the note by fast rider and told the woman to wait for a reply, but the messenger had returned empty-handed, having been sent away by the queen's castellan.

The lack of response could mean nothing or everything. Kedar may have been busy with affairs of state … or affairs of another sort. The image of Chela Quarm hovered before Remeg's eyes – the possessive smile, the almost-touch of the downy royal shoulder. The thought of those awkward hands and lacquered mouth on the queen's flesh …

Remeg's stomach rolled and her fingers tensed on the reins. The horse, confused by her signals, tossed its head and began to slow. She drove it on with her spurs, cursing under her breath. Kedar was playing queen with all of the spite at her command, making certain Remeg knew her place and understood that, at least for now, she was Kedar's servant and nothing more.

Asabi, riding slightly ahead of her commander, raised an arm to signal a halt. She turned to Remeg as the horses slowed. "This is where they left the road to strike out across country."

"Show me."

The two women dismounted. Leaving the bulk of the troop to wait on the road, they crossed a stretch of frost-yellowed grass and stepped beneath the tree canopy. "This way, Captain," Asabi said and led her deeper into the forest. Remeg's eyes swept the area but there was little to see. Any sign of passage had been covered with a dusting of new snow.

Asabi stopped. "We tracked them this far." She held out her hands, open with the palm up, a gesture of defeat. "It's like I said. That damned Banya …" Her voice held a note of admiration.

Remeg's cape lifted from her shoulders like the sprout of dark wings as she turned and called toward the road. "Mestipen!"

The woman who joined them was lean to the point of emaciation and walked with the hunch-shouldered expectancy of a crow, her misshapen nose thrust forward like a bird's beak. Her dark hair, long and coarse, streaked with bands of iron grey, was pulled back in an untidy horse's tail. Mestipen had once been beautiful, but now whorled scars the size of Remeg's thumb disfigured the olive skin of her face where a spear thrust had rammed through both cheeks and broken her nose. What the injury had done to her mind was better left unsaid. Tempered in a kiln of fever and pain, she had changed. Now the other soldiers kept their distance. She could make even the hardiest of them squirm with discomfort.

"Captain." Her voice, cracked and pitted, held the shriek of ice against glass. Mestipen tipped her head sideways and peered at Remeg with mad eyes.

"Find them," Remeg ordered.

Mestipen inclined her head in what was almost a bow and moved away, walking with a swaying side-ways gait as her eyes scanned the ground. Where she came from, no one knew. She had been a soldier for a long time and was lieutenant to the then-captain Morrisy when Remeg first joined the garrison. Morrisy was long gone and her successor Pel also, but Mestipen remained, although a lieutenant no longer by her own request.

Remeg watched her glide among the trees, humming lightly under her breath. Mestipen picked up a rock and turned it over in her hands, ran her tongue across it, held it to her ear, and let it drop. She bent to smell a mound of leaves, rooting her nose through the humus like a pig after truffles. She patted the earth and crooned. Finally, she pointed northwest, where needled boughs interlaced with the fading reds and golds of trees which had yet to drop their leaves.

Remeg frowned. "What's out there?"

Mestipen shrugged. Did she not know or just not care?

Remeg turned to Asabi, who had stood shadow quiet beside her while Mestipen worked. "Get them moving," she said. "North and west."

"With all due respect, Captain, there's a storm coming. We might follow them part of the way, but we'll lose them again in the dark and snow."

Mestipen, fading into the gloom beneath the trees like she was made of the stuff, cackled under her breath. "*I* won't."

It was all Remeg needed to hear.

Thirteen

Cadasbyr had never been a pretty town and the years since Rai's departure had brought nothing in the way of improvement. From a distance, it looked like any other small village turned to gingerbread by a coating of snow. Closer scrutiny revealed roof lines in disrepair amid the random cross-hatching of streets off which narrow alleyways disappeared into unfriendly shadows.

Rai swore under her breath and shifted in the saddle. Her ass hurt and her fingers and toes were cold. "Only for you would I do this, horseface."

"I'm fucking honored. Get moving, will you? I'm freezing."

It was useless to point out that they wouldn't even *be* here except for the Carraid's over-developed need to rescue every desperate individual that crossed her path. Rai swallowed the sour words like a purgative and started down the sloping trail, letting the horse pick its careful away as the snow continued to fall.

Cadasbyr had begun its existence as a group of peasant huts, a tiny settlement banded together for protection and mutual reliance. Those folks had been farmers, though what they had hoped to glean from such arid and rocky soil was anyone's guess. During the reign of the present queen's grandmother Gainestan the Black (so called for the color of her heart), a garrison had been established in the village. A canny woman by all accounts, Gainestan had a keen sense of her own vulnerability and a paranoid suspicion of rebellion from every quarter. Although the threat of uprising in such piss-poor environs seemed implausible to everyone but her, she meant to ensure that the rabble never even considered attempting a coup.

As happens, other folk bent upon business – merchants, hoteliers, and whores – followed the soldiers to Cadasbyr, enlarging the town. This expansion afforded Her Majesty a base from which to run deer for the amusement of her courtiers. They killed with no regard to the gender or age of the animals being culled, took the very best cuts of meat for themselves and left the rest to rot on the field, off limits to all but the most fool-hardy of peasants. Gainestan knew what she was doing. The starving have not the strength to rebel.

Rai was three or four years old the first time she saw the deer run. Sitting astride her father's shoulders with her bony knees bracketing his face and her fists bunched in his hair, she had watched the panicked flood of animals crest a distant hillside and roll down it like a wave. Desperate to escape, the deer wheeled and veered like a flock of birds desperate to escape, antlers back and heads bobbing, thin legs thrusting against the ground, throwing up dark clods of dirt. At their heels had come the hunters on horseback, decked in a torrent of rainbow-hued silk that snapped in the wind. Jeweled crops rose and fell against their horses' sweaty flanks, the tips fitted with broken glass to give the animals incentive.

Giddy with excitement, little Rai had bounced on her father's shoulders and crowed with delight.

"Hush, Rai-bird," Brendie said softly.

The sadness in his voice had stilled her tongue. "Da?"

He turned his back on the butchery and stepped into the shadows beneath the trees, headed for home. "Never take more than you need," he said. "Never take just to have."

The child had turned around for a final look at the bloody field …

… but it was the woman whose teary eyes were now dried by the wind.

Much of Cadasbyr was in ruins – boarded up, half-burned, or partly demolished. The air stank of old soot, despair, and poverty. Vacant doorways gaped like the yawning mouths of corpses. There were a few signs of habitation – a scrap of cloth fashioned into a crude covering over an entryway, a smudge of smoke from a broken chimney – and now and then a pale face pressed to the crack of a shutter as someone inside watched them ride past.

The old barracks area, gutted by fire and vandalism, echoed with the tramp of ghostly feet and the phantom voices of the women who had gone away or gone to dust. Little remained of the buildings but for two charred walls and a stump of blackened chimney. The rest had been reduced to skeletal timbers jumbled together like a child's abandoned game of pick-up-sticks. Something moved in the shadows, a hunched shape, bent and crippled-looking. Rai looked away, just in case she knew it.

"Why was the garrison disbanded?" Banya said.

Rai felt the pain of an old burn beneath her glove as she raised her hand to touch the fine arc of a scar by her left ear. "I don't remember. I left right around that time."

Muire had come home enraged by the news. Gainestan's daughter Plorell, in her dotage and, it was rumored, out of her head and soon to die, had ordered the suspension of the more distant garrisons. The soldiers were being dismissed, thanked for their service, given some pittance in appreciation, and told to leave. Muire had stormed from one end of the kitchen to the other, breaking crockery and scattering cups of thin gruel and watered-down milk. Auntie Windle, the Firstwife, had called her to order but Muire would not be constrained. Her fist had sent the old woman crashing into the wall and the rest of the family had scattered like rats, scrambling to get out of her way. Rai had tried to duck past, but Muire grabbed her by the collar and hurled her into the fireplace. The eight-year-old had hit her head on the stones and fallen with one hand in the coals. When she screamed in pain, Muire had snatched a stick of kindling from the basket and turned on her, but it was Brendie she struck when he tried to intervene; struck again and again until …

Rai's heart felt numb. She would never forgive Banya for this trip, not if she lived to be a thousand. Some memories were meant to stay dead.

An elderly couple, heads bent together in conversation, left off their talk to watch the strangers ride by. A covey of ill-clothed children darted out of an alleyway in front of the horses, startling them, and disappeared between two buildings, swinging their arms and trying to catch snowflakes on their tongues. Another memory threatened to tease a smile from Rai, but she stiffened her lips over it. Anything good about Cadasbyr had died with Brendie.

The town square, such as it was, consisted of a row of abandoned storefronts and a cluster of vacant stalls. Only three of the buildings appeared to be in steady use – a mercantile, a smithy with an attached livery, and a three-storied, sway-roofed inn. A sign over the door of the inn proclaimed it to be 'The Queen's Pleasure.'

Banya's eyes tracked with a wary pendulum motion as she dismounted. "I'll get the horses settled in that livery. You two take our things and I'll meet you inside."

Rai grunted assent and loaded down with rucksacks and bed rolls. As Banya led the horses away, Kinner shouldered his own bags and tried to tuck the sword box under his arm to hide it beneath the long length of his cloak. Rai grinned. "Too obvious," she said. "It stands out like gold on a cheap whore. You may as well carry it outright."

"What if someone asks about it?" he said as he followed her up the front steps.

"I'll come up with something." Rai knocked her snowy boots against the stoop and opened the door.

The inn's ground floor was a single large room with a hearth at one end and a bar for ordering food and drink at the other. An open doorway behind the bar led to the kitchen. Rough-hewn tables and benches were set in something approximating rows and a handful of stools stood before the fire. The ceiling and rafters were dark as peat with years of smoke and the floor was a morass of rotting straw. A funk of tallow, stale tobacco, burning wood, and grease eddied like silt in a pond. Rai took a deep breath and released it on a sigh. "Ah! Smells like home." Kinner looked sick.

As they entered, heads turned and conversation stopped dead. The locals sat gaping, caught in mid-sentence, their drinks and pipes half-way to their mouths and now forgotten. Rai stamped her feet and gave an exaggerated shiver. "Brrrr! Cold out there tonight!" In an instant, it was as if the entire room had blinked. Talk resumed and curiosity appeared to vanish. Rai snagged Kinner's sleeve between two fingers and tugged him along behind her.

"Welcome to 'The Queen's Pleasure,'" said the woman behind the bar. Her apron was filthy, her shirt stained and frayed. The knobs of her wrists and knuckles jutted prominently beneath the skin and her hair hung lank, spiked with grease. "I'm Peterin. I own the place. What's can I get you?" She spoke to Rai, but her eyes were on Kinner and the dark tattoo between his eyes.

He lowered his gaze as he had been taught and stepped closer to Rai, who dropped her packs on the floor. "We need supper for three and rooms for the night."

The innkeeper's wide smile exposed a jaw as gap-toothed as a jack-o-lantern's. "You're in the right place, then. We've ale at six dins, cider for three, and mutton stew for a ku-piece. There's one room vacant, with a single bed. That's a dobler-half."

The prices were extortionary, but Rai knew they had little choice but to pay. It was one thing for her or Banya to sit awake all night in a downstairs corner or find shelter in the barn or an abandoned building. It was something else to ask it of a delicate boy like Kinner. In a pinch, sure, but not unless they had to, not with the way that storm was building.

She made herself smile. "We'll take the room. I'd rather not sleep in the snow."

Peterin's merry face collapsed into a scowl. "Oh, bugger! Is it snowing again?" When Rai nodded, the innkeeper slapped her hand on the bar and bawled. "Keezie! Keezie, get out t'yard! It's snowin' again!"

A florid face appeared in the kitchen doorway, ratty red hair drawn up in a lop-sided top-knot. The girl's ginger eyebrows were singed to stubble and her face was a map of old burn scars and acne. Her right eye was blackened. "I a'nt shovelin' agin! 'S not fair! You send Waddy this time!"

"She's got customers." Peterin raised a fist. "Do as I say 'fore I gives you a second eye to match the first."

The girl glared murder and retreated. A moment later there was a loud clangor as an iron pot was hurled against a wall.

Peterin shook her head. "Bitch a'nt worth what it takes to feed her." She wiped the bar with a filthy rag. "You got horses? The liv'ry'll take 'em for the night. Sen-piece per animal. If you're wantin' hay, grain, or straw, that's extra."

"No, thanks," answered a voice before Rai could speak. Conversation stopped cold for the second time as Banya closed the inn door behind her and strolled toward the bar like a big tawny lioness. She nodded pleasantly at each person she passed and they stared back with unabashed fascination. Most of them had probably never seen a Carraid before. *It's like having a myth come to life right before your eyes,* Rai thought, amused by the effect her partner had on the locals. *This is better than that stupid Weathercock.*

When she reached the bar, Banya nudged Rai aside and leaned her elbows on the scarred wood. "We appreciate your offer," she told the innkeeper. "But the hostler gave us a better deal." She flexed her shoulders.

Peterin followed the tectonic shift of the Carraid's massive frame and reconsidered. "Good, good!" she said hurriedly. "Glad to hear it!" She leaned closer and dropped her voice. "You throw the boy int' the bargain and I'll knock off the price of the room."

"You don't want him," Banya said. "He's sterile."

Peterin snorted. "I got eyes, Carraidlander. I don't give a flyin' fuck if he's dry as the deserts of Jihal. He's able-bodied or looks to be and that's all I care about. I need a pair of hands around here what can actually do some work. Besides …" Her eyes gleamed with greed and her voice dropped to a whisper. "Some women will pay big to lay with a man, fertile or not. It's a lark, you know? Something different. I could get a lot of years out of one so young."

Kinner's eyes were enormous. He glanced nervously at Rai, who casually stepped nearer and closed a hand around his arm. "If he'd bring in that much money, d'you think we'd be idiots enough to give him up?"

The innkeeper laughed. "You don't neither of you strike me as the sort who need a whore to earn her livin.'" She appraised Kinner from top to bottom like a suckling pig at Yuletide. "Let me take him off your hands."

Banya sighed. "Tempting, friend, but no can do. We're being paid to deliver him to Dara. If he doesn't arrive, being compensated will be the least of our worries."

Peterin frowned. "Rich family, is it?"

"Not so much," Rai said, wanting to head off any thoughts of a kidnapping and ransom attempt. "But they have a lot of powerful friends."

"The sort you wouldn't want to meet in a dark alley, if you know what I mean," Banya added. "They'd level this place without thinking twice."

"All because of a sterile?" Peterin looked bemused and tapped her temple with a grimy finger. "Some women get awful queer in the head over their boys, don't they?" She nodded at the box in Kinner's arms. "That's a pretty piece of goods. What's in it?"

Silence. Kinner's eyes rolled toward Rai. She had said she would think of something if this came up, but her brain was empty. She glanced at Banya, always the one with the quick and ready tongue, but saw no help there. She looked back at the boy.

He held the box toward Peterin. "These are my mother's bones. They're going to be buried at Dara. Do you want to see?" He made as if to open the box. "She didn't die that long ago, so they may be a bit smelly …"

Peterin recoiled. "No, I don't want to see!" She waved her hands at them. "Your room's upstairs, down the hall, last on the right. I'll have someone bring up your meal."

Banya tucked a smile into the hollow of her cheek and reached for her purse. "We should settle up."

"Do it in the morning,'" Peterin said quickly and backed toward the kitchen, calling for food and drink to be brought to room six.

The room was what soldiers called 'bijou,' meaning there was barely room enough to piss. It contained a narrow bedstead with a lumpy straw mattress, a chipped and blessedly empty thunder jug, a small battered table, two wobbly chairs, and a cheap tallow lamp. Weak warmth came from an anemic fire. An uncurtained, four-paned window of rippled glass looked out onto darkness and let in a thread of cold air around its cracked frame.

"What a dump," Rai said. She unbuckled her sword belt and hung the weapon over one of the bed posts.

"You don't like it, go sleep in the snow," Banya replied and closed the door.

Kinner put his things down and held his arms straight out from his body. His fingers brushed the opposite walls. "This is smaller than my room back home."

"And over-priced to boot," Rai said. "Well, I'm damned if we'll pay for firewood, too." She yanked apart one of the chairs with ease and tossed a piece onto the fire.

Kinner stared in astonishment. "Can you *do* that?"

She shrugged. "Just did."

A knock on the door heralded the arrival of their food. At Banya's call, the door opened and a young girl with bucked teeth and a wall-eye sidled in. She practically threw the tray onto the table and fled, feet pounding on the stairs.

Banya closed the door and threw the bolt. She picked up a mug of ale, took a long draught, and smacked her lips. "The bed's yours for the night, Kinner. Consider it a reward for that lovely bit you pulled downstairs." She chuckled. "'Mother's bones.' That's one for the story books. They won't sleep tonight for fear of ghosts."

"Thank you." He smiled with pleasure and glanced at Rai.

She fed another piece of wood into the fire and pretended not to see. It didn't bother her so much that he had lied – although men weren't supposed to and Brendie never had. What she found annoying was that he'd been quicker off the mark than either she or Banya; that a *man* had saved their skins. That just wasn't right.

She sat against the hearth stones with her dinner and poked at the supposed stew. Watery broth, soggy whitish lumps that might be turnip or potato, and grey mystery meat that could just as likely be dog as sheep. She swallowed a spoonful and made a face. "This tastes like garbage." She washed it down with ale.

Kinner sat nearby and poked with dubious interest at the clot of food in his bowl. "I've made mutton stew, but it never looked like this. Does it really taste like garbage?"

Rai laughed. "Does it matter? It's what's on the menu tonight. As long as it doesn't give you worms or the collywobbles, consider yourself ahead."

Banya grinned. "My buddy, the philosopher."

Rai spat what looked like a human knuckle-bone into her hand and tossed it into the fire. "You know I'm right," she said.

"I'll die before I ever admit that." The Carraid pointed her spoon at Kinner. "Eat up. Soon as we're done, you and I are going shopping if we can find someplace open in this shit-hole of a town."

"What about me?" Rai said.

"You're going to stay here where it's cozy and warm and keep an eye on our things."

Rai's eyes narrowed in suspicion. "Why me?"

Banya patted her pocket and smiled with enormous satisfaction. "Because I have the money." She drained her mug. "Kinner can't stay alone in case that larcenous innkeeper decides to push her luck. Besides, he needs to try on clothes. I already know what size you wear. Extra puny." She grinned. "Is widdle Wai afwaid to stay all awone in the big scary inn?"

"Go screw yourself."

"Are you two really friends?" Kinner asked, wide-eyed. "I've heard my aunts call each other names, but Mum never tolerated much rough language and I just wondered and … and …" He floundered.

Banya slung an arm around Rai's shoulders and crushed her against her side. "Kinner, I can say with complete honesty that I love this woman like the sister I ate in the womb."

His eyes bugged with horror.

She looked chagrined. "Sorry. Just a little soldier joke." She scooped up the last of her stew. "If you're finished, let's go."

"Get some more blankets," Rai said. "We're heading into worse weather the longer this trip takes. The last thing I want is to have to curl up with your manky carcass in order to stay warm."

"This manky carcass has kept you alive more than once." Banya paused with her hand on the latch. "Keep this bolted and don't go downstairs."

"I have done this before, you know." Rai followed them out onto the landing. "Watch your back."

"I will. You be careful."

Rai grinned. "I'll see you after." The exchange was their old battle mantra. It seemed ludicrous to recite it in a broke-back town like Cadasbyr, but if they had learned anything in their shared life of soldiery, it was not to be complacent. Too many companions had been lost along that road.

She leaned on the balustrade and watched them go downstairs. The inn's main room was nearly empty, most of the locals having gone to their beds. A group of three sat in a corner, occupied in a repetitive game of dice and cards. A pair of drunkards lounged by the fire, heads tipped forward as they snored. No one so much as glanced at the strangers.

Kinner paused at the door to look back and lifted a hand in farewell. She aped the gesture before she could stop herself and then the soldier and the sterile boy were gone.

Not sterile, Rai reminded herself as she closed and barred the door. *And doesn't that open a can of worms?* How could Holan have perpetrated such a betrayal on a rare and coveted child? Then again, she knew from experience that mothers were capable of doing just about anything in pursuit of their own desires.

She tossed the last bit of chair onto the fire and looked around. What to do while they were away? The room had nothing to recommend it, no decorations on the wall, and she was not about to lie on the bed. She knew a pestiferous mattress when she saw one. Rai had shared sleeping space with rampant vermin before, but that had been out of necessity. Choice was another matter.

Her gaze settled on the sword box. She had seen the weapon once, a fleeting glimpse as it clattered across wet cobblestones in a swatch of garnet silk. If she was expected to endure hardship in order to cart it and the boy halfway across the world, she deserved a closer look.

Tugging the box from beneath the other packs, she placed it on the table and lit the tallow lamp. She ran her hands across the polished wood and felt the scuffs and dents, the broken catch. She flipped open the workable latch and raised the lid. Her hand stopped, poised above the silk, and then folded it back to expose the sword.

Rai drew a slow, deep breath of admiration. Never had she seen a weapon of such craftsmanship. The rampant cock was exquisite in detail; each miniature feather in the cage of its protective wings picked out in relief. The bird brandished its spurs and held its wings aloft. Its head was drawn back, poised to strike, and its beak gaped in a crow of … what? Rage? Sorrow? Victory? She had witnessed cock fights; had even bet on a few. She knew how the birds looked when engaged in battle and had seen the damage they could inflict with beak and claw. Holan had captured it all perfectly, rendering this weapon into a deadly work of art.

Rai traced the cool length of the blade with her fingertips. At the faint edge of hearing came the ghostly cry of a fighting cockerel. She snatched her hand away and shivered. "Asshole," she muttered. She slammed the lid closed and chucked the box on top of the packs.

This was stupid. She was never this jumpy. It was all that damned Kinner's fault, him and his talk of mother's bones and ghosts. This town was bursting with specters. You couldn't turn a corner without running into one. And as for her mother's bones … If Rai knew where those were, she'd go piss on them.

She drained her mug, slammed it down, and was reaching for Kinner's when the window behind her burst open. Rai whipped around, ducking the spray of glass as a lean body slithered through the opening like an eel and landed on its feet. Behind it, there was movement on the outside window ledge.

Rai slapped a hand to her hip to draw the blade that wasn't there. Swearing, she threw herself at the bed, hands outstretched to grasp her sword, and they were on her before she got there. She caught a brief glimpse of dark eyes above a scarf and then something slammed into the back of her head.

Malcontent oozed from Remeg like the slow discharge of an infected wound.

The troop had followed Mestipen all night, often with excruciating slowness as the tracker paused to study the trail and then moved on in her stalking, crow-like stride. A lantern swung from her hand and its light flung her shadow behind her like a spray of black blood. She reminded Remeg of the

Ungein, a hunchbacked water-troll purported to live in the east, on Bitanig's Isle, a creature used by mothers to frighten their children into behaving.

Mestipen searched not only the ground, but the sky as well. She read the whirl of wind and snow and fingered the hulking shadows of tree and rock. She clambered high among branches and ghosted low into undergrowth that could not have concealed a weasel. She bent her ear to the wind's whisper and scented like a hound. The long swing of her cloak blurred the line between boot and ground until she seemed to float rather than to walk, moving like a slash of bad dream against the shifting curtain of snow. As the night progressed and the storm worsened, Mestipen appeared less human and more a creature of spirit. The transformation gave even the phlegmatic Remeg a skin-crawling sense of apprehension.

In daylight, the raucous barking of scavenger birds would have led them straight to Holan's resting place. Mestipen found it without the birds' help, her attention caught by something in the darkness which Remeg could neither see nor sense. Without a word, the tracker strode to an old maple and scaled the trunk with the ease of a fisher cat. There was a moment of silence, punctuated by the stamp and snort of the horses, and then a body thumped to the ground.

The horses shied and danced. Soldiers flinched and cried out, tightening their reins and settling their feet more firmly into the stirrups. Mestipen's disembodied voice drifted down from above. "Dead 'un, Captain."

Remeg's heart thudded as she dismounted. Praying against Fate, she knelt and flipped back a swatch of blanket to expose the face. Holan's eyes were open, her thin lips mottled blue and grey, pulled away from her teeth. Her bloodless skin held a waxy suggestion of color beneath the surface, like the blues and yellows hidden inside a cold block of marble.

Not the boy, then. Remeg sighed with relief and sent a silent prayer of thanks to the Goddess. She had hoped for an opportunity to question Holan at length, but what mattered most was the boy. He was the means to Remeg's end. When she presented him to Kedar, all would be well once more.

She made a quick search of the shroud, but found nothing of value. Jerking the blanket back across the dead woman's face, she stood and dusted her gloves together.

"You want her back in the tree, Captain?" said Asabi.

"No. Traitors to the crown should lie where they fall."

Mestipen swung down from the maple's branches. She glanced with disinterest at the body and walked away staring at the sky, the ground, the whirling snow. After a moment, the troop followed.

Now, hours later, they waited once more as Mestipen sought the elusive trail. Day was just a word heralded by a faint change in the light, the sun lost behind thick clouds and the rush of snow. The soldiers took this opportunity to tend to their horses, offering a handful or two of grain or a wizened apple, stooping to dig hardened lumps of snow out of their hooves or pat a weary neck.

"These animals need some rest, Captain." Asabi rubbed her mount's nose and palmed a piece of carrot into its mouth. She hunched her back to a gust of wind, her face turned against the horse's neck to shield it from the worst of the blowing snow.

Remeg nodded. "I know, but Mestipen says we're gaining on them. We can't afford to lose that advantage."

The lieutenant grunted. "Can't afford a troop of lame horses, either."

"Captain Remeg!"

She turned at the call, slitting her eyes against the drive of icy flakes. Tynar waded toward them through the snow. When she reached them, she saluted and held out her hand. "I found this snagged on a bush." It was a white silk scarf, torn and muddied but still recognizable.

Remeg's heart gave a thump. Kedar had given the scarf to her as a token of love, the same love which she now felt perilously close to losing. Had the queen already cast her eyes among her favorites for a new paramour? Did Chella Quarm warm the royal bed or was it some other parasite? The thought raked talons across Remeg's heart at the very instant she realized she was being watched.

Schooling her expression to blandness, she turned to idly scan the hunt and found herself looking straight into Mestipen's eyes. The woman was crouched inside a small root cave formed beneath an enormous pine when flooding had washed away a portion of the soil. Her eyes shone in the gloom, a rabid animal brought to bay. When she saw Remeg looking at her, she cocked her head and grinned like a fox, wide and impudent.

Remeg had a sudden, awful suspicion that Mestipen could read her mind. She looked away and focused again on the scarf.

Tynar held it to her nose and sniffed. "This ain't cheap goods, Captain. Looks like Rai or Banya had a rich lay somewhere."

Remeg ached to take possession of the scarf. Her desire for it bordered on the physical. That silken bit of Kedar was all that remained to her of the queen right now, but she folded her arms to keep from reaching for it and turned to look at Asabi. "This storm will slow them down. They'll have to hole up somewhere. They can't risk the boy in this sort of weather, so where will they go for shelter? What's out here?"

"There's bound to be caves," Asabi said. "But they'd be damned hard to find unless you knew where to look. That Banya, though, I think she could make a shelter out of two sticks and a diaper."

A spectral voice came out of the air. "Cadasbyr."

A cold trickle that had nothing to do with the snow ran up Remeg's spine. She turned around to look at the tracker. "What did you say?"

Mestipen's hands curled around the exposed roots, giving her the look of an evil sprite in a cage. "Cadasbyr's out here," she said. "Where Rai's from."

Remeg heard a voice in her mind. "*I received word tonight from back home in Cadasbyr …*" Her pulse quickened.

Tynar shrugged. "Yeah, she's from there, but so what? Everybody knows she hates it. She never shuts up about it. There's no way she'd go back there."

Mestipen ignored her. She watched Remeg with a disconcerting knowledge in her strange eyes and lifted one bony shoulder in a shrug. It was enough (and perhaps too much) for Remeg. When she nodded, the woman slipped from her den and set out once more.

Asabi sighed and her tired voice rang out. "Mount up!"

Tynar crammed the scarf into her fist and moved away.

Remeg dusted snow from the saddle and swung aboard. She backed the horse a step or two. "Tynar?"

The woman turned with a guilty eye. "Captain?"

Remeg focused on the soldier's face rather than on the bit of cherished history she held. "Throw that damned thing away."

Fourteen

Banya and Kinner hurried along the frozen ruts of Cadasbyr's streets loaded with parcels. Stock at the mercantile had proved to be, in the Carraid's opinion, "worse than balls on a cow" (an evocative phrase Kinner had tucked away for future use), but they found everything they needed in a side street second-hand emporium. The owner, an old woman shaped like a lumpy biscuit, was in the middle of closing up shop when they arrived. A bit of Carraid charm plus the promise of cash for fair prices had induced her to stay open long enough for them to browse the racks and bins of castoff clothing. In addition to purchases for Rai, each had found a second pair of boots and some extra clothing. Kinner's wool cloak, serviceable but hardly sufficient for winter weather, had been augmented by a quilted coat that hung to his knees.

"I bet that belonged to some merc," Banya said as they walked, heads bent against the wind. "Mercenary," she elaborated when he looked confused. "A professional soldier hired for service."

"Really?" He glanced down, liking the way the heavy garment swung against his thighs. "How can you tell?"

"There's a slit on each side that gives easy access to a weapon. That's a modification she probably made herself. Plus there's this." She pointed to a zigzag of miscolored stitchery closing a tear that ran from beneath the armpit of the coat almost to the waist. "That's where a blade got through her defense, poor sod. Plus this faded red stain here? That's not the color of the material."

Kinner's heart took a sick little twist. "You mean she died wearing this?"

"I'd lay odds. Good thing, too, or you'd have a cold trip ahead of you."

Kinner considered this bit of news as he watched the snow-covered toes of his boots appear and vanish beneath the swinging hem. "I'm sorry she died, but I like the coat." He smiled at Banya. "It makes me feel brave, like a soldier."

The Carraid chuckled. "Whatever it takes."

He shifted the bundles in his arms. "Do we have everything we need?"

"Most of it. I'll buy extra oats for the horses before we leave in the morning. We can miss a couple meals if need be, but the horses have to eat if they're to carry us. We lose them and we'll be in a world of hurt." She stepped around a patch of ice. "Do you mind that we sold your mother's horse to the knacker?"

Kinner felt a catch in his throat. "A little," he admitted. "It's another piece of Mum that's gone forever." He blinked rapidly, determined not to cry. "She would have told us to sell it, though. We don't need four horses and the mare was old. She probably wouldn't have survived the journey anyway."

Banya clapped him on the shoulder. "That's a mature outlook, lad. Good for you."

Kinner smiled, warmed by her praise.

The town square was empty, the few tracks reduced to vague outlines by the snow. The townsfolk had retreated to their rickety homes and all were closed up tight against the storm. No street lamps burned, but the occasional flare of a fitful lantern or candle shone though the chink in a wall or shutter. Wood smoke flavored the air.

They helped each other brush the worst of the snow from their heads and shoulders before entering the inn. The main room was vacant and dark but for the glow of embers from the raked fire. A loud snoring came from the direction of the kitchen.

"Is everyone in bed already?" Kinner whispered.

"Seems early to you, does it?" Banya chuckled. "There are only so many games of cards or dice you can play before insanity sets in. On a night like this, it's best to seek a warm bed and sleep through the worst of things if you can. They'll need to be up early to dig out and tend to what stock they have."

Kinner reached into one of his parcels as he followed the Carraid up the stairs. A pair of grey socks patched at toe and heel with black wool dangled from his hand. He had picked them out special. "Do you think Rai will like –"

Banya's out-flung arm caught him across the chest. She glanced at him, her eyes ordering silence, and gestured with her head. The door of their room stood ajar. Stooping, she eased her packages to the floor as quietly as possible and drew her blade from its oiled scabbard with almost no sound. Mouthing the words, "Stay here," she inched along the hallway. Using the tip of the weapon to push the door open, she stood on the dark threshold looking in. "Mother of whores!" she suddenly exclaimed and stepped inside. Kinner hurried after her.

The fire had died to weak embers veiled in ash. Cold air blew in through the broken casement, adding snow to the small drift collecting on the floor beneath it. Shattered glass made a pattern of icy shards around Rai, who lay sprawled on her back beside the overturned table and broken chair. The bedstead was demolished and the mattress lay in a crumpled heap.

Kinner stopped in the doorway. "Is she dead?" he asked in a tiny voice.

Banya sank to one knee beside the prone body of her friend and laid a large hand on her shoulder. "Little girl?"

Rai sat up so fast that Kinner squeaked in surprise. She flung herself across the room, snatched up the fireplace poker, and spun around to put her back against the cold hearth stones. "Get back!" She hefted the long iron rod in both hands and brandished it like a sword. "Get back or I'll kill you!"

Banya snatched the weapon out of her hand. "It's me, you moron. Wake up."

Rai blinked and put a hand to the back of her head. She looked around the room, saw Kinner frozen in the doorway, and sagged to her knees. "Oh, fuck *me*."

"Someone certainly has." Banya motioned to Kinner. "Bring our things in and close the door. And get some wood on that fire. I can't see to fart in here."

He did as he was told, using bits of the chair and bed frame to tease the fire back to life without smothering it. When it was burning well, he righted the table and found the tiny lantern lying on its side in a corner. The base was dented, but the lamp was otherwise intact and only a small amount of fuel had spilled. He trimmed the wick, lit it, and placed the lamp on the table.

"Thank you," Banya said. She knelt beside Rai and put a hand under her chin. "Okay. Let's have a look at the damages." She parted the hair at Rai's temple and whistled in appreciation. "*Nice* goose egg."

"You like it?" Rai touched the back of her head and winced. "I've got another one back here."

"A matched set. Lucky you." Banya rose, pressing a hand against Rai's shoulder as she moved to stand up as well. "Stay put. It's a shorter fall if you go dizzy and take a header."

Kinner watched them, feeling useless. If they were home in Moselle, he'd have known what to do. There was an entire pantry shelf of dried medicinal plants waiting to be made into balms and unguents, tinctures and teas. Comfrey, mountain daisy, and red clover were all good for bruising and contusions, little good that knowledge did him here.

He sat down cross-legged and fed more wood onto the fire. "What happened, Rai?"

She leaned her head back against the hearth stones and sighed. "They came in through the window. Caught me with my back turned. Bowled me right over."

"Probably part of the group that was downstairs playing cards tonight," Banya said. "They saw Kinner and me leave, waited to make sure we were gone, and then came for you, the fly-specked whore-get. How many were there?"

Rai made a tiny motion with her head. "I don't know. Two for sure –

they're the ones that hit me first – but there might have been more. I was all tangled up in broken wood and glass and there's no friggin' space to maneuver in here!" She snatched a piece of wood out of Kinner's hand and flung it at the far wall. It missed his head by a narrow margin and landed on the curl of mattress that lay on the floor like a dead thing.

Though it was useless as a bed, the thin padding might serve to block the worst of the wind and snow coming in through the broken window. Happy to find a way to be of use, Kinner went and picked up the straw ticking. As he fit it against the window frame, something he should have noticed earlier hit him. Dropping the mattress, he looked around the tiny room with frantic eyes. "Where's the sword?"

"Don't shit your drawers," Rai said in a weary tone. "It's gone. *Everything's* gone. Our packs, my blade, and your thrice-be-damned sword." She lurched to her feet, staggered across the room, and wrenched open the door. "Innkeeper!" She thundered down the stairs and swept a chair out of her path. "I'll burn this roach nest to the ground if you don't show your butt-ugly face in two ..." She spun around fast and nearly collided with Banya and Kinner. "Please tell me you checked on the horses when you got back."

The color drained from Banya's face and she bolted for the door.

Cold wind tore the breath from their lungs as it whipped them the short distance across the inn yard to the livery. Inside, two plow cobs swished their tails with languid interest and a one-horned brindle cow eyed them with myopic surprise. At the far end of the ramshackle building a flock of black-faced sheep stared with bland indifference, jaws working sideways as they chewed. The other stalls were empty.

Banya picked up the nearest thing to hand – an old wooden stirrup – and hurled it against the wall. Kinner cringed at the noise and the animals shied, milling about in their enclosures. "I raised that mare from birth! I'm bonded to her, mare's milk to rider's flesh, and I won't lose her like this." She slammed the barn door open with both hands and strode into the storm. The wind wove cyclones of snow about her, snapping her braids around her head. She faced into the maelstrom looking like a goddess from ages past, something so ancient and primitive that it had no name. Putting two fingers to her mouth, she let fly a piercing whistle.

"Don't, Banya," Rai said unhappily. "They're gone."

"In this storm?" Banya's eyes searched the impenetrable roil of flakes. "There are enough hidey-holes in this rotten cheese of a town to hide an entire troop. They must be holed up right here, waiting until the worst of this is over." She shook her head. "I'll give them worst. I'll give them something they never counted on if so much as a hair of that horse is out of place." She whistled again, this one a long blast followed by a tuneful warble. "If she's anywhere close, if she can hear that, she'll bust down doors to get to me."

The wind moaned a hollow, baleful note around the chimney stacks. Kinner shivered, glad again for his new coat, and glanced at Rai who was dusted in snow like a gingerbread soldier covered in sugar.

"This is hopeless," she muttered. "There's no way we're going to find that mare in this storm. Banya," she said a bit louder. "Let's get inside, get warm, make a plan …"

Faint on the wind, a horse whinnied.

Banya yipped. "Hah! You see? I told you she'd come." She whistled again; a sharp, three-note pipping. Now they could hear the clop of hooves, muffled by the snow but definitely growing closer. A vague shadow appeared at the end of the street.

"There she is!" Kinner cried with joy.

A horse materialized out of the storm, but it was not the grey Carraid mare. Nor was it the feisty black or Kinner's mouse-brown steed. This was a buckskin carrying a rider cloaked in leather and wool, snow and wind. A sword hung at her hip and she led a band of warriors.

Remeg drew rein and the troop stopped. For an endless moment, hunters and quarry stared as if not quite able to countenance the other's sudden appearance. Kinner felt the heat of Remeg's eyes upon him and his heart surged in his chest. His eyes darted first to Rai, then to Banya, waiting for them to show him what to do.

With a wordless cry, the troop surged ahead.

"Go!" Banya yelled, and dove down an alley.

Rai snatched Kinner's sleeve and ran in the opposite direction, driving him ahead of her like a dog with sheep. Hooves pounded behind them, drawing abreast. Kinner risked a glance and cried out in fear as Remeg, lips skinned back from her teeth, leaned down from the saddle and grabbed at his collar. Her hand brushed the cloth and he felt the cold caress of one gloved finger against his neck … then Rai stiff-armed him between the shoulders and sent him tumbling. Remeg shot past with an oath and wrenched her horse around for a second pass.

Rai dragged him to his feet and shoved him into a crooked walkway between two buildings, the space too narrow to admit a horse. They raced along it, sometimes having to turn sideways to clear a corner. The cold air burned Kinner's lungs. "If we get to the edge of town," he panted. "Can we hide in one of those burned out buildings?"

"Don't talk," Rai huffed. At a wider spot, she ducked past him to lead the way. They came out on a cross street and she hung back in the shadows, a finger to her lips. Kinner listened, but the snow muffled every sound, making them difficult to place within the labyrinth of streets and alleyways.

A rider galloped past. They cringed back into the shadows and dashed across the street in her wake, unseen and unsuspected. Halfway along another alley, Rai dove into the narrow embrasure of a dark doorway and yanked Kinner in beside her. "Duck your head and put your back to the light," she hissed. They hid their faces against a battered wooden door and tried to quiet their breathing. Hooves at a walk echoed at the near end of the alley, paused as someone peered down the stygian brick throat, and moved on.

Rai released a careful breath. "You all right?"

Kinner nodded, unable to speak for fear his racing heart would burst. His legs trembled and he clutched the doorsill for support. "What's Captain Remeg doing here?" he finally managed to ask.

"She's after us. Me and Banya."

"Why? What did you do?"

"Oh, nothing. Just deserted our post, for starters. That's a hanging offense, in case you didn't know. I hope you appreciate it." She looked along the alley. "We have to find Banya and get our asses out of here."

"How far can we get without horses?"

Rai glared at him. "Men aren't supposed to ask questions like that. Now shut up and let me think."

Stung, he waited in silent obedience for her next orders. After several minutes, when no solution was forthcoming, he gingerly offered, "*I* have an idea."

"Spare me." Rai looked wary. "No offense, but I don't have a lot of faith in the ideas of men."

"Well, no offense, but you're not doing so great yourself right now. Besides, how many men have you ever listened to?" Kinner drew a sharp breath, astonished at his nerve, waiting for the slap that would surely follow such a smart-aleck retort. What had gotten into him? He would never have spoken like that back home.

To his amazement, the blow never came. Rai snorted, sounding almost amused, and said, "Banya's a bad influence. You're turning into a wise-acre just like her." She shivered, turning her back on the finger of wind that sliced through the alley. "Okay, I'll bite. What's your plan?"

"We're almost directly behind the livery."

"Are we?" Rai looked around, clearly impressed despite herself. "How the hell did you manage to keep track of our position?"

Kinner felt a tiny surge of pride. "I guess I have a good sense of direction."

"You're not going to suggest we take those saggy plow cobs, are you?"

When he nodded, she lifted her hands beseechingly to the sky and let them fall. "That's a man for you! Those old wrecks can't outrun a garrison mount, Kinner. Take my word for it."

"They don't have to outrun them. All they have to do is make us look like soldiers from a distance. With all this snow, if we keep back from the rest of the troop, couldn't we pass for soldiers on horseback?"

Rai looked stupefied. She started three times to speak, stopped, and put a hand over her mouth as she thought the idea through. "Okay," she finally said. "I just hope we don't scare Banya off in the process." She gave him a nudge. "Lead the way."

They reached the livery without mishap. The horses seemed vaguely surprised at being accosted in the middle of the night, but they stood patiently while leather bridles stiff with age were fitted over their heads.

"There aren't any saddles," Kinner whispered.

"Then you'd better tuck those family jewels aside or that tattoo won't be a lie." Rai laced her fingers together and boosted him onto a broad back. The animal turned its head and lipped the toe of his boot in a friendly manner. Kinner smiled and leaned forward to pat the horse's neck.

Leading the other animal, Rai pushed open the barn door and took a quick look outside. "No one. Let's do this." Using the edge of the cow pen as a mounting ramp, she settled atop the horse and clucked it into slow motion. The animals stepped into the storm, big heads dropping against the wind as their enormous hooves cast up a drift of snow.

As they turned onto the main street, a horse appeared two buildings away. The rider hailed them, her words shredded by the wind. "See anything?"

Rai tucked her chin and hunched her shoulders. "Nothing," she called back in a deep voice. The soldier waved acknowledgement and rode off. Rai looked at Kinner in surprise. "If this works, kid, I swear I'll never say another bad word about the Weathercock."

"You're on." With the encouragement of drumming heels, they bullied the draft horses into a bone-jarring trot.

Two riders emerged from a side street and started toward them. Kinner, startled by their sudden appearance, sat back and pulled the reins without meaning to. The cob obediently stopped. Panicked, Kinner kicked the horse hard. It looked back at him as if to say, "Make up your mind, why don't you?" and stubbornly refused to move.

Kinner moaned, one eye on the approaching riders. "No, no, no." His heels drummed against the horse's ribs. "Come on, dammit ..."

Rai sat up straight and pointed down the street, behind the riders. "There they go! They're headed for the river!" Swearing, the guards wrenched their horses around and galloped back the way they had come.

"Good thinking," Kinner said. He gave her a shaky thumbs-up.

"Tell that to my drawers." Rai cracked his horse across the ass with the ends of her reins. It jumped and hustled into an awkward trot. Skirting the main avenue, they made for the charcoaled ruins of freedom.

Halfway there, a familiar voice stopped them cold.

"Rai!" Remeg's voice rang out, calling from the center of town. "We've captured Banya!"

Kinner's chest filled with ice.

"She's lying," Rai said with quick assurance. "She's trying to draw us out."

Remeg's voice continued, echoing oddly in the shifting wind. "Surrender and I might be inclined to leniency in the matter of your desertion. Bring me the boy and I most certainly shall be."

Rai looked at Kinner with new eyes. "What the hell? You holding something back on us? What does Remeg want with you?"

He shook his head. "I've no idea."

"Is there any way she could know that you're fertile?"

He shook his head. "That's impossible."

Remeg's voice came again. "His mother's death voids any agreement you had with her, you know. Why don't you turn the boy over to me and let me take care of him, the poor motherless child?"

Kinner whimpered, then yelped sharply as Rai pinched him hard on the leg. "Don't listen to her!"

"Still unwilling to return to the fold?" Remeg called. "Cowardice is hardly surprising coming from you, but I thought you'd have at least a bit of loyalty where Banya is concerned." There was a moment of tense silence, followed by a sharp grunt and a thin cry of pain.

The sound went straight through Kinner. He yanked the reins and pummeled the horse with his heels. The nag sighed, shifted its hips from side to side, and refused to move. "Rai, do something!"

Her face was a mask, cold as porcelain. "No."

He rounded on her, angrier than he had ever been in his life; more furious than he had ever been allowed to be. "What sort of friend are you?"

Rai's eyes filled with a sick dread. "I'm the sort who knows that if you're both dead, no one gets saved." She grabbed the front of his coat and pulled him close, almost clean off his horse. "If you mean to survive in this world without your Household, boy, you'd best lose your romantic ideals. This isn't a story book. People don't risk their lives for each other and there's hardly ever a last minute rescue or a happy ending. Banya wouldn't want us to sacrifice ourselves for her sake. She'd want us to stay free, to finish what we set out to do."

"Hang that," Kinner said with bitterness. He slapped her hand away. "Mum's sword is gone. What business do we have with the Weathercock now? As for me, well, hang me, too. I won't leave without trying to save –" A broken wail shuddered the air, slicing through his words.

Rai's face went paper white. She hauled her mount's head around by force and pointed a finger at Kinner. "You stay here. There's no point in all of us being caught. As soon as Remeg's distracted, you get out of town and head –" she pointed, " – due east, toward Carraidland. If you can get past their border, you should be all right. If anyone will take you in, it's the Carraid." Her eyes were sad. "I'm sorry I can't be more help."

"What are you going to do?"

"I'll come up with something." She raked her heels along the nag's ribs. The horse bucked, probably the first such maneuver since it was foaled, whinnied sharply, and set off at a lumbering canter.

Kinner watched as the storm closed around her. When she was gone, he picked up his reins and turned to face the east.

The wind tore at Rai, turning her hair into a rat's nest as she rode toward Remeg and the waiting troop. She had lied to Kinner. She had no idea what to do to save Banya. She had no weapon, no allies, no means of taking down Remeg or her soldiers. She'd never felt so empty of inspiration in her life.

In the market square, Banya stood trussed between two mounted riders, her arms held away from her body by the pull of taut ropes. Her eyes were half-lidded with pain and her breath came quick and shallow. She was naked from the waist up, her shirt and bandeau lying crumpled in the snow. Rivulets of icy melt tracked her bare flesh and mingled with the run of blood where a strip of skin had been delicately peeled beneath her right arm, along the outer curve of her breast, and down to her waist. Blood stained the trampled snow. Mestipen, standing beside her, paused to survey her handiwork. She juggled a dagger between her fingers like a Tzigane magician walking a coin across her knuckles.

Rai's stomach did a sick flip. She knew what horrors women were capable of in battle, but this was different. She knew these women, some of them well. Alyne, holding Banya's right arm, loved roses. Wyn, on the left, had a feeble-minded younger sister to whom she was devoted. Von smoked too much. They were her friends, or so she had thought, and Banya's friends as well; Banya, who until this moment hadn't an enemy in the world. It was unthinkable that these women would sanction such treatment of one of their own. It mattered little that some of them looked sickened. They weren't doing anything to stop it and that made them as guilty as if they held the knife in their own hands.

It also proved that they would follow Remeg's orders no matter what she asked of them.

"Hello, Rai," one of the riders called as she appeared. The woman thumbed back her hood to reveal Tynar's ratty face creased in an ugly smile. "Decided to join the party after all, did you?"

Remeg's quiet voice was like a lash. "Speak out of turn again, Tynar, and I'll give you to Mestipen as a pet." The northerner subsided as Remeg stepped out of the crowd to face Rai. "I'm glad you saw reason. That boy's of no use to you."

Rai's head snapped around. Several paces behind her, Kinner sat astride his horse. "I told you to leave!"

Remeg chuckled. "You could hardly expect him to follow such orders. He must be scared half to death, poor little soul." She motioned with one hand. "Take her." Two of the guards stepped up and unceremoniously dragged Rai off her horse.

Banya's eyes opened with effort. "Oh, Rai," she murmured. "Why would you do something so foolish?"

Remeg walked slowly toward Kinner and stopped by his knee. "Time to get down, boy," she said in a soft and gentle voice.

His eyes were enormous in his pale and frightened face, but his mouth settled into a stubborn line and when he spoke, his voice trembled only a little. "No," he said. "I'm not yours to order, Captain Remeg."

Her hand snatched his wrist like the strike of a snake and she dragged him to the ground. "I think you *are* mine, little man," she said, twisting his wrist until he gasped. "At least until you remember your manners."

"Leave the kid be, Captain," Rai said. "What's a little sterile to you, anyway?"

"Nothing," Remeg said. "But there are others with quite an interest in our young gentleman here." She pushed Kinner's hood back from his face and ran her thumb across the tattooed mark on his brow. She stroked the side of his face and cupped his chin, turning his head from side to side. "Now that I take the time to look at you closely, you're quite pretty, aren't you, boy?" She leaned down until they were nearly nose to nose. "The queen will be so pleased to make your acquaintance." She smiled at the growing look of horror on his face. "I know your little secret," she whispered.

Kinner stared at her, a fly caught by the spider. It was Rai who responded, speaking hurriedly, her words tumbling as her thoughts ran wild. "We've no secrets from you, Captain."

"Indeed?" Remeg released the boy's chin. "Can it be that your friends here didn't trust you enough to share their secret? How sad. Well, they'll share it with me. During the ride back to Caerau, we're going to have a long conversation about the Weathercock and a certain sword."

"The sword's gone, Captain," Rai said. Her brain spun in confusion. If the weapon and its connection to the Weatherock was Remeg's main interest, that meant she didn't know about Kinner's fertility. "It was stolen this very night."

"Oh, Rai. You must think I'm the most gullible person on the face of –"

Mestipen let out a sudden cry and dropped her knife. One hand clutched the other where an arrow pierced her wrist. The other soldiers brandished their swords, horses dancing beneath them at the hiss of drawn steel, and stared blankly into the storm.

Carried on the wind came a voice accented with the broad vowels of the north. "We'll be havin' no more o' *that* game. Back awa' from the prisoners, if ye please."

Remeg's breath came tight through her nose. Her hand tightened around Kinner's wrist until he cried out. "These women and this boy are traitors to the crown."

"I dinna gie a fig for the crown," replied the voice. "Gie 'em o'er t' us now or we'll be after takin' them. An' just in case you're thinkin' there's no' enough o' us t' do the job …" Bow strings whined like a swarm of summer insects and arrows pierced the ground by Remeg's foot. The horses stamped in agitation. "Believe me when I say we dinna miss by mistake. Now back awa'."

Remeg's hot gaze threatened to burn a hole through the storm. "I can kill them now, right where they stand. What then?"

"Yer welcome t' try if you ken yer fast enou' t' beat our arrows, but know that you'll die as well. You hae until a count o' five. One …"

Rai held her breath. Her eyes darted, hunting in the storm for a sign, just one small sign, of their rescuers. The snow spun in airy circles, hiding motion, blinding her.

"Two …"

"Orders, Captain?" Asabi said quietly.

"Three … four …"

"Release them." Remeg dropped Kinner's arm and shoved him hard, sending him sprawling into the snow. "Back away."

"But Captain …" Tynar began.

"Rot your eyes, do as I say!" She snatched her reins from the hand of the soldier holding them and threw herself aboard the buckskin. Backing the horse in a tight circle, she waved the troop ahead of her down the street. She was the last to go and her fury was a palpable thing long after she had disappeared from sight.

Rai and Kinner reached Banya as she went to her knees in the snow, head bent, breathing in weepy gasps. "You're okay," Rai said over and over, a prayer that it be so. "We'll get you inside somewhere, get you taken care of, don't you worry ..."

"Rai ..."

"Not now, kid. We need to take care of –"

"Rai!"

She looked up. Three snow-covered figures had appeared. Two stepped past them, trailing the soldiers with armed bows held at the ready. The third figure, its only distinguishing feature the ermine-bright eyes that peered above the rough weave of a scarf, approached. "Dinna worry." It was the voice that had challenged Remeg. "You're among friends."

"There's only three of you?" Kinner said, incredulous.

The woman's eyelids crinkled with a smile they could not see. "Aye. But yon captain doesna know that, eh?" She winked, and motioned to them. "Come awa' now."

Supporting Banya between them, Rai and Kinner followed her out of Cadasbyr and vanished into the darkness of the deepening storm.

FIFTEEN

Ren sat beneath the earth, thinking.

She had been born in these caves fifty-odd years ago, on a storming winter's night much like this one. But she wasn't thinking about that.

She sat on a short-legged stool beside a small fire whose thready smoke wafted up a natural chimney to emerge, quite unnoticed, far above ground. There were many such fissures in the mountain chain and several were utilized in this way, but she wasn't thinking about that either. Jak lay at her feet, belly-up and splay-legged, whining and twitching in his sleep.

She clenched her hands between her knees. The fire had burned low in the hours of her thinking; hours when she should have been asleep and wasn't because of what had occurred. Shadows edged the down-turned corners of her mouth. Her hair, grown out since summer's shearing, stuck out in points, disheveled by her hands as she contemplated the hornet's nest of events that had landed in her lap. On the table beside her lay a narrow wooden box. Every so often, she turned to stare at it as though it were something alive that might bite her if she wasn't careful.

That the clan periodically augmented its living by thievery was a thing of which Ren was not particularly proud, but a leader must be pragmatic. What mattered was survival; theirs against the rest of the world. Relations between the hill folk and the Cadasbyr townies had been cordial for centuries, each helping the other to survive when times were rough. It was poor business to prey on one's friends, but a stranger passing through was fair game for anyone.

Two days earlier (and, let it be said, without permission) Ren's eighteen year old niece Marn and some of her friends had decided to check out the pickings in town. They had returned bright-eyed as mice, flushed from the cold and the exhilaration of success. As was required, Ren had been called to come and inspect their booty.

"Who was your mark?" were her first words when she arrived, Jak padding silently at her heels.

Proud beyond all sense or reason, Marn had shrugged one shoulder, the motion just this side of insolent. “Strangers, o’ course. Couple o’ women and a sterile.”

“You kill ‘em?”

“No, just stole and skedaddled.”

“Hm.” That was one bit of good news, anyway. Ren examined the take – a half-dozen satchels, an old sword, a narrow wooden box, and three horses. The black animal was an eye catcher, sure enough, but he snapped at her when she reached out to touch him.

“That ‘uns got attitude,” Marn said with admiration as her aunt snatched back her hand. “He give me a bitch o’ a time.”

Like calls to like, Ren had thought with weariness. “Work him through winter if you care t’, girl, so long as your other duties don’ suffer.” She punctuated the statement with a hard look, promising retribution if Marn failed to comply with that stipulation. Like many teenagers, she was brightly eager to make a big impression rather than take the time required to learn her own strengths and weaknesses. Ren sometimes wondered if she had eyes on becoming Chief one day. If so, the arrogant brat could whistle up the wind. Ren was in no hurry to retire and would certainly not do so in favor of some chitling girl with her brains in her britches. “Come spring, gentled or no’ he goes t’ market at the Thaw.”

“Why? He’d make a grand stud!”

“T’ breed more foul personalities? Use what little sense you hae, girl. We raise sheep an’ goats, no’ horses. If it’s horses you’re wantin,’ go live wi’ the Carraid.” Now *that* would start a war for certain. Balfor would never forgive her.

She stepped around the black to look at the other animals. The ugly mouse-colored beast had blinked sleepy eyes and gently lipped her offered fingers. The muscular grey, however, had stood with its head high, eyes wide and alert, ears pricked to catch every sound.

Ren had rounded on Marn in a fury and thrust a finger at the dappled mare. “By the Cock’s comb, hae you no sense at all? That’s Carraid horseflesh, you half-wit!”

Marn’s face flushed with humiliation. She looked to her friends for support, but they ducked their heads in the face of their chief’s anger and stared at their feet.

“As soon as this storm breaks, you’ll take that mare t’ the valley an’ let her loose, you hear me? She’ll find her way home an’ maybe we’ll keep our heads, no thanks t’ you.” Ren stalked to the haphazard pile of packs and stood looking down at them. “Anything o’ use in this pile o’ shite or is it all garbage as well?”

“We an’t checked yet,” Marn replied in a snippy, ‘I’ve-been-wronged’ sort of voice. "*You* always want first look."

Ren had barely resisted the urge to back-hand her niece for attitude. "Let's hope they're high prizes, indeed, for all your bother." She pushed the bags aside with her boot and tapped its toe against the lid of the box. "An' this?"

One of the other girls spoke up. Luin was younger than the rest, her face rounded with the baby fat she'd yet to lose, her straight hair cut like an upended bowl. "Peterin asked about that. They said it were one o' them …" She hunted for the words. "One o' them bone thingys."

Ren's lips moved. Bone thingys? What on earth … "You mean a reliquary?"

"Aye, that'd be it."

Ren was torn as to whose brains she should dash out first, Marn's or her own. "This gets better an' better. Not only d' we hae the Carraid t' placate, but the Church as well."

"We thought maybe the box would be worth somethin', Chief," Luin said. "It's fine-made."

It was, but that didn't change things. Ren knelt and pulled the box free. "Well, let's see if I can figure out who it is you've insulted." She fingered the broken clasp, flipped back the other, and lifted the lid. At the sight of red silk, her eyebrows had canted in speculation. Using two fingers, she parted a fold of material to reveal the shining point of a blade.

She rose behind the lash of her hand and caught Marn a sharp blow across the face that sent her reeling against the cave wall. "Idiot!" The other girls and the dog cringed in the face of her rage. "Every one o' you is a brain-chilled stupid fool o' a child! Meggity's baby has more sense! By the Weathercock's spurs! No' only hae you stolen from a Carraid, but a warrior at that!" She snatched at her hair, unable to believe they could be so foolish. "Are the lot o' you *blind?* Look at the shine on that thing! D' you think anyone ownin' a blade like that won't do everything t' get it back? D' you think those villagers will keep mum to a Carraid? They'll ha' no choice but t' rat us out!"

"But they're our friends," one of the thieves had ventured in a weak voice.

Ren spat at the girl's feet. "Friends are bought with gold an' food, an' they're turned with iron an' fire an' blood. Someone will hunt for this, you mark me. An' where does that leave us? I've more than half a mind t' truss the lot o' you like deer an' deliver you t' Balfor m'self!" Furious, she had whirled around and kicked the box as hard as she could.

It spun across the floor and upended. Red silk spilled like a fount of blood and metal rang against stone. Torch light raced along the sword like it was drawn to it, blazoning the raging cockerel and making the sightless eyes wink in recognition.

The air in the cave had suddenly felt dense and breathless, gravid with the future. It pressed on Ren's ears like the instant before a thunderstorm breaks. For a moment, all she could do was stare, as she had stared into her fire on that long-ago night when the ashen picture had appeared on her hearth.

Marn, her face marked with the hot blossom of her aunt's hand, gaped. "What *is* that?"

Her voice had broken the spell that held them in thrall. Ren went to her knees and lifted the weapon in reverent hands. Droplets of light scattered across the room like the reflection from a spray of sunlit water.

"By the Spurs ..." someone murmured.

Ren got to her feet still holding the sword. "I need t' meet the woman who owns this." She scanned the group. Who to ask? Certainly not Marn. She could keep out of sight until world's end for all Ren cared. "Luin, you took 'em at the Pleasure?"

The girl's eyes were bright with excitement of the worrisome sort. "Aye, Chief."

"You find Pesk and Swot. Tell 'em t' ski-up fast an' meet me at the south tunnel."

"Weapons, Chief?"

Smart child. "Blades an' bows both. Git!" As Luin dashed away, Ren had turned to those who remained. "The rest o' you, git on w' your chores if you hae 'em." She cast a dismissive eye at Marn. "An' make yourself useful elsewhere if no'. Speak no' a word o' this t' anyone, mind. I dinna want this noised about just yet." With the dog at her heels, she had hastened toward her room to make ready for departure.

So it was that three had left the safety of the caves to brave the mountain slopes and the lashing storm. They found those they sought, although not in the manner which Ren had expected, and returned without sign of pursuit ... which proved that the heartless woman leading that band of soldiers had either more fear in her heart than Ren believed or more sense than she gave her credit for.

"Ren?"

Her head jerked up from her chest so fast that she almost took a tumble off the stool. She had fallen asleep sitting up. A silhouette shone on the curtain covering her doorway; short, and stocky with added clothing. One of the children. "Come in." The hanging parted and Dimnon stepped inside. The ten-year-old boy had been put under her protection by a family who would rather bid their son a temporary farewell than to see him stolen into the queen's whoredom.

The dog rolled over with a startled yip. "Peace, Jak," Ren said, and the animal subsided with his ears cast down. "What is it, child?"

Dimnon's eyes were enormous with curiosity and import. "Ollam says t' tell you they're awake an' askin' for you."

Ren nodded, careful to show neither thought nor feeling on her face. "You tell her I'm on my way, yes?"

"Aye'm." He dashed back the way he had come.

As the echo of his running steps faded, Ren glanced at the dog. "What muddle have we found oursel's in now, eh, Jakky-lad?" Eyes fixed on her face, he thumped his tail against the rug and waited for words or gestures he understood. She stroked the top of his silky head and pushed to her feet. Taking the box which contained the sword, she started down the twisty tunnel after the boy with Jak following at her heels.

The corridor outside the infirmary held more than its usual number of patients waiting for attention. Ren's mouth pursed in annoyance. "Are we after havin' an epidemic, then? Hae you all got the pox?"

Feet shifted and eyes were averted. A few of those present attempted a weak smile of embarrassment, then gave it up as a lost cause and slinked away. Ren did not bother to ask where they had gotten their information. The air fairly reeked of Marn. "Clear out, anyone who's no' sick," she said. "If there's anythin' needs knowin,' you'll be told it, eh?" She waited until all but a few sniffly or injured folk had sidled away before she parted the curtain into the infirmary and stepped through.

The room was shaped like a horseshoe. At the bottom end was the entrance, the fireplace, and six beds for those who needed more tending than a bandage and a kiss would provide. The arms of the horseshoe went off in a gentle curve. On the right was storage for bandages and linens. On the left was where Ollam concocted her remedies for both human and beast.

The Carraid (as easy to spot as a poke in the eye; what was the matter with Marn?), her complexion faded to the color of worms drowned in the rain, lay covered with blankets and propped up on pillows so her feet would not dangle off the end of the cot. Her dark counterpart perched at the foot of the bed, rigid as a sentry that smells trouble. Her fingers, drumming against her knees, stilled when Ren appeared. The sterile boy slouched on a low stool beside the Carraid, but he came off it fast, like an arrow released from a bow. "You have the sword!" He reached for the weapon.

Instinctively, Ren's arms tightened around the box. The boy faltered and his hands slowly dropped to his sides. She cursed herself. *What are ye, Ren?*

No better than the queen, t'take what doesna belong t'you? With only a small show of reluctance, she handed it to him. "On behalf o' that band o' idiots, I apologize for the thievin' of your things. I'm Ren, chief o' the Chesne."

"What's that when it's at home?" the dark women said defensively.

The Carraid kicked her through the blankets. "Don't be rude. Please excuse her," she said to Ren. "She was raised by weasels. I'm Banya Kiordasdotter. The boy is Kinner, lately of Moselle. The ill-mannered lout at the end of the bed is Rai."

Ren nodded greeting. "Peace at your comin,' peace at your stayin,' peace at your goin' awa'." *Although something makes me doubt it,* she thought. "How d' you feel?"

"They'll live." The voice came from deep along the left arm of the infirmary and Ollam waddled into view. The physician's immense body bobbled within the soft drape of a homespun gown like warm holiday pudding wrapped in muslin. Her face was exquisitely pretty, broad and round as a pie with the creamy complexion of a young girl, enormous blue eyes, and a tiny rosebud mouth made generous by laughter. Dark curls streaked with grey framed her face in a halo. "Rai an' Kinner hae some superficial frostburn. Nothin' that canna be cured by a little salve an' a few nights in a warm bed." Her expression darkened and she bent to lay a small, graceful hand on Banya's forehead. "This 'un, she'll carry scars t' the end o' her days. Whoever did the job sliced her as clean as a trapper takin' hides."

"Her name is Mestipen." Rai's voice was tight with contempt. She rubbed one knuckle over and over. "She's a spooky old bitch, but I never took her for the sort who would do something like this, not to Banya." There was pain in her eyes that Ren could almost feel. "Banya gets along with everyone."

"Apparently not," the Carraid said with a dry attempt at humor.

"Was she doin' it for sport or because o' orders?" Ollam said. "Orders is a powerful thing t' some. People can be awful creative when it comes t' doin' what they're told."

"The order came straight from Remeg's lips," Banya said in a dull tone. "But she only said, 'Make them come out, Mestipen.' She gave no actual order to peel me. That was Mestipen's idea all on her own. She enjoyed it, too." The Carraid swallowed hard and looked away. "And not one of them did anything to stop her," she whispered.

"Remeg's the one in charge?" Ren nodded at their noises of affirmation. "That's a mean 'un an' no lie."

"I wouldn't have agreed with you until now," Banya said. "Tough, sure, but fair." Her expression grew pensive. "This sort of behavior isn't like her. There's something else going on."

"Nothing a knife to the heart wouldn't cure," Rai said. She snapped her fingers at the dog. Jak stared at her, hard-eyed, and bared his teeth in a low growl as he slunk behind Ren's ankles.

"What was done t' Banya was a monstrous bit o' work," Ollam said, her voice heavy with condemnation. "But be you glad that yon evil creature is skilled at her sick craft. Your wounds would hae been much worse in th' hands o' an amateur. As it is, they're clean an' dressed. Wi' plantain twice a day, a watchful eye an' some rest, you'll be none the worse for wear in the end." She smiled and patted Banya's shoulder. "But it hurts like all sin right now, eh, little girl?"

Unexpected laughter burst from Rai. Banya arched a sardonic eyebrow and kicked her through the blankets.

Huffing, Ollam bent like a living mountain and picked up a satchel from beside the fireplace. She slung the long strap over her head so that it rested across her body with the bag at one hip. "You're after wantin' t' talk t' our guests in private, Ren, so I'm awa'. Banya, I'll be back a'fore dinner t' change that bandage."

"Thank you, Ollam."

Curls bounced around the healer's face when she nodded. "You're most welcome."

Ren waited until the healer had gone before she took a seat on the bed nearest Banya. Jak circled twice and settled at her feet. He stared at the hand Kinner offered and stuck a questing nose against the boy's palm. Kinner scratched the underside of the dog's muzzle and grinned at Rai when Jak closed his eyes in pleasure.

Ren crossed one knee over the other, a relaxed posture when she felt anything but. "Let's start wi' the sword, eh? Where's that come from?"

"My mother made it," Kinner said, his soft voice full of pride. Jak had inched closer and the boy's fingers were deep in the dog's neck ruff. "She was a blacksmith."

"An' where is she?" Ren said. "I'd like t' talk wi' her."

The corners of Kinner's mouth turned down in sorrow. "She's dead."

The words were like a blow to Ren's heart. According to legend, it was the blacksmith who would know when the Weathercock was born and it was the blacksmith who would lead the Chesne to him. To have the sword but not its maker was an evil trick, something well within the purview of the Triple She. "I'm sorry. Was it this Remeg who –"

The boy shook his head. "No. Mum was sick. She'd been sick a long time." As all tales do, it grew in the telling. The women sat silently throughout and did not interrupt as Kinner relayed all that he knew – Holan's first call to become a blacksmith, life with Kessler and the other women of the Household, bedtime stories of the Weathercock, and his mother's visions. He spoke of her deceit, of the lie she had perpetrated against him to meet her own selfish ends. That was the word he used – selfish – and Ren could not wholly disagree. As he spoke, one hand rose repeatedly to rub the tattoo in what Ren thought was an unconscious gesture. Kinner concluded with his mother's death and then fell silent, with nothing more to say.

The crackle of the fire was the only sound in the room as each pondered their private thoughts. Ren tallied lists in her head – wherefores and whys, how-tos and shoulds, needs and wants. To let impulse drive what might – *must!* – happen next was to invite chaos and failure into the caves and that was something she would not do. The Chesne would die for what they believed, but she would not risk them needlessly.

Banya cleared her throat. "How is it that you happened to show up when you did, right when we needed you?"

Ren sighed. "Much as I hate to, I s'pose I must lay credit for that on Marn." She winced. "Keep mum about that, would you? If word gets out, there'll be no livin' wi' her. She's already puffed up like a woodcock most times." She described what had transpired after Marn's return to the caves and saw the relief on Banya's face when she heard that the Carraid mare was safe. "The instant I saw the sword I knew we had t' find you, an' by grace o' the Weathercock it happened. I hate t' think where yon Mesitpen's little game would hae gone had she no' been interrupted."

"Weathercock, my eye," Rai muttered. "It was pure dumb luck."

Ren felt a stir of trouble in her heart. Jak, attuned to any change in her personality, lifted his head to look at her, seeking the source of unrest. "You dinna believe in the Weathercock?"

Rai's look was level. "No," she said emphatically. "I do not."

Banya gave a cryptic, lop-sided smile. "Not yet, at any rate."

"Not ever, horseface."

"What's Chesne?" Kinner suddenly asked, interrupting. He flushed when they all looked at him. "Rai asked before and I don't know the word."

It was Banya who replied. "It's an old one, from the long ago times. It means 'hidden.'" Her eyes met Ren's. "In Carraidland, we call the Chesne 'those who wait.'"

"Wait for what?" Rai said.

"For the Weathercock," Ren replied.

Rai's strident laughter rang through the cave. "By all that's three-headed and holy! First him." She thrust a finger at Kinner. "Then you." She pointed at Banya. "And now *this?*" She spread her arms wide to encompass the mountain.

"There have been believers in the Weathercock for hundreds of years, Rai," Banya said. "You know that."

"Yeah, but I didn't think they were *organized!* What are you, some sort of welcoming committee?"

Ren folded her arms across her chest and sat back. "In a manner o' speakin.'"

Rai blinked as if she'd been hit with a stone. "You're joking."

"Quit your noise," Banya said in a stern voice. "You're being insulting. Why is belief in the Weathercock less easy to credence than belief in someone with three heads?"

"It's not the same thing at all," Rai argued. "For one thing, look at what the Weathercock stands for. Equality of the sexes? Give me a break! How can they be equal when men are naturally weaker than women in both body and mind?"

Ren abruptly stood up. "If you truly believe that, Rai," she said in a challenging tone. "I hae somethin' t' show you."

Jak trotted ahead of them with a self-important air, feathered tail pluming as it fanned over his back. Now and then, the dog glanced behind to make sure they were still following and his mouth gaped in a canine grin.

Although they moved at a pace slow enough to accommodate Banya's injury, Kinner soon lost all sense of direction in the maze of tunnels. He said not a word, but listened with rapt attention as Ren described the Chesne way of life in and on the mountain, how they followed the turn of the seasons and moved their flocks of sheep and goats between highland pasturage and lowland grazing. Seeing his interest, Ren said, "Is there somethin' in particular you'd like t' know, Kinner?"

He ducked his head, shy in the face of her regard. He wasn't yet used to female attention that did not include sexual overture. "Ummm ..." His eye landed on the dog, strutting along ahead of them. "Where did you get him?"

"Jak?" The dog glanced back at the sound of his name, but faced forward as soon as he realized that his services were not required. "He was born here, one o' a litter 'tween my mam's old dog Sed an' Canter's bitch Neula." She smiled. "Think you'd like a dog o' your own one day?"

"Maybe." In truth, he had little experience with animals beyond those that occupied his dinner plate or the occasional distant sight of the horses that came to the smithy to be shod. Watching Jak wind back and forth across the tunnel, Kinner thought that it might be nice to have a dog, one just like the piebald herder with his intelligent eyes and expressive face.

The idea gave him pause. Until recently, his future had been mapped out by the constraints of his sex, a thing best left to women to decide. Now, just as his mother had said, choice lay in his hands. It scared the life out of him, and yet …

After a while, Ren came to a halt outside the entrance to a cave. "Wait here a moment, please," she said. "I want t' make sure we're no' interruptin.'" She stepped inside, but returned almost at once and motioned for them to join her. "This is one o' our schools," she said in a low voice as they entered.

There were a dozen students present – six at work and six seated along the wall, observing. Kinner was astonished to realize that more than a third of them were boys. A skinny lad about his age, with gingery hair and a bruised cheekbone, stood in the center of the room. He held a long pole horizontally in both hands and his knees were bent in readiness. Five other students, heavily padded for protection, circled him. "They're playin' the part o' wolves," Ren explained in a whisper.

One of the children feinted at the boy's throat and he drove her back with a blow to the ribs. Another came at him from behind, but he turned just in time and whacked her on the leg.

"Sweet spurs, you're a *pack!*" An older woman, obviously the teacher, circled the area in which they sparred. "Act like one! You come at him one at a time like that, he keeps his wind an' his strength." Emboldened, two of the students attacked from opposite sides. The boy whirled, the wooden stick a blur in his hands as he delivered a precise blow to each of their heads. The 'wolves' backed away and the children cheered. "Good," the instructor called. "But don't stop. Keep at him! Don't gie him the chance to catch his breath. Wear him down!"

The attack was renewed, the 'wolves' acting independently as well as together and never giving the boy a break. Whenever one of them managed to get through his defenses, the instructor halted the fight momentarily to query the students on how best to correct the error and avoid it in the future.

Kinner watched with his heart in his throat. At one point, he glanced at Banya and found her watching him. He flashed an enormous grin. She laughed and nodded with understanding.

As the students' attention wandered toward the visitors, the errors on the part of both shepherd and wolves multiplied until finally the teacher was forced to call an end to things. "Pathetic," she said in disgust. "Extra lessons for all." Groans of dismay did not sway her judgment. "You dinna like it? Do better next time. A real wolf willna stand back an' wait while you make up your mind abou' whether t' fight or stare into space." She turned her back on them and saluted Ren by tugging a lock of her hair in greeting. "Hallo, Chief."

Ren nodded. "Torby. I've brought our guests t' see your class."

The woman rubbed her chin. "You chose a day when there's precious little worth seein.'" The class smiled at one another with self-deprecation. They studied the strangers with open, friendly curiosity and, in the case of Banya, more than a little awe.

"There was some nice footwork, though," the Carraid said. "I liked that two-fisted action, bam-bam!" She motioned as if she held a quarterstaff, then winced and held an elbow against her side. "I shouldn't have done that."

"Idiot," Rai muttered. She stood back from the others, close to the door.

"Maybe you ought to take a few lessons, partner," Banya said. "Some thieves might have found you a tougher nut to crack if you knew how to defend yourself." She grinned at the black look that remark earned her and nudged Kinner with an elbow. "What about you? Want to give this a go?"

In the depths of her eyes, he could see his tiny reflection. That Kinner looked older somehow; more self-assured. He nodded. "I'd like that."

"Don't encourage him!" Rai's sudden explosion surprised everyone. She was a little wild-eyed and very angry. "Don't teach him that his life can be different when you know it won't be. Don't lie to him the way his mother did." She flung at hand at the students. "You … you're lying to all of them and it's wrong!" She rushed from the room.

A rill of uncertainty worked at Kinner's new-found resolve like flood waters against a foundation. "What's the matter with Rai?"

Banya's expression had grown sad and thoughtful. She laid a big hand on Kinner's shoulder. "Sometimes, when the things you believe in are challenged, it can be hard to stomach."

"But …" He gestured in an attempt to take in all that had occurred in the past few days. "But that's happening to me and I like it!"

The Carraid's lips settled into a grim line. "You're not Rai."

Head down, Rai hurried through the honeycomb of tunnels, not caring if she ended up lost. All she wanted was to get away from that … that *blasphemy!* Turning swiftly into an intersection, she nearly collided with someone coming the other way. They dodged to avoid running into one another and the shepherd, an older man with grey hair and a brindle-coated puppy under one arm, smiled. "Guess we both need t' look where we're goin,' eh?"

"You shouldn't even exist!" Rai snarled into his startled face and sped away.

A thread of fresh air led her up a cramped stairwell of carved rock to a cleft in the mountain's face. The space was barely big enough to squeeze through, but she forced her way up and out onto a narrow ledge covered knee-deep in snow. The world beyond the mountain had vanished into a maelstrom of white that screamed against the cliff and tore at her clothing. The blast of cold air and icy snow stung Rai's hands and numbed her face almost at once, but at least this was a world that made sense, a world she understood.

In the distance, veiled by the rush of wind-driven snow, came a distant flicker of light. Rai slitted her eyes and peered hard against the storm. What the hell was it? Not sunlight (the sky was clouds from end to end), so it wasn't a reflection off ice or water. What then?

A second flare glowed orange behind the fall of snow, spreading as she watched, and Rai felt a sudden shiver of certainty just before a hint of wood smoke reached her.

Cadasbyr was burning.

Sixteen

Marn coasted down the mountainside on the thin blades of her skis, the *shoosh* of waxed wood on snow lost amid the slicing keen of the wind. The bare branches of trees twisted and dipped in a wild dance. Needled firs whispered as she glided between them. Chesne weather witches had foretold a long, hard storm, but that had not stopped the girl from leaving the safety of the caves.

Her pride burned from the hiding Ren had given her in front of her friends and her emotions churned with conflicting complexity. She resented her aunt, but admired her as well. She craved Ren's approval, yet chafed under her constraints and cautions. Marn thought the Chesne hide-bound, caught in the web of old ways. Tradition may have served them well in the past, but life was about movement, about progress. She meant to lead her people one day; to guide them in a new direction, away from the caves and off the damned mountain forever, never mind the pull of history. To do that, she needed their respect, *Ren's* respect, and today she meant to earn it once and for all. Because Ren would never have agreed to this scheme, Marn had conveniently neglected to ask permission to reconnoiter Cadasbyr.

She could smell smoke on the wind.

Marn did not consider herself foolhardy. She had no intention of waltzing straight into town or confronting the invaders. Although driven by an adventuresome spirit, she understood that any woman capable of inflicting the sort of torture that Banya had endured was no one to trifle with. She would keep her distance, learn what she could, and return to the caves as fast as possible.

Cresting a low, humpbacked hill, she coasted to a stop behind the cover of a thick copse of fir trees. Her breath puffed between the heavy, woven fibers of her scarf as she leaned her ski poles against a tree and bent to free her boots from their bindings. She shrugged off her pack, releasing a shower of snow. Kneeling, she undid the ties and removed the distance-glass she had borrowed (*stolen*) from Ren's quarters. Made of leather and shiny brass, it was a wonderful bit of goods that had once belonged to a great-great-aunt of Ren's, a woman with the good sense to leave the mountains in favor of the sea. (That she had ultimately chosen to return to the caves with her stories and prized possessions was a point Marn chose to ignore.)

Pulling the collapsible sections one from the other, she twisted them to lock them into place. Flat on her belly, she snake-shimmied through the snowy undergrowth to the crest of the hill, where she lifted the distance glass to her eye and trained it on the sprawl of buildings below.

Her faint cry of dismay, muffled by her scarf, was plucked by the wind and borne away. Everywhere she looked, the view was the same. Fire had eaten through Cadasbyr like a purgative. The only buildings that remained standing and unharmed were the inn and the livery. The rest of the town was nothing but blackened ruins trailing smears of oily smoke. Snow patterned the charred wood like rotted lace.

It took her a moment to realize that the oddly-shaped humps covered in fresh snow were bodies.

She looked away, blinking hard to keep back the tears. Cadasbyr was not a big town by any means. How many of those now dead had she known by name? She raised the viewer again and focused beyond the carnage. Horses, looking exhausted and dispirited, were bunched together in the livery paddock. Soldiers moved between the two buildings that remained or hunkered in small groups around fires built in protected corners of the ruins. Smoke rose from the chimneys of the inn and was snatched away by the wind.

Marn stood up, determined to get a closer look so Ren could know precisely what had happened here. The blow took her from behind and she collapsed without a sound, the distance viewer buried beneath her in the snow.

A fist rapped against the door to what had been the inn's kitchen and now served, in part, as Remeg's temporary quarters. She swallowed a mouthful of tepid stew, glanced at the others present, and put down her spoon. "Come."

Rimnir stuck her head around the jamb. "Mestipen to see you, Captain."

"Show her in." She wiped her mouth on her sleeve and did a double-take as the tracker entered dragging a body by its hair.

"The jays told me where to look," the scar-faced woman said. She sniffed and wiped her nose with the back of a glove. "Intruder, they said. I went to look and found the pretty girl watching us through this." She held up the viewer, fingers clenched around it like claws, and handed it to Remeg. "I always listen to the jays," she said. "They speak to me."

Remeg didn't doubt it. She peered through the lens. The sudden, close-up view of one of Mestipen's eyes almost made her drop the thing. "That's a handy little device," she said to cover her discomfort. She collapsed the parts one into the other and set it on end beside her bowl. "Is she dead?"

"Would I waste your time with a dead 'un, Captain?"

"No, of course not." Remeg leaned on her elbows and rested her chin atop her folded hands. Was this girl a local who had escaped the depredation on Cadasbyr or was she, perhaps, someone with a broader accent who knew how to use a bow?

To lose her quarry by such a small margin, to watch the chance of reconciliation with Kedar vanish and be able to do nothing about it, had tipped Remeg into the irrational. She knew it, but berating herself now for an earlier loss of control was like closing the hen house door once the chickens had fled. She hadn't intended for the entire town to be put to the sword, but her rage and frustration had gotten the better of her. She could not breathe life back into the scattered corpses. All she could do was press on toward her goal as best she might and try, in the meanwhile, to repair what damage her actions might have caused her reputation within the troop.

Those who rode with her had been chosen for this duty based upon a general willingness to hunt their own and kill them, if need be. Torture of an adversary was not out of the question in soldiery, but what she had let happen to Banya – what she had *ordered* to happen, let us be honest, even if she hadn't used those precise words – had shaken even the hardiest of those among the troop. She had seen it in their eyes. Sacking a town was one thing; that was part and parcel of what they did for a living. This was something else. She knew that those under her command considered her tough, but fair. Now they looked at her askance, if they looked at her at all, their gazes heavy with judgment. Her actions had made her unrecognizable to them.

"Do you know her?" Remeg said in a soft voice.

The question was directed not at Mestipen or the other soldiers present, but at the innkeeper Peterin, who sat in a corner flanked by Tynar and Sula. Blood from a broken nose stained the torn and dirty linen of her shirt. One eye was puffed shut and her lips were cut and swollen against teeth broken off at the gum line. She slumped against the wall, her expression slack from the beating she had received and the wholesale slaughter she had witnessed. In a failed attempt to ransom the lives of her children and grandchildren, she had babbled everything she knew about the Chesne. Her reward had been to watch her family die.

Tynar kicked her in the leg. "Answer Captain Remeg!"

Peterin lifted her head as if it were a ponderous weight and blinked her one good eye. "Will you kill me if I tell you?" Her voice was flat and atonal from the swelling in her nose and mouth. The question sounded like a plea.

"You'll die regardless," Remeg said.

"Good." Peterin swallowed, coughed, and spat a wad of blood onto the floor. She shifted her gaze to Mestipen's prisoner. "If it weren't for them, you'd not have done this. You'd have stayed a night or two at most, spent your money, and gone away. If it weren't for them my family …" Her thick tongue flicked across the dried speckles of blood on her lips. "Her name is Marn. She's one of them cavers, them Chesne."

Remeg had been unfamiliar with that word when the first of those to be killed had spoken it, but Mestipen had known. Mestipen seemed to know *everything.*

Remeg pushed back her chair and stepped from behind the desk. At her nod, Tynar and Mestipen hauled the slack-jawed girl upright, slumped between them with her head hanging. Remeg removed one glove and placed her naked hand beneath the girl's chin.

She never expected her to come awake fighting.

Marn jerked an arm free and clawed a row of furrows into Remeg's cheek. Mestipen did something to her then (no one saw what) and the girl collapsed with a shriek of agony. Remeg touched the wound on her face with a careful hand and rubbed her bloody fingers together. "You've more talent than skill, Marn."

The girl's eyes widened to hear her name. "Peterin, you didna' tell 'em!"

"They're all dead 'cause of you!" the innkeeper shouted. She sprang at Marn and was forcibly restrained by Sula. Peterin's eyes rolled toward Remeg. "Let me have one go at her! Just one! Please!" Bloody spittle flew from her lips. "One go before I die!"

"Shut up," Remeg said calmly. She pressed her sleeve against the injury, wondering if it would scar. "Three prisoners were stolen from me, two women and a boy. The women are soldiers in the uniform of Caerau. The boy is a marked sterile. Where have you taken them?"

Marn raised her chin, foolishly obdurate. Her eyes blazed defiance.

Remeg nodded to herself, wearily unsurprised by the girl's ardor. "I know your sort, Marn. Proud and foolish. Those traits will get you killed sooner or later." She scratched a spot on her nose that she thought might be frostburn. "The absence of a garrison in Cadasbyr has obviously bred outlawry. I would recommend to Her Majesty that she remedy the situation if there was going to be anyone left here to which it might be applied." She glanced at Peterin. Sula drew a knife from her belt and pressed the length of it against the innkeeper's throat, just beneath her chin. Remeg raised an angular eyebrow at Marn. "Well?

One word saves the innkeeper's life."

The girl's breath came fast and tight through her nose. Her jaw clenched and she pointedly shifted her gaze away from the unfortunate innkeeper. "You lie," she whispered.

"You're right," Remeg said agreeably. She made a slight gesture with her bloody fingers.

The blade bit deep. Peterin neither struggled nor voiced protest as the knife cleanly sliced through skin, meat, and gristle. Blood flowed, filling the room with its acrid tang as her knees folded. The body landed at Marn's feet, spattering her boots with gore. Gagging, the girl lurched forward and spewed all over the corpse. Tynar wound a free hand in Marn's long hair and jerked her head up. The girl was fish-belly white. Her eyes were circled with pale green shadows and her chin was shiny with vomit. The sour smell mingled unpleasantly with the metallic scent of so much blood.

Remeg pinched the bridge of her nose between two fingers. She had a headache and longed for the comfort of her own bed. "I ask again, girl. Where are those I seek?"

Marn's head shot forward and she spat. The gobbet landed just short of Remeg's boot, a bright bead of spittle against the scarred wooden floor.

"Oh, child." Remeg shook her head in mock sorrow. "What you're doing isn't bravery, it's foolishness. It won't be remembered past today and no one will ever sing songs to your memory. Are you certain you won't cooperate? No?" She gave a weary nod.

The thin-bladed weapon that appeared in Mestipen's hand as if by magic was different from the one she had used on Banya. Remeg wondered with vague interest just how many of these little toys the tracker possessed.

Marn's eyes widened in terror. She jerked and thrashed, fighting to get free, but her captors' grips could not break free.

Mestipen smiled. "Care you to reconsider?"

When it was over, the vermillion spread of Marn's blood across the kitchen floor looked very much like a bird's wing. The girl had proved to be stronger than any of them would have guessed. For that she received full points, much good might it do her. Mestipen, however, had been stronger still ... not to mention patient, persistent, and creative in technique. Towards the end, Marn had happily told them whatever they wanted to know.

Well, perhaps 'happily' wasn't quite the correct term, Remeg conceded. But why quibble over semantics?

Kinner limped along the tunnel toward the room he shared with Banya and Rai. He favored his right ankle where he'd sprained it in a fall, and his lower back ached from a thump in the kidneys he'd received that afternoon from Danika, a girl half his size and three years his junior.

The past few days among the Chesne had been a long blur of almost constant activity and an education in every sense of the word. At Banya's instigation, he had asked if he might join the other children in their studies. Ren was agreeable, so Torby had set him to running tunnels and working with weights to strengthen his muscles. He'd tried his hand at archery with dismal results, was slightly better at swordplay, and found he enjoyed the odd ballet of the quarterstaff. He learned that there was more to overcoming a larger foe than he'd ever suspected and that a greater mass was not necessarily required. Armed with nothing but a tree limb, he could become almost formidable. Well, maybe not *yet,* but he had promised himself that he would get there. Each evening, bruised and exhausted, he sucked down his dinner like it was water and collapsed into bed, asleep almost before his head touched the pillow. He awoke at dawn aching in every muscle and eager for more.

What the Chesne did (what they had done for centuries), flew in the face of everything Kinner had been taught about a man's proper place in society. In the world he knew men were property to be discarded like cattle if they failed to perform. Among the Chesne, however, they had worth and useful lives to fulfill beyond the question of fertility. Individual talents and interests were given recognition and utilized in the best possible way. Consequently, each member of the community put forth their best efforts to keep the clan alive and well.

And he was making friends; something he hadn't realized was missing from his life. Holan had been his companion, protector, supporter, and confidant. Now strangers approached him with an open-handed geniality born out of something other than a desire to breed and he met them in kind.

Dancing sideways with quick steps, Kinner feinted and shadow-boxed the wall – one, two, three! – and stepped through the open doorway to their room. Banya looked up from where she sat reading and whistled. "Yow. Where'd you get the mouse?"

"What?" he said, confused.

"The eye."

"Oh." He touched beneath his right eye where a lavender bruise puffed the skin and spread along his cheekbone. He grinned. "Danika."

Rai, stretched out on her bunk, shook her head. "That little spit-fire is gonna kill you one of these days."

Banya laughed. "Or marry you."

Kinner held up a warning finger. "Don't start with me," he said and limped toward his bed.

"Ooo-hoo!" Banya let the parchment roll shut. "Someone's full of himself." She shoved back her chair and stood, careful not to move too fast. She was healing, but the wound inflicted by Mestipen remained tender. "Do you know what we do to cheeky buggers?"

He dropped onto the bed and stretched out on his back. "Leave them alone to get a good night's sleep?" he suggested hopefully.

Banya grinned. "Rai, tell him what we do to –" She broke off as Ren entered the room with Jak in tow. "'Evening, Chief," she said with a nod of welcome. "We're just about to start torturing Kinner if you'd like to join in."

Ren smiled. "'Tis a tempting offer, but I think I'll pass."

"Thank you," Kinner said with such heartfelt relief that the women laughed.

Rai pushed up onto her elbows. "Have you found Marn?"

Ren shook her head. "I told you afore, this isna' the first time the wee hot-head has gone off in a snit for a few days t' hide an' stroke her ego after she's had her hand slapped. I'm damned if our lives will be turned upside-down on the whim o' a spoiled girl." She turned a chair around and straddled it. Jak leaped onto Kinner's bed and snuggled against him, sighing with piggish contentment as the boy's sword-nicked hands stroked his head and gently tugged the feathery black-and-white ears. "You've spoiled that dog useless," she said with a fond smile.

"I think he's wonderful." Kinner scratched the dog under the chin.

"If you come back through here one day, perhaps you'll take a pup. We'd be honored." Arms draped over the back of the chair, Ren laced her fingers together. "I came t' tell you the storm is breakin'. Weather witches say it's soon time to be awa', if goin' is what you're after. The good weather won't last. If trouble comes from below, it'll happen at snow's end. If you're leavin', you need to be well awa' before it arrives."

"I'm sorry we brought this on you," Kinner said. He thought of Remeg, that woman Mestipen, and what they had done to Banya. His hands went still on the dog's body. Jak looked up in silent inquiry and nudged the boy with his nose to resume.

"What you brought us is hope," Ren said. "Never apologize for that. If yon Remeg comes, we'll hae her an' her bloody troop turned 'round six ways from Yule." She winked. "An' if a few meet their demise in the process, well, it's a terrible thing the way accidents happen on a winter's trail."

"Don't play with Remeg," Banya said in warning. "If she gets her hands on one of you ..." She stopped and her mouth hung open. "I'm sorry. I wasn't thinking."

Ren waved away the apology. "I told you, don' fret yourself o'er Marn. She's no' in Remeg's hands, she's jus' gone off t' pout." She rubbed her knuckles. "We'll provide you wi' provisions, a tent, an' a map o' the area to see you on your way. The Chesne hae more trails than your Captain Remeg realizes. We'll set you on the doorstep o' Dara before she knows what's what."

Kinner's fingers trailed through the dog's fur. "I don't want to seem greedy, but may I ask a favor before we go?"

"Well, you canna hae me dog!"

He grinned, but almost immediately sobered. He pushed Jak aside, swung his legs off the bed, and leaned toward Ren with his elbows on his knees. "I've been thinking about the sword, about what it means to everyone who believes in the Weathercock. It doesn't seem enough to take it to Dara, especially when we don't know what will happen to it once we get there." He glanced at Rai and Banya. He had not discussed any of this with them and wondered how they would react to what he was about to say. "After we've gone, would you spread the word and let the others know about the sword? Will you tell them that something is finally beginning to happen?"

Rai's mouth dropped open. She sat up fast, but before she could protest, Banya reached out and clapped a hand over her mouth. There was canny speculation in the Carraid's eyes.

Ren nodded, eyes shining. "Aye, I can do that."

Rai shoved Banya's hand away. "While you're at it, make sure you tell everyone not to expect the Weathercock any time soon. It's not like he's actually shown up or anything."

To Kinner's surprise, Ren smiled at the jibe. "Hae a care, Rai. We've already shaken some o' your dearly held beliefs. Who's to say we won't rock your entire world by the time we're through?" With a nod, she whistled the dog to her and was gone.

Rai's pillow thumped against the wall above Kinner's head. "What the hell was that?"

"You do realize you've stepped over the line into deep water?" Banya said. "This goes beyond fulfilling your mother's last wish, lad. You're talking open rebellion now. Do you understand what that means?" Her arms swept wide to indicate the lattice of tunnels and caves beyond their room. "Are you prepared to shoulder responsibility for their deaths, if it comes to that? You can't talk big and get everyone riled up, then step aside and let others do the work. If it comes to it, will you lead the vanguard? Will *you* go into battle for what the Weathercock stands for even if he never shows up?"

Kinner stared at them. Banya's words echoed in his head and lifted the hair on his arms in a rush of gooseflesh. He felt a lot of things – fear and worry being the most prevalent – but doubt was not one of them. Rai sat hushed, awaiting his reply.

He nodded. "Yes."

Seventeen

Morning was less than half gone and already Remeg was exhausted. Slumped in the saddle, she fought to keep her eyes open against the rocking motion of the horse beneath her as it broke trail. Behind the clouds, the sun glowed like a grey pearl, lending a sheen to the snow that made her eyes ache.

The storm that had blown her troop into Cadasbyr (and blown her quarry out) had moved on at last, leaving every trail into the high country closed. When word came that the storm was lifting (Asabi's hand on her arm in the dark hours of the night; Remeg coming instantly awake, her hand slipping beneath the cloak she used as a pillow for the dagger hidden there), she had roused the troop. Using horses, shovels, and buckets, they labored to break through the wind-sculpted drifts to open a way out of town. Remeg had worked alongside her soldiers not merely out of a desire to get the job done, but to regain their respect. Having them on her side was not a necessity – their job was to do as she ordered; they didn't have to like her in the process – but neither would it hurt.

After serious deliberation, she had divided the troop. Four soldiers would remain in Cadasbyr under Rimnir's command. Their job was to find a way into the Chesne caves and determine if what Remeg sought was still hiding there. If so, they were to take custody of the three fugitives and send word to Remeg at once. If their search proved unsuccessful, they were to rejoin the troop as soon as possible, but only after destroying any sheep or food larders they discovered. Remeg realized that there was no hope of killing the Chesne all at one go, but slow death by starvation had a certain appeal. Meanwhile, she would take her riders across the Lon and along the western foothills of the Garadun Mountains in the event that her quarry had fled. If the miscreants had any hope of achieving Dara, there was no choice but for them to go south and east where travel would be easier. The boy's presence would demand it.

On the odd chance that Remeg failed to intercept them and heard nothing from Rimnir, her intention was to catch the road above Taran Falls where the Sower River plunged its icy waters over a sheer rock face to become the Calleigh. The wide river foamed out of the foothills and spread into the lowlands, where it eventually slowed on its meandering path toward the twin cities of Kell and Kiarr. Remeg knew that the track above the Falls, known locally as Snake Belly Road, often remained navigable in all but the worst of winter weather. That route would take them through the mountains to the village of Risley. From there, it was a day's journey to Dara. In clear weather, one could look north from the village and see the monastery perched on its mountainside like a peregrine on a cliff, fierce in dark stone, sheltering a nest of men whose sole purpose was to serve the Goddess. Her memory of that view remained all too clear.

Twelve years earlier, she had made that trip with her eighteen-year-old son. Every moment of that journey was burned into her soul, particularly the trek up the mountain from Risley to Dara. The air had been crisp that day, rarified despite the grip of summer's fist on the lowlands, and she and Tearlach had worn jackets over their lightweight shirts. As Dara's walls loomed nearer, Remeg (although that was not yet her name) had fallen silent and stared straight ahead, wondering at her inability to slit the child's throat and be done with it. Would he be worse off as wolf food than to spend his days marking time in a stone keep at the edge of a distant sea? Why could she not do what countless mothers before her had done? As her own mother had done to Remeg's sterile brother?

As though it were yesterday, she remembered Tearlach's birth and the unanticipated swell of emotion which motherhood had brought. To Remeg had come the honor of bringing forth a son to bestow wealth and prestige on a family too long without a Husband of their own. To her had come the ridicule of failure for having produced a sterile.

When Remeg refused to kill him, Toreg (Firstwife and Remeg's mother), had ordered one of the Secondwives to do it. Remeg had fled with her son, leaving behind her birthright and the world she knew to cross the continent and hand Tearlach over to an anonymous priestess. She had not hugged him goodbye at the gate (although he tried to embrace her) and she never spoke a word of farewell. She slung him to the ground, tossed down his few belongings, and rode away without once looking back. Had Toreg shown even a spark of empathy for Remeg's position, she would have returned home to bury her memories beneath hard work. Instead, she turned her back on the west coast, changed her name, created a new identity, and took a lowly post in the Caerau garrison.

Tearlach.

Tall and dark like her, thin and angular, with nary a whisper of his father about him. All hers. Was he still alive? Did he remember her? Did she care?

The last thing Remeg wanted to see were the walls of Dara rising over her again. She had no desire to confront the past, let alone risk meeting it face to face, but what alternative did she have? Long ago, love had brought her to Dara and it was love (coupled with an increasingly obsessive sense of vengeance) that sent her back there now.

"Something troubling you, Captain?"

She glanced at Mestipen, who had ridden up alongside her without Remeg having realized it. A soiled bandage covered the wound inflicted by the Chesne arrow. "Not particularly," Remeg said. She wondered what stray expression had given away her mood.

Mestipen stuck a loose strand of hair behind one ear. "You don't worry, Captain. We'll catch them."

"Yes," she said, the word clipped. "We will." They rode in silence, the horses breaking through knee-high drifts of dry snow. Remeg wished that Mestipen would go away, drop back into the body of the troop where she belonged. When it became obvious that she had no intention of doing so, Remeg nonchalantly asked, "What do you know about the Weathercock?"

Mestipen chuckled. "Bless you, Captain. What's brought that old legend to mind? Mercy me, that story's been around as long as I can recall and prob'ly goes back farther than that." She settled more comfortably in her saddle. "It tells of a man who will rise up among the common folk to take the land by force and create a balance of power." She winked. On that ravaged face, it was a grotesque expression. "I don't imagine there's been too many queens particularly fond of that tale. It tends to paint royalty in an uncomplimentary light." Her hand curled into a fist and beat soft time against her thigh as her voice deepened and took on the cadence of a chant. "He rides from the sun like a burning brand, dark of hair, forged steel to hand. The blacksmith finds him in the flame …" She broke off. "Captain?"

The words had wrested a shiver from Remeg. "I'm cold," she said. Her voice sounded brittle to even her ears. "Asabi!" she called out. "Let's stop before these animals fall in their tracks." A collective sigh went up from the troop. As the soldiers dismounted to feed their horses a scant handful of grain and dig through the snow for withered forage, Remeg found a lee of stone out of the wind, turned her face into it, and closed her eyes.

At the juncture where two tunnels merged and turned from the darkness within the mountain toward the filtered light of the outside world, Rai and the others waited for the return of the reconnaissance scouts who had gone out earlier to check the trails and note any activity among the scorched remains of Cadasbyr.

Rai marked the restless shuffle of Ren's feet and the tense angle of her shoulders. The lines on the older woman's face had deepened over the past few days, evidence of the worry she carried. The soldiers billeted in the valley below were bad enough, but Marn had not returned and was now considered missing.

"I ken where she went," Ren had said the night before as she shared a final meal with Rai and Banya. (Kinner had gone off with his new friends.) She poked at the food, moving it around her plate, but had eaten little. "The distance viewer is missin' from my room. She went t' scout Cadasbyr, mark me; thought she'd go an' make a big name for hersel'." Ren's fingers had gripped the rim of her plate so tightly that Rai thought she might hurl it across the room. "I dinna think she'd be that stupid. Why could she no' do as she was told, just this once?"

Now, in the pallid light of a new day, Ren stood with her gaze trained on the faint nimbus of light that marked the entrance and said not a word, but her grief was like a living presence. She knew better than any the meaning of Marn's continued absence.

The black horse nudged Rai's shoulder and she obliged by giving his velvety nostrils a rub, ready to clamp down if he seemed likely to neigh. The jackdaws and jays would be bad enough once they left these caves, screaming in black and blue flashes among the dark green shadows of the pine trees. Many a soldier had learned too late to pay attention to those nosy birds and the raucous way they had of making everyone's business their own.

A few feet away, Banya hunkered with her back against her mare's forelegs. The Carraid's hair was silver-gilt in the pale light, her eyes washed to grey. Though she gave every impression of being at ease, Rai knew better. She worried that Banya was pushing herself to travel too soon. Ollam's care had gone a long way toward healing her, but Rai had caught her friend wincing more than once when she over-did.

Kinner stood draped in shadow but for his eyes and the bold tattoo. In the short time they had spent with the Chesne, he had begun to change from a scared child into a young man Rai scarcely recognized. The idea of him being trained for combat still stuck in her throat like a chicken bone gone sideways and the fact that Ren had gifted him with a sword and dagger only contributed to her uneasiness. The kid would probably lop off his own ears at the first sign of trouble and then bleed to death in the bargain.

A chickadee piped a brief snatch of tune and silent expectation rippled through the group like a shared shiver. When two snow-covered scouts appeared at the mouth of the tunnel, Ren went to meet them.

A light fall of snow dislodged as one of the women tossed back her hood. “The high trails are closed. There’s no goin’ that way.”

The other scout nodded and scrubbed a gloved hand through her hair. “They head north, we’ll be diggin’ their bear-chewed bones out come spring, make no mistake.”

Banya stood. “Where’s that leave us, then?”

Ren stared at the growing light of morn. “You’ll hae t’ head east, cross the Lon. If the snow’s no’ bad, you can stick t’ the hills and keep out o’ sight o’ the lowlands until you reach the Falls.”

Rai pulled a map from her saddlebag and handed it across to Ren. “Show us.”

Ren unfolded the supple sheepskin on which she had drawn their route. Using her finger, she traced a line south and east of the trail they had originally hoped to take. “This route will take ye as far as the foothills below Taran Falls. From that point, you head north an’ west along the river. I know it’s out o’ your way,” she said, cutting Rai off before she could speak. “I dinna see another alternative.”

“Except to stay here and that puts all of you at further risk,” Kinner said. “I won’t have that.”

Banya gave a lop-sided grin. “He’s the boss.”

Rai rolled her eyes. “Spare me.” She scowled at Kinner. “Risk is here, like it or not. Our leaving makes not a jot of difference, so don’t salve your conscience with that, Mister Big Talk.” She put the map away. “Let’s move if we’re going.”

“May the Weathercock watch o’er you,” Ren said. Gesturing the other Chesne ahead of her, she started down the gloom of the tunnel and did not look back.

By mutual accord Banya rode point, the broad chest of the hardy, Carraid-bred mare breaking through the worst of the drifts for the smaller, more lightly built animals. It was slow going and cold. The storm was ended and the clouds had cleared, but the blizzardy wind remained. It bit the bare skin of their faces and taunted them with blinding sheets of thrown snow.

They reached the Lon as the pale sun dipped the last of its watery radiance behind the mountain peaks and washed the world with a cloak of plum shadows. The river was grey and sluggish in the dusky light, the water flecked with ice. They set up their tent in the shelter of a stand of firs and Banya prepared dinner while Kinner and Rai cared for the horses.

Kinner ducked his head as he entered the tent. Coming in behind him,

Rai wondered if it was her imagination or had he actually grown a couple of inches? "No fire?" he said a bit wistfully as he settled onto his bed and received his share of way-bread and venison jerky.

"Not until we're well away," Rai said. "The less mark we make on our surroundings, the better our chances that thrice-blasted Mestipen won't find us. We'll be warm enough if we pig-pile. You'll just have to forgive Banya her snoring."

The Carraid slapped the inside of her thigh. "Forgive this, shithead." Her jaws worked around a chewy bite of venison. "I'd rather sleep with the horses than with you."

"Sleeping beats what you usually do with them." Rai tipped Kinner a wink fat with innuendo. For all his new-found worldliness as a steely-eyed killer, the boy blushed and looked away.

Banya kicked her partner's foot. "Just for that, you take first watch. Kinner'll come after and I'll take the last."

Kinner smiled, happy to be included. "That sounds gre –"

Rai held up both hands. "Whoa, now. He is *not* going to stand watch."

"Why not?" Banya and Kinner said together.

"Because he'll either fall asleep or rouse us at every little noise."

"Thanks for the vote of confidence," Kinner said. He bit off a chunk of bread. "I'm not entirely useless, you know."

"I'm not saying you are. But you've had four days of training, bucko." She held up her fingers. "*Four.* They may have been stiff days and you may have learned a lot, but to my mind that makes you worse than useless. It makes you dangerous. You've had just enough instruction to make you believe you're pretty hot stuff. That sort of thinking could get us killed easier than *that.*" She snapped her fingers.

Banya scratched an eyebrow. "You … you mean the way *you* almost did the first time you took up a sword?" She wrenched off another bite of jerky with her back teeth and chewed with bovine equanimity.

Rai glared at her. "I think I hate you so much because you remind me of my mother."

Banya smiled sweetly. "The dead one?"

In the end, it went just as Banya had said it would. Kinner took his turn at watch, no one was murdered in their beds, and everyone but Rai got a decent night's sleep. She had to admit that Kinner did his best to behave like a seasoned veteran. He had woken immediately at her touch on his shoulder and had roused Banya when it was her turn. As the Carraid stepped out of the tent, he had slipped off his boots, crawled into the warm hollow of her vacated spot next to Rai, and was asleep in seconds.

Morning found them early away. It was colder than yesterday and the horses snorted plumes of hot breath. Banya glowered at the sky. "We're in for more snow."

Rai frowned, cranky from lack of sleep. "It's winter, you dumb schlub. Of course it's going to snow."

"Bite me, bitch."

At noon they paused for a short break, eating in the saddle while the horses pawed the snow in a half-hearted attempt to forage. To the north rose the Corydon Mountains, rank upon serried rank of peaks, each steeper than the last, grey and ochre and violet, disappearing behind a low veil of clouds. To the south lay a range of high hills, not yet mountains but not quite foothills. Beyond those were the flat plains that led to the sea.

The second night passed much like the first. Kinner stood watch and reported seeing a red fox, although he never glimpsed the owl that left the marks of wing-tips in the snow where it snatched a mouse from its chilly warren. Banya saw the red reflection of a weasel's eyes and heard the growling rush of a fisher cat somewhere in the branches overhead. When it was Rai's turn, she listened to the crunch and squeal of snow under her boots and paused once in dread at what sounded like the distant whinny of a horse. When none of their own animals reacted to the noise, she heaved a gigantic sigh.

The next morning was colder still. Rai and Banya looked at each other, communicating in their silent partnership, and broke camp early. They both knew what the lock-down of cold meant.

They were on the trail no more than a couple of hours before the snow arrived. It began as a few anemic, breeze-borne flurries, but quickly developed in a sly and sinister way into a steady drive of thick flakes that softened the sharp edges of rock and tree and turned the world into a moving wall of white.

"Wait," Kinner called from the rear.

Rai drew rein and turned in her saddle. "We can't stop here. We need to find a place to hole up."

"My horse is walking funny." He slung a leg over the round curve of the animal's rump and dismounted into snow that reached past his knees.

Colorful invective came from the broad expanse of Banya's snow-dusted back as she jumped to the ground and walked back to join him. "Which leg?"

"I don't know."

It turned out to be the right rear, although Banya checked them all just to be certain. With the hoof cocked up and secured between her knees, she showed him the underside. "See this spot here?" She pointed. "That's called the frog. Don't ask why, 'cause I don't know." She prodded it with a gentle finger and the mare flinched. "She's caught a piece of ice and it's cut the skin. It's not bad, but she'll be dead lame if she has to walk all day. I can put something on it as a temporary fix, but she needs to rest and keep off it."

Rai's summation was succinct. "Fuck." She looked around. "You want to make camp here?"

Banya blew a sigh that temporarily vanished her face behind a cloud of smoky breath. "It's not my first choice, no." She slit her eyes against the wind. "This storm's coming out of the east. We're riding straight into it. Let's head south a mite. The going should be a little easier in the lowlands and we can make camp to sit this one out." She lowered the mare's hoof and watched the animal cock the leg to keep from putting weight on it. Frowning, the Carraid slogged back to her horse, pulled some supplies from the saddle-bags, and set to work making the animal comfortable.

What she did was arcane and Kinner said as much. Even Rai, who had watched her perform such tasks countless times, did not understand everything that went into one of Banya's horse-related potions. She watched her bind the concoction of powders together with a familiar greenish ointment. "Is that some of the stuff Ollam used on you?"

The round apples of Banya's cheeks rose into view above her scarf as she smiled. "The plantain? Yeah. Amazing stuff. She gave me a jar and the recipe. I'm going to send it home to my mother." She winked. "Maybe we'll deliver it in person, eh?"

Rai, in truth, had never felt any desire to go to Carraidland, but now she nodded. It was nice to think about a future away from these mountains. "Sure. Whatever you say."

"Which is the way it should always be." Cradling the mare's foot, Banya coated the injury with the poultice, then packed the cavity with padding and tied a length of white cloth around the hoof to keep everything in place. Eyeing her handiwork, she straightened and patted the mare's rump. "That should ease it until we find a place to camp. Kinner, divide your packs between me and Rai so the mare doesn't have to carry any weight but you. We'll go easy, but you tell me the minute she seems any worse."

They remounted and rode south.

With little sleep and nothing to look at but the back of Banya's coat and the hypnotic fall of snow, Rai's eyes canted to half-mast. She slumped in the saddle, her mind wandering in a lazy state between wakefulness and sleep. She was so relaxed that she nearly fell off her horse when Banya's mare suddenly stopped and the black ran into her.

The mare pinned her ears and gave a little kick. "Quit it," Banya said. She drew her reins in tight.

"What's wrong?" Kinner said from the rear.

Banya shook her head. "I don't know. She's picked up on something. Could be a herd of deer or …"

The black's nostrils fluttered wide as he scented the wind. "Oh, shit!" Rai cried and lunged too late to stop his trumpeting cry. The mares joined in and were answered.

The garrison troop materialized out of the storm like horse-prowed ships breasting the white foam of the sea, riding breakers of ice and snow. A bow's *twang!* was all the warning they had before an arrow rammed into Rai's saddle just above her knee. In one move, they wrenched their horses' heads around and drove in their heels. From behind, a cry went up like the bay of hounds on the hunt.

At first, Rai and the others managed to out-strip their pursuers. Banya's mare forged ahead fleet and strong, with the black close behind. The injured mare did her best to keep up, but suddenly she wallowed. Kinner cried out in desperation and kicked her hard, but the poor beast had no more to give.

Aware at some visceral level that he was no longer with them, Rai hazarded a glance over her shoulder in time to see the mare stumble to a halt. Swearing, she yanked the black around in an arc, almost tearing the bit from his mouth, and came at the mare from behind, determined to drive her forward. The animal cringed and shuddered beneath the lash of the reins, but would not move.

Kinner was nearly sobbing with fear. "She can't! She's hurt!"

"We'll be more than hurt if they catch us!"

Ahead of them, Banya hauled rein and stood in the stirrups with the Carraid mare dancing in agitation beneath her. "The river's just ahead! If we can get across, maybe we can lose them on the other side!"

Snarling, Rai beat the mare. Crying out, the animal leaped forward, hobbling on three legs, and the black drove her toward the water.

The Sower was like something out of a nightmare. Miles below the falls, this raging water slowed, changed its name, and grew tame, bringing custom and merchandise to those lands beyond the waiting sea. Here, though, the river was insane, a roaring and hungry thing that plunged untamed in a cascading bellow of sound and deep green water over the breach of Taran Falls.

Kinner's mount stopped short at the sight of that torrential churning. Eyes rolling in terror, she tried to back away from the river's edge and an arrow took her high in the rump. Screaming, desperate to escape the pain, she sprang through the pelting drive of icy spray and into the torrent, taking Kinner with her.

The black plunged into the river like a *shoopiltee,* the water-horse that Rai's father had said lived in the lake near Cadasbyr. Rai's mouth and nose filled with water as they submerged, then the stallion broke the surface and struck out for the distant shore. Spitting water, Rai clung to the saddle with both hands and glanced back in time to see the dappled mare and her rider launch into the river like it was a brook they could step across.

Banya waved to let Rai know she was all right and that was when the arrow struck, slamming hard into the small of her back. The Carraid jerked, eyes wide with shock, and collapsed forward, clutching the saddle to keep from slipping off into the river.

"NO!" Rai screamed and sawed at the black's mouth, trying to turn him, but he would have none of it. Neck out, he ignored her and forged ahead, overtaking Kinner's mare just as her hind legs gave out. She slewed sideways and Kinner screamed, hauling on the reins. Torn in two directions, Rai thought she would go mad. "Leave her!" she bellowed to the boy and thrust out a hand. "Come on! Leave her!"

Dropping the reins, he grabbed Rai's hand, kicked free of the stirrups, and threw himself toward her. The mare floundered and the river, roaring like a beast, claimed her as prey. In a spindly thrashing of dark legs against the pelt of snow, she rolled onto her back and pitched over the falls.

Hungry for more now that it had fed, the river seized the black. Whinnying in defiance, he battled for the far shore. Rai's left hand, knotted in a tangle of reins and mane, clutched the saddle for all she was worth as frigid water surged above her shoulders and spume brought the metallic taste of grit. She leaned sideways, dragging Kinner against the pull of the river. Her shoulder, canted backward, felt like it might erupt from the socket.

A log whirling out of the maelstrom slammed into Kinner, tearing his hand from Rai's. She caught a single glimpse of his terrified face, white against the surging roil of dark water, before he was sucked over the falls. His dying wail rang in her ears as the black lurched ashore.

EIGHTEEN

Torqua Bin hunched deep in her furs and glared at the twisting fall of snow. There should have been six more weeks in which to make this journey, six more weeks of doing bits of business, stockpiling northern goods and stories in anticipation of half a year or better spent trading in the southern climes. Winter had played them a great dirty joke, catching them while they were still in the mountains. In an emergency she supposed they could winter-over in one of the hill towns, but months of looking at nothing but the same indigent peasant faces would drive her to homicide.

The Tzigane gypsies depended upon travel for their livelihood. The loss of those precious months in the south would not only upset their trade and travel schedules, but also deny them the wares that made them welcome in the north. Because this was so, Torqua had started the wagons south, moving in a slow single file along the meandering bank of the Calleigh when anyone with a lick of sense was battened down somewhere warm.

There were twenty of them in the tribe, broken into five somewhat inter-related families, each with its own wagon. Nineteen women and one man. Old Mander Nicabar was toothless and no longer able to sire children, but he had his uses and the tribe was fond of him so Torqua let him stay. The other male in the tribe, Asker Sim, had died eight years ago this month, just after the birth of his son Tig to Mur Zayac.

Memories of puppy-eyed Tig fanned the hot coals of Torqua's heart. There had been rumors that the queen's agents rode in search of men, taking them without paying, but she had discounted those stories as hearsay until direct experience had taught her differently. Wee Tig (barely eight years old, his fertility as yet unproven) had been stolen from Mur's wagon three months back while the rest of the tribe was busy entertaining the evening's crowd in Lach. The gypsies had searched the town from church steeple to dank cellar, but the boy had vanished like a dream. Since then, Mur had been worthless, vacant-eyed when she bothered to wake at all. Meanwhile, Torqua fed her outrage and entertained cheerful thoughts of evisceration.

"May Blas, Goddess of Fire, roast Trevelyan's guts before her dying eyes," she muttered. "May Erda, Lady of Soil, stuff her mouth so that she drowns in dirt. May Kern of the Waves let crabs to feast on her womanhood. May …"

The swaying curtain behind her parted and a kerchiefed head poked out. "Did you say something, Mama?" Nepter's black eyes were bright with interest.

"Nothing worth listening to, child."

"Oh." The teenager nodded. "Tig again?"

"Among other things."

A sobering look came into the girl's eyes. She chewed the inside of her cheek in thought. When she spoke again, it was not about what Torqua thought was on her mind. "Can I go for a ride?"

Her mother gestured at the sky. "In this? Are you out of your mind?"

The pretty girl wrinkled her nose. "I'm bored. All Narain wants to do is play with the cards and Aunty Lordibi is snoring and farting from all those beans she ate at lunch." She waved a hand in front of her nose. "*Phew!*" She put on her most beseeching face. "May I *please* ride, Mama?"

Torqua hid a smile. Her twins were seventeen. She adored them and indulged them more than was wise, but not today. "Save the theatrics for the paying customers, girly-girl."

Nepter leaned her forearms along her mother's well-padded shoulders and rested her chin atop Torqua's head. "Chat could use the exercise," she wheedled. The stocky white pony had been a gift to the girls in celebration of their spring birthday. Nepter had instantaneously fallen in love with the beast. Narain, who was more inclined to quiet boyish activities than her sister, had little interest in the animal beyond braiding its mane and tail.

"He's getting plenty of exercise tied to the back of this wagon. I'm not having you get lost in this storm."

"I won't get lost. I'll ride just ahead."

Torqua sighed. "Girl, do not push your luck with me today. If you're so eager to be out-of-doors, plunk your pretty ass down on this seat and give me a rest." She offered the reins. When the girl did not take them at once, Torqua gave them a shake. "I'm not asking."

Nepter's mouth twisted. Resigned to her fate, she climbed over the back of the seat and took her mother's place on the thin pad of cushion.

"We want another couple of hours if we can manage it. Keep along the river and stay well to the middle of the road. Don't let the horses stray or you'll have us bogged."

"I know the trail, Mama."

Quick, strong fingers found the girl's earlobe under the woven covering of her kerchief and tweaked it hard. "No back talk or you'll spend the next couple of hours knee-deep in snow walking point. Then we'll see how well you know the trail." Torqua released her daughter and parted the canvas curtain to step into the wagon. She wrinkled her nose. Nepter had not been joking. The place stank.

A small stove kept the inside of the wagon warm and a chimney pipe through the roof saved them all from being smoked like a side of meat. Drying laundry hung from lines strung front-to-back. An overhead lantern swung back and forth with the motion of the wagon, dancing light and shadow across the interior, giving a sense of movement to the stowed boxes and trunks. Ancient Lordibi slept in a tied-down rocking chair with her head tipped forward, wattled chin pillowed on the loose softness of her ample bosom. Her snores carried the ear-twanging whine of a cicada's buzz and one side of her mouth wiffled on the exhale. Her bitch dog Rat, hardly bigger than the rodent for which it was named, lay curled around the old woman's feet.

Narain sat on the bed with her legs tucked beneath thick woolen skirts. Shuffling a deck of dog-eared cards from hand to hand, she looked up and smiled brightly as her mother entered. "Hello, Mama."

"Aunty stinking you out, daughter?"

"No. I just raise a flap and air things out when it gets bad."

"You lose heat that way."

The girl made a face. "It's worth it."

Torqua chuckled and shrugged off her outer coat. She watched as Narain's deft hands, slender fingers decked with numerous cheap rings, laid out the cards in a wagon-wheel pattern. "Practicing?"

One of the girl's narrow shoulders lifted. "Sort of. I wanted to tell fortunes, but Neppy's being a toad and Aunty's asleep, so we can't even play pretend." Finishing the spread, she turned up the first card. Her lips pouted into a moue of disgust.

"What's that face for?" Torqua unwound her scarf and hung it over one of the many wooden pegs that stuck out of the wagon uprights. Chafing her hands together, she settled down on the bed beside her child.

Narain gestured. "I've done this spread half a dozen times and the Drowned Man keeps coming up in the center."

"In the Questioner's spot?" The lines and faded colors of the cards were familiar to Torqua from birth, although she had only a rudimentary understanding of what the symbols meant and absolutely no talent for divination (not even of the pretend sort). In the middle of Narain's spread lay the Drowned Man, his card all faded greens, purples, and silvers where he'd lain too long under water. His eyes were closed and his brown hair waved in the paper current. "Is that bad?"

"Not bad so much, but damned strange."

"Is it something we should worry about?"

"I don't think so."

Torqua knew by the way she said it that Narain was uncertain *how* to take it. She considered waking Lordibi to let the talented old soothsayer have a go, but let the whim slide. If there was trouble coming to the tribe, it probably could not be avoided by the turning of a few cards. "Who'd you have in mind when you did the spread?"

"All of us." Narain swept the cards together into a hasty stack and wrapped them with the silk cloth in which they were kept when not in use. "I know you're not supposed to have more than one focus, but it was only play-work."

"And the same card came up every time?" When her daughter nodded, Torqua said, "Well, what's it mean, the Drowned Man?"

Narain tucked a strand of hair behind one ear. "Change, mostly."

"For good or naught?"

"Could be either. The outcome depends upon how the other cards influence that one."

"Bollocks," Torqua said, not quite meaning it. She pursed her lips and wished she had stayed outside where her worries consisted of the weather and the whereabouts of a missing child. Cold of the flesh beat cold of the spirit any day.

The wagon lurched suddenly and stopped, leaning to one side. Torqua steadied herself with a hand against an overhead beam as Narain leapt up to keep Lordibi from jolting out of her chair. The old woman blinked in confusion. "What is it?" she said, querulous from the abrupt awakening. "What's the matter?"

"The matter is your grandniece! *Blast!*" Torqua snatched her coat from the peg. "I said not to let the horses stray, didn't I? Oh, but she knows everything about everything, doesn't she, just?" She thrust her arms into the coat and did up the front. "Now she's gone and put us into a hole! How long will we have to muck about with that?" She wove her scarf around her neck and headed for the door. "Nepter!" She thrust her head into the frigid air. Much to her surprise, the girl was not on the wagon seat nor anywhere to be seen. "Nepter! Where in the blazing hells are you?"

"Down here!" The cry came from over the side of the riverbank.

"I'll kill her," Torqua muttered. "Stone dead, I'll kill her." She jumped from the listing wagon and waded through the snow in the direction of her daughter's voice. She rarely beat her children (and could not, in truth, recall the last time she had been forced to employ more than an ear tweak or a dark look to alter their behavior), but that was about to change. "'I know the trail, Mama,'" she spat. "You'll know it once you've walked it from here to Emeram." She stopped on the crest of the steep riverbank and looked down.

A body lay face-down on the wet, snow-capped rocks. Nepter crouched nearby, prodding it with a stick.

"That's what you drove us off the trail for?"

The girl dropped the stick with a flush of guilt. "I'm sorry, Mama. I was trying to keep an eye on it until we got closer and I guess I didn't pay attention to the road."

"You guess?" Torqua jerked her chin. "She alive?"

Nepter slid a hand along the neck and felt for a pulse. After a tense moment, her head bobbed an affirmation.

Torqua sighed. "Drat." The rules of the road demanded she offer aid where it was needed. This was a code to which every Tzigane adhered. You never knew when you might be on the receiving end and gold passed from hand to hand as easily as shit. A live body required warmth and food. Then again, a live *unconscious* body would never know that its pockets had been turned out. "Any money on her?"

The girl felt inside the pockets she could reach and came up empty. She tucked her hands beneath the body, shoved to roll it over, and drew back in surprise. "It's a man!"

Torqua called over her shoulder to the tribe where they waited on the road. "Make camp!" She glanced at the sky and sighed. "We won't get the damned wagon freed before dark, anyway," she muttered and started down the bank toward her daughter. *Here's your drowned man, Narain,* she thought. *I wonder what it means.*

Kinner woke to darkness, his mind a confusing welter of half-remembered images. He listened, but heard nothing to indicate that anyone in the house was awake. *Good.* Perhaps he could cadge a few more hours' sleep and get rid of this pounding headache before he had to get up and make breakfast. He shifted, stretched … and froze with the realization that this was not his bed. This lumpy tick mattress was wider and longer than his own, as if meant to hold more than two people. The room smelled differently, too. In place of the briny scent of the sea, the air carried a dry and smoky odor, dusty with herbs. He struggled to sit up, but the pain in his head dropped him back onto the pillow with a groan.

"So you've decided to live after all." The voice came from beyond the end of the bed. The wick of an oil lantern was turned up slightly, brightening the room, and he saw a broad-shouldered woman sitting in a wicker-work chair.

"Banya?"

"No." She rose and stepped closer. For a moment Kinner thought it was Rai, but this woman was olive-skinned, taller and heavier than his friend, dressed in colorful, mismatched clothing. Her long black hair was pulled back in a braid and a series of gold rings spangled each ear. "I'm Torqua Bin."

Although he had never seen the Tzigane, Kinner had heard enough stories from his aunts – how the gypsies peddled their wares and simples, sold lies, and stole you blind – to recognize one when he saw her. She sat on the edge of the bed and laid a palm across his forehead. "No fever," she said with a nod of satisfaction. "How do you feel?"

"Terrible." The warmth of her hand felt good against his face. It reminded him of Holan. "I have a headache and my toes and fingers are prickly."

"That's frostburn. Jibben got to it in time, so it isn't likely you'll lose any dangly bits." She crossed one knee over the other. "Found you beached like a salmon. This is an interesting time of year to be swimming."

Despite the sick pounding in his head, memory rolled over Kinner like a breaker. "My horse went down in the river. Rai grabbed me, but I lost my grip."

Torqua leaned close, peering into his face. "You went over Taran Falls?" She sounded like she did not believe him.

He pressed the heel of his hand between his eyes. His head *really* hurt. "I think that's what Banya called it."

"Hm." She pulled her bottom lip, lost in thought. "This Rai and Banya, they your family?"

"Sort of." Sleep wound smoky fingers around his brain and tugged with gentle insistence. "Where am I?" he asked around a yawn.

Torqua ran a hand over his hair and did not answer his question. "You have a name or should I make one up for you?"

"Kinner," he mumbled, eyes half-closed with weariness.

She patted his shoulder. "Well then, friend-Kinner. You rest easy. We'll talk more when you're up to it." She rose to leave, but paused with a hand on the door. "At least I'll talk. Maybe you'll just listen." There was a faint dance of firelight beyond the open door, but Kinner was sound asleep by the time it clicked shut.

When he woke again, it was to the rolling sway of a wagon in motion. He blinked at the ceiling, getting his bearings, and bit by bit the world came together. There were gaps in his memory, but he could recall the cold and eely smell of the river and the warmth of Torqua Bin's hand on his forehead. He knew they had spoken, but could not remember the details.

Daylight filtered through hairline chinks in the walls and rimmed the edge of the rear door in a bright rectangle. From outside came the jingle of harness and the snort and stamp of horses. A dog barked and a woman's sharp voice called it to order. The voice sounded a little like Rai's.

Kinner's heart clenched. Where were they, she and Banya? Had they escaped Remeg or had they fallen, sliced to bits by arrow and sword?

The sword!

He groaned and rolled onto his side, knees drawn to his chest. Banya had taken the weapon when his horse came up lame. Was it in Remeg's hands now, reward for the lives taken in Casasbyr? Had it crossed the water to safety or did it lie on the riverbed, the box wedged among rocks, the brilliant sword drowned beyond all hope of recovery?

Was the Weathercock doomed to remain empty-handed because of him?

In a sudden burst of resolve, he threw back the covers and swung his legs over the side of the bed. His feet danced on the cold floor as he hunted for his clothing. What he found was a thunder jug that his over-taxed bladder greeted with enthusiasm. When the pressure in his abdomen was gone, he resumed the search for his clothes. Against the sounds of the moving wagon, he did not hear the creak as someone swung onto the outside stair nor did he realize anyone was there until the door opened and pinned him, naked, in a spill of daylight.

White teeth flashed in a dusky-hued face as the figure outlined in the doorway paused. "You'll do," Torqua said in appreciation. She stepped inside and closed the door, cutting off the light only for the moment it took to turn up the overhead lantern.

In that bit of darkness, Kinner dove for the safety of the bed, pulling the covers up to his chin as he backed into a corner. Blush heated his face as the light came up, and he knew by Torqua's grin that she saw it. "You could have knocked."

"It's *my* wagon, boy."

"I was looking for my clothes."

"All in good time." She placed a covered basket on the bed and gestured. "That's breakfast."

"Thank you." He took it onto his lap and lifted the lid. Inside was a billy can of tea and some corn bread. An earthenware bowl contained a spicy mixture of beans and onions. Kinner's stomach growled audibly.

Torqua chuckled. "That's a good sign. I guess you'll live after all." She dragged a chair to a spot in front of the door and sat down. "Go ahead. I can talk while you eat." She waited until he had downed a wedge of bread and a half-cup of tea before she began. "Tell me about this 'sort of' family of yours, this Rai and Banya."

"They're my friends." He realized with a start that the words were true. They were his friends, the first real ones he had ever had. "Friends who are like family," he amended. He ate a spoonful of beans. "My real family …" He paused to chew, swallow, and think. With no Rai or Banya to claim him, would the gypsies send him back to Moselle? "My real family lives north of Cadasbyr." That, he realized, was also true.

"In the hills?" When he nodded, Torqua pursed her lips in consideration. "You don't strike me as hill folk get."

His heart gave a thump. He shrugged and concentrated on the meal. "I'm adopted."

Torqua grunted. "Rough time of year to be traveling."

Kinner nodded. "We got caught out by the bad weather coming early."

She snorted. "I know all about that. Where were you headed?"

"To the monastery at Dara. I'm sterile."

"I can see that." She leaned back in the chair and stretched her legs out in front of her. "We played there this past spring. Not the monastery, mind, but Risley. We camped in the meadow. Some of the monks came down to watch the show and buy a few items, thread, buckets, useful sorts of stuff. My but they're a silent and hollow-eyed bunch. You sure you want to go there?"

Why such a seemingly innocent question should send a flicker of warning along every nerve, Kinner did not know. "What choice do I have?" he said guardedly. He drained his cup and refilled it.

"Plenty, last I heard." Her dark eyes gleamed in the lantern light. "Hill folk don't send their sterile sons to Dara, Kinner."

The food went to ashes in his mouth.

Torqua crossed her legs at the ankle and steepled her fingers beneath her chin. Her sleeves pulled up from her wrists at the motion and Kinner saw bright tattoos. "We saved your life. We've tended you and fed you. It's pretty unfair of you to meet such generosity with lies." Before he could respond, she added, "The world works in strange and mysterious ways, don't you think?"

No longer hungry, he put aside the rest of the food. "How do you mean?" he said cautiously.

"Well, you've no way of knowing this, but some time back a little boy was stolen from our caravan."

Kinner's heart clenched in compassion. "Was it the queen?"

"So you've heard the stories, too." Torqua nodded. "That's our best guess." She spread her hands open, palm up. "Where one is taken, another is given."

Kinner drew the blankets up further. "I told you. I'm sterile."

"I heard you. Men can be used for other things besides making babies." Her smile was gilt over cheap goods. "You'll learn to like life with us. Behave yourself and you'll be well treated. And you'll get to see the world in the bargain."

Weeks ago, he might have accepted the offer with eagerness. Certainly it was better than what his aunts had proposed as his Fate. Thanks to Banya and the Chesne, however, Kinner understood there were possibilities open to him that he had never imagined. "I appreciate the offer, but I can't accept."

Torqua's smile faded. "It's no *offer,* boy. You'll do as you're told. You're found goods, free and clear for the taking."

He sat up straight. "You can't just keep me like some sort of pet!"

She laughed. "Of course we can! That's what men are! What makes you think differently?"

His fingers clenched in the blankets. "If you do that, you're no different than those who stole your boy."

Before Kinner had met the Chesne, Torqua's slap would have found its mark. Now he ducked under the swing of her hand ("*You're fast,*" Danika said in his memory. "*You just don't know it yet.*"), and threw himself from the bed. Scrabbling across the floor on all fours, he gained his feet, yanked the door open, and leaped to the ground, landing knee-deep in an explosion of cold that took his breath away. There was the brief impression of two pairs of startled eyes from the next wagon, then he darted off among the trees. Frigid air chewed his naked body, tasting tender flesh. Without proper clothing there was no hope of survival, but new instincts had taken hold of him and he let them have their way.

A shout off to his left and the baying of a hound told him he was spotted. He cut to the right and raced along a ridge, searching for a place to hide. From the corner of one eye he caught a blur of motion. Seconds later, the side of his head exploded in pain and he crashed to the ground in a spray of snow.

Pain had taken Kinner out and it was pain that brought him back, pulsing in his temple with an intensity that bordered on nausea. The first thing he saw when he dared to open his eyes was a man's wizened and ancient face just inches from his own. He recoiled with a grunt of surprise and the oldster smiled, exposing gums as naked as a newborn baby's.

"Little Feeny's a killer shot with that sling, ain't she?" said the old man.

"My head hurts."

"I imagine it does. She hit you with a fair-sized rock. Brought you down like a struck goose, she did. You're lucky she didn't want you dead."

Kinner filed that bit of information away for later consideration and raised a tentative hand to his forehead. A lump the size of a small apple met his questing fingers with another bleat of pain. Gentle old hands took hold of his and pressed it back against the mattress. "Leave that alone. Don't you have any sense?"

"If I do, I don't know where I put it." Kinner looked at the old man, with his long white hair pulled back in a horse's tail and bushy eyebrows bristling like scrub forest. "Who are you?"

"Mander Nicabar. You thirsty? Jibben said I was to give you something to drink when you woke up." A cup appeared before Kinner's eyes, bobbing and weaving with the faint palsy of the elder's hands.

The motion made him feel more queasy. He steadied the cup with his own hand and drank. The water was warm and carried a bitter flavor. "I didn't know there were Tzigane men."

Mander laughed. "Where do you think Tzigane babies come from?"

"I meant –"

"I know what you meant." The old man sobered. "There's just me now that Tig's gone. I'm too old for much good, but they keep me around." Mander grinned suddenly with the impish expression of a child and a small silver coin appeared in his hand. Kinner watched in fascination as it walked across the spotted, shaking knuckles and back again. "I can still do a trick or two. You like tricks?" Mander's voice was hopeful.

"Maybe later."

The old man looked disappointed and put the coin away. "Why'd you run? You'd just die out there and what's the use in that?"

Kinner's brain spun like a child's whirligig. "I don't want to be a whore."

Mander snorted, spraying Kinner with saliva. "Posh! That's a good line of work, that is. Ain't no hardship." His lined face screwed up into a frown. "What would you rather do?"

Kinner waved the question aside. He pressed his hand tight against his temple and willed the pain away with no success. "By the Comb, this *hurts.*"

Mander offered the cup again. "Drink this up. There's willow bark in it. That'll take the pain away in time, and there's something else to help you rest." He watched while Kinner drained the cup. "You believe in the Weathercock, eh?"

He had uttered the oath by accident. "Do the Tzigane worship the Three-Headed Goddess?" he said to avoid the question. Sleepiness circled his head.

Mander shook his head. "We don't need her or your Weathercock."

Kinner fought against the pull of the drugs to keep his eyes open a few moments longer. "What do the Tzigane believe in?"

The old man's expression was hawk-proud. "Ourselves."

Nineteen

Rai was stirred from the light doze into which she had fallen by a boot nudging her foot. She raised her head, blinked sleepily at the face bending over her, and scrubbed a sleeve across her eyes. "Eir." She cleared her throat. "Is something wrong? What time is it?"

"Does it matter?" The Carraid physician shook her head in annoyance. "I told you to go to sleep hours ago. I didn't mean for you to do it here." She gestured at the low wooden bench on which Rai lay. "We purposely don't pad these seats so people won't be tempted to roost, but every time I come by, here you are."

Rai looked chastened. She could not seem to pull herself away from this spot for more than a few minutes at a time. What if Banya needed her? She sat up and swung her legs off the bench, her eyes straying to the door across the hall. "I, um, I didn't have anywhere else to, uh, go."

"Have you slept in a bed at all the past few days?"

Rai stared at her feet, feeling somewhat like a wayward girl. "A bit."

"A bit." Eir snorted. "Are you eating?"

She shrugged. "Some. It's just … I'm not very hungry and …" Her voice trailed off.

Eir laid a compassionate hand on her shoulder. "I know," she said gently. "No matter how good the meal is, it still tastes like dirt when you're worried." She sighed. "Well, since you seem determined to loiter," a smile removed any sting from the words, "You may as well come in and make yourself to home. Banya's not awake, but you can sit by her if that will help."

Rai returned the smile with enormous relief. "Thank you. Yes, that would help a lot."

The physician opened the door and ushered Rai inside ahead of her. Soft-footed in slippers, terrified she might disturb sleeping the patient, Rai tip-toed across the room and stood at the foot of the bed. Banya's face was waxy against the pillow case but for a patch of rosy color high in each cheek that reminded Rai uncomfortably of Holan and the false vigor the blacksmith had displayed until the very end.

"Will she live?"

Eir checked her patient's pulse and stroked a hand across Banya's brow. "Lung wounds are chancy things, Rai, and difficult to predict. She may be here awhile." A slight smile dimpled both cheeks and made the middle-aged doctor suddenly look like a teenager. "You'll be here, too, yes?"

Rai gently touched the tip of one finger to the lift of blankets that was Banya's left foot. "I've no place else to go," she said softly.

"Then sit you down." The doctor patted the back of a chair drawn up close beside the bed. When Rai had settled into it, Eir shook open a colorful blanket and draped it across her lap. "Who knows? If you get comfortable, you might even take a nap." She withdrew and the door clicked shut behind her.

It had been three days since Banya was struck by the arrow; three days since they had fled across the Sower and passed beyond the western borders of Carraidland. Banya had ridden for as long as she could before she lost her grip and slid from the saddle, collapsing into a boneless heap on the ground. Unable to get her friend back on the horse, Rai had wrapped every blanket they owned around Banya and left her to seek help. The mare, responding to the odd symbiosis which all Carraid shared with their mounts, had lain down beside her rider.

Rai had not found the Carraid, they had found her. They challenged her presence and listened to her rattled explanation, then half of them raced off in a thunder of hoof beats while the rest escorted Rai elsewhere, under protest, to be further interrogated. When she was finally allowed to ask questions of her own, she learned that Banya had undergone surgery and the consensus was that the wound was very bad. Her family had been sent for. The words had laid a freezing hand across Rai's heart.

As Eir had hoped, Rai slept. When she woke, she found that someone had brought in a tray with a plate of biscuits and a glazed brown teapot shaped like a grass-fattened pony. She yawned, stretched the kink out of her back and neck, and sat up. Banya had shifted in her sleep, but otherwise things remained unchanged.

What would my life have been without you? Rai wondered, looking at her. Ten years ago, Banya had discovered the frightened, bedraggled, half-starved child that was Rai hidden in the garrison barn, pilfering grain to eat and chewing it dry without the wherewithal to make gruel. It was Banya who coaxed her out of hiding and got her a bath and a hot meal; Banya who had taken Rai under her wing and then vouched for her to Captain Pel in order to get her a job and a bed.

"If you die, you dumb blonde," she whispered. "I'll never forgive you."

She stood up and walked back and forth a few times to clear her head and get the blood circulating. On a cloudless day, this many-windowed room would be filled with light. Today it was draped in shades of grey, a decor that fitted her mood perfectly. Returning to her chair, she poured a cup of tea, chose a biscuit, and sat back to eat.

Motion beyond one window caught her eye, halting her breath. For an instant she saw what she feared most – Remeg and her soldiers galloping across the rolling hills of yellow grass. Then she blinked, the image faded, and she realized that what she was looking at was a great river of horses – white, chestnut, bay, black, grey, sorrel, splotched and freckled. Their manes and tails flicked and tossed like spume on a wave as riders circled and called and drove them on.

It had been explained to her that this was the Fall Roundup, an occasion for much celebration among the Carraid. The vast herds of Carraidland grazed mountain-wild all summer and required neither the constant tending of a shepherd nor a dog's watchful eye. Speed was their protection and the strike of a well-placed hoof, which could crush to pulp the flesh and bones of any predator foolish enough to hazard an attack. Riders checked the condition of the herds every few weeks and most of the animals would come to hand if called. There were always a few who resisted, believing themselves to be truly wild, but their challenge was sport and play to the Carraid and no animal went ungentled. As winter approached, the horses were brought to the lowlands where they were less likely to mire and starve in deep snow. This year the early snowfall had made the work difficult. A couple hundred horses had been gathered so far, with more to come. In the spring, after the birthing of the foals, the cycle would begin anew.

Banya had once recounted to Rai the process by which a Carraid bonded with a foal. Throughout the chosen mare's estrus, the joining with the stallion, and the quickening of the pregnancy, the future rider waited with impatience for the first glimpse of tiny hooves and soft wiffling nostrils beneath the mare's tail. Banya had been the first to lay hands upon the dappled filly as it slid warm and wet from its dam. With a handful of straw she had worked alongside the rasping lick of the mother's busy tongue to wipe the foal dry, murmuring words of love and encouragement in a sing-song accompaniment to the mare's grunts of pleasure. Banya's hands had guided the questing mouth to the nipple for its first suck. Warm milk had dribbled over her fingers and across the foal's hungry lips, giving the baby a taste of both mother and rider-to-be.

"If you wanted to come to Carraidland so blasted much, all you had to do was say so. You didn't have to almost kill me to do it."

Rai lurched forward, spilling her tea as she grabbed Banya's hand in both of hers. "I am *so* sorry," she said.

Banya raised a weary eyebrow in an expression of surprise. "Are you crying, little girl?" she whispered.

"No." Rai sniffed loudly and swiped her nose against her sleeve. "Be a cold day in Hell before I cry over the likes of you."

"Good. For a minute you had me worried I might be dying."

Rai bit her lip. "Um … they've sent for your family."

Banya's eyes widened. "*Am* I dying?"

"Eir says she doesn't know."

"That's encouraging." Banya's fingers fluttered in the closed circle of Rai's hands. "You look ridiculous in that get-up."

Rai grinned down at herself. Her clothing had been taken to be washed and repaired and in its place she was given traditional Carraid garb to wear. The wide-legged, somewhat billowy pants felt slightly indecent, but she liked the embroidered shirt very much. "Black Hirn always said, *'When in savage lands, dress like a savage,'* but I drew the line at the boot bells."

"Shit, the boot bells are the best part." Banya licked her lips. "Is there any water?"

"Sure." Rai poured a cup from the ewer beside the bed and held it while Banya drank. A few sips was all it took to exhaust her. She shifted slightly and grunted with discomfort.

Rai's hands danced above the coverlet, afraid to touch for fear of adding to her friend's pain. "Should I call Eir?"

"No." Banya's voice was a breathy rasp between clenched teeth. "No, it's …" She squeezed one eye shut and drew a slow, shaky breath. "Okay," she said on the exhale. "Okay, it's a deal. I won't move again. Sit back down, will you? You're making me nervous."

"*I'm* making *you* nervous? That's a joke."

"If it is, I'm not laughing." Banya looked around the room. "Where are we?"

"Someplace called Eachan's Rest."

Banya nodded. "One of the stopping points on the Roundup. We gather here before the big push to Riddock. Is Eachan around?"

"Here and gone." When Rai had first appeared, the ham-fisted, bear-shaped woman had terrified her by grabbing the front of her shirt and bawling "*What's going on?*" into her face. "Do you know that all you Carraid look alike?"

Banya smiled, acknowledging the jibe without the energy to make a comeback. "How did we get here?"

"Pure dumb luck." Rai retrieved the dropped cup, threw down a napkin to soak up the worst of the spill, and poured more tea. "Once we crossed the river, your mare took off and it was all I could do to keep up."

"Not dumb luck then, just a well-trained horse. How long have we been here?"

"A few days."

"What happened to Remeg?"

Rai sipped her tea. "Eachan and some others dealt with her. She'd gotten across the river and was coming after us."

Banya's head made a slight motion from side to side. "She's nothing if not persistent."

Rai chuckled. "Eachan says she's crazier than a shit-house rat. Apparently, Remeg invoked the queen's name, thinking that would make a difference, and Eachan told her to shove it up her ass."

"I'll bet that went over like a fart in church."

Rai's expression sobered. "Someone in Remeg's band – I don't know who – tried to push the point and got killed for it before the Carraid drove them back across the water."

Banya closed her eyes. "What a fuck-row." She was silent for so long that Rai thought she had fallen asleep again. She had drifted into a light doze when the Carraid's voice brought her awake once more. "How's Kinner?"

Dread sluiced through Rai's body like cold water. Her throat felt tight and dry. How else to say it but straight out? "He's gone."

Banya's eyes opened. "Oh, Rai," she said in admonishment. "You didn't let him go off to Dara alone? I know he's a bit full of himself right now, but he's hardly ready to –"

"I mean *gone* gone," Rai said in misery. Who would have thought the little shit could get so far under her skin in such a short time? "He went over the falls."

Banya struggled to sit up, but a wave of pain hammered her back against the pillows. "You have to find him!"

"There is no finding." Rai drew a shaky breath. "We tried. Eachan thinks his body is lodged somewhere under the ice sheet."

A tear broke from the corner of Banya's eye and trickled past her ear. She uttered a low moan, the cry of a beast in pain.

"For what it's worth, we, uh, we still have the sword," Rai said. "As soon as you're out of danger, I'll take it to Dara."

"I thought you didn't believe in the Weathercock."

"I don't, but it would mean a lot to Kinner to know the job was done."

"But he won't know," Banya said sadly. "Dead is dead."

"Well, somebody has to pick up the pieces and it's the only thing I can think of!" Rai thrust herself out of the chair and stalked across the room to stare through the window at the grazing herd.

After a moment of taut silence, Banya said quietly, "You're not going to Dara without me."

"Don't tell me what to do. You're in no condition to ride and won't be for weeks, maybe months according to Eir. If I leave soon, I have a good chance of getting there before the snow closes every pass until spring."

"And what then? Spend the winter at the monastery?"

"There or in Risley." Rai drew herself up tall and turned to look at Banya. "I'm not entirely without tradable skills, you know. I'll get by." She shoved her hands into her pockets and tried to look stern. "I'll be back here in the spring and you'd better be ready to ride by then or I'll kick your lazy ass all over Carraidland."

"You'll try." A faint smile lifted one side of Banya's mouth. "That's all right, then," she said and drifted off to sleep before Rai's eyes.

Unable to restrain herself, Remeg paced from one end of the room to the other, her steps quick, her turns tight. Each time she passed before the fire, her clothing steamed a little in the heat, still damp from the river dunking she had suffered. She had allowed the troop neither food nor drink during the freezing rush south to Kell. Now, while her soldiers ate and rested in a tavern across town, she waited impatiently for an audience with Oofa Lorn, the provincial governor.

Humiliation and rage brought Remeg near to putting a fist through one of the decorative wall panels. Her quarry had escaped again! When the troop had reached the river, the boy was already gone, across and vanished, no sign of him anywhere. Rai's horse had just gained the far shore and Banya … well, Banya had made it across as well, barely. The sight of an arrow embedded in her back had brought Remeg some cheer. The soldiers had struggled across the raging water, losing time as their horses panicked in the frigid torrent, but they gained the far bank en masse and set off in pursuit.

Then the Carraid had arrived.

Remeg's mouth curled into a sneer. The blasted horsefolk had sent them packing like a band of penniless tinkers. That hot-headed idiot Tynar had been killed in the confrontation and Duan – a decent soldier, not terribly bright but useful – had perished in the retreat across the Sower.

Remeg's angry thoughts were cut short as a liveried servant entered bearing a tray holding a pitcher of mulled wine, two well-made cups, and a plate of expensive pastries. The woman placed the offering on a low table between two chairs, bowed, and withdrew. A moment later, The Lorn arrived.

Remeg had made it her business to know the histories of every landed family in the realm. The Lorns, fishmongers in ages past, had scratched and clawed their way out of the gutter and never looked back on their plebian roots. Having risen from nothing, they over-compensated with pretentious homes, flamboyant clothing, and personalities which might, on a good day, be described as rapacious, conniving, affected, and sybaritic.

Lorn's flesh quaked within a garish and low-cut gown as she crossed the room with mincing steps and presented a well-padded paw to Remeg. "Be welcome, Captain."

Remeg took the sausage fingers and bowed over them, lightly kissing the back of the powdered and perfumed hand. "Thank you, Governor."

Lorn withdrew her hand slowly from Remeg's grip. "You're a fair distance from Caerau. How fares our belovéd Kedar?"

'Belovéd Kedar' would slap you silly for calling her that, Remeg thought. She smiled politely. "Her Majesty seemed well when last I saw her."

"You appear travel-worn, Captain." Lorn gestured toward the table. "Please take your ease. May I offer refreshment?"

"Again, my thanks. That would be most welcome." Remeg waited until the woman was seated before she took the other chair. Curling her fingers around the handle of the pitcher, she looked straight into Lorn's eyes. "May I serve?"

The double-entendre was not missed. Lorn simpered beneath the layers of face paint she wore in a farcical attempt to hide her true age and stroked a wanton hand across her prodigious cleavage. "Perhaps we can serve each other," she said with a lubricious smile. She picked up the plate of finger-sized pastries and held it out. "Tidbit?"

Remeg's gut churned at the thought of sweet confection instead of real food. She wanted meat, bread, ale. Instead, she took the smallest bit of pastry and placed it on her plate. "Thank you." She filled the cups with wine, waited until Lorn had raised hers to her mouth, and then drank deeply. The warm and honeyed alcohol hit her stomach hard, for which she was grateful. She would need that numbness in order to carry out her plan.

Once they had tasted the wine and pastries and Remeg had offered compliments on both, Lorn leaned forward to display the chasm between her breasts. "Winter has arrived so early this year, Captain," she complained in a pouty whine. "It has completely destroyed my plans for an autumn hunt and I am quite put out about it. I imagine it must have caught you unaware as well." Her heavily kohled eyelids drooped. "Is it Her Majesty's business that brings you to Kell?"

"Yes, Governor. My troop and I seek three fugitives."

Lorn's ears practically perked. "*Fugitives.*" She rolled the word in her mouth like a succulent bit of candy.

"Traitors to the crown."

"Oh, my." One hand played with the pendulous jewel nestled at the base of her throat. "And they are in my city, you say? Am I in danger, Captain?"

Had Rai or Banya been any threat to this piggish oaf, Remeg would have kissed them both on the lips and bestowed a full pardon. "As far as we know, they are not in Kell at the moment, Governor, but one must never underestimate criminals. If you'll pardon my saying so, it would be foolhardy on your part not to take every precaution. You are, after all, the power in this area. Desperate women, by their very definition, are liable to do anything."

"Indeed." The canny look Lorn gave her reminded Remeg that this woman had not attained her position through stupidity. "But you will catch them?"

"That is my intent." Remeg looked downhearted. "Unfortunately, my troop is small and has become smaller still. Two have died, leaving just five besides myself, and we are all pushed beyond exhaustion."

Saliva had gathered in the folds of Lorn's bottom lip. A languid finger traced circles between her upper chest and triple chins. "Surely if you inform the queen of your difficulties, she will send more soldiers."

"Her Majesty has not the soldiers to spare, Governor. What remains of my garrison must guard Caerau, and the queen's personal body guard may not leave her side until these traitors are apprehended. If they were to double back and make an attempt on the Crown …" She shuddered at the thought.

Lorn's doughy hands bracketed her astonished, porcine eyes. "Think you they might?" She sounded titillated, both eager and repulsed by the thought of Kedar's murder.

For two sens, Remeg would have wrapped her hands around that corpulent throat. "There are those who will stop at nothing to get what they desire. You know this."

Lorn's nod set her entire body quivering like a pot of jam. "Better than most, Captain. But, tell me this – how does your search involve me?"

The swiftness with which Remeg moved startled the woman. She squealed in surprise as Remeg dropped to her knees and sought Lorn's hands amid the folds of the opulent gown. "Please, Governor! Give me soldiers! Help me to capture these brigands!"

Oofa Lorn stared thoughtfully at the entwined fingers in her lap and then met Remeg's desperate gaze. "I would like nothing better than to help you, but if my soldiers are with you then who will protect me?"

Remeg swallowed an inappropriate retort. "Imagine Her Majesty's gratitude when she learns how you selflessly aided me, putting yourself at risk in order to keep her person safe." *Imagine what she'll do to you if she discovers you did not, you swollen whale.*

An entire minute passed without response. Remeg swallowed hard. She had hoped that mere flirtation would get her what she desired, but she was prepared to go further if need be. Now she laid her cheek against Lorn's knee and stared up into her painted eyes. "Please help me. I'll do anything you ask in return."

Oofa Lorn looked back at her … and smiled.

When it was over, Remeg kept her face averted while she dressed, pretending shyness but concealing disgust. She had done what she must in order to win Kedar back, but she would rather have bedded a corpse than The Lorn. It was not Lorn's weight that put her off. Remeg had coupled with large women before and to great satisfaction. Her contempt stemmed from the knowledge that this woman would eat you alive given half a chance. Sex with Lorn was not a pleasurable partnership, but the assimilation of one individual by another. Remeg longed for nothing more than a hot bath and a stiff scrub brush.

"I shall have Captain Sheel choose the very best soldiers to send with you." Lorn, sprawled naked on the sex-tangled rug, ran a hand through her hair. "Fifty should serve."

Remeg would rather it were a hundred or more (*that* would show the thrice-be-damned Carraid!), but she knew better than to quibble over numbers. Besides, more soldiers might precipitate the need to bed Lorn a second time. Much as she wanted this venture to succeed, Remeg didn't think she had the stomach for it.

She finished tying her pants and smiled with gratitude. "My thanks."

"The thanks are mine." Lorn's fingers played across her body in a way that turned Remeg's stomach. "When your hunt is successfully concluded, I hope you'll stay a few days here as my guest." She licked her lips.

Returning to the sink-hole of those arms and legs was something Remeg intended to avoid. She smiled, trying to convey the correct combination of pleasure and embarrassment in order to placate this wallowing, obscene bloodsucker. "When we return from Carraidland with our quarry, I will certainly try to –"

Lorn sat up fast. Her hair, broken free of its combs and ornate styling, fell in a ratty tangle over one bare shoulder. "Carraidland?" she squawked. "You can't go there!" She whipped her head back and forth in denial and lifted her hands in appeal. "The horseclans are crazy! We have a very tenuous truce between our two cities and each keeps to its own side of the river." She pawed her hair, combing it with her fingers. "It's stupid, I know. We should be able to trade openly, but Kiarr belongs to the Carraid and Kell does not and that's the end of it." She shook her head, flapping loops of loose hair against her ears. "I can't afford to upset Balfor. No, absolutely not. I'm sorry, but I won't take the risk."

Remeg's jaw tightened. "Her Majesty requires the risk, Governor. And you promised me soldiers."

Lorn drew herself up and reached for the tumble of her discarded robe. "Do not use that high-handed tone to with me, Captain. It's you who came a-begging."

Remeg's fingers curled into fists. What had happened to her ability to master her temper, to be diplomatic? "Pardon, Governor. I didn't mean –"

"You should have been clearer in your explanation when you first asked for help. If I'd known you meant to invade Carraidland, I'd have refused right from the start."

"Without those soldiers, Governor, I'll have no choice but to abandon the hunt, return to Caerau, and report your refusal of aid to Her Majesty."

Lorn's thick cheeks trembled, flushed with anger. Her eyes were tiny, bitter currents in the dough of her face. "Don't you dare threaten me! The queen will understand everything once she learns the particulars. She has no more desire to anger the Carraid than do I."

"That's true." Remeg picked up her jacket and put it on. "But how will she feel when she learns what you've been up to here in your pleasure palace?"

Color drained from Lorn's face. Her smeared make-up stood out stark against the pasty skin like paint on a boiled pudding. She drew herself up and collected her clothing around her. "I've no idea what you're talking about."

"Oh, yes, you do." Remeg pretended to flick a bit of dirt from the front of her jacket. "It's amazing how much information one can learn in the corridors of powerful houses merely by the application of an open purse and a willing ear." She bent down and slid a hand along the side of Lorn's neck. Her fingers went up into the woman's hair and yanked her face close. "Does the queen know that you've taken a page from her own book? Does she know that you seek out men and boys for your own pleasure rather than send them to her?" The last of Remeg's tenuous control fractured. Her fingers clenched in the matted hair until tears sprang to Lorn's eyes. "You'll give me the soldiers I need or the queen will know everything. And if you think to get rid of the threat by getting rid of me, keep in mind that there are those in this city who can make you vanish even quicker, and they are in my employ. If I develop so much as a cough, they will move against you."

She shoved Lorn away. Without looking at her again, Remeg left the room, closing the door behind her. The strike of her footfalls echoing through the governor's palace was like the sound of a broken heartbeat.

Twenty

By the sounds coming from outside the wagon, Kinner knew the gypsy caravan had arrived at a city. Putting his eye to a thin crack in the wall, he peered out but could see little beyond a brief glimpse of buildings and a mass of people and animals moving about. From the level of noise he judged this to be a place of some size or at least one which possessed a thriving market district. Voices called to one another in inquiry, jest, and greeting. Cows and oxen lowed. Sheep and goats blatted. Pigs shrieked like murdered children. Hooves clopped against cobblestones and horses whinnied. There was the clucking and honking of chickens and geese, and dogs barked; even a donkey brayed. He could smell ale, roasted meat, and hard, ripe cheeses.

Kinner settled once more into Lordibi's chair and drew a blanket across his lap. Torqua had returned his clothing as clean and fresh-smelling as if he had laundered it himself, but she had refused to give him back his socks or boots. "To keep you from going rabbit on me again," she had said. "This weather will freeze your feet black. Your toes will drop off like the balls on a castrated lamb. Can't have that, now, can we?"

He watched the lazy swing of the oil lantern as the wagon made its way along the street. All he need do was dash it to the floor. One little 'accident' and the wagon would be in flames. Torqua, one step ahead of him, had read his mind and warned him not to try it. "You mess with that lamp, I'll bar the door with you inside and listen to you burn." He believed her.

After falling to Feen Bin and her handy little sling, Kinner had spent several days in the back of Lel Nicabar's wagon under the care of old Mander and the caravan herb-witch, Jibben Tem. Repeat applications of a cool mint-smelling poultice had brought down the swelling over his eye, although the bruise remained and he had frequent low-level headaches. As soon as he could sit up without feeling ill, Torqua had moved him back into her wagon and sent the twins and Lordibi to ride with the others. Locked in, Kinner spent his restless days pacing the confines of his prison and his nights huddled in bed. At all times, Rai and Banya were on his mind. He imagined their joy when they discovered he was alive and day-dreamed endless scenarios of rescue and reunion, but days passed with no sign of them and doubt began to work a troublesome finger into his vitals.

They won't come because they think you're dead, it wrote on the walls of his heart. *They can't come because* they're *dead.* Hard on the heels of those thoughts, another voice spoke. Sometimes it sounded like Holan or Ren or even Banya, but most often it was a voice he recognized as his own. *What are you going to do about it?* He had no clue.

The wagon lurched to a stop and shifted as someone climbed onto the outer stoop. A key rattled in the lock and the door opened only far enough to let Torqua duck inside. "How's the head?" she said.

The last time she asked him, he had played sick. She had seen through the chicanery at once and spent some little while making sure Kinner understood how badly he could be made to feel if he continued such foolishness.

"Better than it was," he said. "But I still get dizzy sometimes."

"Then it's a good thing you'll be spending so much of your time laying down, eh?" She tugged off her gloves and tossed them onto the bed. Taking his chin in one hand, she peered closely at his face. "A little paint should cover that bruise nicely. Customers don't want battered goods after all." She crossed the wagon, unlocked the rounded lid of a large trunk, and rummaged through the contents. "Done up right, I think you'll be a very popular boy." She shot him a grin. "Don't worry, now. I don't mean to exhaust you. There'll be a set limit each evening, no more than five or six couplings a night, with time in between to take a wash and a breather."

Kinner's gut clenched. This was no better than it had been at home. Worse. At least back in Moselle it had been his family that was involved or people they knew from town, not a bunch of strangers. "Please don't make me do this."

"You've no say in the matter, lad. You're found property. Unless someone with a prior claim that they can prove comes calling, you're mine and you'll do as I say. What else are you good for, eh? Ah! Here we are!" She brought forth an armload of cloth and tossed it to him.

He caught it with both hands. The cascade of gossamer fabric, pale verdigris shot through with gold, slipped across his fingers like the touch of fog, as insubstantial as a dream. It was gorgeous stuff and obviously expensive. Kinner hated it on sight. "What am I supposed to do with this?"

"Wear it, fool." Torqua closed the trunk, locked it, and sat on the lid. "That's your costume."

"My what?"

"That shot to the head make you stupid? *Costume,* I said." She shook her head in dismay. "Good thing you're sterile. The last thing I need is a caravan full of half-wits." She dusted her hands together. "Most of the fun in a liaison is the fantasy, Kinner. A few strategic trappings can make all the difference between dissatisfaction and a customer who comes back for more. There're plenty of women, Tzigane or otherwise, who'll pay good money for a go at you regardless of your fertility."

Kinner kept his expression bland, but his mind raced. *And when the first baby comes, what then? Raise the price?* Once his fertility was proven, as it surely would be, any chance he had at a new life on his own terms would vanish forever. The Tzigane would breed him until he could breed no more and then sacrifice him like a worn-out ram. He was not family, like Mander, and could not expect similar treatment.

Torqua stood up and raised a finger in warning. "Wear that robe, play the part, and please your customers. Otherwise I'll beat you senseless and work you anyway. There are women in the world who don't care a fig if you're coherent, only that you can perform. You bear that in mind. I'll be back later to do your face." She went out, locking the door behind her.

Kinner flung the shiny fabric at the wall. It wafted to the floor with a soft and wholly unsatisfactory sigh. "I am *not* wearing that thing," he said and folded his arms across his chest. "Let her beat me if she wants to." He glared at the cloth for a long while, then blew a gusty sigh of frustration and began to undress.

The outfit was no more than a single length of cloth doubled in half and sewn up the sides, with openings for his head and arms. His skin dimpled with gooseflesh as he dropped the sleek fabric over his head. The silken touch brought a pleasurable thrill to his manhood and he stared in horror at his body's obvious and unintentional enthusiasm. He sat down fast and crossed his legs, feeling more naked with the robe on than he had without it.

Torqua returned a few hours later with a tray of food and a small leather pouch. In a fleet moment of fantasy, Kinner imagined knocking her aside and making his escape. He might have succeeded, but the untimely foolishness of his earlier attempt had made her watchful and she never let down her guard.

She paused in the doorway and gave an appreciative whistle. "My, but you clean up nice." She kicked the door shut and placed the tray on the bed. "Here's dinner. Jibben's put in some special herbs to give you staying power so you clean that bowl, understand?" She pulled a chair close, straddled it, and plopped the leather bag into his lap. She loosened the ties and reached inside. "This," she said, shaking a dark-glassed bottle before his nose, "is scented oil. Roses, I think. Rub it on your skin. You'll stink like a brothel."

Kinner took the bottle and thumbed up the cork. The smell of flowers scented the air. "It's lilac," he said, filled with a sudden and wistful memory. Auntie Distel had grown lilacs.

Torqua shrugged with indifference. She uncapped a circular tin and, using her finger, daubed some pale ointment onto Kinner's temple. The unguent felt cool against his skin and carried a faint odor he could not place. Her finger moved in quick circles, blending it against his flesh. "This will hide most of the bruise. It's shadowy enough in here that the rest should be hardly noticeable." She grinned. "Besides, if you do your job right, she'll be too busy to pay attention to your face, eh?" Finished, she closed that tin and opened another, this one half-filled with something red. Catching him by the back of the head, she held him steady while she smudged a line of rouge along each cheekbone. "When the weather's fine, we'll chain you outside to get some sun, keep the roses in your cheeks, but this'll do for now. When you're done eating, put a dab of it on your lips as well, you hear?" She opened a final tin, dusted his eyelids with purple and gold, and leaned back to survey her handiwork. She smiled and made a noise of admiration. "You're every woman's fantasy, Kinner, mark my words."

"Oh, good."

She grabbed his chin in her strong fingers and shook it in warning. "Here now! You lose that attitude and do what you're meant for or I'll hamstring you and let them at you anyway. You think I won't, just try it. I'm going out to check how many customers our advertising has brought in. You eat up." She released him and the door closed behind her once more.

"Is there anything else I should know? Some little tidbit you've forgotten to share?"

Seated on the end of Banya's bed, Rai gave the question due consideration. If she left out anything important, even by mistake, the enormous woman standing before her might see fit to break her in two. "No, that's all of it." She nudged Banya's foot through the blankets. "You?"

Banya shook her head. It was a tiny motion, but she winced nonetheless. Her face was wan, her expression listless. She was responding to treatment, but healing was a slow process hampered by an infection lodged deep in her lungs. Every four hours Eir brought in a bowl of boiled water and herbs over which Banya had to sit for thirty minutes with a blanket tented over her head. Rai didn't think it was helping much.

Balfor Oldinsdotter, leader of the Carraid, looked skeptical and rubbed a hand along her jaw. Her hair, wheaten gold with a swath of silver at each temple, twined down her back in a single thick plait made of three joined braids. Her bi-colored eyes, one blue and one green, studied the wall as she mulled over all they had told her.

Banya's parents sat at either side of the bed. They had remained in quiet attendance on their daughter since their arrival the day before, bathing her, helping her to shift position, to use the chamber pot, and cajoling her to eat.

Banya had obviously been a late-life child, for her mother Kiorda was older than Rai had expected. Her spine was bent with arthritis and forced inactivity had thickened her waist. Her hair, stick straight and cut very short, was a stark white cap around the lined, bronze skin of her face.

Rai was less startled by Banya's father than she would have been prior to meeting the Chesne. Ruarc was tall, lean and muscular despite his age. Silver hair flared across his shoulders and his features were almost ascetic, unusual in a Carraid. The lower half of his right leg had been replaced by a wooden peg.

Her friend's present disinterest in food worried Rai far more than her injuries. She knew from experience how much Banya could pack away in the course of a meal. Eir had assured her that the malaise was perfectly normal and would pass in time, but Rai refused to set out for Dara while Banya's health remained in question. With Kinner dead (she felt a twinge around her heart every time she thought about it), what difference did it make if the sword arrived in Dara a week from now or in several months?

Balfor drew a deep breath. "Let me see if I have the gist of this sorted. You got into trouble in Caerau with Captain Remeg …"

"*Rai* got into trouble," Banya said. "I had nothing to do with it."

"Thanks," Rai muttered.

Balfor ignored the interruption. "Then this blacksmith and her son –"

"Holan and Kinner," Rai supplied.

Balfor glowered at her. "They showed you –"

Banya lifted a finger. "Showed me, not Rai."

"– the Weathercock's sword and asked for your help taking it to Dara." Balfor frowned. "Which makes no sense at all," she said more to herself than to anyone. "Then, in a fit of brilliance the likes of which I've never seen, you *both* decided to desert your post, only to run into the same Captain Remeg you had pissed off earlier. Have I got it right so far?"

"Pretty much," Banya said with a deprecating smile.

Balfor nodded. "Then the blacksmith died and you went to Cadasbyr where you got into more trouble –"

"That was Rai's fault, too."

"Cut me a break, will you?"

"– and were then taken captive by the talented Captain Remeg. The Chesne, having robbed you, now rescued you and set your feet on the road to Dara. But Remeg found you again and chased you over the Sower into Carraidland."

Rai held up a tentative finger. "Except for Kinner. Don't forget he …" Her voice trailed off and she looked away as Balfor turned a baleful gaze upon her. "Nothing."

Balfor stood with her hands on her hips. "This is a hell of a thing you lay on my doorstep, little girl."

Rai looked up, thinking Balfor meant her, but it was Banya who answered. "I know, Carraidleader. I'm sorry."

"Sorry doesn't buy grain." Balfor ran both hands over her face and then pointed a finger at Banya. "You chose to leave Carraidland! What you do out there among the Others is your business, although I'd expect you to behave in a way that doesn't bring shame to your motherline."

Banya looked chastened. "Yes, Carraidleader."

Balfor placed both hands on the footboard of the bed. The wood creaked as it took her weight. "This Remeg must be one quick study. I don't know many who could see that sword for an instant – and in moonlight yet! – and connect it with the Weathercock. I guess talk of the old boy is one thing, but someone going to the trouble of forging him a weapon is something else. That's *tangible,* that is. That's proof." She pulled at her lower lip, musing. "It's belief and it's threat. That's why she's after you. To protect Kedar Trevelyan." She said the name with disgust. The single sharp *crack!* as her hands came together made everyone jump. "And you bring this to me!"

"I'm sorry …"

"Not a word!" Balfor turned away. "I need to think." Into the silence that followed came a discreet tap on the door. She gave it a smoldering look. "I'm busy!"

The door opened and Eir looked in. "I don't want you. I want Banya."

The muscles along the Carraidleader's jaw bunched in annoyance. "This isn't a mid-winter revel we're having in here, Eir. I told you I didn't want to be interrupted."

The physician stood her ground, utterly unperturbed by Balfor's tone. "And I told you that Banya gets her breathing treatment every four hours without fail, whether you're done talking or not. I have a pitcher of hot water out here and unless you want it dumped over your head, Carraidleader, you'll let me do my job."

Balfor glared at her. "You're pushy for a doctor."

"Thank you. Now if you don't mind …" She entered the room and began to set up the treatment.

Balfor rolled her eyes and made a shooing motion with her hands. "All right, everyone out. Let's leave them alone for a bit." She snagged Rai by the elbow and pulled her along. "That goes for you, too, short stuff."

Rai gestured toward the bed. "But I ..."

"Need to have the stink blown off you." When she got her out into the hallway, Balfor's tone gentled. "How long has it been since you stuck your nose out of doors, Rai?"

"I don't know."

"That's what I thought." Balfor patted her shoulder. "Don't worry so much about Banya. She's a good strong girl and Eir is an excellent physician. Before you know it, you'll both be on your way again. Thanks be to the Weathercock," she added in an undertone. She started off down the hall.

"It's because of the Weathercock that this happened." Rai's tone was accusatory.

Balfor stopped and turned to look at her. "I know you don't believe in him, Rai, and that's your business, but you might want to give some consideration as to why he's chosen to appear in your life with such persistence." She winked and walked away. Her last words drifted up the stairs as she descended. "Go do something useful."

"Like what?" Rai said to the empty hallway. With a backward glance at Banya's closed door, she wandered away. Fresh air did sound like a good idea. Perhaps she would pay a visit to the black, maybe bring him a treat. He was keyed up by the proximity of so many mares. She had fallen asleep last night to the sound of his horny declarations of love.

She stopped in her room long enough to change into boots and grab a jacket. The sword box lay on the floor beside her bed, but she refused to even look at it. The Weathercock had caused enough trouble.

She was halfway down the stairs when a voice hailed her. "Rai!"

She leaned over the banister. A six-year-old version of Eachan dressed in dirty britches, muddy boots, and a hand-me-down sweater several sizes too big stood in the front hall looking up at her. Two blonde braids stuck out from the sides of the child's head like the feelers on an insect.

"Hello, Briot."

"Are you coming outside? Are you going to ride the black today?"

"I might do, yeah."

The child met her at the bottom of the stairs. "Can I ride him?"

Probably better than me, squirts. "That depends."

"On what?"

Rai, being unfamiliar with children, had not expected that question. "On ... well ... all sorts of things. Mostly on what Eachan or your mother have to say about it."

"Oh." Briot made a flippy little gesture with her hand. "Gran won't mind and Mummer is busy with Seula." She stood with her feet spread wide, hands on her hips, and looked up at Rai. "What's his name?"

"The black?" Rai thought a minute and shook her head. "I don't know. No one ever said. Banya might know, I guess."

The girl's face registered undisguised annoyance. "You ride him and you don't know his *name?*" She flapped her arms as if Rai had just proved herself to be a hopeless case. "Are you going to keep him?"

Rai smiled as they headed for the door. "Why, do you want him?"

Briot looked both surprised and grave. "No. He's nice, but he's not Carraid-bred and that's what I want."

Rai opened the door and let the child slip out ahead of her. "Then I guess I'll keep him, if that's okay with you."

"If you're going to keep him, you should name him."

Rai's child-saturation point had been reached. As they stepped down from the porch, she looked around to see if there was anyone on whom she could foist the kid, but the area was suspiciously vacant of adults. "Like what?"

Briot paused to think with a small forefinger pressed against the point of her chin. "Dog," she finally said.

Rai sputtered laughter. "You want me to name my horse *Dog?* Why?"

"'Cause when it's really dark out an' there's no moon, Gran says it's dark as the inside of a dog an' your horse doesn't have any white on him, so *he's* dark as the inside of a dog." The little girl grinned. She fitted her hand into Rai's and pulled her along in the wake of her enormous personality.

A discreet tap on the wagon's door brought Kinner bolt upright in the rocking chair, his heart knocking with anxiety. Torqua peeked in at him. She nodded her approval at the empty bowl (the contents of which had been dumped into the chamber pot and pushed deep under the bed), gave him a cursory once-over, and held the door open as a figure came up the stairs and into the wagon. "Have a good time," Torqua said and closed the door.

Caped and cowled, the woman stood unmoving in the middle of the floor. Kinner waited, his mouth dry. For several moments nothing happened, then the figure straightened its shoulders and pushed back the hood. Instead of a grown woman, it was a girl younger than Kinner, no more than eleven or twelve and as darkly beautiful as only a gypsy could be. Her long hair was coiled around her head like a crown and dangly silver earrings sparkled in the lantern light. She took a deep breath, raised her eyes to meet his, and expelled a word like a sigh. "Hello."

He knew beyond a doubt that, of the two of them, she was the more frightened. Could this possibly be her first time? If so, it made what he was about to do absolutely reprehensible, but he did it anyway.

Goggling his eyes, he leered at her. "*Nuhnuhnuh,*" he said in a panting grunt and waved a limp hand. The girl's eyes widened and the color drained from her small, sweet face. She darted a glance at the door and slid one foot backward. Kinner shuffled toward her, head hanging to one side, and rolled his eyes. His tongue worked and a line of spittle dangled from his bottom lip. "*Nuhnuhnuh.*"

The girl shrieked and burst from the wagon. Torqua was up the steps in two seconds, had hold of Kinner in three, and shook him hard. "What did you do?" she hissed, mindful of those gathered outside. She reached back with a foot and shoved the door closed.

"Nothing," Kinner said. "She must have changed her mind."

"Not with what her mother paid for the privilege, she didn't. What game are you playing at?"

"Nothing! I swear! She said hello and then she got all scared looking and ran away!"

Torqua released him and stood for a moment in thought. "Wouldn't be the first time a girl got scared her first go-around with a man," she said in a musing tone. Her crow-bright eyes studied him. "You swear you didn't do anything to help it along?"

Kinner shrugged and held his hands palm up.

"All right." She pointed a finger at him. "But one display like that is all you get, laddy-buck. The next woman who comes in here had better stay awhile or I'll ride the rough spots out of you myself."

There was a tap on the door and it creaked open. "Torqua." It was Lel. She looked worried. "You'd better come sort this." Beyond her shoulder Kinner glimpsed a knot of very angry-looking women.

The gypsy leader flung a black look at him and left the wagon. A dozen heartbeats later she blasted back through, nostrils white with rage, and grabbed him with both hands. "Playing the idiot, are we?" She slammed him against the wall. "Drooling?" She slapped him hard and he tasted blood. The blow released something inside Torqua and she struck him repeatedly until someone grabbed her from behind and hauled her off him.

Kinner slid down the wall and curled into a ball, covering his face with his hands, fingers tacky with tears and blood. His lips were swollen and his ears rang with pain where Torqua had clipped them with her big rings.

"Let go of me!" she railed, and then repeated it in a calmer tone. "Let go of me. I won't kill the glutter-slut quite yet." When her tribefolk released her, she jerked her clothing back into order and gestured them out of the wagon. On the stoop, Torqua leaned out into the night. "Preta?"

A woman stepped from the edge of the crowd to the foot of the steps. She seemed familiar to Kinner, although he could not place her. Torqua made an expansive gesture. "Preta, my friend. I apologize for the insult laid upon your daughter."

A voice rose from among those gathered. "I think Biet had another sort of laying in mind!" The crowd laughed.

"Shut up!" Preta spat. She scowled at Torqua. "You owe me more than an apology, Bin."

"I do," Torqua agreed at once. "Your family has been insulted and should be recompensed appropriately. Since Biet has lost interest for now, why don't you take her turn? Please, help yourself."

Kinner's guts turned to ice. He scrambled to his feet and backed as far away from the door as the jumbled interior of the wagon would allow.

Preta's grin exposed a tooth that sparkled gold. "That will do, friend Torqua. That will do, indeed." She came up the steps and into the wagon. It took a moment for her eyes to adjust to the dim interior, then she spied Kinner. "Come here, pretty boy," she said, smiling broadly, and closed the door.

Twenty-One

Sheel, captain of the Lorn militia, leaned back in her chair and laced her fingers behind her head. "It's a question of technique," she said. "It doesn't help matters that you went clod-hopping into Carraidland as if you owned it."

Remeg fought to keep her expression passive. When Oofa Lorn had promised to lend her soldiers, Remeg hadn't realized that their commander was part of the bargain. She and Sheel had hated one another on sight, not that it mattered. The success of this endeavor required cooperation, not friendship.

It also demanded there be one commander.

"Kedar Trevelyan rules Carraidland," Remeg said. She circled the rim of her tankard with a forefinger as the noises of the pub went on around them. "Since I ride at her behest, I go where I must."

Sheel lifted her mug in wry salute. "You and Kedar Trevelyan have a lot to learn about the Carraid."

Remeg's smile was thin. "Enlighten me."

Sheel grinned and leaned forward with her elbows on the table. "Stop me if you know all this." She took a moment to order her thoughts. "Time was when every little plot of land had its queenlet. Folks gathered around those with the most charm or power, the greater land or brains. Little kingdoms sprang up. So did rivalries, pacts, and broken treaties." She signaled for another round of drinks. "You know how it goes. Bit by bit the smaller so-called realms merged into a greater one. On this side of the river it was Queen Uan, from whom our gracious Majesty descends in a direct line." She paused to smile at the barmaid who brought their drinks and pressed a coin into the girl's waiting palm. "On the other side of the river it was Sker Slakkisdotter. It's she who gave the Carraid their name and brought them together under one banner. She's the one who made them what they are."

Remeg sipped her ale. "Barbarians?"

Sheel's look was as sharp as her laughter. "You don't think that or you're a bigger fool than I'd have credited."

Remeg dipped her head in slight acquiescence but said nothing.

Sheel continued. "Holding the greater area of land, Uan felt it only right that Sker bend knee to her. As you might guess, that notion wasn't exactly embraced with enthusiasm by those across the river."

"Is that what caused the rift between Kell and Kiarr?"

"In a round-about way. Early on, the two cities were like twins who share the same womb, divided down the middle by the river that brings them both life. They traded back and forth and relations were on a mostly even keel. When Uan came to power, she chose Kell as her capital. For various reasons that made relations a little more tense, but things were basically fine until her child drowned in the river. Her only child." Sheel's dark eyes gleamed over the rim of her mug. "Her *male* child." She paused to drink and then continued the tale.

"Uan's gardens bordered the river. She liked to sit there and watch the water, entertaining friends or those whom she wished to impress. I daresay she had ordered the child's caretakers to keep him away from the river, but I hear tell that he was spoiled and headstrong." Sheel cocked an eyebrow. "At any rate, the little nipper went missing."

"And Uan blamed the Carraid?"

Sheel nodded. "Oh, yes. She accused Sker of kidnapping him for breeding stock and demanded his immediate return or she would bring an army into Carraidland and take him back by force." She chuckled. "Sker's response was about what you'd expect. She said that she wouldn't taint good Carraid blood with any of Uan's get and that Uan should think long and hard before crossing the border." Sheel rolled her eyes. "Oh, yes, it was *very* pleasant. Before Uan could retaliate, the kid washed up downstream quite a bit *less* attractive than when he went in. Uan went insane with grief. She accused the Carraid of murdering him and called up an army to invade." The Lorn captain shook her head.

Remeg was intrigued despite herself. "And?"

"Got her ass killed by the Carraid." Sheel drained her mug and set it aside. "Greatest number of casualties in any battle before or since. Sker and her riders drove them back across the river and burned most of Kell before they turned around and went home. After that, Sker posted guards at the Carraid end of the bridge and it's been that way ever since."

"I'm surprised she didn't choose to burn the bridge as well."

Sheel laid a finger against the side of her nose. "Ah, but you see, Sker was a forward-thinking sort of woman. You know the old adage about burning bridges, don't you?"

Remeg did. "So where does that leave us? How do we get into Carraidland without being detected?"

Kinner's cousins had whispered amongst themselves about women who liked their sex spiced with violence. Preta's hands were tender at the beginning, arousing him with skill despite his fear and turning his unwilling body traitor. Then her touch grew heavier, her caress less gentle. She was careful what she did and where. Small welts could be excused away, but no lasting damage should come to the goods. Kinner struggled and cried out, but she muffled his mouth with her hand, her lips, her body … whatever worked.

When she was finished (rocking back on her heels with a cry of pleasure), she rolled off him and dropped onto her back. Shifting her naked hips in a languorous motion, Preta closed her eyes and stretched. Trembling, sore with the memory of her weight across his hips, Kinner inched away from her to the far edge of the bed.

A hand grabbed his wrist. "Where you off to, lovey?" Preta whispered. Her dark gaze was sleepy with contentment.

"Torqua told me to wash …" He swallowed, startled by how small his voice sounded. "I have to wash." She nodded, released him, and settled back with a happy sigh.

His first attempt to stand proved fruitless and he tumbled back onto the bed. Preta, in a half-sleep, muttered and rolled away from him. Kinner tried again to stand and managed to hobble as far as the wooden bucket and bit of flannel that had been left for his use.

He bathed with tender care, unable to watch the cloth as it slid across his body. His brain played an endless loop, powerless to stop. Outside, in the real world, voices were raised in song. There was music, the money-like *ching* of a tambourine, and the heady smells of roasted meat and spilled ale. His gaze wandered the wagon's interior, noting each item but incapable of understanding what any of it could possibly mean to him. Rocking chair, door, boxes and trunks, a lantern, tumbled bedding, a naked woman's sprawled form, and a tray with an empty bowl.

Knuckles rapped the door. "Time!"

The plan flashed into his mind in that instant. He did not pause to think it through (to hesitate would be to find the chink in its logic), but took the empty bowl from the tray and swung it hard against the wall. Preta, startled from sleep by the shatter of crockery, sat up with a confused cry as Kinner turned the piece of broken bowl that remained in his hand and gouged his cheek. Screaming, he shoved the bloody shard into Preta's hand. Her fingers reflexively closed around it as the door burst open and Torqua rushed in.

Wailing, Kinner flung himself at her and clutched the cloth of her shirt. "Don't let her hurt me again!"

Torqua stared at him in astonishment and then at the woman sitting in the middle of the bed. "What the bloody hells is this?" she demanded.

Preta stared in bafflement at the broken pottery in her hand, then dropped it and wiped her fingers on the sheets. "I didn't do anything! He's a lying little whore!" She scooted toward the side of the bed.

Kinner shrieked. He dodged behind Torqua as if to hide and stiff-armed her in the small of the back. As she hurtled into Preta, knocking them both onto the bed, he leapt from the wagon and dashed naked through the crowd. Behind him, the caravan erupted into mayhem.

In the end, it proved surprisingly easy for Remeg to buy information about Carraidland. There were always people willing to sell anything, *everything,* depending upon the offered price. This was particularly true in times of conflict and the air between Kell and Kiarr had been boiling for centuries. Sheel knew who to contact and which palms to grease in order to learn the safest routes into and out of the Carraid stronghold.

"Fugitives from one side slip across to the other all the time," she told Remeg as they saddled their horses. "They find sanctuary because the cities refuse to aid one another."

"That's one way to keep a thriving economy alive," Remeg replied in a dry tone.

Sheel laughed, nodding in agreement. "A body of horse such as we've got can't move about without rousing notice. We'll divide as if we're going in different directions, but meet at the same place." She mounted and waited for Remeg to do the same. "There's no point in sending some of us across the river by night, others to the south and north. We'd be forever waiting to catch up. We'll leave town in twos and threes by the north road, meet, and cross at the Falls."

"We already tried that," Remeg reminded her. "And were driven back."

"Aye." Sheel nodded. "Because you crossed *above* the Falls. There's a path carved into the rock *behind* the water. We'll cross there and be at Eachan's Rest before you know it."

Remeg frowned. "What's Eachan's Rest?"

"A way station on the Roundup and home to the very woman that sent you packing. My sources tell me that's where you'll find those you're hunting."

"You seem to know an awful lot about the Carraid, Captain Sheel. That's rather extraordinary given their natural reticence."

The Lorn captain smiled. "Let's just say that I have friends in high places."

For the first time, Remeg was glad to have Mestipen at her back.

She gave her horse a jig with her heels to keep it moving behind Sheel's as they passed through town. Despite the cold, the street was thronged with merchants and shoppers alike, for the gypsies had arrived. The crowd jostled and surged around the soldiers, making the horses toss their heads with irritation and snap at anyone who came too near.

Sheel swung a hand at the brightly painted wagons drawn up in a semi-circle to their left. "I *love* the Tzigane! Interesting stories, unusual wares, and hot cheap sex!" She grinned wickedly at Remeg's silent and unsmiling response. "Torqua Bin!" she suddenly called out and waved an arm.

A broad-shouldered woman rose from her seat on the stoop of one wagon and shoved through the press of people to grasp Sheel's offered hand. "Captain Sheel! Always a blessing and a pleasure!"

Much to Remeg's annoyance, Sheel drew rein. "You're down from the hills late this year, aren't you?"

"It's not us that's late, but the snow that's early. Caught us in the mountains and near-about froze us all to death." The gypsy woman glanced at Remeg and sized her up in an instant. She tipped her head in greeting and tugged her forelock. "You ladies out for some enjoyment this evening? I've something new in the wagon to tempt you,"

Sheel sighed with heavy regret. "Some other time, I'm afraid."

Torqua Bin snorted. "Off on business for that boss of yours, eh? Leave it to the rich to send the rest of us out into weather like this while they sit by the fire fat, dumb, and happy. I wouldn't trade my life for all the gold in their coffers!" She stepped back as Sheel lifted her reins to move on. "If we're here when you get back, Captain, I expect a visit. I've lots to tell!"

"It's a date!"

They rode on. As they passed out of the market area and into a more residential district, a hullabaloo went up behind them. Remeg turned in the saddle to look, but saw nothing beyond the glare of torch-fire and the jostle of the crowd. She faced forward again and followed Sheel along the city streets. As they moved into the countryside, they were joined now and then by a handful of shadowy riders until the troop was once again complete.

"... by surprise."

Remeg blinked. "Pardon? What did you say?"

Sheel gave her an amused look. "Sleeping in the saddle, Captain Remeg?

That's not a good sign by half. I was saying that you wait and see. We'll take Eachan by surprise and no mistake."

"We had better," Remeg said. She knew there would only be the one chance.

TWENTY-TWO

Kinner's escape from the gypsies fell to surprise and dumb luck.

The Tzigane caravan was doing a brisk business that evening – fortune telling, juggling, dancing … and the dark exchange of money for flesh. As he catapulted from the back of the wagon, his frightened mind registered bright torch light and noise, drunken singing and a sea of confounded faces. He landed hard, stumbled, nearly went down on all fours, scrabbled to his feet, and ran as if the Goddess herself was after him.

Behind him, the gypsy camp exploded into pandemonium. Someone yelled incoherently as a confused jumble of voices lifted like a rising tide. There was the sound of running feet, a melee of haphazard intent, and then someone shouted, "There he is!"

Mindful of Feen Bin and her accuracy with a sling, Kinner put on a burst of speed and dove into an alleyway. Remembering their flight in Cadasbyr, he took the first passage that opened off it, swerving around piles of refuse and bouncing off walls as he sped along. He pulled up short at the other end, breathing hard. The freezing night air burned his bare flesh and his feet were cut and bruised. Blood, going tacky in the cold, stuck his toes together as he danced from foot to foot in the packed and dirty snow. Arms wrapped tight across his chest, he shivered violently and tried to listen past the banging of blood in his ears and the juddering clack of his teeth. There was noise on every side and no way to tell the difference between revelry and pursuit.

"Hey, hey," spoke a rough and broken voice from the ground and something brushed his ankle. Kinner jumped away with a wordless cry. Crumbling mortar bit into his naked back and buttocks as he pressed against the wall. Inches from his foot lay a hand, palm up, the fingers loosely curled. It belonged to an arm which belonged to a woman who lay against the opposite wall. Her fingers moved feebly as if to find him again. Her eyes were closed. "Money for a beer, sister?"

"I haven't any money."

"Oh, dearie, dearie, me," the woman singsonged. With effort, she rolled onto her back and blinked stupidly at the sky. Her eyes were blank and unfocused, the pupils huge, drugged with liquor or narcotics. "No help for the needy? A din is all I ask, sister, just a din." A finger brushed his toe.

"Get the fuck away from me!" Kinner shouted. He gulped, surprised by his choice of words.

The woman patted the air with a placating hand. "No worries, sister, no worries. No need to be so …" The rest of the sentence was lost in a snore.

Shuddering with the cold, Kinner watched her with a wary eye. When she made no move, he bent and fished around in the dark. What came to hand was a broken off barrel stave. He poked her with it, a short jab to the ribs. She snorted, muttered something that sounded like "ducks," but did not rouse. He stood looking at her, torn and undecided, not quite willing to admit what it was he meant to do. When he reached for the buttons of her coat, she never stirred.

The woman was beefy, so nothing fitted him properly. The boots were worn through at the sole and down at the heel, but the socks were in surprisingly decent shape. The rest of her clothing was threadbare, filthy, and pest-ridden. The movement of insects against his flesh was horrifying, but not half as much as the idea of freezing to death.

A length of dirty rope served as a trouser belt. He had to wrap it around his narrow waist three times to keep the pants from dropping around his ankles. The hooded coat was enormous, big enough to fit two of him, and the sleeves hung long enough to shield his hands from the brunt of the cold. He experienced a brief pang of sorrow for that other coat, the lovely quilted garment that Banya had bought for him. He had wanted to keep that coat forever, if only as a memento of the kindly Carraid and all that she had done for him. Now it belonged to the Tzigane. He hoped they would take good care of it.

Using a sleeve, he wiped the worst of the makeup off his face. "I'm sorry," he whispered to the sleeping woman in her holey underwear. "This is a vile thing to do. You'll probably die from exposure, but I – thank you." He stepped into the street, turned left, and began to walk.

From beyond the dark alleys to his right came the glint of moonlight on moving water and the sucking sound of waves against rock and piling. This was a wharf area of shops and warehouses, all of them locked and shuttered against the night, with several taverns tossed in to cater to the merchants, sailors, and whores who patronized the district. Those establishments stood with their doors open to the cold. Vague light spilled into the street along with the sounds of raucous voices, a caterwauling fiddle, and an asthmatic concertina.

Kinner kept to the far side of the street and walked in shadow with his head down, minding his own business. He tried to move with purpose, like someone dangerous who could not be trusted. Those he met he gave a wide berth. He turned a callous shoulder to the figures huddled in doorways, the muttering addicts and the rustling, grunting clot of lovers as they humped against a wall.

What should he do? He had no idea where he was, no money for food or shelter, and no means of transportation save shanks mare. Remeg might be next door or a thousand miles away, for all he knew. The same could be said for Dara, but what was the point of going there now with no sword and nothing to offer in its place but his tattooed and decidedly fertile self?

His steps faltered as a rush of indecision threatened to overwhelm him. "Oh, Mum," he said, his voice a low moan of loss. "What do I do?" The only response was the hollow ringing of a bell and the nearby *lap-dub* of water. The bell reminded him of the chimes from the little church that served Moselle. For no other reason than homesickness, he turned toward the sound and soon discovered that the bell belonged not to a church, but to a boat. The vessel, anchored several yards off-shore, rocked with the motion of the river. Each sideways dip was punctuated by a brassy clang.

There was also a bridge.

Made of stone, it spanned the water like the arched back of a cat. At this end it was dark, but oil lanterns began mid-point and lighted the way to the opposite shore. Drawn by the sight, Kinner set foot to the bridge and started across, determined to put the river between him and the Tzigane.

As he neared the far side, he saw that the way was barred by a stout pole and two figures made bulky with heavy clothing. A voice called out, "State your business!"

Kinner slowed. He glanced nervously over his shoulder, but quickly faced forward again as a second voice rang out. "You deaf, woman? State your business!"

He ducked his head as a wind-lashed spray of river water hit him in the face. "I want to come across." Why else would he be on a bridge?

"Ooh, very funny, that," the first voice said. "And *why* do you want to come across?"

"Umm ..." Kinner lifted his shoulders. "To get to the other side?"

One of the guards laughed, a stiff bark of sound. The second voice spoke. "We've got ourselves a comedian. Okay, joker, shog off. Get your crapulent ass back to Kell."

He stepped closer. "I'm not joking. I just want to get across the river."

"It's trouble you're in, is it? What sort?"

Kinner hesitated. Into his indecision stepped the first voice. "Come here." He inched nearer. "*Closer,*" the voice wheedled. Kinner drew a deep breath and walked right up to the barrier.

The two women whose job it was to guard that end of the bridge reminded him so much of Rai and Banya that he almost cried out at the sight of them. One was big and beefy. Her hair, shorn to a fine, pale fuzz, exposed a lurid, curved scar that ran along the side of her head from her right temple all the way to the back of her skull. Her counterpart, child-sized, was whip-thin and dark as mud. Before he knew what to think, she grabbed him by the collar and shoved back his hood. Her eyes widened. "Shit, Saldis! Look at this, willya!"

The large woman studied him with a pensive expression, beginning with the too-large, mismatched clothing and ending with the tattoo. She sucked a tooth. "What are you doing out here, boy?" The question was put forth with such kindness that tears prickled behind Kinner's eyes. When he failed to respond, she snapped her fingers in front of his nose. "You got brain matter in that head of yours or straw? State your business or get you gone. It's too damned cold to stand out here and shilly-shally."

"You're running away, I'll bet," said the dark one. She gave her tall companion a look. "What say you, Saldis? Does Carraidland need another runaway?"

Kinner's heart gave a leap in his chest that nearly suffocated him. "*Carraidland?*"

Saldis looked amused. "Where did you think you were, sonny?"

"I didn't know!" He babbled, fear mixed with joy. "I was sick and then I was hurt and then I was in this wagon but they wouldn't let me out." He gasped for breath. "I know someone from Carraidland!"

Saldis leaned on the barrier. "Do tell. And who might that be?"

"Her name is Banya!"

"That's a common name around here, lad. This Banya have a mothername?"

Kinner wracked his brain and came up empty. "I don't remember it."

"Your loss, then," the dark woman said. She made a shooing motion.

Saldis laid a hand over hers. "Wait a minute, Tannis." She looked at him. "You know about the two sides of the river?"

He blinked. "I don't understand the question."

She pointed back and forth between the cities. "These two sides?" When he shook his head, she nodded. "They don't get along. If Kell caught fire tonight, the folks in Kiarr," she thrust out a thumb to indicate the dark city behind her, "would line the river to cheer the blaze." She folded her arms across her chest. "Would anyone in Kell be pissed if you was to disappear over here?"

He thought of Torqua – her dark face suffused with rage, her fist raised to strike – and nodded. "Oh, yes."

"That's good enough for me." Saldis grinned, exposing the gaps where several teeth were missing on one side. "Come on under, boy. Welcome to Carraidland."

The Kinner who had departed Moselle with his mother would have spilled his guts to these two friendly souls. He would have told them everything and left it for them to sort out, happy to turn his problems over to a woman. The fellow who dipped beneath the pole and planted his feet firmly on Carraid soil for the first time was a different Kinner altogether, one who was stronger in both body and spirit, a newly-formed creation made up in equal parts of Holan's death, a little Chesne training, the loss of his friends, and the abuse he had suffered at the hands of the Tzigane. This Kinner kept his own council and the women (who could have easily overpowered him and did not) accepted his reticence without question.

"Thank you," he said. He took two steps, stopped, and stared at the black bulk of Kiarr. Chill wind whistled from the north and skirled random snowflakes around his head. "Which direction is Dara?" he asked over his shoulder.

"Carraidland's not such a bad place for someone like you," Saldis said.

He nodded. "I know, but I have to go to Dara first. Maybe I'll come back later."

"Suit yourself." Tannis surprised him by producing a chunk of bread and thrusting it into his hand as Saldis took him by the shoulders and turned him so that he stood with the river on his left hand. "I don't know how you'll get there, boy, or even if you will, but follow this river to where it splits above the falls. If you take the right fork, you'll end up stranded on the shores of Ooshka Bay with nothing but seals for company, so mind to keep to the left leg. That's the Sower and that road will take you most of the way if you don't freeze to death first." She winked at him with black humor. "Someone with the balls to step out on his own just might make it."

"Thank you." Kinner put the bread in his pocket, straightened his shoulders, and walked into the night.

It was amazing how knowing where he was made such a difference in his outlook. No longer lost, he was in *Carraidland.* The world of the horseclans might not know him, but he knew it, if only through Banya's fireside talk. That alone made him feel more confident.

He broke off a hunk of the bread and chewed as he walked, sorry now that he had wasted Torqua's stew by tossing it in the chamber pot. Thoughts of her brought images of other things he would rather not contemplate. He pushed them aside with an almost physical effort and concentrated instead on searching for a livery stable, barn or stockyard, something with animals in it.

Fearful he might lose his bearings if he wandered too far down a side street, he stayed on his present course, the river always to his left, never more than one street away. He passed homes and shops with darkened windows, and dingy little pubs lit by cheap tallow. Next to one of these, he found what he was searching for.

A striped cat with wild green eyes hissed and dashed off among the stalls as he entered the barn. A sleepy-eyed cow lay on dirty straw and chewed her cud with bovine disinterest. Half a dozen horses raised their heads at the intrusion and one or two nickered a greeting before turning away to lip half-heartedly at the fodder in their racks. Kinner chewed his lip with indecision. Stealing a horse in Carraidland was tantamount to pissing on someone's religion. His life wouldn't be worth squat if he were caught.

Motion in a stall at the far end of the row drew his attention. Because no equine head peered over the side, he had thought it was empty. Now a dark-coated beast with tan points lurched onto its feet, gave a brisk shake, and looked at him with an expression of such benign curiosity that he began to laugh. Almond-shaped eyes beneath a prominent brow ridge bracketed a coarse and scraggly forelock. Straight-up ears, larger than those of a horse, swiveled as the mule's nostrils fluttered to catch the boy's scent.

Kinner walked toward it. The miller who sold flour to the Household had an animal much like this one but without the lighter points. Kinner used to feed it apples while the miller made her delivery and he liked to think the beast watched for him every week. This mule, happy for some attention, sniffed his fingers and rubbed its nose against the front of his coat as he patted its neck and scratched beneath the mane. "You're perfect," he murmured.

It was the work of moments to get the animal saddled and ready to go. Kinner found an old pair of saddlebags in the tack room and filled the pouches with grain. If nothing else, he and the mule could share the food on the road. He led the beast outside, secured the livery door, and climbed aboard. With Saldis's directions firmly in his mind (*river on the left, town on the right*), he lifted the reins and clucked his tongue.

They departed Kiarr without incident. Beyond the city limits, the moon sketched a dim path over his shoulder, here and then gone behind a welter of racing cloud. After the first couple of meandering miles, Kinner no longer noticed his surroundings. Though he fought hard against it, exhaustion overcame him at last. His chin tipped toward his chest as his body rocked to the john-mule's easy sway. Freed of his guiding hands, the animal followed the winding course of the river until, smelling distant kin on the air, it left the waterside and chose its own route cross-country as the boy slept on.

Banya stepped onto the front porch of Eachan's Rest. The weather had turned again and the day was balmy, full of the cheater warmth of autumn but touched with a hint of the winter to come. She drew a deep breath, taking in the scent of hay and horses, the smell of home.

"Well, this is an encouraging sight," Balfor said with a smile. She perched on the porch railing with her back against a support post and her legs stretched out before her.

"Doctor's orders," Banya said.

"Which she'll follow to the letter if she knows what's good for her," tiny Kiorda said from behind her immense daughter. She hovered at Banya's elbow. "Are you all right?"

"I'm fine, Mumma." Banya eased into a chair and sat back. "I can't say it doesn't hurt to move, but I'm grateful to be out of bed."

Kiorda kissed the top of her daughter's head. "Eir said a few hours only, mind. Don't over-do it because it feels good. You don't want to exhaust yourself."

Banya snorted. "Hard to do that when you spend the day on your ass. I haven't been this inactive since I was an infant. Speaking of kids, has there been any more word on mine?"

Balfor smiled. "You're worse than a first-time mare. You read the letter from Bergdis, same as me."

Actually, Banya had been over the note so often that the parchment now threatened to tear along the seams from repetitive folding and unfolding. The letter had arrived by fast rider at Balfor's home in Avenal and been sent on to her at Eachan's Rest.

"*Carraidleader,* (it read) *Six children have arrived here from Caerau. Said they were told by Banya Kiordasdotter to find you if they ran into trouble back home. Am sending them to Avenal with the next supply train. They're good workers and they know horses. If you don't want them, I'll take them back.* (signed) *Bergdis Dagnysdotter, Dagnysteading, Emeram.*"

It hurt Banya's heart to think that things had gone sour for her barn rats. The mention of six meant that two of the girls were gone, probably dead. The letter gave no details as to who was missing, why they had left Caerau, or how they had reached Carraidland, but that news could wait until she heard it directly from them. All Banya wanted right now was to count fingers and toes and hug the stuffing out of them, but Eir would not release her for travel. The children would have to come to her. What that intent, Balfor had written that the children should be sent on to Eachan's Rest with all haste.

Stretching her legs out before her, Banya looked across the open yard to a large round pen made of split rails. Eachan stood in the center of the pen with a long handled whip in one hand. Making circles around her, Briot rode bareback astride a big slate brown mare with black points (what the Carraid called a *grulla*), her arms straight out from her shoulders, holding on with just her thighs and knees, heels down, as the horse trotted. On the other side of the ring, perched on the back of a small chestnut roan, Rai was attempting to do the same.

"How's she doing with the riding lessons?" Banya said.

Kiorda hesitated just a second too long. "She's, uh, she's doing … *well,* yes, well." She patted her pockets as if looking for something and hurried back into the house.

Banya sighed as the door closed behind her mother. "Rai's hopeless, isn't she?"

Balfor smiled and nodded toward the pen. "What do you think?"

Banya studied her partner's form. "She looks like a turd on a stick."

The Carraidleader laughed and nodded. "Well, little girl, you can't get piss out of an egg. Not everyone is a rider."

"But she's my partner! You'd think riding would've rubbed off by now." She watched Rai slide sideways, grab two handfuls of mane, and right herself. At this distance, the profanity was a low, indistinguishable mutter. "This is embarrassing."

"Think how Rai must feel."

Banya chuckled. She watched Briot twist around to ride backwards, leaning forward with her elbows on the horse's rump as she spoke, but could not make out the six-year-old's words of sage advice to the fledgling equestrian. "Any sign of Remeg ?"

"Nothing. Last report placed in her Kell." Balfor glanced at Banya. "At the house of Oofa Lorn," she added. A dark tone edged her words.

"The Provincial Governor? That's not good."

"No, it isn't. Someone saw her in town with that Captain Sheel who works for Lorn, but now she's gone to ground. I don't like not knowing where that woman is or what's on her mind." She looked directly at Banya. "What *is* on her mind, little girl?"

"You're asking the wrong person, Carraidleader. Remeg's a folded card, a blank slate. I'm not privy to her thoughts and I'm not sure I'd want to be." Banya stroked a finger along her top lip. "I can't figure it. The issue with Rai and our desertion are enough to make Remeg mad, sure, but angry enough to hunt us down with this sort of rabid intent? I wouldn't have thought so. Certainly Kinner isn't – wasn't," she amended unhappily, "an issue. What would Remeg want with a sterile kid?"

"Do you think she found out he's fertile?"

"I can't see how."

Balfor snorted. "What about that sword? There have been stories of the Weathercock for longer than, well, longer than there have been Carraid. Factions have risen in his name before and been swept low. None of them ever drew interest like this."

"Maybe it's the sword that's done it." Banya shifted in her chair and tried not to wince. "I don't know. I feel like there's more going on here, that there's something at risk with Remeg, I mean."

"I'm not sure I like the idea of that woman feeling threatened." Balfor twined her hands around a cocked-up knee. "Anyone else, we'd take them on and be done with it. This one will drag herself dying past the hellgate to get what she wants."

"You're frightening me."

Balfor shot her a look. "You should be frightened. Your Captain Remeg is like one of those ice mountains in the waters around the Kern Waste. What do they call them?"

"Icebergs?"

Balfor nodded. "She's like an iceberg. Most of what's going on with her is beneath the surface."

Out in the round pen, Rai lost her grip, slid sideways, and hit the ground. Banya moaned. "What am I going to do with –" Distant movement caught her eye and she raised her head to look.

Briot saw it as well. With perfect balance, she stood up on her horse's back and pointed at a rising plume of dust. "What's that, Gran?" Eachan turned to look as Rai jumped to her feet.

Balfor shielded her eyes with a big hand. "That's not enough dust to be Signy's herd."

"She's not due in until later today." Banya eased up out of her chair and cast a worried eye toward her leader.

Balfor's eyes never left the horizon. "Eachan!" she called. "I want you here with me. Briot, Rai, you both get inside." She looked at Banya. "You, too, in case this turns out to be bad."

Kinner woke to daylight and a sore neck where his head had dragged on it as he slept astride the mule. Grimacing, he massaged the back of his neck, stretched, and yawned wide enough to make his jaw creak. Sitting up straight, he blinked at his surroundings. Where was the river?

The shock made him yank hard on the reins. The mule, unruffled, halted with quiet obedience and dropped its head to graze. Kinner stood in the stirrups and looked around. In every direction was rolling grassland, marked here and there by stands of scrub trees, jumbles of rock, and random clumps of early snow. Nothing looked familiar.

"Dammit, mule! Where have you taken us?" He wanted to weep, to rail, to kick his heels and tantrum like a toddler. Could nothing in his life go right? Could something please happen in his favor just once? "*Oh!*" He clutched the saddle as the john-mule suddenly threw its head up. Ears canted with interest at something beyond the horizon which Kinner could neither see nor hear, the beast drew breath and a noise – part horse's whinny and part grunting wind-down of a bray – burst forth. With a happy-sounding chuckle, the animal broke into a bone-jarring trot.

"Wait a minute! Hey!" Kinner pulled back on the reins, but the mule ignored him. Tossing its head in annoyance, it gave a small buck to let him know who was boss and fell into a smooth, rocking-chair canter.

Although the sky was cloudless, a sound like thunder slowly grew at the edge of Kinner's hearing. As the mule sped across the plain and came up a long rise, the sound rose to a percussive drumbeat. Beyond the crest of the ridge, dust rose like smoke. The mule mounted the slope and a great moving river of horses suddenly closed around them.

Kinner cried out in terror and clutched the saddle. Dust choked him and turned the sun a muddy gold. The animals, built to the pattern of the classic Carraid draft, towered over the mule and quickly outpaced it. As the horses drew ahead, seeming to run for the sheer love of speed, their long-lost cousin fell to the rear.

A shrill whistle cut through the din of hooves and the horses began to slow. At the same instant, a rider unexpectedly appeared beside Kinner, scaring him a second time. She leaned from the saddle, grabbed the mule's bridle, and towed him to the edge of the herd and out. When the animals were safely past and had dropped their heads to graze, she released the mule and turned on Kinner.

"What the hells are you playing at?" Her young face was florid, furious. "You trying to mess things on a lark or did some idiot put you up to it? Are *you* an idiot? You look like one. You could have fouled things royal, you know that? I don't care two figs if you and this cockeyed, mal-formed jigger-beast mule go down under those hooves, but if just one of those animals had fallen because of you, I'd break your puny …" She stopped. Staring at him as if she were really seeing him for the first time, she reined her horse around in a tight circle and reached out to shove Kinner's hood back from his face. "By all that's …" She blinked in astonishment. "You're not Carraid."

Kinner thought that might be the understatement of a lifetime. Before he could respond, she grabbed his arm and gave it a hearty shake. "Who are you? What are you doing here?"

He had no wit or imagination for anything but the truth. "Kinner. My name is Kinner. I'm headed to Dara, but I fell asleep in the saddle and the mule brought me here by mistake." He patted the sweaty brown neck. "I didn't mean any harm."

She released him and sat back in the saddle. "Dara?" The fury had bled from her voice. Curiosity took its place. "At this time of year? That's not a trip I'd make on a bet. It may already be too late. Winter's come a tad early this year and fuckered up everyone, including the Carraid." She leaned down to fondle the mule's ears. "I'm Signy Solveigsdotter. You hungry?"

"*Yes.*"

Laughter at his enthusiasm transformed her serious young-old face. "Well, come you on, then, Kinner. We'll get you something to eat and you can help me sort out what I'm supposed to do with you."

Rai stood just inside the front door of Eachan's Rest, where she could peer through a crack in the jamb to watch and listen. She glanced at Banya, who stood close to the stairs. "If this turns out bad," she said in a whisper, "You'd better run. You're no good in a fight right now."

Banya's expression was grim. "I'm no good at running, either."

"This is no time to be brave!"

"Who's talking brave? I'm talking lung injury. I *can't* run. I can hardly walk."

"*Shhhhhhh!*" Briot, balanced on a newel post that brought her to eye-level, thrust a stiff finger against Banya's lips. "I can't hear!"

Out on the porch, Eachan raised a hand to shield her eyes. "Two riders," she said, loud enough for those inside to hear. She glanced at Balfor and quirked an eyebrow. "Pretty small for an invasionary force."

"Don't be a smart-ass." Balfor, too, squinted into the distance. "One of 'em's riding Carraid horseflesh. That's a good sign."

"Unless they killed and ate one of us."

Balfor gave Eachan a sour look. "Maybe you ought to go inside and send Briot out instead."

Despite her concern, Rai smiled as Briot bounced on her perch and whispered, "*Yes!*"

The elder Carraid watched the riders draw near. "Is that Signy's palomino?" Balfor said.

"Sure looks like it, but what's that with her?"

Rai changed position, angling to get a better look. Like desert *djinn* who arrive on a cloud of sand, the animals came to a halt in front of the porch. There was a golden horse with a white mane and tail and a dark-colored, long-faced mule. The horse's rider waved away the dust and lowered the neckerchief that covered the bottom half of her face. "Hello, Carraidleader!" she said in surprise. "I didn't think to see you here. Eachan, I've brought you a present."

"Not that mule, I hope."

Balfor frowned. "What's going on, Sig?" she said as the other rider pushed back his hood and pulled down his neckerchief.

Rai shrieked like a little girl on Yule morning. Flinging open the door, she threw herself across the porch and dragged Kinner out of the saddle. He froze in shock, but as soon as he realized who had grabbed him, he hugged her hard enough to make her grunt.

She held him at arm's length. "I don't know when I've ever been so happy to see ..." Her brows peaked in a tiny frown. "By the Comb, what happened to you? You're all beat up." She licked her thumb and applied it to the corner of his eye. It came away smudged with purple. "And you're made up like a two-bit whore."

Kinner's smile crumbled. His chest hitched around a sob and big sad tears rolled down his face.

Rai raised her hands in defense. "What'd I do?"

"I don't think it's anything you did," Banya said in a thoughtful tone. She came down the stoop one step at a time and drew the boy to her. "Don't squeeze," she whispered in his ear as his arms went around her. He nodded and, crying softly, rested his head against her shoulder.

Briot pushed past the adult legs and stopped beside her grandmother. "Who's that?"

Eachan lay her hand on the child's head. "A guest, pet."

"What's the matter with him?"

"Just run and tell your mama to bring hot food and drink to the common room."

"But I ..."

"*Now.*"

With a squeal, Briot dashed away. Eachan grinned at her leader. "She'll have everyone thinking we're under siege."

Balfor did not return her smile. Her gaze slid past the huddle of reunited friends and studied the horizon. “Perhaps we are.”

Twenty-Three

Although the common room at Eachan's Rest had been built to accommodate a Carraid's oversized proportions and zest for life, it retained an air of homey intimacy which Kinner found immediately soothing. The wooden walls, polished to a muted sheen, lent the room a honeyed glow scented with beeswax. A large field-stone fireplace dominated one end of the room, with a low round table and several pieces of very comfortable-looking furniture placed in front of it. The floor was strewn with colorful woolen rugs. Kinner felt an enormous desire to curl up inside one of them and stay there until spring, snug as a caterpillar inside a cocoon.

"Eachan, Rai, Banya, you stay," Balfor said. "Kinner, you have the seat of honor." She ushered him into the chair nearest the fire. "Signy, if you go back to the kitchen, I think you'll find that Sobity has a bowl of soup waiting for you."

"That's all the incentive I need," the rider said with a grin. She nodded at Kinner. "Good luck," she said and was gone before he could thank her.

As everyone settled into their chairs, Briot ran in and climbed into her grandmother's lap, straddling Eachan's knee as she would a horse. A moment later, a young woman with wheaten braids and Eachan's square chin appeared with a tray of food and a steaming pitcher of wine. The slight mound of a mid-stage pregnancy pushed against the long-tailed shirt she wore over loose breeches.

"Ah, Sobity, thank you," said Balfor. She tapped the table with her hand. "Put that here, if you please."

Briot leaned sideways and poked Kinner in the knee to get his attention. She pointed at her mother's belly. "That's my little brother."

"Or sister," Eachan said and jostled her knee to bobble the child up and down.

Briot giggled as her head whipped back and forth, snapping her braids. "No, it's a boy," she said with unshakeable faith.

"Congratulations," Kinner said. "You must be very excited." He tried not to stare at the food, but the aroma that came from the warm slices of stuffed bread had his mouth watering.

The child looked at him and a fine crease picked out between her brows like a line of embroidery. The frank gaze was unsettling, as if every secret Kinner had ever held were bared to view. Briot picked up a piece of bread and put it into his hand. "Here," she said with kindness. "You're supposed to eat this."

Tears again watered his vision. He ducked his face against his shoulder to blink them away.

"Please, everyone," Eachan said. "Help yourselves."

For the next little while, it was all about the food. Praise was heaped upon Sobity until she blushed with pleasure and retreated to the kitchen, taking her protesting daughter with her.

Briot's voice whined down the hallway. "But I want to *stay!*"

"It's big people talk," her mother said. "That's not the business of little ears."

"How can I learn to be Carraidleader if I can't listen to big people talk?" The sound of a closing door cut off Sobity's reply.

Eachan chuckled. "Looks like someone's after your job, Balfor."

The Carraidleader rolled her eyes. "She can have it. Kinner, have you had enough to eat?"

He leaned back against a cushion with a sigh, the worst of his anxiety in abeyance. "Yes, thank you." He was fed, among friends, and Rai had told him that the sword was safe. For now, so was his world.

"To business, then," Balfor said without preamble. She took a moment to refill her cup. Into that silence, Banya asked. "What happened to you, Kinner?"

He met her eyes across the table. The look lasted only seconds, but something passed between them, something understood and acknowledged beyond the use of words. Without being asked, Rai refilled his cup with wine and put it into his hand. He gave her a small, grateful smile and took a sip. When he spoke, his voice started out soft and grew stronger with the telling. He described his plunge over the falls, waking among the Tzigane with no memory of how he got there, and Torqua's plans for his future. He never intended to go into detail – certainly not with strangers present – but once the words began they fell out of him like rain. When he was finished he felt wrung dry, limp as an old dishrag.

"I'd like to teach those gypsies a thing or two," Rai said, white-lipped with anger.

Banya cocked an eyebrow as she handed Kinner a fresh napkin to dry his face and blow his nose. "You've been corrupted by the Chesne, pal-o-mine."

"And the damned Carraid, too," she said. "What of it?"

"What about you?" Kinner asked. "What happened to both of you?"

Their story was far shorter than his. When they were done, Kinner said, "What made Remeg think she could invade Carraidland with a handful of soldiers?"

"Arrogance," said Balfor.

"Stupidity," said Eachan.

"I'm not convinced she was thinking at all," Banya said.

Balfor looked at her. When she spoke, her words sluiced the peace and safety from Kinner's soul like a dose of salts. "That's a perceptive observation, little girl, and a frightening one. A beast that no longer thinks is a beast gone mad." Her expression darkened. "A beast gone mad is capable of anything."

Having spent the day in bed per Eir's orders, Banya was antsy from inactivity. Although she insisted that she felt fine, Rai had agreed with Eir that her friend's color was off and had been since before Kinner's arrival a few days earlier. The smudgy brown shadows that gathered beneath her eyes worried Rai no end. Banya looked older than her years, careworn and haggard, and she had developed an old woman's fretful petulance.

"I can't believe you're going to ride off to Dara and leave me here to rot. Some friends you are."

"Put a sock in it." Rai took each piece of clothing that Kinner had carefully folded and crammed it into her rucksack. "Look at it from our perspective. You get to stay inside in a nice warm house where everyone spoils you rotten while we'll freeze our asses off riding through the mountains in the dead of winter."

"It's hardly the dead of winter, Rai," Banya said in a dry tone.

"I realize that, Banya," she replied in the same sarcastic manner. "But it will be if we don't stop jawing about this and get a move-on." She stuffed more clothing into the bag, yanked the ties closed, and tossed it onto the pile at the foot of Banya's bed. The Weathercock sword, its box latch repaired, lay on the table by the window. "I'm not exactly thrilled about this either, but we all agreed it was the best way to go. The sooner we put an end to this sword business, the sooner we can get on with our lives."

Banya nodded and picked at the bedspread. "I know. I'd just feel a lot better if I was going with you."

"Me, too." When Banya raised grateful eyes to her face, Rai added, "You're big enough to hide behind when the wind blows."

"Fuck-face."

"Could you two quit bickering, please?" Kinner said in exasperation.

Rai snorted. "Listen to who's giving orders."

"Oh, shut up." He walked to the window, but there was little to see outside in the dark except his image tossed back from the rippled glass.

The house was quiet. The Roundup had moved on toward Riddock with only half its usual riders. Eachan had held some back for what she called 'insurance.' Kiorda remained at the steading, as did Eachan, her immediate family, and those in her employ. Balfor had gone south taking Ruarc with her, but before her departure she had posted additional sentries along the Carraidland border and sent word to the steadings around Ammon, Camshron, Avenal and Riddock that riders were needed in the west at once. So far, there had been not so much as a whisper of Remeg or her troop, but that did nothing to change the fact that she was out there somewhere.

Rai studied the watery pattern of Kinner's reflection. Who was that lanky, half-grown boy with the guarded expression? Surely not sweet little Kinner of Moselle. She shared a look with Banya and hid a smile as he rubbed a finger along his top lip. Somewhere along the road from home to here, he had sprouted the beginnings of a moustache and the faint fuzz of a beard. It was obvious that he liked it and she wondered if it reminded him of his father. Some day, she would have to ask.

He turned away from the glass. "I appreciate all the trouble you've gone through for me. I wish more of what Mum said made sense."

"That's what happens when you deal with visionaries," Banya said. "One has to act on faith. You having second thoughts?"

His laughter was a breathy burst of sound. "Mum asked me the same thing once. I'm *always* having second thoughts!"

"Then why bother finishing this?" Rai asked, curious. "Why not give it up, sell the thing or give it away?"

"Oh, believe me, I've thought more than once about chucking the sword into some deep lake and just walking away, but ..." Whatever else Kinner might have said was interrupted by the sound of rapid steps coming up the stairs.

A second later, Eachan opened the door without knocking. Her features were drawn tight with anxiety. "Rai, Kinner, I want you downstairs. There's something amove in the night. It's only sheer damn luck that Cobin heard something on her way back from the privy. I've sent her on to Riddock to see if she can meet their riders coming and Tobelin's gone south to rouse Balfor. I don't dare deplete our strength any more than that." She shook her head in worried bemusement. "I'd love to know how they got past the border sentries."

Still muttering, she left the room in a hurry, closing the door behind her. Her steps went along the hallway to the next room. They heard the door open and soft voices speaking in a rush.

"I bet I know how they did it," Rai said. "First chance I get, I'm killing that ugly bitch Mestipen."

"Get in line," Banya said. She laid a gentle hand over her bandaged side.

Rai nodded. "Sit tight. We'll handle this. Come on, kid."

They split in the hallway, each to their own room. Rai had not worn her sword since their arrival in Carriadland and it was with an odd mix of feelings that she buckled it on now. The blade settled at her left hip with a weighty familiarity that was oddly comforting and yet … she hadn't missed the weapon.

She was the first to arrive downstairs. Kinner appeared a moment later with a Carraid-made sword Eachan had given him when she learned that his Chesne weapon had been lost to the river. Seeing him armed, Rai sighed and shook her head. "Just so long as you keep in mind that you're not the Weathercock."

Kinner rolled his eyes. "Believe me, Rai, no one is more aware of that than I am."

They joined Eachan outside. A moment later, several Carraid riders appeared on horseback and arranged themselves in front of the porch. In the distance, there was motion against the darkness of night. Eachan nodded. "That's them."

"Why is there no sound?" Kinner said. "Why can't we hear their horses?"

"Because they've muffled the harness with rags and wrapped the horses' feet in burlap," Rai said. It was an old soldiering trick she knew well. She stared into the night, willing it to part and reveal their enemy. "Remeg had only a small troop in Cadasbyr. This feels …"

"Bigger," Eachan finished for her. "I know. She must have profited from her visit to the Lorn, damn them both." She stroked her chin. "The question is will she play this by force or with care? Will she risk open battle or try for intimidation and a show of strength?"

Rai snorted. "It's impossible to intimidate a Carraid."

"I'm glad you think so." Eachan's smile had no humor in it. "Remeg invaded once and was turned back. Now she's come again, without invitation or provocation. That puts Kedar Trevelyan in a precarious position, politically speaking; the sort where she could owe Balfor restitution if it turns out you're not here." Her eyes cut to them. "Which is what I want."

"What?" Kinner sputtered.

Rai grabbed her arm. "Eachan, I'm not leaving you to hold off a troop of soldiers with –"

Eachan cut her off. "My riders can handle things without your help. I'm telling you to get off my place." She took them each by a shoulder, turned them around, and gave them a firm shove. "Get your stuff and get you gone while there's still time. If you're not here, I don't have to lie about it. The less I have to lie, the more my real deception will ring true."

"What about Banya?"

"I'll not risk Banya any more than I'll risk the others who can't fight. Now go!" For a moment, Eachan's worried expression softened. "And may the Weathercock protect you."

"Weathercock, my ass," Rai swore as they took the stairs to the second floor two at a time. "I'd like to tell this Weathercock of yours to shove it straight up his –" They burst into Banya's room and found her out of bed and dressed. Rai stopped so fast that Kinner ran into her. "What the blue fuck do you think you're about?" she said. "You're no bloody good in a fight right now! Get back into bed!"

Banya slung her sword belt around her waist and cinched the buckle tight. "They're not taking me flat on my back."

"No one's taking anyone! Eachan and her riders will handle it." Rai snatched up their packs and threw one to Kinner. "She's sending us away before …"

"Before they get here. Good." For a moment they just looked at each other. "You be careful, little girl."

Rai nodded and finished the mantra. "I'll see you after," she said softly.

Kinner approached Banya. "I'm afraid to hug you. I don't want to hurt you."

"Let me worry about that." She tucked an arm around him. "You take my mare, you hear?" She laid a finger against his lips. "Don't argue. She's the finest there is and you'll need a mount you can trust. Rai, make sure he takes her."

"He'll take her."

Banya kissed the top of his head. "You be careful, too," she whispered into his hair.

"I'll see you after," Kinner replied in a voice tight with unshed tears. He stepped out of her embrace and followed Rai downstairs.

They departed via the back door, grabbing their coats on the way. Hunkered low well behind the line of Carraid riders, they hurried from the house to the barn. The night seemed full of sound and threat. Every insect creak was an approaching horse; each shadow was an armed assailant. Rai had never felt so spooked. *I know why that is,* she thought as they reached the back wall of the barn. *Banya's not with me.*

The barn smelled of sweet hay and grain. The horses, sensing the approach of strangers, circled in their box stalls. Heads tossed. Hooves stamped and pawed the ground. In a corner enclosure, the black chuckled low in his chest, a dark sound of warning.

Rai laid a hand across his nose. Did he know Remeg was out there? Did he hate and fear her as much as Rai did? "Keep your fat mouth shut for once, dingbat." His ears canted to catch the sound of her voice and his lips moved as if he meant to reply in words.

With swift fingers they made ready to ride. Kinner rubbed the grey mare's forehead as he settled the headpiece behind her ears. "Will you bear me?" he whispered to her. "Will you leave Banya behind?"

"They're not attached at the hip, Kinner," Rai said, and wondered belatedly if that was true. Carraid were strange with their horses. She eased open the door to the black's stall and led him into the aisle. Reins gathered and one foot in a stirrup, she paused and cast an eye toward the front of the barn. "I can't do this. I can't just leave. I have to know what's going on."

"Eachan told us to go."

"You always do what you're told? Look, stay here. I won't be a minute." She handed him the reins and hurried to the front of the barn to peer through a window.

Eachan's Rest blazed with light. Every lantern had been kindled to tell Remeg that any hope of ambush was lost. Eachan stood on the porch in full view as the riders appeared. Rai's heart went cold at the sight of Remeg, riding in front with Asabi and Mestipen to her right. To her left rode a woman Rai did not recognize, dressed in blue and white livery. Close to three-score soldiers had swelled the ranks of the detachment. They halted short of the porch and Eachan spoke, but at this distance Rai could not hear what was said. "Shit."

"What?" Kinner spoke softly into her ear.

She jump in surprise, whirled around, and punched him hard in the shoulder. "I told you to stay put!"

"Fuck that," he said, rubbing where she'd hit him. "You always do what you're told?" He pushed her aside to get a better look. "Who are those soldiers in blue and white?"

"I'm guessing Lorn levies." She peered out beside him, their heads close together. "I swear I don't understand any of this. How could what we've done be bad enough to bring on all of this?" She tugged his sleeve. "Let's go."

They exited from the rear of the barn and were riding away from Eachan's Rest when a flare of light made them both turn in the saddle. Torches had been kindled among Remeg's soldiers and several bows were lifted with their arrows nocked.

"They're going to kill Eachan!" Kinner cried.

"No, they're not," Rai said. She felt cold and bloodless. "They're threatening to set fire to the buildings." She thought of Sobity, awkward with pregnancy and Kiorda, so crippled with arthritis that she could hardly get out of her own way. Briot might escape if she could be made to leave, but Banya never would.

Kinner turned the Carraid mare around. "I'm going back. Mum once said that a lot of people would die because of the Weathercock, but they aren't going to die because of *me.*"

Rai grabbed his reins and pulled the horse up short. "Who do you think you're dealing with? Noble sentiment won't stop Remeg. She has no heart for sacrifice, if she has a heart at all. If we surrender, she might still put them to the torch for no other reason than because it pleases her to do so."

Before Kinner could respond, the soaring arc of a burning arrow lit the night. Seconds later, the dry thatch of Eachan's Rest burst into flames.

Hand resting on the hilt of her sword, Remeg sat her horse easily and watched the angry Carraid woman on the porch. *How does it feel, Eachan?* she thought. *To be on the receiving end?* Behind her, bowstrings creaked as they drew taut in readiness.

Eachan's face flushed with anger. "Fulfill that threat, Captain Remeg, and Carraidland will not be held accountable for what follows."

"The aiding and abetting of traitors to the Crown is a crime that will damn you in any number of courts, Carraid or otherwise," Remeg said.

"Whose crown would that be, Captain?"

Remeg thought her teeth would crack from the tension in her jaw. "You know whose crown, Carraid."

Eachan nodded. "Ah. Your queen. The she-goat."

A ripple of shock went through the troop. Remeg's fingers tightened on the reins. The horse, sensing her tension, tossed its head in fretful motion. "Like it or not, Byrsdotter, Carraidland belongs to Kedar Trevelyan. This land is subject to her laws."

"You've neglected your politics. Although we maintain a tenuous peace, Carraidland has *never* been subject to the Crown." Eachan rested a hand on the porch railing. "I wonder what your queen will think when she learns that you've threatened that peace by crossing our borders like petty sneak thieves? You might have blundered among our herds and caused irrevocable damage. Would Kedar Trevalyan compensate us for horses ruined because of you?"

Remeg held taut, her face a bland mask. She felt the weight of Sheel's presence at her side – silent but watchful, judgmental and sardonic. How would Kedar take the news that her lover had invaded Carraidland? Would she see it as proof of Remeg's devotion or as the foolhardy action of a woman desperate for reconciliation? Would Kedar praise or condemn her?

Unable to guess the mind of her beloved, Remeg swayed, caught between emotion and action like a fly stuck in an airy web. "There's a simple way to end this, Byrsdotter. Hand over the fugitives and we'll be on our way."

"I told you. They've gone."

Remeg's lip curled. "The last time I saw Banya, she had an arrow in her lung. Rai would never leave her in that condition."

"Banya's dead," Eachan said bluntly. Remeg heard a stir behind her as the troop took in the news. "She didn't last the first night. Rai and the boy left days ago. They're well away from here and well away from you. Good luck finding them."

"Oh, I think I can flush them out," Remeg said. "It's not as if I don't know where they're going." Her fingers moved. At the rear of the company, an arrow ignited. It burned a fiery trail across the sky and rammed home in the heavy thatch of the house, setting the straw alight. Seconds later, another arrow sliced out of the darkness and impaled the archer through the throat.

Like beasts born of legend, half-woman and half-horse, Eachan's riders charged from the darkness into the lurid dance of flames, riding with hands free to better wield blade and bow. The Carraid mounts, trained to obey every nuance in the shift of their rider's body, lent their aid to the battle, rising up to strike out with their hooves.

Sheel cursed. "Remeg, you imbecile!"

Remeg's face burned. She drew her sword, half-intending to plunge it into the Lorn commander's breast. Instead, she swung as Eachan hurtled toward her, blade drawn. The horsewoman's weapon was hammered aside in the last instant by Mestipen, and Remeg's stroke sliced into Eachan's arm. As she roared in pain, two voices joined hers, both battle-pitched to carry above the sound of combat.

"EACHAN, GET DOWN!"

Banya plunged from the house, blue eyes lit with icy fire. She struck at Mestipen as a black animal Remeg recognized only too well careened between them. Rai leapt off the horse and slammed Eachan behind the knees, dropping her to the ground as the return parry of Mestipen's blade whistled over their heads. They rolled together amid a forest of dancing hooves and scrambled to get out of the way as the horses pitched and reared, riders yowling as sword blades tore their flesh and arrows brought them down. The air filled with smoke and the reek of blood.

A child's wail rose over the hungry crackle of flames. Eachan, wild-eyed with panic, tossed Rai aside and rushed into the inferno that had been her home.

Sheel, proving to be a better soldier than Remeg had thought, reined her horse around tight and drove it across the melee, hacking from one side to the other. Rai met her halfway, sweeping her blade before her like a scythe, and opened the horse's breast with one stroke. The pain maddened animal screamed and collapsed, taking Sheel with it.

"Who's the imbecile now?" Remeg muttered. She drove her mount toward Rai as another blazing arrow split the sky.

The barn roof went up with a hungry *WHOOSH!* and the doors sprang open. A torrent of terrified horses boiled out, splitting like a river to either side of the fray and disappearing across the grassland.

A vision appeared in the gaping doorway.

The grey horse, made hazy with drifting smoke, stood firm and resolute in the face of combat. The thick neck bunched as the animal tucked its chin close to its chest and danced its feet in the battle dressage of the Carraid. The rider, cloaked and cowled, swung the bright nimbus of a blade into the air as a voice rang out, not in the thin, high tones of an adolescent boy, but in the full clear tenor of a man.

"WEATHERCOCK!"

Remeg's scalp crawled as the cry slashed across the battle, bringing everyone up short. Into that window of silence the Carraid roared, baying like hounds, and fell on the invaders with renewed vigor as the grey horse dropped its head and joined the fight.

Blade slid against blade with a screeching cry as old as time. Women raged with pain and horses screamed. Sweat and blood flew; smoke blinded the eye. Those who foolishly pursued Carraid riders into the darkness beyond the lick of flames, perished.

Remeg fought like a machine, a thing devoid of emotion made for no other purpose. Slowly, she worked her way toward Kinner. His skill with a blade was rudimentary at best. Any success was by dint of surprise and the natural hesitation of women to kill a man unless absolutely necessary. Nor did Remeg wish to kill him. Banya and Rai, yes, by all means, but right now, she wanted to get her hands on that child and send him to Caerau as fast as possible.

Face grey with fatigue, Banya stepped into her path. Her breathing was labored, her eyes glazed with pain. The side of her shirt was crimson where she'd either taken a blow or ripped free her stitches. "No, Captain," she said. "He's not yours to take."

Remeg's vision narrowed with gall. Snarling, she drove her heels hard into the horse's sides. As it sprang forward, she let her weapon fall.

Grunting, Banya parried the stroke with both hands, staggering with exhaustion. Remeg turned the horse around and came at her again. Once more, Banya deflected the sweep of Remeg's blade, slicing past her guard and delivering a shallow cut across Remeg's sword arm. Cursing, feeling the well of blood and the dense heaviness of injured muscle, Remeg shifted the weapon to her left hand and came at Banya from her wounded side. The Carraid stood tall, dashing blood and sweat from her eyes with a snap of the head, and brought her sword up with both hands as Remeg bore down on her. Silent as the black wings of death, Remeg stood in the saddle and put every ounce of strength she had into the blow. The blade knocked Banya's aside and sheared into her chest, splitting muscle and shattering bone with the ease of Black Hirn cutting steaks. For an instant, Banya stared with confounded fascination at the wet tide of blood spilling across her chest. Then she crumpled forward onto the churned ground.

An inarticulate scream shattered the night. Rai, her face a gory mask of loss, stared at her fallen partner. Remeg backed her horse around and lifted her sword in salute, the blade glistening with Banya's blood. Incoherent, uncontrolled and unthinking, Rai charged. Smiling, Remeg drew back her blade –

– and a grey fury barreled into her, knocking her horse clean off its feet. Remeg threw herself free of the saddle, rolled, and came up empty-handed. Casting around for her sword, she froze, unable to believe what she was seeing.

Asabi – *Asabi, of all people!* – had hold of Rai and was slinging her, limp and unresponsive, across the back of the dancing grey and into its rider's lap. Some brief words passed between them – at this distance, Remeg could not make out what was said – and then the dark warrior stepped back and slapped the mare with the flat of her blade. As it galloped away, Asabi turned and faced Remeg.

TWENTY-FOUR

The hardy dappled mare was miles from the carnage of Eachan's Rest before Rai regained consciousness. She came awake fighting, flailing her arms and legs until Kinner had no choice but to let her go. She slid off into ankle-deep snow, lost her balance, and came down hard on her rump. The fall knocked her teeth together, but she struggled back onto her feet and slapped a hand to her empty hip.

"It's gone," he said. His voice was raw from screaming during battle. "All we have left is this." He touched the Weathercock sword where it rode at his knee. Rai eyed it like an animal deprived of food and Kinner backed the horse away from her. "Don't even think about it."

"I could take it from you."

"You could try."

She looked as if he had slapped her. Her face crumbled with agony. Turning away, shoulders hunched against the cold, she began trudging back the way they had come, following the broken trail in the snow.

"Rai, don't be stupid!" When she neither stopped nor responded, Kinner turned the mare around and went after her. "What are you going to do?" he said, walking the horse beside her. "Take Remeg on alone with an entire troop at her back?"

She did not reply. There was no sound save the crunch of snow underfoot and the foggy chuff of their breathing.

He urged the mare on ahead of her and halted the animal cross-wise to block the path. "You stubborn, motherless half-wit," he swore, wishing he had a soldier's facility with profanity. "Remeg will cut you down where you stand."

"All I need is one chance." Her eyes flicked again toward the blade on the saddle.

Kinner curled a proprietary hand around the hilt. "*No,* Rai. You had your chance."

"And you stole it from me!" She punched him on the thigh hard enough to numb the muscle. "You owe me this! Don't you even care that Banya is …" Her entire face constricted. She could not say the word.

"You'd have died, too, if I hadn't gotten you out of there!"

"*I DON'T CARE!*" she shrieked. She threw another punch, missed, and grabbed the saddle to keep from falling. Clutching the leather, she hid her face against the grey's warm shoulder and bawled like a child.

Kinner heard the echo of those words in his own heart and thought they might hold the greatest truth Rai had ever expressed. They had for him. When Holan died, he might have stayed right where he was, pinned to the spot by grief, had it not been for Rai and Banya.

He placed a gentle hand on her heaving shoulder. He knew from experience that there were no words of comfort he could offer, nothing that would make even the slightest bit of difference to her pain. There was no wish strong enough, no magic powerful enough, to bring back the bright and witty Carraid, no matter how much they both wanted it.

Kinner dismounted into the snow. This was the moment when she could overpower him if she chose, take the sword and the horse and head down the trail toward her death. He put his arms around her. "Come with me," he said gently. "We have to give up Remeg for now, but not forever."

She looked at him. Her face was a mess – mottled skin, swollen red eyes, and a river of snot. "Why did you stop me?" Her voice was small and hopeless, a hurt child crying in the night. "I had her."

Kinner's lips pinched into a chapped and bitter line. "You had nothing. You were so intent on trying to kill Remeg that you didn't see the Lorn commander coming at you from the side. She'd have skewered you before you made the first thrust." He glanced at the sky, trying without success to gauge the passage of time the way Banya had taught him. He rubbed his forehead with a balled-up fist. Had he learned nothing? "Anyway, it wasn't me who saved you. One of Remeg's soldiers did it."

That brought her up short. "One of Remeg's – ? *Who?*"

He shrugged. "How would I know? Tall. Slender. Skin dark as peat." He pictured the woman as she had first appeared to him, striding through the melee with her weapon at the ready. He had thought she meant to kill them both, but she had cuffed Rai behind the ear with her fist, grabbed her as she collapsed, and slung her across the mare's withers like a deer carcass. "She was bald, but very beautiful."

"Asabi." Rai's voice was both certain and confused. "I don't understand. She's one of Remeg's lieutenants and loyal as hell."

"Apparently not."

"She'll pay for this." Rai's voice dropped. "Everyone pays."

"If that's true, then so will Remeg." The honesty of those words and his belief in them set fire to Kinner's bones. "She's followed us this far. If she survives Eachan's Rest, she'll follow us again. The next time we meet, let's have it be in a place of our choosing, where we have the advantage."

"Yeah? Where's that?" When he didn't respond, Rai palmed the tears from her face and wiped them on her pants. "You're turning into quite the warrior, aren't you? I don't think your family would recognize you now."

The comment both surprised and pleased him. "Thank you. I'll take that as a compliment." He gave her another brief hug, then they remounted and rode north.

When night came, they sought shelter within a tumbled cairn of rock. The comfort of the small fire they kindled in a secluded corner was more spiritual than physical. The Carraid mare – trained, experienced, and smarter than either of them – laid down on a patch of ancient bracken and let them curl against her broad, warm back. They ate sparingly of their meager stores, slept in fitful turns, and were up and away before first light.

They spoke little, for there was no need to rehash the recent and terrible past or their present predicament. Alone with his thoughts, Kinner traced them in circles as worry gnawed his guts. Half their food stuffs and fodder were gone, left behind along with Rai's spare clothing and bed roll when the black horse had bolted. They had not enough to sustain them until Dara, but where in this wilderness could they hope to find more?

What of Eachan's Rest? Had the Carraid won the day or were the buildings collapsed into black and smoky ruins, hiding the bones of those who had perished within? He thought of Eachan, blustery as a winter's storm but exceedingly kind; Briot and her six-foot personality; Sobity, soft-spoken and nurturing; competent Eir ...

And Banya.

Had she been healthy and strong, she would easily have killed Remeg. As it was, all that remained to Kinner were brief memories of her generous spirit and a final image of her standing brave and glorious despite her injuries.

He glanced over his shoulder at Rai, but her attention was on the distant mountains, her expression one of pensive calculation. She would continue to survive as long as Remeg endured. Beyond that remained to be seen.

They found the Taran River impassible, the fords above and below the falls swollen with foul, rolling grey water. Rai stood well back from the bank and watched as clods of soil tore loose and were washed away in the tumult. "We'll have to keep going north, find a way around the river or over it closer to its source." She pointed to show the way. "There's no way we're going to try crossing this."

Kinner stood even further back, giving the boiling tumble of water a wide berth. "Fine by me."

Rai nodded, remembering the frigid suck of that deadly river and what had happened here. "All right, then. Let's go." They continued on.

The hardy souls who inhabited the mountainous region between Carraidland and Dara kept to themselves. Protected by the forest, the mountain valleys and narrow passes, they eked an existence from the rocky soil, growing just enough to get by from year to year. Far from the depredations of those who served the queen, they hunted and trapped at will, taking deer and mink, beaver and bear. Those who farmed the sea – the beach pickers, fisherfolk, and sealers who made their living on the great cold waters from Ooshka Bay to the Kern Waste – paid scant attention to anything beyond the circle of their clans and the turn of the seasons that dictated their lives.

Late on the second morning, they happened across a stone hovel roofed with hunks of sod. The dooryard was deep in old, crusty snow. A narrow trail, packed slick and glossy by the passage of feet, led from the door and around the side of the hut. Smoke emerged from a small hole in the roof and vanished amid the slant of flakes.

Kinner stopped the mare. "Who lives here?"

"Who cares so long as they know the meaning of hospitality." Rai slid backward over the mare's rump, dislodging a thin layer of newly fallen snow, and knocked a fist against the plank door. "Hello? Anyone there? We could use some help." When there was no answer she tried the door, but the latch was either stuck or barred from inside. A single window, shuttered with a plank of wood, also refused to open.

"Leave them alone, Rai. I don't blame them for being scared." Kinner fingered the ends of his hair where the blood of battle had dried into stiff points. "I bet we don't exactly look reputable."

"What do looks have to do with anything? I'm talking about common courtesy to the wayfarer." She kicked the door hard. "Fuckers. Come on. Let's check around back." She followed the path and he came after her, riding the mare.

A stack of wood taller than he was ran from the hut to a rude lean-to that served as shelter to an anemic cow and three skinny goats. The cow, her bag flaccid, lowed when she saw them and nudged her hayrick. The goats (nanny, billy, and kid) stared with yellow-eyed boredom and *maaa*-ed. Rai rubbed her hands together. "This is more like it. Give me the sword."

Kinner laid a protective hand on the weapon. "Why?"

"Because I'm going to kill one of those goats." She rolled her eyes at the expression on his face. "Don't get your knickers in a twist, Grandpa. I won't insult your delicate male sensibilities by murdering the little baa-baa in front of you."

"For your information, I've seen animals killed before."

"Then what's your problem?"

"Rai, you can't just take someone's livestock and kill it. These goats could be all the food these people have for the entire winter."

"Your mother's ass. With a cow and three goats, *'these people'* are rich by local standards." She raised her voice to carry to anyone who might be hiding inside the house. "They probably have smoked venison hanging inside the chimney and maybe a barrel or two of salt pork or dried fish tucked away in a corner. I bet there's even a crock of honey in the larder and a cask of ale, and a root cellar with turnips and spuds, *none of which they've offered to share!*" She kicked over an ice-rimmed bucket used to water the cow and snatched it up by its rough, woven handle. She held out her free hand and wiggled the fingers. "Now are you going to give me that sword or do I have to kill the thing with my bare hands?"

He gave it to her without further argument. She chose the kid, thereby leaving the breeding stock, and took it behind the lean-to where she clamped it between her knees, drew back its long neck, and finished things with a single quick slice. She upended the corpse by its hind legs to drain off some of the blood into the bucket, then she beheaded, skinned, and gutted the beast as best she could. She left the head and most of the viscera for those in the house, but kept back the liver and heart.

"That didn't look too difficult."

She was surprised to find Kinner standing behind her, looking more curious and less nauseous than she'd have expected. "You've never killed an animal?"

"No, my aunts always did it." His boots crunched in the snow as he squatted beside her and reached out to touch the naked meat. "They said men were too delicate to take part in such things."

Rai chuckled. "They should see you now. You'd give 'em a heart attack." She sawed at the carcass, cutting it into packable joints. "My aunts did the killing, too, but they left the butchering to my father. That's who I learned it from. I thought once about becoming a butcher, but …" She shrugged. "Guess it happened, just not in the way I thought it would." She piled the cuts of meat in the center of the open skin. "You know, I've worked with better tools."

He gave her a sardonic look. "Mum didn't exactly make that sword with butchery in mind."

"Not of the goat variety, at any rate." Rai sat back on her heels and reached for the bucket. She held it toward him with a bloody hand. "Have a drink."

He leaned away. "No, thanks."

"Suit yourself." She lifted it with both hands, took a swig, and licked her gory lips with a lurid tongue. "If you're going to survive without a Household, Kinner, you'd better learn to make use of whatever comes your way. You've eaten blood pudding, haven't you?"

"Yes, but that doesn't mean I want to drink blood."

"I don't see much difference. Besides, 'want' has little or nothing to do with it." She took another swallow. "You might miss this if we end up in a tight spot and the only alterative is an empty stomach. You sure you don't want to try it?"

He hesitated. She thought for a moment that he might take her up on it, but his expression closed. He crossed his arms and shook his head. "Not this time."

"Your loss." Rai sighed at the waste (she could only drink so much of the stuff herself without upchucking), and put the bucket aside. She finished cutting the meat and wrapped the pieces inside the skin. She cleaned the sword with snow and handed it to Kinner. "Let's go. We'll eat as we ride." She grinned and licked the blood from her teeth. "And, yes, I mean raw."

The storm followed them away from the steading, haunting their steps and intensifying as the hours passed. The trail grew steep for a time and then evened out into a long valley where it dipped between two peaks. Here they were able to pick up speed, moving at a gentle canter through soft snow that reached the mare's knees. At the far end of the valley, the ground rose again. Here the wind sharpened and changed direction, blowing directly into their faces from the north. Icy snowflakes pecked their red cheeks like tiny birds.

Kinner, riding behind Rai with the skin of goat meat in his lap and his arms around her waist, lifted his face from the protection of her back and drew a long, deep breath through his nose. "Do you smell that?"

She sniffed. "Pine," she said with a shrug.

He poked her in the hip. "It's not pine, that's salt, that is. We must be near the ocean."

Rai turned her face aside as a particularly strong gust pelted them. "Ooshka Bay, Eachan called it."

"Where the sealers live." Kinner bent his head against the wind. "Rai? What's a seal?"

"Beats me."

They rode on. The snow deepened with creeping inexorability, blurring the line of tree and rock and erasing all features of the landscape except those which lay directly ahead of them. The trail grew slippery and their pace slowed. By mid-day, they were forced to seek shelter against a cliff where a divot had been worn in the rock by wind and rain. With the mare picketed behind some scrub, they hurriedly gathered what few bits of wood they could find and climbed into the cramped aerie, prepared to make the best of it.

Rai cobbed together a tiny fire. When it was burning to her satisfaction, she jabbed a hunk of goat meat onto a stick and handed it to Kinner. "Give that a sear and get it into your gut, then roll up in the saddle blanket and get some rest. I'll take first watch."

He dutifully took the stick from her hand and hunkered down beside the fire. Fat dripped from the meat onto the flames and sizzled. "If Remeg's on our trail, won't she smell this on the wind?"

"You'll give yourself nightmares thinking like that."

"*Rai* ..."

"How the hell do I know? Depends upon the wind and what direction she's coming from. *If* she's coming." Rai hoped she was coming. She wanted the satisfaction of killing Remeg with her bare hands.

Buckling the Weathercock sword around her hips, she took up her station at the entry to their lair. The wind tugged at her hair and wormed icy fingers inside her clothes. It was going to be a long night. There had been many such nights in her career, but there had always been someone with her. There was someone with her now, yes, but it wasn't the right someone.

She braced one hand against the pommel of the sword and wondered how many times in her life she had taken this stance. "What do you think of battle now that you've tasted it?"

"I hate it." The bitter tone of Kinner's voice was marred by a mouthful of food. He handed her a piece of the meat. "The sound. The smell. It's awful."

Rai nodded. She remembered her first time and how close she had come to death but for Banya. She took a bite and chewed. "But you survived."

"Not by my own skill." He stared at the meat on the stick, turning it back and forth, watching fat bubble and drip. "You were right, you know."

She turned to look at him. "About what?"

"I know just enough to be a danger to myself and everyone around me. Oh, I got in a lick or two, but you know damned well the only reason I didn't die was because Remeg didn't want me to."

So it was back to Remeg. "Eat up and get some sleep," Rai said in a brusque tone. She did not speak again, not even to respond to his soft "good night."

There was no flicker of shadow against the fall of snow, no clue as to what stalked the night. The wind murmured through pine boughs with the cold sound of the sea against pewter-colored sand. Limbs creaked like footsteps on a stair, the soft tread of an ancient goddess on her rounds or the shade of an absent friend come to stand watch at Rai's side.

She fed the fire, walked to keep warm, and only gave up the vigil when she caught herself nodding off on her feet. She gave Kinner a poke with the toe of her boot. "Your turn." He shivered beneath her hand, but did not respond. She shook him. "Wake up."

He stirred with a confused and jerky motion. "Wha'stit?" His voice slurred. "… meg?"

Rai grabbed him by the arms and yanked him to his feet. "You're freezing to death right under my nose! Move!"

He sagged against her. "'m so tired."

The sluggish, passive sound of his voice frightened her. The threat of losing the only other person she cared about in this stupid ordeal was more than she could bear. "I'll give you tired, soldier! You walk or I'll kick your ass all the way back to Moselle! My boot will be so far up your jacksie that you'll need a horse and tackle to take a shit!"

His head moved against her shoulder in a listless nod. "Okay," he mumbled. With her supporting most of his weight, he began to shuffle in a small circle.

"What do you think this is, some stroll by the river? Move, you bone head! March! Lift your knees like you mean it, soldier! One, two, three, four … step, step, step, step!" Rai tried to recall every biting epithet Banya had ever used on her. "You … you pig's knuckle! You sperm-burping gutter slut! You don't have the brains of head lice!"

She harangued and pleaded and time blurred into one long moment of fear as they trod back and forth across the shelter's tiny confines. Their feet wore a path in the leaves and ancient dust, their steps matched like a couple of old drays at the plow …

… until all at once Kinner was moving under his own power.

Rai stepped back, hovering to make sure he was steady on his feet. Night had faded to grey as they walked, a wintry precursor to dawn. She could see the fine line of his profile and the opening to their shelter. What she saw beyond that rocky portal took the breath and heart out of her.

During the night, the world had disappeared behind a heavy, wind-shifted curtain of white that obliterated the forest and mountains, rendering visibility to little more than a hand's breadth. "Oh, fuck me to tear drops," she moaned. They had no tent, no sleeping furs, and little food. The brave Carraid mare, for all her skill, would only go so far before she bogged down in the heavy snow. What then? Make camp and tough it out with nothing? And what if the storm persisted, locking in for a week or more? Kill the mare for food? Banya would have said yes, no matter what it cost her, but the pain of that thought tore another hole in Rai's heart. They should never have left Eachan's Rest. Hell, they should never have joined this fool's mission in the first place. She should have behaved herself, should have stayed in bed with the covers pulled over her head and nailed Banya into a feed barrel the first time the Carraid laid out this idiot plan. Except Banya had been determined to go and what choice did Rai have but to follow?

She heard Holan's voice in her mind. *There are always choices.*

"Get fucked," she said aloud. The wind moaned in response, swirling and eddying the snow like water and bringing with it the faint, but unmistakable ring of harness.

The mare stirred in her enclosure and whinnied. Rai cursed an oath that sent the blood rushing to Kinner's cheeks. She grabbed his sleeve and bolted from the shelter, dragging him with her as she sprang down the rocks like a rabbit flushed from its warren. "When that stupid Weathercock of yours finally shows up, I'm gonna smack him in the mouth!"

The mare whinnied again as they crashed into the bramble enclosure. Rai shoved the bridle over her head and thrust the cold bit into her mouth without warming it. Grabbing the reins in one fist, she boosted up onto the broad back and reached down a hand. "Get up!" she ordered Kinner.

"The saddle … our packs …"

"There's no time!" She grabbed his arm and all but dragged him up behind her. He was barely seated when she jammed both heels into the horse's ribs. Unused to such treatment, the mare crow-hopped in outrage. Kinner swore in surprise and grabbed Rai's waist as the horse dropped her head and plunged into the storm. Behind them, and too close by far, a cry went up.

Rai had neither Banya's gentle way with horses or her ability to teach them special whistles and hand signals, but she knew how to drive one with brute force. Bent low over the animal's neck, she lashed her shoulders with the reins and menaced her with every dire threat at her command. The horse responded by laying her ears flat against her skull and fleeing as if Blas herself was behind them, her black raven's robes flowing in the wind.

It was not the landscape for a race. Steep heights and hummocky hollows were tailor-made to break a horse's leg and spill its rider. Somehow the nimble mare found her way, sliding down inclines on her haunches like a dog, front legs braced. From the rear came the growing drum of hooves muffled by snow and the occasional clang of iron shoe against an unsuspected rock. There was a sudden sharp *crack!* behind them and a horse shrieked in agony.

The Carraid mare's hooves skidded along hidden stones and old leaves, tripping over surface roots. She grunted and lunged, front legs clawing them up a slope as her rear legs pushed. Rai clutched her mane to keep from sliding backward and Kinner lay against Rai's back, arms locked around her waist.

At the summit, the trees suddenly ended as if a giant had come along with a huge bread knife and sliced them all away. Ahead lay a steep downward grade littered with bracken and wrack. Thin, bent blades of pale, frost-seared grass blended with wet, snow-backed rocks, pebbled like a cobbled street down to a stretch of pale, narrow beach. An enormous mass of grey water surged and heaved like a living thing, chewing the shoreline with hungry teeth.

The mare never paused. Haunches bunched, she took the slope sideways, hooves clicking and sliding against the icy rock as she descended toward the water. Freezing wind tore the breath from their throats.

Kinner thrust an arm past Rai's shoulder, pointing. "What's that?"

Out on the ocean, two small rounded shapes danced across the waves like walnut shells spinning on a freshet. Black-garbed figures, wet and shiny, bent their backs to the storm and pulled on the oars. "Coracles!" she yelled. "Fishermen or sealers. They must have gotten caught out by the storm."

The Carraid mare gave a sudden, savage cry as an arrow bloomed in her shoulder. A second shaft took her deep in the broad, muscular slope of her rump, just behind Kinner, followed by a third. Her hindquarters collapsed and she fell, screaming, spilling her riders in a wild tumble down the scree-littered slope.

Twenty-Five

As she had been taught under bruising tutelage seemingly a million years and another lifetime ago, Rai tucked her head as she fell and rolled. There was the sharp report of bone snapping like dry kindling and for half-a-second she imagined Kinner lying dead at the bottom of the slope, his neck at an impossible angle and his skull cracked wide open, brains sprayed across the wet and rocky ground.

She caught up hard against a boulder and darkness bled inky fingers across her gaze as corkscrews of bright pain darted against the shadows. Moaning, certain that a rib or two must be broken, she staggered to her fee and cast around in bewilderment. A little ways above her, Kinner lay flat on his back, arms and legs splayed like a prisoner about to be drawn and quartered. She started toward him, certain he was dead, but he sat up with a jerk and struggled to his feet. Arms out, he wobbled in a shaky circle and froze, staring up the hill in transfixed horror.

The injured Carraid mare – bonded to Banya from birth; that had carried her in both battle and joy; that had saved their lives more times than Rai could count – lay in a slight dip in the slope, caught on her back like a tortoise. One leg flopped in the air like a child's broken toy. Flecks of white bone and gristle shone stark against the grey hide.

Rai gave a shuddering cry of despair and started up the slope just as a troop of mounted horse topped the crest and poured toward her in a surging wave of eerie silence, the drumbeat of their hooves drowned out by the raging surf. She took one look at Remeg riding in the fore with the Lorn commander and Mestipen not far behind, and bolted toward the sea and its narrow rocky shoal. The coracles were closer now, pitching and yawing in the swell a few yards from shore. Their crews rode the lashing waves with the aplomb of ducks and silently watched the drama on the beach unfold.

Kinner bolted past her and hit the water. Rai flung a prayer skyward and followed. The ocean's deep cold surged across her belly, snatching the breath clean out of her. A second wave hit her full in the face, filling her with the taste and smell of salt. She remembered belatedly that she didn't know how to swim

Neither did Kinner, apparently. He flung himself forward through the water like a spastic, half-walking, half-swimming, bobbing like a cork at the end of a fishing line and slapping the waves with his open hands like it was a pack of dogs to be driven back. He waved at the coracles. "Help!" He gulped water and choked. "Please, help us!"

A figure in the nearest boat brandished an oar like a weapon. "Help you ownselfs!"

A second voice spoke with sharp-toned authority. "Massak!"

"What dey to us, den?" the first challenged. "We could be kill' jus' as well as dey!"

"Yes, Kaskae!" a voice called from the other boat. "Lander trouble be none of ours. Let's us be puttin' out and move on!"

"No!" Kinner cried out. "Please!" He threw himself the last few feet and slung both arms over the side of the boat as it dipped precariously with his weight.

One of the sea-folk poked him hard with an oar. "Here now! You be leavin' off dere or you be swampin' us!"

"Not if you help us, I won't!" He struggled and got one foot up and over the gunwale. "Why did you come closer?" he said and glared at the nearest set of dark eyes, all he could see in the covering of oilskins. "Just to watch us die?"

Rai floundered as the ocean washed her legs out from under her. Grabbing the back of Kinner's coat, she hung on for all she was worth as the Weathercock blade dragged at her hip, pulling her down. She swallowed brine and spat. "This bastard sword is going to kill me." Clutching Kinner with one hand, she used the other to work the scabbard buckle loose. The leather, made oily with salt water, came free all at once and slid through her fingers. At the last instant, her hand closed around the sword hilt. The blade slipped free with a smooth, clean motion and the scabbard sank, the belt writhing behind it like an eel. Heaving hard against the drag of water, Rai flung the weapon into the boat.

A strong wave hit her broadside, breaking her grip on Kinner. The ocean closed over her head with a green roar and she upended, mouth flooding with the bitter tang of salt. She flailed, desperate to find the surface, but in every direction there was only water. Black spots burst before her eyes as her screaming lungs failed and her last breath expelled in a single bubbling rush.

Firm hands plucked Rai from the sea and dropped her down beside Kinner on the coracle's woven bottom. Trembling, she crouched there, hair and clothing streaming with water, and hacked up brine. Her stomach clenched and roiled in greasy accompaniment as the vessel pitched and swayed. The sea-folk moved around her as if the ocean was as still as mirrored glass and she no more trouble than a coil of rope.

On shore, the soldiers charged their horses into the surf, yelling and brandishing their swords, but the boats were out of reach. Arrows fought the wind, fell short of their mark, and sank. The sailors responded with derisive cat-calls in a strange tongue. One of them stood and dropped her trousers to smack her naked buttocks at those on shore.

The coracle spun on the surging tide. Rai buried her head in the circle of both arms and curled into a tight ball against Kinner as the ocean raged.

Her eyes opened to the gloomy confines of a cramped shelter and the press of vague memories – landfall in the dark and wet, and the swift erection of a hut. She blinked at the ceiling where springy poles formed a low, domed space roofed with cured animal hides. A small opening at the peak served as a chimney draw.

A half-dozen figures garbed in black ringed a small fire kindled in a shallow depression in the sand. Shiny dark hair was cut in a short cap around each head, and broad expressive faces shifted with conversation and the play of firelight. Their voices were soft, their language composed of high fluting notes, whistles, and low grunts.

They turned to look at her when Rai sat up. One removed a long-stemmed pipe from her mouth and grinned, her teeth a startling white against the ruddy red-black of her skin. "So you decide to stay wit' us, eh Little Sister? *Good.*" She pointed behind her with the pipe to where Kinner lay curled on his side, sound asleep. "I tol' da Little Brudder dere dat you would, but I don' t'ink he believe me." She said something in her own tongue and the other women chuckled. "Dis one, he got wore out waitin' for you to come back to us. He were some worried, but I tol' him you was just be needin' time to get Mother Sea out of your lungs. You hungry?" She produced a communal bowl. "Come an' join us here. Dere's plenty for all." She nudged the figure next to her to shift aside and make room. That woman, a girl hardly out of her teens, flicked her dark gaze across Rai and looked aside in sullen dismissal.

Rai settled down cross-legged and accepted the bowl. The contents smelled of grain, fish, and something she could not name, a dark brown meat rimed with a thick, red strip of fat. When she tried a piece, the rubbery flesh released a smell and taste so much like brine that she felt as if she were consuming a piece of the ocean.

A meaty elbow nudged her in the ribs. “You eat up now and don’ be mindin’ that eel of a girl beside you dere. She being Massak. She don’ much like nobody any time.” A dark hand, the long fingers corded with strong tendons, made a circle of those gathered and then splayed against a skin anorak. “We being Turaaq, Children of Mother Seal. I being Kaskae, leader here. Cross ways dere be Kanut, Nauja, Palartok, an’ Suka.” She pointed to each woman in turn.

Rai dipped her head in greeting. “I’m Rai. Hello.”

Kaskae laughed with robust good will. “Hello she say! Well, hello, indeed we be sayin’ back! Fishin’ we come an’ to hunt Oogrooq. Dat be Mother Seal, may she grow sleek an’ fat an’ breed many babies. We never t’ought to pull two such sorry creatures from da water, no!” Kaskae tilted her head sideways and studied Rai with shrewd eyes past the swirl of her pipe smoke. “You so puny, I t’ought to t’row you back, but, hey! Mebbe you grow!” She laughed and kicked her feet with delight.

Kinner stirred at the noise, murmured in his sleep, and burrowed deeper beneath the covers.

Kanut thrust a finger at Kaskae. “You wake that chile wit’ you walrus noise, I give you a slap back da head.” She was older than Kaskae by several years and a massive woman, even taking into account the thick layers of protective clothing that she wore. Her face, seamed with wrinkles, made Rai think of the dried apple-headed dolls her father had once made for her.

Kanut gestured at the bowl. “You eat what you want of dat now, Little Sister. We be havin’ our fill. An’ don’ you mind any gull chatter you be hearin.’”

Kaskae grinned and rolled her eyes. “Aye,” she said. “Talk can wait.”

While Rai ate, the sealers spoke quietly among themselves. It was a fluid tongue, rippled like the surface of the water, and a little seemed to go a long way. As they talked, nimble hands braided line, cleaned hooks, and sharpened harpoon heads of bone and metal.

When Rai had finished eating, Kaskae produced a fat-bellied leather flask with a long neck stoppered with a cork. She worked the plug free with her back teeth and passed the container to Rai. “You be tryin’ dis, Little Sister. Jus’ a sip, mind. Dis take da last of da sea chill from you bones, oh my yes.”

A sip was all Rai could tolerate. Grimacing – the strong liquor had the viscosity of warm molasses and a pungent, meaty odor – she swallowed, coughed, and blinked the tears from her eyes. Kaskae chuckled, took the bottle back, and tapped home the cork. “Dat’s what Little Brudder t’ought when he try it. What he say, Suka?”

The woman’s round cheeks lifted in a smile. “Dat it take some gettin’ use’ to.”

Kaskae barked laughter again. She cast a guilty look toward Kinner’s recumbent form and put the bottle away. "Now den." She tapped the pipe bowl against her palm, flung the spent ash into the fire, and murmured something as the smoke rose through the hole in the ceiling. "Little Brother d'ere, he tol' us what happen."

"How much did he tell you?" Rai said cautiously.

Kaskae shrugged one shoulder. "All of it, so he say."

Several colorful barracks curses swarmed through Rai's mind. She suppressed the desire to thump the boy good and hard. Telling their story to just anyone was a good way to end up dead … or worse. There was absolutely no way to tell who they could trust and who might sell them to Remeg at the first chance.

Kaskae set about refilling her pipe. "You be relaxin' dere, Little Sister. We da least of your worry. Dat Kinner-boy, he know what he be talkin' 'bout. Dat Weddercock, we don' have much to say 'bout him, no. He has not'in' to do wit us. We prays to Oogrooq an' to Kern in her water home. It's dem who care for da fisherfolk an' sealers. That Weddercock, now, him is bein' somethin' different altogedder. Him don' mean much to us, no, but him mean a lot to our friends."

"Friends?" Rai felt as if the world had galloped on ahead of her while she slept and now there was no hope of catching up.

Kinner's drowsy voice rose from the tumble of blankets. "They know the monks at Dara, Rai."

She turned to look at him. "But the monks don't believe in the Weathercock."

Kaskae threw her head back in a hearty laugh, no longer mindful of disturbing the boy. The other women joined in. Even sour-faced Massak allowed herself a slight smile. "Oh, you be seein'!" Kaskae giggled. "You be seein,' yes, indeed!"

Being on the short end of things made Rai feel stupid and angry. "Be seeing what?" she said, snappish. When all the women did was laugh more, she reached around behind Kaskae and swatted Kinner hard. "Be seeing what?" she demanded.

He pushed aside the blanket and came up onto his elbow. "I don't know, but they've agreed to take us all the way to Dara."

"Really?" She let his words sink it. Was it possible that this ordeal could end, that it would soon be over and her life could return to normal? Well, as normal as it could ever be again without Banya. "What about Remeg?"

Kaskae's head swung from side to side in deep negation. "Dat Captain Remeg, she got gills? Fins an' tail? She not come dere, no, not on dis sea. Dis sea, she love her children, all her babies. She do right by us. That Remeg, she crazy-bad fish. She try dis sea, it eat her up, *oh* yes. Da only way to dis beach where we go be by water." Her hand swung in a circle above her head. "All aroun' be mountains and cliffs. No way up dere 'cept a steep climb nobody know. Dat's why Oogrooq Seal Mother bring her children dere, yes. For dat Remeg, dere's nowhere to go but inland, and inland be a long way. And dere's da storm. You hear dat?" She cocked her head.

For the first time Rai paid attention to the noises outside the tent, the wind's low moan and the skitter of ice and sand against the shelter's outer skin.

"Dat storm, she bein' our friend. She come in off da sea, hit da land an' leave da sea alone. Oh, she happy-dance the waves some, yes, but not so bad dat we can't ride dem out come daylight. Dat Remeg, she have to fight da whole storm. Wind, snow, ice. She have to stop an' rest, even if she don' want to. Get tired, can't see, might fall off da mountain." Kaskae's face drooped into a mournful expression. "Oh, my, so sad, dat, eh?" She laughed. "You hear me. Dat Remeg, she be more dan a few day comin' to Dara, if she come at all an' not be et up by da storm. By den, long den, you be dere, you an' da Kinner-boy. We let you off on da beach, you climb da cliffs." Her fingers air-walked a steep incline. "Get to top. What you do den, dat be your choice." She slapped Rai soundly between the shoulders. "Since you up now, we be movin'." Her words set the other women into motion. "We give you seal skin to wear, keep you warm, dry as bone." Kaskae kicked damp sand over the fire and stamped it out. "Believe it."

Whether by luck or the will of the Seal Mother, the storm behaved just as Kaskae had predicted, staying well to land where it beat the mountains with blinding sheets of snow and ice. Although little snow fell at sea, the fierce wind knocked hell out of the light boats and danced them across the tops of the waves like skipping stones. More than once, Rai felt certain that they were as good as drowned, but each time the sealers bent to their work, hands strong and sure on tiller and oar, and the obedient coracles followed their command.

It was a mystery to Rai how they kept afloat, let alone on course in all the blowing darkness. There was not a single star by which to steer or anything remotely like a landmark. There was only the raging sea, yet the sailors seemed confident and at ease.

With nothing to do but stay out of their way, she could keep Banya at bay no longer. There would be no more stupid jokes and arguments, no late-night talks and too much beer, no more kittens and snot-nosed barn rats and someone always at her back. Why had she not been able to save Banya's life, when the Carraid had saved hers and had hauled her ass out of the fire so many times since? Where had Rai been and what had she been doing when Remeg's blade fell?

Leave off, little girl. The voice in her head was so clear that Rai's head jerked up. Her hands clutched the gunwale as she looked around, half-expecting to see the Carraid perched in the stern like a queen. *'No bloody good in a fight,' you said, and you were right. I had no business picking up a sword, but that was my choice, so let be.* Rai wiped her eyes with the back of her hand and looked forward. Kinner crouched in the bow with the sword between his knees, one wing of the enraged cock pressed against his cheek. If he harbored any fears or doubts, they didn't show. He seemed to just *be,* caught in this moment for all time like a fly stuck in amber.

Kinner blinked the salt spray out of his eyes. Thoughts ran through his head like water down a sluice. His journey was almost over. Everything Holan had lived for, everything she had envisioned, would soon come down to a single moment in time when he relinquished the sword to its next keeper.

He could hardly wait.

A sudden thought intruded on that bucolic vision. *What if they don't want it? What if they laugh at me for coming all this way to leave the sword in a place built to honor everything the Weathercock stands against? What if they take it and destroy it?* His hands tightened around the weapon's hilt. Suppose his mother's visions had been nothing more than the disease at work in her brain? What if her stories, like his infertility, had been a lie?

"No." He said it softly, but with a firmness that could not be denied. "Mum lied about a lot of things, but she would never lie about this." *Are you sure?* his traitor mind asked. He bent his forehead against his hands. He thought to pray to the Weathercock, but had no idea what to ask for. His fear was suddenly too immense.

They sailed through the night. With no work to occupy them, Kinner and Rai slipped in and out of sleep by turns. When dawn came, the sun lay hidden behind ominous clouds that covered the world from edge to edge in a cap of leaden grey that turned the sea black. Cold mist rode the water like a gossamer veil.

Kaskae sang out a caroling note from the stern where she sat with the tiller snugged firmly into her armpit. "Hah! Morning being come, no worry. Look you dere, yes!" She pointed and both Rai and Kinner turned to follow the thrust of her finger. "Tol' you we bring you in jus' fine. Tol' you dat Mother Seal, she be seein' us safe away."

At first, they saw nothing; then, bit by bit, a rocky shoreline appeared from out of the fog. Battered and gouged by wind and sea, the stony cliffs towered against the sky in a twist of fantastic shapes. A fingernail of tawny beach bent in a crescent at the base of the rocks.

Kinner looked at Nauja, who sat directly behind him. “Is that Dara?”

The sealer shook her head. “Dara be up top dem cliffs. We get some closer, you see da stairway up da rocks, oh yes. It be wet going in dis, so you make to be careful.”

Kaskae nodded and laughed. “You fall dere, you be splat like da crab drop’ by da gull. We be scrapin’ you off da rocks for use as bait!”

Chirruping back and forth in their strange language, the sealers brought the boats to ground on the minuscule beach and let their passengers disembark. Kinner made to undo the ties of his borrowed coat and Kaskae shook her head. “No, now leave dat be. You be soak right t’rough widdout it in dis drivin’ wet, yes. You leave dat wit’ Brudder Sellin. He know where to keep it for us, oh yes. We get it anudder day.” Bright teeth flashed in a grin and she flapped her hands at them. “Go away! You want ta drown on land after we come all dis way makin’ you safe on sea? You ask for da Lady. She see you fine, just yes.” She slipped her fingers into the corners of her mouth and shrilled a piercing whistle. The coracles put to sea and pulled away from shore with long, even strokes. Kaskae waved once from the stern and then they were lost to the fog.

Kinner started toward the base of the cliffs and the narrow steps carved into the rock face. Rai followed, craning her neck back to view the soaring tower of rock to its summit. “I hope we didn’t come all this way just to get killed climbing a stupid flight of stairs.”

The stone was wet and slick under their boots, forcing them to go slow and place their feet with care. The stairway followed the contours of the rock wall, wending back and forth across the cliff like a trellised vine of ivy. Kinner was smart enough to not look down, but he did glance once across the water to see if he could spot the seal folk. “Do you realize that the Turaaq are the first people to help us who haven’t had to pay a price of some kind?” he said.

Rai snorted, breathing hard. “The day’s young,” she said. “Give it time.”

They were both panting when they reached the summit and Kinner’s thighs trembled with fatigue. Beyond a narrow patch of open ground rose Dara’s dark walls. The monastery looked as ancient as the mountain from which it sprang, organic and impregnable. A gravel path led to a small arched wooden door set beneath a deep lintel of mossy stone. A brass bell, patterned with verdigris, was bolted to the door. Kinner glanced at Rai. When she nodded, he set his hand to the bell pull and tugged. The clapper swung and a single sonorous note rang out.

The response was instantaneous. A small panel set into the door snapped aside and a pair of eyes bright as a chipmunk’s peered out. “What do you want?"

"We'd like to come in, please," Kinner said politely. "We've come a long way and –"

"Go away! I don't know you."

"No, you wouldn't," Kinner continued, trying to explain. "We just got here and –"

"No one comes this way." The peep hole began to slide shut. Rai thrust two fingers into the narrow slot and wrenched it open. Behind it, the dark eyes were huge with surprise. "Here now!" the voice squeaked. "You can't do that!"

"I just did." Rai leaned close so that her face filled the small space. "If no one comes this way, why is there a door? Not to mention that neck-breaker of a stairway that we almost killed ourselves on. Kaskae said it was okay to come this way and we –"

"Kaskae?" The eyes darted back and forth. "Why did Kaskae send you this way?"

"Oh, I don't know," Rai said. "Maybe because she couldn't sail the boats to the front door." She gritted her teeth. "Listen, you idiot. We've come a long way and it's damned cold out here, so open this door before I –"

Kinner elbowed her out of the way. "My name is Kinner and this is my friend Rai. We need to speak to –"

"Kinner?" the voice behind those eyes exclaimed. "But you were supposed to come by the meadow road!"

Rai flung up her hands. "Does *everyone* know our business?"

The eyes vanished and the slit closed. From behind the door came the rapid beat of a voice talking to itself. In a moment, a bolt slid back and the door creaked open to reveal a short monk with a blue triskele tattooed on his forehead. The round beginnings of a pot-belly pressed against the drape of his brown robe like a tiny pregnancy. "Come in!" His hands fluttered nervously. "Come in! I'm sorry I made you wait, but I had no idea! You weren't expected. I mean, you *were* expected, just not this way. The back way, I mean. They said you were coming by the meadow road."

"So you said," Rai remarked as he closed the door behind them and engaged the lock. "Who's 'they'?"

He turned around to answer and shrieked instead. Rai and Kinner both spun, hunting danger, but found nothing behind them but an empty stone corridor lit at intervals by tarry sconces.

Rai's eyes slid toward the monk. "What is it now?" she said through gritted teeth.

He patted a hand over his heart, round eyes fixed on the sword balanced in the crook of Kinner's arm. "Oh, my. That's it, isn't it? That's the Weathercock's sword."

Rai and Kinner shared a look. "Why is this so important *here* of all places?" she muttered to Kinner.

He shook his head, admitting his own confusion, and patted the head of the hilt cock like it was a prized pet. "This is it."

The monk stared, hands pressed against his mouth.

Rai's expression turned impish with amusement. "You want to touch it?"

"No!" The monk clapped his hands to either side of his face. "I couldn't! I shouldn't! I mean … *could I?*"

"Sure." With a magnanimous gesture, Rai took the sword from Kinner and held it out across both palms. The monk's eyes were enormous, his breath rapid and shallow. After some hesitation, he touched the blade with a single finger and sighed.

Kinner undid the toggles on the front of his wet coat and shrugged it off his shoulders. "We're looking for either Brother Sellin or –"

The monk's scream echoed off the close walls. He cowered back, ink-stained fingers clutching his throat, and stared at them in horror. "Who told you to find Brother Sellin? The Weathercock?" His voice squeaked on the name.

"No, you numb fuck," Rai said in disgust. "Kaskae. She said we could leave these coats with him."

"Oh." His disappointment was unmistakable. "I'm Brother Sellin," he said with resignation. He held out his hands for the coats. "I'll take those and make sure they get back to her."

"Thank you." Kinner took the sword from Rai. "Kaskae also said we should ask for someone called 'The Lady.'"

Brother Sellin nodded. "I think she's in the refectory. I can take you."

"Sellin!" The cry echoed down the corridor. There was the sound of running feet and a half-dozen men and women rounded a distant turn in the corridor. Each was robed as a religious, but all of them carried weapons.

Sellin flushed pink. "It's all right," he called to them. "Everything's fine."

"But we heard a scream," said the man in front. Like the hapless Sellin, he was short and tattooed, but there the resemblance ended. He was trim with muscle, spoke with authority, and carried himself with grace and confidence. Grey hair bespoke an age that his face did not show. His expression grew sardonic. "Several, in fact."

Sellin lowered his eyes in chagrin. "That was me, Brother Corlinn. I apologize. I was startled." He gestured at their guests. "This is Kinner and Rai."

Corlinn blinked in astonishment. "Praise be!" He lowered his sword and clapped Sellin on the shoulder. "Faced with such a miracle, I'd have screamed as well." His face creased into a delighted smile and he held out his hand to first Kinner, then Rai. "We've been watching for you to come –"

"By the meadow road," Rai finished for him. "We heard."

Corlinn peered past them into the shadows. "We were told to expect three of you."

Silence radiated from Rai like a disease. Kinner held out the sword to forestall any mention of Banya's death. "This is for you." Now that the moment had come, he felt an embarrassing amount of relief.

All eyes riveted on the magnificent weapon. Flickering torchlight once again worked its magic, bringing to life the hilt cock, his throat stretched long with a deep breath, poised on the edge of a warrior's cry.

Corlinn, although captivated, did not take the sword. He closed his eyes and bowed with reverence, his expression one of awe and gratitude. "Not for me, but for one far greater than I. I am but one of its caretakers." He smiled and touched the boy's shoulder. "Don't look so worried, Kinner. We'll ease you of this burden soon enough." He swept his hand before them. "Come with me, please. The rest of you, back to your duties."

He led them along the main line of the many-branching corridor to where it emerged onto a cloister. Icy wind and whirling snow buffeted them as they hurried along the covered walkway to a group of three attached buildings. Corlinn pointed to each in turn. "Calefactory, refectory, and kitchen." He paused briefly to wash his hands in the frigid, ice-laced water of a lavabo and waited as they did likewise. When all were clean, he lifted the latch on the refectory door and ushered them inside.

The room was hung with tapestries woven with scenes from scripture. Trestle tables lined the walls, dark wood polished to a shine by centuries of use. At the far end of the room stood a raised dais carved with an emblem of the Three-Headed Goddess. Light from the tall, unadorned windows was augmented by oil lamps, candelabrum, and a wide hearth where two women sat talking. They broke off their conversation as the door opened, and one of them sprang to her feet. "By the Comb, you're a sight!"

Kinner's jaw dropped in astonishment. "*Ren!*"

The Chesne leader bore down on them and he sprang forward to meet her hearty embrace. She swung him around twice, set him on his feet, and turned to his companion.

Rai held up both hands. "You try that on me and I'll hurt you."

Ren laughed and grasped Rai's offered hand in both of hers. "I'll take ye at your word." Her eyes searched past them. "Is Banya no' wi' ye? Ye canna say she chose ta stay in Carraidland! I dinna thought she'd want ta miss the end o' this adventure."

Kinner hated the empty look that came into Rai's eyes every time their friend's name was mentioned. He swallowed with difficulty, his heart weighty with loss. "No."

Ren understood at once. All expression dropped from her face, leaving it pale and blank as a slate. "Remeg?" she whispered.

"Who else?" Rai snapped. She turned away and rubbed hard at both temples, her pain held against her heart like a clenched fist.

Kinner went to her and placed a careful arm around her shoulders. She tensed for an instant, and then relaxed into his embrace in acceptance of what he had to offer. He tipped his head against hers.

A gentle voice spoke into their silence. "Come sit by the fire." The woman seated with Ren had joined them. Well beyond middle age, her face was lined with years but pink-cheeked with vigor. She wore a plain robe the color of old wine and her long grey hair, braided into a single plait, was coiled around her head like a crown. Her smile was as compassionate as her voice. "I'm Min'da, Lady of Dara. Be welcome here." She gestured to Corlinn. "Our friends could use some refreshment, my dear. Would you ask that food and wine be brought in?"

"Certainly, Lady," he replied with a bow and left the room.

Beneath Kinner's arm, Rai began to tremble. He drew her toward the fire and eased her into the chair nearest the blaze. Taking the seat beside her so as to stay close, he laid the sword on the rug at his feet. In this light, he could see that the blade was scratched, marked with dried salt and sand. It needed a good cleaning, yet still the rampant cock managed to shine as if newly cast. There was dried blood caught in some of the more intricate work and he wondered if all of it belonged to the hapless kid goat.

Min'da took a seat across from Rai. Her hands, folded together in her lap, were large-knuckled and latticed with old scars that Kinner recognized as the marks of swordplay. Ren took the seat beside her. Something about the Chesne made her look lost, a little empty, and Kinner suddenly realized that Jak was not with her, curled in his habitual place by her feet. He yearned to ask about the dog, but was afraid he might see in Ren's eyes the same expression of loss that Rai carried.

Corlinn returned, followed by another monk. Both carried trays which they placed on a table between the chairs. While the nameless monk withdrew, Corlinn pulled up a chair to join the women. They ate in silence broken only by snippets of inconsequential conversation.

Kinner pared a slice of cheese from the rind and suddenly heard Bug's voice in his head: *It were all hairy.* He smiled at the memory.

Seeing that smile and taking it as a sign of encouragement, Min'da curled her hands around a cup of warm wine and settled back in her chair. "Kinner, would you tell us of your journey?"

He glanced at Rai. When she nodded, eyes fixed on the moving flames, he took a deep breath and a moment to order his thoughts. Little by little, the words came as he retraced their steps from Caerau to Cadasbyr. When he was finished, he leaned across the space between them and touched Ren on the knee. "What happened after we left you?"

Her mouth turned down. Ren laced her hands together between her knees as if to keep from striking out and studied the floor as she spoke. "Marn's dead, though we kenned that afore ye hied." The words were blunt, a brief flash of pain already dimming for a woman who had learned to hold onto life's lessons but not their agony. "They tortured her, did her wi' less care then ye'd gie a dumb beast. That Mestipen, she'll be mine one day."

"Not if I get to her first," Rai said. The thick tension of her voice was a promise.

Kinner laid a hand on her wrist to belay any argument. "I'm sorry, Ren."

The Chesne leader shook her head, a quick jerk back and forth. "Sadness willna bring her back. It willna return any o' those who were lost to us."

Rai met her eyes. "How many?" she said in a dead-sounding voice.

Ren shook her head again. She would not give numbers or names. That alone spoke of how extensive the loss of life had been in the Chesne caves.

Kinner's heart felt cold. What of Ollam? Where were Danika and his other friends?

"Remeg left some soldiers behind when she moved on." Ren picked up a cup of wine and turned it between her hands. "They found their way into the caves an' set flame t' the stores, killed the flocks. They were good at their job. Very thorough."

"'Were'?" Rai said.

Ren's lips curled like the rictus of a corpse. "Aye, we did that much."

"What ..." Kinner's voice clicked and he had to swallow before he could continue. "Where are the others?"

"In the hills," Ren said. "Recoupin', callin' in favors, rebuildin'. We'll no' be driven awa' by the likes o' Remeg or her bitch queen. I've brought Torby wi' me, an' Swot. I could spare no others."

Min'da refilled their cups whether or not they seemed to want it. "Kinner, what happened after you left the mountains?"

He told of their trek east and the flight to the river. Beyond Taran Falls, the tale diverged. Kinner took them to the Tzigane camp, although he chose not to elaborate on his time spent among the gypsies, and ended with his arrival in Carraidland.

Silence fell again. Kinner waited, toying with his cup and watching Rai from the corner of his eye. Would he have to tell all of it? Was there nothing she wanted to say?

"Banya should have stayed out of things."

Rai's words came scratched and broken, ruined with battle cries and sorrow. She drained her cup to the dregs in one swallow and placed it on the table. Words poured from her then, a breached dam of emotion that made the Taran Falls look like a watering can. "You should have seen her! She was beautiful! Eachan's Rest was burning and it was chaos, utter fucking chaos, and she had no business being there, no business taking up a sword no matter what the odds, but she did it anyway, the crazy stubborn bitch, and she faced Remeg. Faced her!"

Her words ran on and as they did, Kinner felt Banya's legend taking root in the soil of Dara. Her life and death would not be remembered only by those few who had known her. Generations yet unborn would know of the brilliant and loyal Carraid warrior who, although wounded, had faced Remeg to protect those she loved and defend a belief she held dear. Perhaps one day, Banya would be as famous as the Weathercock.

He thought he heard laughter on the wind.

Rai's narrative brought him back from his reverie. "And you never knew what would take her fancy. Could be anything, usually something cute and defenseless." She glanced at Kinner and he ducked his head, blushing. "She loved ..." Rai struggled for words. "Everything. Nearly everything. I mean, not stuff like meanness and stupidity, she had no tolerance for that shit, but she had a way of seeing value in just about everyone." She spoke of the kindnesses great and small, the horrid jokes, the atonal singing and musing philosophies. She told of Banya's annoying habits (*"She sucked her teeth when she was thinking"*) and her great strengths (*"There wasn't a thing she couldn't do with horses"*). "She was a good soldier," Rai said. "Maybe even a great one. I'm glad we were on the same side. Oh, we riled each other, but I never had to face her when she was in full ire. We had this thing we used to say to each other right before battle ..." Her words stumbled. A wounded look came over her face and the story came to an abrupt end. She would not – or could not – say those words. Kinner wondered if she ever would again.

"I wish I had known her," Min'da said. When Rai looked up in an almost challenging way, The Lady did not smile or flinch, but stared straight into her eyes to reinforce the truth of those words. They had not been said in a lame attempt to soothe Rai's loss, but because the priestess meant them. Rai accepted the compliment with a slight nod. She reached for her cup, found it empty, and put it back.

Corlinn leaned forward to refill it from the pitcher. "I harbor no sympathy for Captain Remeg, nor do I understand the madness which drives her, but I *will* pity her the day the Carraid catch her. The destruction of Eachan's Rest will not go unpunished. Balfor's wrath will be like the Weathercock's own justice."

Kinner picked at the table's rough grain where a name – *Tearlach* – had been carved a long time ago. "Speaking to that," he said. "Mum never understood why the visions told her to bring the sword to Dara. This monastery is devoted to the Goddess, so of what possible use to you is a weapon made for the Weathercock?"

Min'da's lips curled into a smile.

She led them along a passage cut through bedrock, the entrance masterfully disguised to hide in plain sight against the rough texture of old stone walls. They passed from the upper levels of Dara to the cellars, into the sub-cellars and beyond. Min'da spoke as they walked. "Long ago, the tide ran higher than it does now. It carved out caves in the rock far beneath Dara. As the water retreated and the ground dried, our earlier brothers and sisters converted those areas into storage. Over time, another use was found for them."

A bit further on, the way was barred by a young monk standing in front of a door beneath the light of a wall torch. He bowed as they approached. "Lady. Brother Corlinn."

The older monk grasped his hand. "Brother Tearlach, these are our friends Rai and Kinner. You know Ren, of course."

He dipped his head. "Blessings and welcome on you all."

"Tearlach?" Kinner said. "I saw your name carved on a table in the refectory."

The monk screwed up his face in mild embarrassment. "A childhood transgression, I'm afraid. I've learned better manners since then."

Although his expression was open and friendly, the sharp peak of Tearlach's brows and the shape of his nose shockingly reminded Rai of Remeg. The resemblance was so pronounced that she caught herself staring.

His pleasant demeanor faltered under that scrutiny and his eyes darted toward his superiors. "Is something wrong?"

Rai shook her head. "Sorry. For a second, you reminded me of someone." She glanced at Kinner. He frowned, looked again at Tearlach … and his eyes widened. It wasn't her imagination, then. Could it be that her reticent former commander had another card hidden up her sleeve?

Tearlach's broad smile banished the likeness. "Someone nice, I hope."

Rather than perjure herself, Rai gave a noncommittal grunt and cocked her head to listen to the faint sounds issuing from behind the closed door. "You have a forge in there?"

"In a manner of speaking," Min'da said with a cryptic smile. She gestured for Tearlach to open the door.

The chamber beyond retained a heavy odor of brine from ages past. Faint through the intervening rock came the hollow boom and rush of waves against the outer cliffs. The room, an egg-shaped, high-ceilinged area lit by torchlight and lantern, held perhaps a hundred …

"*Fighters?*" Rai burst out. Beside her, Kinner stood transfixed.

"Yes," Min'da said with pride.

The combatants ranged in age from striplings to adults. Some were dressed in knee pants and sleeveless tunics, others in loincloths or short singlets. Still others wore chain mail or armor, and every one of them was male.

Kinner's face glowed. "This is wonderful!"

Rai's mouth gaped open and then snapped shut. "Warrior monks," she said in a toneless voice. "Why am I not surprised?"

Ren nudged her. "Careful," she said with a grin. "Your prejudice is showing."

Emotion squeezed Rai's heart. "It's not that," she said, her eyes still on the fighters. "I've learned that things can be different. Hell, everything I thought I knew about life has been turned upside down." She could not put into words what she felt, the extreme sense of sorrow and regret and loss that was hers. It wasn't only Banya. If Brendie could have had this chance, if her father had been allowed to pursue the things he loved, the life *he* chose, and been valued for his strengths, he might still be alive today. Instead, that good man had endured the lash of his wife's fury and died under the weight of her drunken rage.

Min'da laid a hand on Kinner's arm. "You asked what the Weathercock has to do with us. I'm not sure where or when the legend first appeared. I'm not sure anyone does. At the risk of sounding blasphemous, I'm not even certain it matters. What does matter is that there have always been, and always will be, those whose sense of justice demands change."

Rai tore her gaze from the men on the training ground. "Are you saying that the Weathercock is nothing more than an excuse for social action?"

The Lady shrugged. "I'm in no position to judge, but things cannot continue as they have, with Kedar Trevelyan stealing men and discarding them like last year's fashions." She rested a hip against the stone buttress that protected them from a long fall to the cave floor. "There are books, subversive to some, books that were once burned and have since been hidden. They speak of a world – *this* world – in which things were not always as they are now." She gestured at those on the training ground. "Our present society sees men as weak and in need of protection, fit only for household chores and the breeding of children. But what if their weakness, their frailty, and their oft-times sterility are the *result* of having been coddled instead of allowed to face rough work and adversity? What if they need those things in order to thrive? Should the opportunity for a full life and all that entails be denied to them based solely upon their sex? Upon an accident of birth?"

Rai held up both hands. "Hey, you're preaching to the converted." She rolled her eyes at Kinner. "Hard as that is for me to admit," she said under her breath.

He patted her arm. "You'll get used to it."

Corlinn gestured over their heads. "Dara was built long ago as a place to put away sterile men forever so they could be forgotten. We've chosen to turn that circumstance to our advantage."

"Warriors we are," Min'da said. "Our allegiance pledged to a deity of our own making, one who encompasses the aspects of both male and female and holds them in equal honor."

Her fervent tone made Rai uncomfortable. So did the rallying light that shone in the eyes of Ren, the monks, and even Kinner. "It's going to take a lot more than a bunch of warrior priests to change the world."

"Ah, but you forget," Min'da said. "We have not only the Goddess, but the Weathercock on our side. When he crows – whether or not he actually *comes* – we'll be ready."

Twenty-Six

At the back of Remeg's mind lurked the notion that she had gone insane.

She could recall having once been in control, but that dim and unfocused memory belonged to a different woman. Now she felt helpless – *led* – swept along with no more grasp on the situation than a leaf in a high wind. The single-minded core of her pursuit had gone beyond the rational, but she could not stop.

The deaths in Cadasbyr had been only the beginning. In battle, certain behaviors were anticipated, even excused. Buildings could be pillaged of their goods and women tortured and murdered. Children could be taken as slaves or killed outright if they appeared weak. As for men, well, any number of things might happen to them in the heat of battle and its coal-hot aftermath.

But there had been no battle in Cadasbyr. What had occurred there was an eruption of Remeg's frustration, a childish temper tantrum of such proportion that it became a turning point in the minds of those she led. Odd as it would seem to those unacquainted with garrison life, there existed a code of honor among soldiers by which they lived. Remeg had broken that code. Now she heard imagined whispers and felt the strands of words coil and twist about her like skeins of braided rope, a hangman's noose: *This ain't no war. It's gone too far. All this for a couple of runaway soldiers and a sterile boy?*

Cadasbyr's fiery doom and wholesale slaughter had been nothing compared to the destruction of Eachan's Rest. Timbers fell with a roar as the house and barns burned, trapping those within, roasting them alive. The blaze rose against the night sky in a fountain of flame as the Carraid fought not only to repel the outsiders who had invaded their land, but to quench the sailing embers that threatened to turn the whole of their country into an inferno. Remeg had stayed her hand for no one, yet still her quarry had escaped … except for Banya, whose death had been sweet recompense.

The memory of that battle caused Remeg to flex her injured arm and glance over her shoulder at Asabi . The dark warrior, markedly less beautiful after a session with Mestipen, rode at the rear of the company trussed to a horse like a pig meant for the butcher. Her betrayal galled Remeg like hot iron against unprotected skin. The woman's voice still rang in her ears, pitched to carry above the clashing din of swords.

"Enough, Captain!" she had cried. "This is beyond all sense!"

Remeg was well aware that Asabi had let herself be taken captive. Someone with her skill in arms was not so easily subdued. Her refusal to escape had bought a little time for Rai and the boy. Her decision to remain in battle rather than flee as well, leaving her compatriots to their fate, had proven her loyalty. Her behavior had made a *statement,* one which stayed Remeg's hand when her first inclination had been to kill the traitorous bitch. The last thing Remeg needed right now was a martyr. When the Carraid were routed and had been driven to abandon all that had once been theirs, Remeg had partially satisfied her rage by stripping Asabi of all rank and giving her to Mestipen.

Now Eachan's Rest lay far behind them. Remeg drove the troop with the lash of her tongue and the strength of her will, stopping to rest and seek shelter only when forced to by Sheel, who had stated her position baldly and without hesitation.

"What happens to you and yours is none of my affair, Captain." The Lorn commander stood so close to her that Remeg could smell the stench of her unwashed body. Sheel's voice, kept low so as not to be overheard, thrummed with emotion. "Those under my command are another matter. They have been conscripted by my employer for your use, but that is a promise which I am bound to honor only up to a point. Death is part and parcel of what we do, but I will not gamble their lives against foolhardy single-mindedness." Having spoken, she had turned her back and walked away.

Remeg watched her go … and thought about death.

Thanks to Mestipen's uncanny skills, they were able to track the fugitives despite the bad weather that moved in like an intervening hand. The soldiers forged ahead, working beyond exhaustion, aware that the longer they kept to the hills, the greater the risk of being trapped in some snowy pass for the winter … where they would have no choice but to shelter as best they could, consume the horses one after the other, and then eat their own dead. Their perseverance paid off. The sight of the fugitives running down the beach in helpless terror warmed Remeg's heart as nothing else had … for those few moments until her quarry, heedless of danger, had plunged into the frigid sea and were rescued – *rescued, Goddess rot it!* – by some thrice-be-damned sealfolk.

Such serendipity almost made her believe in the Weathercock.

Five days of storm and bitter cold had pushed the troop so far beyond exhaustion that there were no words to describe it. Battered, numb, and starving, soldiers and horses died on the mountain trail and were left where they fell as food for scavengers once the bodies were stripped of anything useful. The faces of the living grew lean. Tempers frayed. Predators stalked their back trail, drawn by the smell of blood and desperation. Haunted by failure and the overwhelming shadow of Kedar's threat, the underpinnings of Remeg's carefully crafted existence continued to shake and fracture.

In late afternoon of the fifth day, they paused at the crest of a rise to rest. Aware that she was no longer welcome in the company of those she led, Remeg stood apart, leaning against the smooth grey trunk of a beech as she gazed at the snowy valley below. To the west sprawled a broad expanse of snow-covered meadow. Once the site of a long-ago battle, it was now used as grazing land. Straight ahead lay the village of Risley.

Remeg lifted a hand, closed one eye, and covered the entire village with the ball of her thumb. The pokey backwater had changed little since her last visit. Beyond Risley, cut into the very stone that anchored it, stood Dara.

It was curious how the roll of years could change one's perspective on a place. The last time she was here, the monastery had seemed sinister and foreboding. Now the edifice harbored little of its old menace. The small bit of her past that might still lurk behind those ancient walls was a ghost and nothing more, its power over her subsumed by what she suspected might harbor there now – a traitor soldier, a presumptuous boy, and that damned sword. She would tear the place down stone by stone until she had all three in her grip. And then …

Footsteps crunched through the snow behind her, announcing the approach of Captain Sheel. The Lorn commander halted beside Remeg, sharing the view but not her thoughts. Much the worse for wear, the Lorn commander's smart uniform was torn and dirty and her face was scratched and chapped from the cold. A tiny patch of frostburn graced the side of her neck just below her left ear. "So that's Dara," Sheel said. "Home of the unwanted."

"Yes."

Sheel glanced at her. "Satisfy my curiosity, Captain Remeg. Why are we really here? And please don't waste my time with some story about apprehending traitors to the crown." She folded her arms across her chest and shifted her weight onto one hip. "I'm not calling you a liar, of course, but it seems that there must be more to your fervency than meets the eye."

Remeg's glance was cool and distant. "You're under my command, Captain. I don't owe you an explanation for anything."

Sheel's gaze pulsed like a poisoned wound. "As you like. When the time comes that an explanation is required of me, I can state with total honesty that I had absolutely no clue what was going through your head." She scratched her dirty hair and stared at Dara. "Your 'traitors' probably aren't even there. It's a safe bet they drowned." She clicked her tongue. "Heavens. What then will Remeg do with her rage?"

"I could show you, if you like."

Sheel snorted dry laughter through her nose. "You speak with such confidence. If I didn't know better, I'd think you were perfectly sane."

Remeg's reply was cut off by a single, sonorous note tolling from the monastery bell tower. She took it as a signal. "Let's go visit Risley, shall we?"

At the far end of the chapel's very last pew, Rai sat in attendance on services similar to those she had witnessed in the cathedral at Caerau. Once built in honor of the Triple She, this church had been subtly changed over time into something else. In the cathedral, Her emblem hung alone above the altar, stark and bare, both balm and threat. Here the wood of Her sigil was so clothed in ivy, fir, and pointed holly bright with berries that Rai hardly recognized it. Shiny brass oil lamps hung from chains above the altar sent up tendrils of soot to mix with the light perfume of incense. Candles in tall iron holders lit the center aisle as the religious community filed in to take their seats. Ren nodded to Rai as she entered, but opted to sit nearer the front, determined to miss nothing of what was about to happen. Behind the altar, Brother Corlinn and the Lady Min'da, dressed in rich ceremonial robes heavy with embroidery, waited to begin the internment ceremony. Kinner, clad in the borrowed robe of a monk and looking startlingly grown up in it, stood between them with the Weathercock sword cradled in his arms. In the choir, the high tone of a single boy soprano brought goose flesh to Rai's arms.

When all were in attendance, the doors closed. Corlinn raised his hands and intoned, "I bind unto myself today the virtues of the star-lit heavens."

The congregation stood, responding as one, male and female voices joined like flesh. Rai, after a halting start, joined in. "The glorious sun's life-giving rays and the whiteness of the moon at evening."

"I bind unto myself today the virtues of the star-lit heavens."

"The flash of the lightning free and the whirling wind's tempestuous shocks."

Corlinn's voice echoed from the ceiling's stone buttresses. "I bind unto myself today the virtues of the star-lit heavens."

"The stable earth, the deep salt sea, and old eternal rocks. In the Weathercock's name," Rai's voice stumbled again, caught by surprise, "I bind this day to me forever."

As the chant ended and they resumed their seats, she thought, *What am I doing here?*

Where else would you be?

The question felt a little like Banya. She wished it *were* Banya, that the Carraid were sitting next to her (although knowing old horse-face, she'd have probably been right up front with Ren, loathe to miss a thing).

Rai had to admit that the words were hers alone. They belonged to the child she had been, the child left behind when she ran away in fear of her life and in grief over her father's death. They were the words of the woman she had become and the one who had changed as each long-held belief was challenged and brought low. There was no going back to the old ways, not when those hide-bound lines of thought had cost her two of the three people she loved most in the world.

Min'da raised her hands, palms turned toward the ceiling. "Today is a great day!" she said in a ringing voice. "A wondrous day! A day that each of us has prayed for, but few thought ever to see in their lifetime. We have been blessed." She smiled at Kinner, who stepped forward and lifted the sword into the air, point down, his hands curled carefully around the blade. A whisper of awe moved through the congregation.

Cleaned and polished, bright as a newly-minted coin, the boisterous cock fairly crowed jubilation. Brilliant light caught every carved feather, ran like liquid fire along his gleaming spurs, and jumped from the unfurled wings. His open beak glimmered, battle-ready, and his carven eyes blazed with potent energy.

"Here, under the protection of the Goddess, this blade shall rest until the Weathercock claims it," Min'da said.

Rai sat up straight and frowned. That was it? After all they had been through to get the damned thing here, it was going to be hidden away? What about … about … Her head made a jerky, petulant little motion. She hadn't really believed that some heroic figure called the Weathercock was going to stride forth from the shadows, lay claim to the sword, and finish the battle in one fell swoop, but there ought to be more to it that this! Was this what Holan had wanted? Was this little nothing what Banya had died for?

"Know you that its journey here was not an easy one," Min'da continued. "Peril and death have dogged the steps of those who struggled to bring it hence. We inter this blade today with thanks to Kinner of Moselle." She and Corlinn bowed to him. "And to Rai of Cadasbyr." Their eyes found her, hidden at the back, as they bowed again. "Likewise, we thank our friends the Chesne and Carraid and Turaaq. Know you that the sword's safekeeping shall honor the memory and sacrifice of all who have died to protect it, but especially the memories of the blacksmith Holan of Moselle and the Carraid Banya Kiordasdotter, who fell in its defense."

Mollified, Rai folded her arms tight across her chest and sat back. *Big showoff,* she thought with sorrowful affection.

Lady and priest moved to either end of the altar, bowed to one another, and shifted the capstone sideways to expose a long, narrow niche like a shallow grave carved into the pedestal. Corlinn gestured Kinner forward. The boy stared into the opening for a moment and then he nodded, as if in answer to some silent question, and placed the sword within the altar. There was a final flash of silver, bright as a promise, and the capstone slid back into place.

A last prayer and benediction released the congregation. As everyone streamed out of the church, voices raised in animated conversation, the bell tolled a single note. Rai sat where she was and let the others leave ahead of her.

Cheeks flushed and eyes bright with enthusiasm, Kinner pushed down a side aisle to join her. "Rai! Wasn't that wonderful?" He threw both arms around her in a massive hug. "Mum would be so proud!"

She tolerated his embrace, grateful that the overriding worry had been lifted from his shoulders and heart at least for awhile. He moved with a lightness of spirit at odds with the boy she had met in Caerau. With this journey over and the promise to Holan accomplished, his life stood wide-open. He had every right to feel marvelous.

He released her, smiling fit to crack both cheeks, but sobered when he saw her pensive expression. "What's the matter?"

She shook her head and took the liberty of ruffling his hair. "Nothing, kid. I'm happy for you." She gave him a once over. "You look pretty good in that get-up. You sure you don't want to become a monk?"

"Don't feed me a …" He looked around, leaned toward her, and lowered his voice. "A ration of shit. We've been through too much together. What's wrong?"

She waved the question away. "Just my usual loosey-goosey." She glanced at the tall windows. Beyond the stained glass, the shadow of snow fell thick and fast. "I can feel Remeg out there like a boil on my backside."

"That's an image I could have lived without." Kinner touched her arm. "So what if she is? We beat her, Rai! We did what we set out to do and she *lost!*"

Rai's response was forestalled as Tearlach appeared in the church doorway, moving fast against the tide of those who crowded the narthex. Her eyes followed him as he pushed past the congregants and hurried up the aisle, disappearing into the vestry where Min'da and Corlinn had gone to change out of their robes. In a moment, the three of them emerged, heads bent together in rapid conversation. As Tearlach hurried away, Corlinn and the Lady sought out Rai and Kinner.

"Soldiers have been seen on the road to Risley," Min'da said without preamble. "They've just emerged from the trees on the ridge that overlooks the village."

A trickle of dread curled in Rai's stomach like an icy serpent. "Shit." She grimaced. "Sorry, Brother. Lady."

"Don't apologize," Corlinn said. "I'm tempted to say a few choice words myself."

"It's us she's after," Kinner said. He looked at Rai. "If we leave, we'll draw them away."

"You can't martyr yourself on Remeg's insanity," Min'da said in outrage.

"The Lady's right," Rai said. "If we leave, it'll be Cadasbyr all over again. It might be anyway." Her eyes strayed toward the front of the church. "I don't suppose any of you could convince the Weathercock to show up and lend a hand?"

Corlinn smiled. It was an expression so filled with emotion – worry, sorrow, bravery, and belief – that Rai felt her heartbeat slow. He glanced around at the ancient stone work, old benches, stained glass windows, and vaulted ceiling. His gaze lingered longest on the altar and the Goddess sigil draped in heavy garland. "I've given quite a bit of thought to your story over the past few days, Rai. Like it or not, you must accept that the Weathercock has laid his hands on you. Why else join your fate with Kinner's?" He looked at them. "No one forced you to become guardians of the sword. You chose that path." He sighed and scratched an eyebrow. "It seems to me that the Weathercock is already here, whether or not he's taken the aspect we anticipated."

"I agree with Corlinn," Min'da said. "And since he's come, the least we can do is dance to his tune."

Rai stood atop the wall that surrounded the monastery and looked across the dusk-shrouded distance toward Risley. The troop of soldiers had ridden into town, but not emerged. "Where are they?" she muttered. She glanced at her companion. "You don't suppose the villagers killed them, do you?"

"Don't sound so hopeful." Tearlach, cloaked and hooded like her, studied the town, its outlines made vague by heavy snow and encroaching night. The sword belted around his waist was an incongruous sight against the dark brown of his robe. "No, they did nothing. Nor, I think, have the soldiers enacted any violence. We'd have heard screams otherwise or seen smoke if they set fire to the place." He pulled at his top lip in pensive thought. "Who was it?" he said after a moment.

She glanced at him in confusion. "What?"

"That I reminded you of when we first met."

"Oh." She shrugged. Snow sifted from the shoulders of her borrowed cloak. "Someone I knew from the garrison."

"Captain Remeg?" He grinned at her obvious surprise. "It wasn't hard to figure out, Rai." He returned his attention to Risley, now all but invisible in the gloom. "I don't remember a lot about my mother. I was seventeen when I came here, but that's a long time ago. I'm not certain I'd even recognize her were we to meet. We came from Ronan. Do you know where that is?"

"West coast, isn't it?"

"Close enough. It seemed like we rode forever to get here. I didn't want to come. How many do?" He rubbed the tattooed mark between his eyebrows. "The Lady met us at the gate. She invited Mother inside, but she wouldn't come. She didn't want to see the place, didn't want to know where and how I would live out my days. She just put me off the horse, handed me my little bundle of belongings, and rode away."

"That sounds like Remeg. All the compassion of an in-grown toenail." It sounded like Muire, too, but she was not about to say so.

Tearlach shook his head. "I've learned not to judge my mother. It can't be easy to let go of your child knowing that you will never see him again or know what becomes of him. My mother must have loved me in her way, otherwise she'd have left me in the forest to die or killed me. I think those mothers who choose to give away their children still love them. Maybe the ones who kill them love them, too. They're just too afraid to take a stand against the rest of the world." He shrugged. "It seems to me that love is a very complicated thing."

Rai thought of Banya and her heart filled with emotion. "What do you remember?"

He glanced at her. "About my mother?" When she nodded, he pursed his lips in thought. "Her name was Sorinha and she smelled of spices." He smiled at the memory. "Our family were fishers mostly, but we also owned a bakery. It was my mother's job to make the fancy cakes. I used to help her shell nuts and chop fruit." He chuckled. "Her hands were always sticky with frosting." Tearlach folded his arms as if to hold the remembrance close to his heart. "No matter what my mother has done or where she's gone, no matter who she may have become, I have that little bit of her. It's enough."

A bell began to toll. "That's None." When Rai raised her eyebrows in question, he smiled. "Not a church-goer, are you?" he said in a teasing tone.

"Mid-afternoon prayer. Hard to believe it's so dark at mid-afternoon, isn't it?"

"I can stay on watch if you have to, you know," she wiggled her fingers. "Go do something monkish."

He laughed. "Religious obligations are suspended until further notice. We can certainly go if we like and I probably will do at some point, but right now our focus is elsewhere. Don't worry. The Weathercock won't mind."

"What about the Goddess?"

Rai had meant it as a joke, but the monk grew serious. "The Lady teaches that the Weathercock and the Goddess are part and parcel of one another. I hope she's right."

Two figures dressed in heavy cloaks emerged from the refectory. Heads bent against the weather, they hurried across the courtyard and up the stone steps to the parapet. As they got closer, Rai saw that it was Kinner and portly little Brother Sellin.

"We're to relieve you," Kinner said. "Brother Corlinn wants you to get something to eat and then try to sleep."

"I won't feel safe to close my eyes until that bitch is dead," Rai said. She leaned her elbows on the balustrade and stared in the direction of Risley. "What's she up to?" she mused.

Kinner tugged on her arm. "Get out of here, Rai. Let the rest of us have a turn."

"You've gotten awfully pushy lately."

"I take after you." He ducked the cuff she aimed at his head.

"Come along, Rai," Tearlach said. "We know when we're not wanted. Brothers …" He bowed and led the way down the stairs and across the courtyard to the entrance of the refectory. "I'll leave you here," he said as she pulled off her gloves to dip her fingers in the icy water of the lavabo. "I need some time alone in chapel."

She wiped her hands on her pant leg. "Did our talk upset you?"

"No, but it has given me some things to think about." He bowed low to her and walked away.

Twenty-Seven

Vespers rang and Compline. When the church bell tolled Matins, somewhere in the deep hours of the night, Rai got out of bed in the tiny monastic cell given over for her use. Restless, she had tossed and turned as the hours passed. Unable to sleep deeply or well, she had skimmed the surface of repose like a bug on water, her fleeting dreams fractured and chaotic.

She stamped her feet to bring some warmth to her cold toes. Soldier to the core, she had lain down fully clothed atop the thin pallet with her borrowed sword under her hand. Her dirty boots she had let hang off the end of the bed so as not to soil the scratchy wool blanket beneath her.

She fumbled in the dark, found the curtain which served as a door, and stepped into the corridor. A candle burned low in a sconce at either end of the hallway, silent hint to the flow of time. All up and down the passage were alcoves like the one she had just quit. From behind their curtained doorways came the sounds of sleep, soft voices lost in conversation or prayer, and the suppressed sounds of lovemaking. Loathe to eavesdrop, she went down a short flight of stairs, stopped briefly to use the garderobe, and continued to the ground floor where she opened the heavy door and stepped outside.

Thick snow beat against her face. Squinting, she drew her scarf up over her mouth and nose. Her breath condensed in a frosty rime on the outer layer of wool. Harried by the wind, snow had piled high drifts into odd corners and along window embrasures. Faint trails showed where people had passed back and forth in the night, but those were rapidly filling as the storm advanced.

She was reminded again of her father. Once, when Muire was away, Brendie had shown Rai how to make a snowbird by laying on her back and flapping her arms and legs. She raised a gloved hand to her teary eyes. This sorrow was beyond all reason. Why did she still miss him so much after all these years?

Across the courtyard, the church was lit from within. The dim glow of candles muted the colors of the stained glass and gave the rose window the look of dried blood. Lighted more brightly were the refectory and the kitchen where the pragmatic cooks (who understood that people must be fed, no matter what the day brought) were busy with breakfast preparations. The smell of fresh bread set Rai's mouth to watering. She started in that direction, hopeful that a lay-person might cadge a morsel from whichever brothers were manning the ovens, but paused in the courtyard as the church door opened and a single figure emerged.

"Kinner?"

Closing the door, he hurried to meet her. "Good morning." He glanced at the black sky as snowflakes frosted his eyelashes. "It is morning, isn't it?"

She yawned. "Only just. Quite the storm, eh? Maybe Remeg'll get snowed in and the villagers will eat her." She jerked her head toward the church. "What's going on in there?"

"A few of the brothers and priestesses are at prayer and Corlinn's giving Communion to any who want it. I needed some time to myself." He hunched his shoulder against a gust of wind. "I didn't want to be alone, but I didn't feel like talking, either. I needed time to ..." He hesitated and rubbed his bearded jawline. "To make peace with Mum, I guess." He drew a deep breath. "What about you? Can't sleep?"

"I never sleep before battle." She took his elbow and steered him toward the kitchen. "You do realize a battle is coming, don't you?"

"Yes." He looked around at the monastery, its outline blurred and hidden behind the storm's windy cloak. "I'm not sure they do, though."

"Corlinn and the Lady do. These others ..." The cloud of Rai's sigh was snatched away on the wind. "They're well-trained from what I can tell, but they've never tested those skills in real combat."

"Like me with the Chesne. They know enough to be dangerous."

Rai nodded. "They've never confronted someone who really and truly wants to kill them." Her brief laughter was black and humorless.

Kinner cocked his head. "What's funny about that?"

"I was thinking of something else. There used to be a sergeant in the garrison named Steg. She was a small, angel-faced, bandy-legged runt of a thing, hardly bigger than a ten-year-old. She looked like a harsh thought could knock her over and she had the kindest disposition you could imagine ... until she got you on the training floor. That little half-pint commanded arms training back then and you learned two things real fast: never to be late for practice and never to assume that she didn't have your death as her goal." She shook her head at the memory. "She trained some really good fighters, that Steg. These monks could have learned a thing or two from her."

"What happened to her?"

Rai shrugged. "Died in battle, just like she wanted to."

They mounted the steps to the kitchen together, forsaking the lavabo which had frozen solid. Rai's hand was on the latch when a sound borne on the wind made her turn. From beyond the monastery's high stone walls came a wailing cry. She snatched Kinner's sleeve. "Come on!"

They plowed furrows of snow across the courtyard and climbed the slippery steps to the parapet. As one of the monks on watch leaned out over the stonework to speak to someone outside the gate, his partner held a lantern high.

Rai slapped it out of his hand and it flew over the wall. "Are you insane?"

"We need to see who it is!" he said, insulted by such rude handling.

"What you need," Kinner said sharply, stepping between them, "Is to not get shot by giving away your position. What's your name?"

"Brother Jorosh," the monk said with a touch of reluctance. "That's Brother Kabel," he added, as if to spread the blame.

Kabel looked up at the sound of his name. "It's Fause, from the village. There's been an accident." A fist pounded the door beneath them.

"This Fause," Rai said. "You know her?"

Kabel nodded. "Aye. She's the blacksmith."

Rai's eyes met Kinner's. "Do you trust her?" she asked the monk.

Jorosh bristled with outrage. "Of course we trust her! Why on earth would she come out in this weather unless it was an emergency?"

"That question shows how little you know about anything," Rai snapped. She called out. "You! Blacksmith! What's your problem?"

"It's my daughter!" the voice cried from below. "She's hurt!"

Rai bent low and sneaked a look over the parapet. All she could see of the woman below was a huddled shape with a bundle in its arms. "What's wrong with her?"

"She's bleeding!" The pale oval of the blacksmith's face tilted toward them. Shifting the child in her arms, she pounded the gate's heavy wood.

"How did that happen?" Rai called down.

"Oh, for the love of all that's holy!" Brother Jorosh sped toward the stairs, his robe and cloak flapping like wings in a surge of wind.

Rai's voice lashed out. "Stop him!"

Kinner tried, but the monk was more agile than he expected. Jorosh leapt the stairs, letting the ice help him along, and reached the postern door ahead of Kinner. He wrenched it open and ushered the woman and her burden into the monastery. His voice was a quiet murmur over the blacksmith's hysterical babble as he parted the blanket to look at the child. The weight of his shock was so immense that Rai felt it where she stood on the parapet. "They've cut off her fingers!"

Dark shapes poured out of the night and hit the postern door. Fause and her child were knocked aside and trampled in the rush and Jorosh was dead before he could draw breath, gutted like a perch, standing in momentary shock with his hands full of his own entrails before he toppled into the snow.

Rai's blade sang as she whipped it free. Shoving Kabel, she screamed, *"GO!"* He reeled along the parapet, crying the alarm. From across the courtyard the church bells began to peal, waking the community to war.

In the broad courtyards and twisting, dimly lit corridors of Dara, iron sang a clarion cry as old as forever. Drunk with the taste of blood and the fleet passage of souls through the sharp bones of her skeletal hands, Blas – a goddess of an older time – spread her sable wings over the monastery and harvested death.

The thrust and parry of Rai's sword arm had taken on a familiar rhythm all its own when she found herself in the gardens facing someone she recognized from the garrison. Fallon was small and slight, a non-descript woman with an almost fanatical admiration of Remeg. A decent fighter, she spent her off-duty hours painting thumbnail-sized pictures that were striking in their detail.

Rai saw the move before Fallon made it, saw it in the shift of her grip and the flick of her eyes. Filled with a heavy sadness (she had liked Fallon and admired her paintings), Rai parried the first stroke. A cold and business-like calm circled Rai's heart, at odds with her usual berserker rage. Their swords clashed and cried as she drove Fallon backward into the frost-burned vegetation which was all that remained of the monastery's bountiful garden. Vines and bushes crackled beneath their boots. Rai's gaze never wavered as she cut past Fallon's guard and laid open her cheek from the base of the left ear to the corner of her mouth.

Fallon dropped her sword and clutched her face with both hands in a ridiculous attempt to hold the separate pieces together. Rai wound up and – two-handed, putting all the power of her shoulders behind the blow – sliced Fallon through the small of the back. The soldier let out a tiny, breathy *yip!*, the sound of a mouse surprised by an owl's talons, and toppled. Breathing hard, Rai stooped to touch a hand to her old comrade's head and moved on.

She could guess how it had gone; she could see it in her mind. The troop had taken the tiny population of Risley captive while Remeg bided her time and thought her dark thoughts. Was it she who had conceived the notion of mutilating a child as a means of getting inside the monastery or had that bit of evil been Mestipen's, with her putrid delight in butchery? Which of them had severed the child's fingers? Who had sent the terrified mother into the snow with her child bleeding to death in her arms, vanguard to the black force that ghosted along behind her? How surprised the troop must have been when the monks did not fall back in terror as expected, but met the attack with ferocity and – yes, she must admit it – skill. Had that moment of astonishment stayed a single hand, even for an instant?

She had lost track of Kinner almost at once. Corlinn had emerged from the church and Min'da from the refectory. Ren had stumbled out of the dormitory armed with a bow, followed by Torby and Swot. Even mousy little Brother Sellin had appeared, transformed by the twin short swords he brandished. That was the last she had seen of any of them. Where they were now (*if* they were) was anyone's guess.

In the darkness of a pillar, Rai paused to catch her breath and wipe her face with a sleeve. All through the monastery, voices rose and fell in jubilance, pain, and fury. The noise should have been sharp and bright on this cold night, but it seemed muted somehow, as distant as the echoes inside a seashell. The storm had eased to an occasional squall borne in on the glacial north wind, but the surcease was momentary; she could feel it in her bones. Clouds shredded to fleecy standards admitted an occasional wayward shaft of moonlight.

It was this that saved her.

The tail-end of her eye caught the flash of light along a blade as it fell toward her. She spun, evading the blow, and caught up against the hard stone corner of a crypt.

Mestipen smiled at her from insane eyes. Her black hair, pulled free of its customary tail, churned wild and witchy around her head. "Hello, Rai," she said as if they had chanced to meet on market day and stopped to pass the time. "I didn't know it was you standing here with her back all lovely and unprotected. Fancy me being the one to find you."

Fury burned a kernel of heat in Rai's heart. "Maybe teacher will give you a gold star." She inched to one side, jockeying for position.

Mestipen did not counter the motion. Instead, in a slow and almost exaggerated manner, she sheathed her sword.

Rai frowned. What was this shit?

The corner of Mestipen's mouth lifted, her lips pulled sideways by the scar. Without taking her eyes off Rai, she opened one side of her coat. Reaching inside like a Tzigane magician about to produce a bouquet of paper flowers, she drew forth a tempered needle of steel.

Rai's vitals slithered with ice.

"Our captain, she wants you whole." Mestipen held up the dagger, her hand snug beneath the guard, and turned it back and forth. Nebulous light flashed as if the sharp blade were slicing it, *peeling* it, from the fabric of night. "She has plans for you, plans what don't include Mestipen." Her left eye narrowed as Rai sidled another step and she edged sideways to match the maneuver.

"Remeg won't like it if you kill me, Mestipen." Rai's hand flexed around her sword grip. She stepped.

Mestipen did the same, a longer one this time to cut off Rai's escape. The knife flicked out and Rai felt the prick of steel in her sword arm. She gasped, a short, in-drawn hiss of pain. How could the woman be so *fast?*

"Think I care what Remeg likes?" Mestipen said. "Use Mestipen, but don't reward her, not with what she wants. If I keep you for myself, I can do as I like." She lunged, ducking under the swing of Rai's blade with the oily grace of a mink. Rai's sleeve and the flesh inside it parted under the star-twinkle-flashing-bright-burning-fire of the dexterous blade. A heavy line of blood welled from the gash and her vision greyed at the edges. The muscles in her arm felt flat and stupid.

"I can tell Remeg you escaped, send her running. I can say you fell in battle, lost off the cliff. I can say …" Mestipen shrugged, lips pursed in a moue. "*Anything.*" Her gaze was that of a crazed beast – a weasel or stoat, a polecat – hungry for blood. "I can put you away for later. Take you out to play with like a doll." She struck. The dagger cut into Rai's bicep and sliced crossways against the run of muscle. Hot blood surged and agony danced black spots like boils before her eyes. Rai screamed and her dead fingers opened like the petals on a flower. Her sword dropped away and there was the faint sound of metal on stone, muffled by snow.

Mestipen stepped back, slipped, and did a little jig of happiness to catch her balance. "When I'm done, Remeg will have to take you as she gets you. No choice. Dead is dead." That smile again, wider this time, more unctuous. "Like Banya."

Rai's vision smeared red. "Don't you dare say her name. Not you."

Mestipen capered with glee. "Banya, Banya, Banya …" she sang, hopping toward Rai and back again. The wind lifted her cape and turned it into raven wings. For an instant, as if guided by a spectral hand, it swung low and slapped her hard across the face.

The point of Rai's left shoulder, turned at the last moment, caught Mestipen high in the solar plexus and she shot backward as if yanked by the hair. The air burst from her lungs in a solid *whump!* that was joyful to hear. Mestipen landed hard and the menacing little dagger flew free of her hand.

Rai dropped to her knees, right arm held against her chest, and scrabbled with her left hand through the snow, searching for her weapon. "Where, where …" The words were a sobbing, frantic litany. Mestipen lay stunned, whooping for air but struggling to rise, to come at Rai and finish it.

A wall of wind slammed into them as if wrenched from the mountains and flung at Dara in a rage. It lifted the snow in a dense wave, whirling it around like a cyclone, and out of that pillar of white stepped a figure as dark as shadow and as lean as a river eel.

Asabi bent at the waist, hooked her fingers into Mestipen's matted nest of hair, and yanked her head back. Without hesitation, with no opportunity for comment or supplication, she sliced her throat from ear to ear and dropped her like so much carrion.

Rai thumped backward onto her ass and stared.

Rising, Asabi threw her a decidedly jaundiced look. "Why do I keep having to save your life?" Her voice, once earth-brown and sweet, sounded flat and atonal, stuffed like a snotty nose. Her face was a swollen parody of its former self, her regal nose broken and the nostrils slit. The corners of her mouth had been sliced as well and there were patches below both eyes where it looked as if the skin had been peeled away.

Rai swallowed hard and tried not to stare. "Where the fuck did you come from?"

The corner of Asabi's mouth twitched, but Rai would have been hard pressed to call the expression a smile. "No time for that. You all right?"

Rai cradled her arm against her chest. "No."

Asabi's nod was a sharp peck, an economy of motion. "Good." She squatted beside Rai and opened the rent in her sleeve to look at the wound. Voices lifted somewhere on the grounds and she raised her head to listen. "I'm going to try and turn things, see if I can get our old mates to rally to me instead of to Remeg; maybe even those Lorn levies. If you're bright, you'll get yourself someplace safe if there is such a thing, snug that wound down, and wait this out." A glimmer of humor touched her eyes. "Not that I expect you to." She rose and another gust of wind carried her away.

Rai struggled to her feet. She spared not a single glance at Mestipen, whose body was already coated with snow. She wanted to feel angry for having lost the chance to avenge Banya, but couldn't work up the energy. "What the hell," she muttered. "Horseface won't care so long as it's done."

Arm held tight against her chest, she moved away hugging the wall of the crypt. Her feet slid on the ice, each time knocking her against the stonework. With every impact, she let rip a storm of execration such as had never been heard within the walls of Dara. "Wait this out," she groused. Who was Asabi to give her orders? She had to find a weapon and someone to bind up this stupid arm.

She rounded a corner into the courtyard and stopped dead, her pain forgotten as her attention riveted on two figures facing off on the steps of the church.

Kinner.

And Remeg.

During his time among the Chesne, Torby had taught Kinner to watch an adversary's eyes rather than her weapon. He recalled that training now and his eyes fixed on Remeg's as she came slowly up the steps toward him.

"Give it up, boy," she said. Her voice was gentle, soothing. She held her weapon low, the point toward the ground. *There's no threat here,* the stance was meant to convey. *Nothing to worry about.*

Kinner kept his blade raised and on guard. The wrought iron handle of the church door dug into the small of his back. He was trapped with no room to maneuver, mouse to her cat, while Remeg stood halfway up the stairs with all the room on the world. How long before he tired? How long before his guard slipped or his feet on these icy stones, and she cut him down?

Remeg turned one hand palm-up, a conversational gesture at odds with the circumstances. "Don't be a fool. This is over. Surely you can see that." She ascended a step. "You gave it good play, I'll grant you that, but the game is done. I don't want you damaged and I most certainly do not want you dead. The queen would be most displeased and we can't have that, can we?"

Kinner, surprised, couldn't help his question. "What does the queen want with me?"

Remeg's smile was so oily he could feel it on his skin. "You're young, boy, but not *that* young. Why do you think?"

In an unconscious gesture, his free hand went to his forehead. "But I'm sterile."

Remeg shrugged and came up another step, smiling faintly as he tried to back away with nowhere to go. "All that concerns me is that the queen gets what she wants and, thereby, so do I." She went for him.

Kinner saw it coming and stepped forward to meet it. Their swords clashed and the impact traveled from the steel blade all the way up his arm. He was trained (*just*), but Remeg had years of experience. She pushed the offensive and in a move too fast to capture, caught the tip of her weapon on one of the turnings of his hilt. A flip of the wrist was all it took to disarm him. The sword snapped from his hand, sailed clear of the steps, and plumped into a snow drift. Kinner pressed back against the church door and stared at Remeg with huge eyes.

"Now then," she said in a chiding tone. "We'll have no more of that."

He shifted from foot to foot. There was motion in the shadows behind Remeg and his heart clenched with gratitude. One of her own would not move toward her with such furtive intent. He forced his eyes to stay on Remeg and not betray whoever it was. The Chesne had taught him to face down hunger-maddened wolves. Where was the difference between that and Remeg?

She never expected the attack. Kinner's surprise kick took her just above the knee at the same instant that Rai grabbed her by the back of the coat and flung her down the steps. Not waiting to see where she landed, Kinner shoved open the church door and dragged Rai inside, slamming it shut behind them.

Her hands fumbled at the latch. "There's no lock!"

"It's a religious community," he said needlessly. "They trust each other."

"Fuck that!" Rai cast about in a frenzy. "What about the pews?"

"They're stone. We'll never move them." His hand brushed the marble font of holy water. It could be repositioned, but would not hold the door for long. "We have to hide." He grabbed her arm, her bad arm as luck would have it, the one he now realized she carried tucked into the open front of her jacket.

Rai howled and slapped him hard across the top of the head. "Leave off!"

He stared at the blood all down her sleeve and the thick crust of it on her hand. "What happened?"

"What's it look like? I had a knitting accident." She caught hold of his sleeve with her good hand and dragged him up the center aisle toward the front of the church. Behind them, the door burst open.

Remeg had once been a commander of some consequence, but now her reputation and her sanity were in ashes. Riddled with madness and soaked in the blood of those she had slaughtered, she came up the aisle in a blind rush, intent upon nothing but the quarry which had turned to bay at the altar.

Rai grabbed one of the heavy brass candlesticks and hefted it in her good hand. Short and squat, it looked about as dangerous as a salt cellar. Kinner reached for the other one, knowing it would be of little help against Remeg …

… and saw in his memory Corlinn and the Lady, resplendent in ceremonial robes, shifting the capstone.

He flung the candlestick at Remeg. "Rai! The stone! Move the stone!" He braced his feet and shoved on one end of the altar. The capstone shifted slightly, scraping against the base, and stuck. "Rai!" he pleaded, sobbing.

She flung her candlestick at Remeg's head and joined her strength to his. The capstone slid in its groove and crashed onto the floor, shattering. Rubble careened into the aisle and Remeg skipped back, dancing sideways to avoid tripping over it.

Kinner thrust his hand into the opening, past the covering of red silk, and swept up the Weathercock sword in a swinging arc. The feeble candles that lit the church flared as if with fresh air and the sword reflected back their glory like a song.

Remeg growled like a rampant beast and brought her weapon down two-handed. The blades clashed, shrieking an eerie, almost animal cry that raised the hair on Kinner's scalp. The magnificent weapon, made by the hand of a zealot for that of a legendary hero, twisted in his grip and tore free. It sailed high, struck the wall beneath the holly-wreathed image of the Goddess …

… and broke. The pieces clattered to the floor, their beauty and magic destroyed forever. The embattled rooster lay lopsided on one broken wing, silent and dead, devoid of fury or the wink of bright, bedazzling eyes.

Remeg laughed. "That's the weapon that was going to change the world? That's what you tied all your dreams to, what you risked everything for?" She chuckled with delight. "Wonderful! Well, so much for that." Her voice thickened with mocking contempt. "And so much for your Weathercock."

"I am the Weathercock."

Kinner's words rang clear in the cold air of the church and silenced everything – heartbeats, breathing, even the clangor of battle that raged through Dara.

The women stared at him in bewilderment. Kinner looked back, at peace for the first time in his life. He felt light, almost lacking substance; unafraid of what was to come and unsurprised by what he had done. He knew the words were true.

Remeg's perplexity was fleeting. "Give it up, boy!" she snarled. "You –"

"I am the Weathercock," he said again, louder this time. His words sliced across hers like a honed edge of steel. He stepped toward Remeg and her gory blade. "So is Rai. So are Banya and Marn, the folk of Cadasbyr, and the Chesne and Carraid you murdered. So are the monks and priestesses here. You're the one who's to blame for the Weathercock rising, not us."

"He's got you there, Captain," Rai said. "It wasn't the sword or Holan or a peasants' tale that brought him to life. It was *you.* You've released the Weathercock into the world. I wonder what the queen will have to say about that?"

The comment was a jibe; ridicule for the political mess which Remeg had brought to Kedar Trevalyan. Neither Rai nor Kinner could know the strength of those words or that their truth – in an instant's flash of white heat – would obliterate any remaining vestige of hope Remeg held for reconciliation. She gaped at them, stunned. The tip of her sword lowered … wavered …

With a howl of rage, Remeg brought the blade up and around, knocking

Rai aside and bearing down on the unarmed boy who was the symbol of her ruined life.

Two arrows took her high in the back, so close to the same mark that their feathers – one set black, the other blue and white – blended. Eyes wide with shock, Remeg slowly turned and tried to raise her sword. A third shaft *thunked!* deep into the meat of her chest, driving her backward onto the open altar. The weapon dropped from her hand and she collapsed to the floor.

TWENTY-EIGHT

Stupefied, Kinner and Rai stared at the crumpled body of their adversary, then turned and looked into the choir loft. At either end of the balcony stood an armed warrior – one in a filthy blue and white uniform, the other in a monk's robe and mail.

In a blur of movement Tearlach nocked another arrow, drew it taut by his ear, and sighted down the shaft. The longbow never wavered. "Please be so kind as to put down your weapon."

Sheel shook her head over the linked arms of the loaded crossbow. "I think not, Brother, with all due respect. You've nothing to fear from me."

"Tell us another, why don't you?" Rai called from below.

The comment made Sheel smile. Without taking her eyes off Tearlach, she made a slight bow. "Captain Sheel of the Lorn Levies, at your service."

"I don't understand," Kinner said. He gestured at Remeg's torn and bloody remains, but could not bring himself to look at them. "You rode with her. You helped her attack Eachan's Rest."

"And I'd have killed her then if your troublesome friend hadn't intervened."

Rai looked flummoxed. "Are you talking about me?"

The Lorn commander inched backward, her weapon still aimed at Tearlach. Could she beat him? Kinner wondered. The monk excelled at the longbow, but Sheel was clearly no slouch. She had shot her bolt and managed to reload the weapon in the time it had taken fleet Tearlach to deliver two rounds into Remeg.

"I was sent on this fool's errand with one purpose," Sheel said. "To turn Remeg's success into our own and then do her in. My employer hopes to ingratiate herself with Kedar Trevelyan. If she could aid in the capture of traitors to the crown, it could not help but work to her advantage."

"Traitors to the crown?" Rai said. Kinner shushed her with a wave of his hand.

"But it all went to shit at Eachan's Rest," Sheel continued. "It wasn't you I was trying to kill there, but that crazy bitch commander of yours. Ah!" She made a sharp exclamation, but her weapon never wavered. "Watch that bow of yours, Brother! I'd hate for there to be an accident."

Tearlach's expression was as cool and immovable as marble. "By God's grace, there are no accidents with this weapon."

The Lorn captain smiled. "What a relief. I'd hate to die by mistake."

"You had plenty of time to kill Remeg on the road to Dara," Rai said. "Why didn't you?"

"Politics, my dear girl," Sheel replied. "If I'd killed her when I first tried, the Lorn would have been hailed a hero for narrowly averting a war with Carraidland. As it was, the damage was done. Imagine crying 'oops' to the Carraid. My one chance to resolve this debacle in any sort of favor to the Lorn was to accompany Remeg to Dara as planned, capture the prize, and then get rid of her. In that way the queen would have you, my employer's honor would be avenged, and Remeg would be exposed as a traitor." Sheel's eyes widened with feigned innocence. "Imagine being so foolish as to invade Carraidland! Why, my poor troops and I were caught in the middle by the actions of a madwoman. We never had a chance; we *had* to fight." Her expression turned sardonic. "Which, by the way, happens to be the truth," she added in a more normal tone of voice. "Handing Remeg's body over to the Carraid is the least I can do."

"All very tidy," Tearlach said with sour admiration. "But if you think I'll just let you take Kinner and Rai …" His bowstring groaned a low note as he drew it back a tad further.

A hullabaloo rose outside the church. Stepping carefully over the fragments of broken altar, Kinner hurried to one of the windows and boosted up into the embrasure. He bent forward and cupped his hands around his face to peer through a break where some of the stained glass had shattered and dropped away. "It's Carraid!" he cried after a moment. "Lots of them!" A pause, then, "There's Signy!" He gave a sudden shriek of rapture. "Eachan!" He dropped from the sill and ran for the door.

From overhead came the twang of a bowstring, the deadly sound of a hurled missile striking home, and an unexpected (and thoroughly un-monkish) oath from Tearlach. Kinner stumbled to a halt and Rai, who had started after him, caught up short with a cry. "Tearlach?"

"Missed!" came the monk's voice. "I can't believe it!"

"Are you hit?" Kinner called.

Tearlach peered over the balustrade. "No. Sheel didn't shoot; she just ducked and ran. Looks like goodbye to her grand scheme of glory." He leaned on his bow, glanced briefly at Remeg's sprawled body, and looked away. If he had any thoughts on the subject, he kept them to himself. "Why don't you go greet our friends, lad?"

Kinner's face split into an enormous grin and he ran to throw the church doors open to the wind.

Rai sat on the refectory steps and watched as the Carraid made final preparations for departure. The last horse in the train, a red roan with a clever eye, carried a corpse rolled in cloth; Remeg, bound for Caerau, where Balfor intended to unroll the gift at Kedar Trevelyan's feet and lodge a complaint against the realm demanding restitution on behalf of not only Carraidland, but also Dara, the Chesne, and all of Cadasbyr. Rai wished she could be there to see the queen's face when it happened.

A mantle of new snow had muted signs of the battle that had been fought here weeks before. The bodies of the dead lay bundled in the coldest of the lower levels to await burial. Blood had been scrubbed from the stones and broken windows sported wooden shutters until new glass arrived.

Inside the church, voices lifted in song. It was Corlinn they sang for, and Holan. It was for Jorosh and the other monks and priestesses who had fallen to the blade that terrible day. The song was for Fause and her child, for Banya and those who had died at Eachan's Rest (Eir and Sobity's unborn child among the count), and for the Carraid who braved the storm to pursue Remeg across the bleak hills only to lose their lives at Dara. It was for the Lorn levies, dead every one, and for their commander, whose body was never found. The song was for the poor soldiers of Caerau, whose loyalty had bid them follow a madwoman to their doom … all except Asabi who, having been released by the villagers in Risley, had fought against Remeg. In exchange for a pardon from Balfor, she was going with the Carraid to Trevelyan's court to offer testimony against her former commander. What would happen to her afterward, where she would go, was anyone's guess.

The hymn was even for Remeg and Mestipen too, although it was the intoning of their names during mass that had sent Rai out into the cold. She could pray for all the others, but not those two, not for the dark-haired enigma who had been her commander nor for the blood-soaked harpy.

The church door opened and Kinner stepped outside accompanied by Tearlach. They paused with their heads bent close in conversation, then Kinner nodded and started towards Rai while Tearlach went off in another direction, raising his hand to her in greeting.

Rai returned the wave and rose to meet Kinner, dusting the snow from her rump. "Had enough religion for one day?"

"Maybe a little." His expression sobered. "I'm trying, Rai, but I don't feel much inclined toward charity right now."

"I know what you mean." She jerked her head in Tearlach's direction as the young monk disappeared around a corner. "He okay? It's pretty heady stuff to kill your own mother."

"Well, it's not like he knows for sure that she was his mother." Kinner shrugged at her look. "Okay, so, yes, he knows, but he's fine. Well, not *fine,* maybe, but he's at peace. He told me that Remeg wasn't his mother; that was a woman named Sorinha and she died a long time ago. Remeg's just a stranger who took her place. The fact that she never knew it was her son who killed her helps him, I think."

Rai nodded and shoved her cold hands into her pockets. She had lost her gloves somewhere and would need to borrow a pair. "I'm sorry about the sword. Who'd have thought it would break?"

Kinner grinned. "I know. Mum would be mortified."

"Why aren't you upset about this?" Rai said, startled by his response. "That sword represented everything Holan lived for, everything she made *you* live for. Now what's the Weathercock supposed to wield when he finally arrives?"

Kinner folded his arms across his chest and hunched his shoulders against the cold. His beard, clipped short along the curve of his chin, had come in dark. His expression reminded Rai once more that he was no longer a boy. "The sword was only a symbol, Rai. It served its purpose. It struck the first spark of change."

She snorted. "It's a big world out there."

"Then I guess it's up to us to fan the flames."

She held up her hands. "Leave me out of it."

He laughed. Looking down, he watched the toe of one boot jab repeatedly at a hunk of ice. "I wish you'd stay."

Rai cleared her throat. "Yeah, well, don't make me feel any more guilty about leaving that I already do, okay?" She fidgeted, taking her hands in and out of her pockets, scratching her chin. "It's crazy-serious to travel at this time of year, but Eachan says she can't afford to stay away, especially with Balfor heading to Caerau. The Carraid need to get back, recoup as much of the roundup as they can, and I … I want to help. I'll stick out like a sore thumb among all those bubble-headed blondes, but maybe Briot can finally teach me to ride the right way." The thought of the pigtailed go-getter made her smile even as her heart clenched around the memory of Kiorda, lost in the fire at Eachan's Rest. "I think Banya would like that. Besides, her barn rats are waiting for me." She shoved her hands back into her pockets. "What about you?"

"I'm staying here," he said simply. "There's a lot to be decided. The queen won't drop this matter now that it's begun. That'll mean trouble in the future."

"Oh, goody."

He shot her a look that was half-humorous, half-annoyed. "There's talk of establishing outposts, more schools where men can learn to be something other than what they've always been, where they can be given a choice."

Rai nodded sagely. "I see. And after you change the face of the world as we know it, then what?"

His smile grew wistful. "Then I'll head south to the Chesne. That's home … at least for now."

Rai thought about those distant hills. It was a hard life but a satisfying one, steeped in tradition and, more importantly, a sense of community. "Maybe I should go with you, get set up with a dog and a flock of sheep."

Kinner's look turned droll. "Yeah, I can see that. You and a flock of stinking, witless sheep." He shook his head. "Banya always said that like calls to like."

Rai gaped at him. Then she laughed and punched him hard on the shoulder.

"Ow!"

"You deserved it." But she liked the teasing. It reminded her that not everything had been lost.

A sharp whistle sounded and they looked round. From across the courtyard, Eachan waved an arm. "Time to go!"

Rai raised a hand to let her know she was coming. "You going to say goodbye?"

"Did it last night."

"Oh." She stuck out her hand. "Well … so long."

He pulled her into a tight hug. "You be careful out there," he murmured in her ear.

Rai's chest tightened. She pressed her face against his shoulder to hide the sudden tears. "I'll see you after," she whispered back.

From overhead came a creaky whine. On the top spire of the church a weathervane shaped like a crowing rooster shifted in the wind, changing direction and pointing the way, all of the ways, to the future.

At the age of five, Melissa Crandall asked for a typewriter for Christmas. She never looked back.

A resident of New England, she loves to travel and is available for interviews, books signings, readings, conventions, and workshops. She particularly enjoys working with children and young adults who are enthusiastic about writing.

Melissa Crandall can be contacted via her website, on her blog, or through the email address listed below:

www.melissacrandall.com
www.melissacrandall.wordpress.com
mcrandall50@yahoo.com

Coming soon from Melissa Crandall:

Call of Blood

In Kirian's dream, black tinged with copper and brass swirled in the air like watered silk, stirred by a breeze that stank of corruption. She grimaced and pressed a hand over her nose and mouth. She knew – the way one sometimes knows things in dreams – that this stench was born of an evil vast enough to destroy worlds, leaving people shuddering in piss and blood. The air reeked of pain concocted with glee, hatred dispensed with joy, and a deep and abiding rage that fed on itself like internal worms on soft organ meat.

All at once, she felt a *presence,* large and monstrous. The darkness around her swelled like a lung drawing breath and folded back on itself in two halves, parting down the middle like theater curtains.

He stood revealed, eyes lifted toward the dark sky. On his face was an expression of insane joy almost sexual in the depth of its pleasure. As if sensing her presence, he turned to face her. His smile echoed of bedlam and the shrieking agony of someone locked away forever in the dark. A graceful hand extended in invitation …

Kirian sat bolt upright, wide awake and screaming in terror as sudden light spilled a circle of illumination around her. The front door slammed open and Ned rushed onto the porch brandishing the iron fireplace poker. He stopped short when he saw that she was safe and cast about in the night for what had frightened her. "I heard you talking," he said. "Soft, I couldn't make out what, and then you were moaning like something was hurting you and I heard you say no, and then you …"

They stared at each other, both breathing hard – he confused and disheveled from illness and sleep, eyes bleary and face puffy; she pale as paper, her eyes huge with fear – and then she flung herself into his arms with a wordless cry and buried her face in his shoulder.

Ned dropped the iron bar and gathered her to him, hugging her tight, stroking her hair and back, murmuring the odd nonsense phrases that everyone uses to keep panic at bay. Shivering, Kirian turned her cheek against his shoulder to stare at the dark forest. Neither she nor Ned would have been surprised to learn that the very same words were going through their heads at that exact instant: *That's it. This has to end.*

Unfortunately for them, it was only the beginning.